Praise for *Fifteen Minutes*

"Kingsbury has produced a new riveting page-turner of
relatable characters and situations and the best ways to hang onto
our faith in a world that no longer sees its value."
—*CBA Retailers+Resources*

"Bestselling author Kingsbury drives straight to the heart
of her characters as always in this excellent tale of desire and faith,
digging beneath the surface of her plot to fuel an emotionally
driven story set within the exciting world of reality TV."
—*Booklist*

"Christian novelist Kingsbury offers a faith-based look
at an *American Idol*–style show and the inherent spiritual
risks placed upon the contestants."
—*Kirkus Reviews*

From #1 *New York Times* bestselling author Karen Kingsbury comes a dramatic story about fame, true love, and the cost of having it all.

Zack Dylan made a promise to God and his college sweetheart as he left his family's horse farm in Kentucky to compete on the popular reality television show *Fifteen Minutes*: If he makes it, the fame won't change him.

Overnight, Zack is the nation's most popular contestant, a country singer with the looks and voice of a young Elvis. As his star rises, Zack is asked to compromise and quiet his beliefs, and also something more. Something Zack could never have imagined. Just as America is falling in love with Zack, just as he's on the verge of winning it all, his choices lead him to the brink of personal disaster.

At the same time, Reese Weatherly, a therapeutic horse instructor, is no longer sure about her relationship with Zack, or the wedding they had dreamed about. While Zack advances from one round of the competition to the next, an offer comes to Reese—one that will take her to a home halfway around the world.

Then Chandra Olson—reigning diva pop star and one of the *Fifteen Minutes* judges—intervenes. Chandra has suffered so much public pain and private agony since her days as a *Fifteen Minutes* contestant. Now she wants just one thing: meaning.

Can Chandra's private losses help Zack find his way, or will his fifteen minutes of fame cause him to lose the life he once loved? *Fifteen Minutes* is a story of character, compromise, and the cost of having it all. A story that raises the question: Who are the real winners?

What Readers Are Saying About Karen Kingsbury's Books

"Karen Kingsbury's books inspire me to be a stronger follower of Jesus Christ, to be a better wife, mother, sister, and friend. Thank you, Karen, for your faithfulness to the Lord's gentle whisper."

—Tamara B.

"It's as simple as this: God's heart comes off these pages—every line, every word. You can feel the love and redemption of Christ through every character's life in each book. The message is a message of hope, hope in the One who has saved us and reigns victorious!"

—Brenae D.

"Karen's books are like a personal Bible study—there are so many situations that can be applied directly to the truths found in God's Word to help strengthen and encourage me."

—Laura G.

"I have read many of Karen's books, and I cry with every one. I feel like I actually know the people in the story, and my heart goes out to all of them when something happens!"

—Kathy N.

"Novels are mini-vacations, and Karen Kingsbury's novels are my favorite destination."

—Rachel S.

"Karen Kingsbury's books are amazing! They are inspirational, encouraging, heart-touching, and definitely life-changing. Thank you, Karen, for sharing your gift with us."

—Lisa M.P.

"The best author in the country."

—Mary H.

"Karen's books are like chocolate—very addicting! You can't just eat one piece at a time, you have to eat the whole thing—you can't just read one chapter at a time, you have to read the whole book!"

—Sarah M.

"Karen truly has a God-given talent. I have laughed, cried, and rejoiced with your characters as if they were real people! Please keep writing, Karen. I can't put your books down! God bless you!"

—Rebekah H.

"The stories are fiction; their impact is real."

—Debbie L.R.

"It was my lucky day when a friend introduced me to Karen Kingsbury's books! A day without KK isn't complete. . . ."

—Bette O.J.

"My daughter and I 'fight' to read Karen's books first. She has even said, 'Mom, I'll do dishes. *You* go read the latest Karen Kingsbury book!'"

—Terry S.

"Recently I made an effort to find *good* Christian writers, and I've hit the jackpot with Karen Kingsbury!"

—Linda O.

"Karen Kingsbury books are like my best friends—they make me cry, laugh, and give me encouragement. God bless you, Karen, for using your talent for Him."

—Tammy G.

"Every time I read one of Karen's books, I think, 'It's the best one yet.' Then the next one comes out and I think, 'No, *this* is the best one.'"

—April B.M.

"Karen Kingsbury's books are fantastic! She always makes me feel like I'm living the story along with the characters!"

—Courtney M.G.

"Karen's books speak to the heart. They are timely, entertaining, but, more important, they speak God's love into hungry souls."

—Debbie P.K.

"Whenever I pick up a new KK book, two things are consistent: tissues and finishing the whole book in one day."

—Nel L.

"When I was in Iraq, Mrs. Kingsbury's books were like a cool breeze on a hot summer day, and they made the hard days a bit easier to bear. By the end of my tour, all the ladies in my tent were hooked!"

—Olivia G.

"These books are the *best*! I have bought every one of them. I love getting my friends 'hooked' on Karen Kingsbury!"

—Dana T.C.

"Not only do Karen Kingsbury books make you laugh and make you cry, they will leave you begging for more. I stay awake all night when a new one comes out, reading by flashlight while my family sleeps!"

—Hellen H.

"Reading a Karen Kingsbury book is like watching a really good movie. I just can't get enough of her books."

—Esther S.

"The lady who orders books for our church library shakes her head and laughs when I tell her, 'Okay, Karen Kingsbury has a new book out! I get first dibs when you get it!'"

—Jeannette M.B.

"Each new Karen Kingsbury book is like a visit home. Nothing beats time with family and friends, which is just what Karen's characters are!"

—Erin M.

"As someone who has struggled with health issues over the last two years, Karen's books have been such an encouragement to me. They remind me that God is with me and will never leave me. Please keep writing; I need that reminder."

—Carrie F.

"Pick up a Karen Kingsbury book, and I guarantee you will never be the same again! Karen's books have a way of reaching the deepest parts of your soul and touching places of your heart that are longing for something more."

—Becky S.

"Karen Kingsbury's books make a way for God to get a hold of your heart and never let go!"

—Jessica E.

"Karen Kingsbury really brings fiction to life, and I'm longing to read the next segment. Real men really do read KK!"

—Phil C.

"God's love, mercy, and hope shines through every one of Karen Kingsbury's books. She has a passion for the Lord, and it shows in every story she writes. She is amazing!"

—Kristi C.M.

"It is hard for me to walk out of a bookstore without a Karen Kingsbury book in my possession. I am hooked."

—Shilah N.

"Karen Kingsbury is changing the world—one reader at a time."

—Lauren W.

"Karen writes straight from the heart and touches each of her readers with every new story! Love, loss, family, faith, all the struggles we each face every day come to life in the characters she creates."

—Amber B.

Other Life-Changing Fiction™
by Karen Kingsbury

Stand-Alone Titles

The Chance

The Bridge

Oceans Apart

Between Sundays

When Joy Came to Stay

On Every Side

Divine

Like Dandelion Dust

Where Yesterday Lives

Shades of Blue

Unlocked

Coming Home—The Baxter Family

Redemption Series

Redemption

Remember

Return

Rejoice

Reunion

Firstborn Series

Fame

Forgiven

Found

Family

Forever

Sunrise Series

Sunrise

Summer

Someday

Sunset

Above the Line Series

Above the Line: Take One

Above the Line: Take Two

Above the Line: Take Three

Above the Line: Take Four

Bailey Flanigan Series

Leaving

Learning

Longing

Loving

9/11 Series

One Tuesday Morning

Beyond Tuesday Morning

Remember Tuesday Morning

Lost Love Series

Even Now   Ever After

Red Glove Series

Gideon's Gift   Sarah's Song
Maggie's Miracle   Hannah's Hope

e-Short Stories

The Beginning   I Can Only Imagine

Forever Faithful Series

Waiting for Morning   Halfway to Forever
Moment of Weakness

Women of Faith Fiction Series

A Time to Dance   A Time to Embrace

Cody Gunner Series

A Thousand Tomorrows   This Side of Heaven
Just Beyond the Clouds

Children's Titles

Let Me Hold You Longer   The Princess and the Three Knights
Let's Go on a Mommy Date   The Brave Young Knight
We Believe in Christmas   Far Flutterby
Let's Have a Daddy Day   Always Daddy's Princess

Miracle Collections

A Treasury of Christmas Miracles   A Treasury of Miracles for Friends
A Treasury of Miracles for Women   A Treasury of Adoption Miracles
A Treasury of Miracles for Teens   Miracles: A Devotional

Gift Books

Stay Close Little Girl   Forever Young: Ten Gifts of Faith
Be Safe Little Boy   for the Graduate

www.KarenKingsbury.com

Fifteen Minutes

A NOVEL

Karen Kingsbury

HOWARD BOOKS
A Division of Simon & Schuster, Inc.
New York   Nashville   London   Toronto   Sydney   New Delhi

Howard Books
A Division of Simon & Schuster, Inc.
1230 Avenue of the Americas
New York, NY 10020

Scripture quotations taken from The Holy Bible, New International Version® (NIV®). Copyright © 1973, 1978, 1984 by Biblica US, Inc.®. Used by permission.

Published in association with the literary agency of Alive Communications, Inc., 7680 Goddard Street, Suite 200, Colorado Springs, Colorado, 80920, www.alivecommunications.com.

First Howard Books trade paperback edition April 2014

HOWARD and colophon are trademarks of Simon & Schuster, Inc.

For information about special discounts for bulk purchases, please contact Simon & Schuster Special Sales at 1-866-506-1949 or business@simonandschuster.com.

The Simon & Schuster Speakers Bureau can bring authors to your live event. For more information or to book an event, contact the Simon & Schuster Speakers Bureau at 1-866-248-3049 or visit our website at www.simonspeakers.com.

Designed by Davina Mock-Maniscalco

Manufactured in the United States of America

10 9 8 7 6 5 4 3 2

The Library of Congress has cataloged the hardcover edition as follows:

Kingsbury, Karen.
Fifteen minutes : a novel / Karen Kingsbury.
 pages cm
I. Title.
PS3561.I4873F54 2013
813'.54—dc23
2013008054

ISBN 978-1-4516-4705-1
ISBN 978-1-4516-8746-0 (pbk)
ISBN 978-1-4516-4706-8 (ebook)

To Donald:

Do you feel it, how the years are picking up speed? With Kelsey into her second year of marriage and Tyler racing toward college graduation? Isn't our Lord so faithful? Not just with our kids but in leading our family where He wants us to be. I love the sign that hangs in our kitchen: "I wasn't born in the South, but I got here as fast as I could." Nothing could be truer about our new home, our new life, here in Nashville. It remains so very clear that God wanted us here—not just for my writing and to be near Christian movies and music, but for our kids and even for us. I love how you've taken to this new season of being more active in my ministry and helping our boys bridge the gap between being teenagers and becoming young men. Now that you're teaching again, we are both right where God wants us. Thank you for being steady and strong and good and kind. Hold my hand and walk with me through the coming seasons—the graduations and growing up and getting older. All of it's possible with you by my side. Let's play and laugh and sing and dance. Together we'll watch our children take wing. The ride is breathtakingly wondrous. I pray it lasts far into our twilight years. Until then, I'll enjoy not always knowing where I end and you begin. I love you always and forever.

To Kyle:

Kyle, you have become such an important part of our family. You are now and forevermore will be our son, the young man God planned for our daughter, the one we prayed for and talked to God about and hoped for. Your heart is beautiful in every way,

Kyle: how you cherish simple moments and the way you are kind beyond words. You see the good in people and situations, and you find a way to give God the glory always. I love watching you lead Kelsey, growing alongside her in faith and life and the pursuit of your dreams. Constantly I am awed by the wisdom you demonstrate, so far beyond your years. You are an example to our boys and a picture of how a husband should love his wife. Thank you for that. Even still, I am struck by the way you look at our precious Kelsey. It's a picture that will hang forever on the wall of my heart. You look at Kelsey as if nothing and no one else in all the world exists except her. In your eyes at that moment is the picture of what love looks like. Kyle, as God takes you from one stage to another—using that beautiful voice of yours to glorify Him and lead others to love Jesus—I pray that you always look at Kelsey the way you do today. We thank God for you, and we look forward to the beautiful seasons ahead. Love you always!

To Kelsey:

My precious daughter, I'm so happy for you and Kyle. Your dreams of acting and singing for Jesus are firmly taking shape, but it is your beautiful heart that best defines you. I've never known you to be so happy; time and again I point to you and Kyle as proof of God's faithfulness. Now, as you two move into the future God has for you, as you seek to follow your dreams and shine brightly for Him in all that you do, we will be here for you both. We will pray for you, believe in you, and support you however we can. With Kyle's ministry in music and yours in acting, there are no limits to how God will use you both. I rejoice in what He is doing in your life, Kelsey. He has used your years of struggle to make you into the deeply rooted, faithful young woman you are today. Keep trusting God; keep putting Him first. I always knew this season would come, and now it is here. Enjoy every minute, sweetheart. You will always be the light of our family, the laughter in our hearts, the one-in-a-million girl who inspired an entire series. My precious Kelsey, I pray that God will bless you mightily in the years to come, and that you will always know how He used this time in your life to draw you close to Him and to prepare you for what's ahead. In the meantime, you'll be in my heart every moment. I love you, sweetheart.

To Tyler:

It's hard to believe you're well into your third year of college, ready for the next season of challenges and adventures. Watching you on the stage, performing *Les Misérables,* will remain one of the highlights of my life. I can imagine your papa watching from a special spot in heaven. He'd be in the front row if he could be, right next to your dad and me. What's incredible is how you have become such a great screenwriter while singing so beautifully from the stage. So many exciting times ahead, Ty. I can barely take it all in. I believe with all my heart that God has you right where He wants you. Learning so much about performing for Him and becoming the man He wants you to be. You are the rare guy with a most beautiful heart for God and others. Your dad and I are so proud of you, Ty. We're proud of your talent and your compassion for people and your place in our family. And we're proud that you are completing your college degree. However your dreams unfold, we'll be in the front row, cheering loudest, as we watch them happen. Hold on to Jesus, son. Keep shining for Him! I love you.

To Sean:

High school is behind you now, and your dream of playing drums for a Christian artist is firmly in sight. That's a wonderful thing, but even more wonderful is the way you've grown into a godly young man, a leader for your friends and an example to others. God will bless you for how you're being faithful in the little things. He has such great plans for you. Sean, you've always had the best attitude, and now, even when there are hard days, you've kept that great attitude. Be joyful, God tells us. In our family you give us a little better picture of how that looks. On top of that, I love how much of your heart you share with us. Stay close, Sean. Remember, home is where your heart is always safe. Your dreams are right around the corner. Keep working, keep pushing, keep believing. Go to bed every night knowing you did all you could to prepare yourself for the doors God will open in the days ahead. I pray that, as you soar for the Lord, He will allow you to be a very bright light indeed. You're a precious gift, son. I love you. Keep smiling and keep seeking God's best.

To Josh:

Soccer was where you started when you first came home from Haiti, and soccer makes up much of your life now. I never for a minute doubted that you'd play NCAA Division I soccer, but watching it happen has been one of my greatest joys ever. I pray that as you continue to follow the Lord in soccer, He will continue to lead you so that your steps are in keeping with His. This we know: there remains for you a very real possibility that you'll play competitive sports at the next level—the Tim Tebow of the soccer world. Even with all your athleticism, I'm most proud of your spiritual and social growth this past year. You've grown in heart, maturity, kindness, quiet strength, and the realization that time at home is short. God is going to use you for great things, and I believe He will put you on a public platform to do it. Stay strong in Him, and listen to His quiet whispers so you'll know which direction to turn. I'm so proud of you, son. I'll forever be cheering on the sidelines. Keep God first in your life. I love you always.

To EJ:

EJ, it's hard to believe that you're a senior in high school. I'm so glad you know just how much we love you and how deeply we believe in the great plans God has for you. I know you are a bit uncertain with new opportunities spread out before you. But I see glimpses of determination and effort that tell me that with Christ you can do anything, son. One day not too far off, you'll be applying to colleges, thinking about the career choices ahead and the path God might be leading you down. Wherever that path takes you, keep your eyes on Jesus, and you'll always be as full of possibility as you are today. I expect great things from you, EJ, and I know the Lord expects them, too. I'm so glad you're in our family—always and forever. I'm praying you'll have a strong passion to use your gifts for God as you head into your senior year. Thanks for your giving heart, EJ. I love you more than you know.

To Austin:

Austin, I can only say I'm blown away by your efforts this past school year. Through shoulder surgery and the flu, through growth spurts and adjusting to high school, you have continued to excel. From the first day you stepped on the football field this fall, you have given one hundred percent of your special heart to the task at hand. Nothing can hold you back now, Austin. The dream is yours to take. Along the way, you are becoming such a godly leader, determined to succeed for Him, standing taller—and not just because you've grown several inches lately. Austin, I love that you care enough to be and do your best. It shows in your straight A's, and it shows in the way you treat your classmates. Of course, it absolutely shows when you play any sport. Always remember what I've told you about that determination. Let it push you to be better, but never, ever let it discourage you. You're so good at life, Austin. Keep the passion and keep that beautiful faith of yours. Every single one of your dreams is within reach. Keep your eyes on Him, and we'll keep our eyes on you, our youngest son. There is nothing sweeter than cheering you boys on—and for you, that happened from the time you were born, through your heart surgery until now. I thank God for you, for the miracle of your life. I love you, Austin.

And to God Almighty, the Author of Life,
who has—for now—blessed me with these.

Chandra Olson made the trek every July.

She inked it on her calendar and told her manager and staff so that everyone in her camp knew she was off-limits. For two days midsummer, nothing was more important to America's premier black vocalist than leaving Los Angeles, flying to Birmingham, and driving out to the old country cemetery where her parents were buried.

Nothing.

She would spend the day here, same as she did each July for the last four years. No driver or entourage or fanfare. Just Chandra Olson, a fold-up camping chair, a cooler of smartwater, and a journal. Always a journal.

That way Chandra could write her parents a letter they would never read, and express in words her thanks for their support and her regrets at the cost of fame.

The very great cost.

She parked her rental car in the corner spot and surveyed the area. Oak trees dotted the couple acres of grass and tombstones that made up the graveyard. A few worn-out bouquets and the occasional American flag pressed into the earth over the grave of a soldier's sacrifice. A quick look around confirmed what she hoped to find. She was alone. Except for her, the place was empty.

Chandra stepped carefully through the freshly mowed grass, between markers, to the place where her parents lay. She set down her cooler and opened her chair. For a long moment she simply stared at the etchings in the modest gray stones, letting the truth wash over her once more. Martin and Muriel Olson. Young and vibrant and full of life. Her dad, forty-eight. Her mother, forty-four. Weddings, grandbabies, retirement—all of life ahead of them. Shot down just when their beautiful story was at the best part.

Tears blurred Chandra's eyes. Their death dates were the same: May 15, 2009.

A song burned in her heart this morning, a lyric that had been swimming to the surface for weeks. It would come together here, Chandra was sure. Here, close to the bodies of her parents and with the auditions for season ten of *Fifteen Minutes* set to begin later in the week. The song would be a ballad. A warning to be careful what you wish for, be careful what you dream.

In case it actually happens.

Chandra took her seat and studied the gray clouds slung low over the cemetery. She'd been part of the audition process in seven cities across the country over the last two months. Atlanta would be the last one, and the contestants who moved on would go straight to New York.

Yes, somewhere in houses across America, they were getting

ready. Thousands of them. Saying good-bye to family and friends and heading off for a weekend of auditions in the heart of the South. Looking for a shot at fifteen minutes of fame.

Six years ago, Chandra was that wide-eyed singer, working at a state-subsidized day-care center and taking college classes at night. Nineteen years old with a dream bigger than Texas. What did she know about *Fifteen Minutes* or where it might lead, where the journey would take her?

Chandra closed her eyes and saw herself the way she was back then. No one had been more excited about her audition than Chandra's parents. They were longtime hard workers, both of them office managers for sales firms in downtown Birmingham. Martin and Muriel grew up in the projects, too poor to eat some days. They spent their lives trying to give their kids—Chandra and her brother, Jalen—everything they never had. Jalen's dream had been soccer. He was playing now, a senior at Liberty University in Virginia. But only because her parents had worked years of overtime to pay thousands of dollars in club soccer fees and private coaching and gym memberships. It was the same for Chandra—only her passion wasn't soccer, it was singing.

She opened her eyes and looked at her mother's tombstone. *You used to tell me I was born humming. Remember that? You gave me every advantage, Mama.* It was true. Chandra took voice lessons from the best teachers. She'd attended a private arts school on the south side, and when she wrote her first song, her parents took her to Atlanta and had it produced by a legend known for turning out R&B hits.

Nothing opened the door to her singing career the way *Fifteen Minutes* did. Chandra blazed through the audition process; even with the show's manufactured drama, there was never really any contest. On the show's finale, when dapper host Kip Barker smiled at the cameras and rattled off the famous line "The next fifteen minutes of fame go to . . . Chandra Olson!" there wasn't one surprised person in the audience or at home.

"You might be the best singer to ever grace the *Fifteen Minutes* stage." That's what longtime judge Cullen Caldwell had told her, and the comment was plastered across the Internet, everywhere from the *Today* show to *People* magazine.

Chandra remembered a private moment with her mother a week later. "You realize how big this is, baby girl?"

Beneath the warmth of her mother's words, Chandra's heart swelled. She hugged her mama for a long time. "It's big."

"It's more than that!" Her mother put her hands on either side of Chandra's face and looked deep into her eyes. "*Fifteen Minutes* is the biggest show on television, baby. And you're the best singer they've ever seen! God's gonna use you, child. He's gonna use you like none of us can begin to imagine."

Her mama was right about *Fifteen Minutes*. The show had been on the air for ten years, and though other voice talent programs competed for a share of the market, nothing compared to *Fifteen Minutes*. Between the judge's comment and her mother's praise, the future seemed brighter than the sun, Chandra's potential unlimited.

Anyone could see the success ahead.

But none of them saw coming what happened two years later. The second autumn after Chandra's win—with her first album topping the charts and her fame far surpassing what even Cullen Caldwell expected—an Alabama stalker stepped into the picture. He found Chandra on Facebook and asked for a loan. Money to help him and his mother buy a house. Chandra let the comment pass.

The request quickly became harassment, with the guy posting daily demands for money. His most chilling post was also his last. *What if something happened to your parents, Chandra? Maybe that would get your attention!*

Chandra blocked him from her Facebook page and filed a report with the Birmingham police.

"The guy's annoying," the Birmingham officer told her. "But anyone can make a Facebook page. We can't even prove he's a guy or that he lives in Alabama. People like this are rarely serious." The officer added that there wouldn't be enough hours in the day to investigate every crazy threat made against a celebrity. "It comes with the territory."

Yes. It came with the territory. Another aspect of being in the public eye. Chandra tried to believe the officer's words. The threat was nothing. Her concert schedule rolled on, and Chandra talked to her mother every night before she took the stage, same as always. Once she even shared her fears about the guy.

"I should get you a bodyguard, Mama. I have one."

"Don't be silly." Her mama's calm never wavered. "God's in control, baby. Me and your daddy are fine."

"I wish you were with me." Fear made the drafty wings of the arena colder than usual. "You and Daddy could come out on the road."

"Aww, Chandra." Her mom's smile rang through her words. "When we retire we'll be front row at every show."

Chandra had two minutes before her first song. "I love you."

"I love you, too. Do me a favor, baby."

"What?"

"Out there tonight, picture me and your daddy in the front row. We're with you, baby girl. We're always with you." Her emotion got ahead of her. "I'm so proud of you, Chandra."

Her mama's confidence kept Chandra sane, helped her forget the stalker's awful comment. But one warm night later that week, her parents pulled into their driveway after a church service and climbed out of their car. One of the neighbors was outside getting her mail and saw everything. Chandra's parents were laughing and talking, full of life. Her father had just taken her mother's hand when a spray of bullets exploded from the front porch, ripping through their bodies and dropping them to the ground. They were dead before the neighbor could call for help.

The man turned out to be certifiably insane, an escaped patient from a mental hospital. He waited on the Olsons' front porch until the police arrived, at which point he handed himself over and readily admitted to the killings. "I wanted Chandra's attention," he told police.

It worked.

Life would forever be measured as before and after the shootings. No question, a part of Chandra was buried right here with her parents. In the wake of their murders, she took two months off and became a recluse, handling her parents' affairs, afraid to leave their house. Eventually she hired two additional bodyguards and returned to the limelight.

She had no choice. The stage owned her now. It was where she belonged.

Questions plagued her then the way they did four years later, here at the cemetery. What was the point of fame and celebrity? All the record sales and accolades and awards? The money and houses and vacations? None of it could take her back to that moment, her mother's hands on her cheeks.

Her parents' faith had been strong and foundational, a key to Chandra's life before *Fifteen Minutes*. Now only one Bible character allowed Chandra a sense of understanding, a point of relating.

Solomon.

The king who had everything but finished his days believing the most desperate of thoughts—that all of life was meaningless. A chasing after the wind. Chandra had read the book of Ecclesiastes again on her Bible app during the flight here, and once more she had found her life verse, the only one that applied, Ecclesiastes 2:17, a nugget of sad truth tucked in the mix of a host of depressing Scriptures. She remembered the verse word for word.

So I hated my life, because the work that is done under the sun was grievous to me. All of it is meaningless, a chasing after the wind.

Her newest album was number one on iTunes, and she'd been asked back to *Fifteen Minutes*. This time as a judge. She had ten million Twitter followers and daily requests for movie and book deals. But here, in the warmth and quiet of the cemetery, she could only agree with King Solomon. Where were the real winners? Life was meaningless . . . a chasing after the wind.

All of it.

She opened her journal and began to write. The lyrics came easily, pouring from the gaping holes in her heart. It would be a hit, she was sure. Even that was meaningless. Only one thing kept Chandra going, kept her engaged in the daily trap of celebrity and fame, through concerts and autograph seekers and handlers and bodyguards. It wasn't her new role as judge on *Fifteen Minutes* or the countless hopefuls heading out to audition this week.

It was the twenty finalists.

The ones whose lives were about to change forever. The unsuspecting contestants who would never be the same, who could never go back to life the way it had been. Just maybe among them was a singer like she used to be, someone with faith and family and a quiet, happy life.

If she could warn just one about the false illusion and prison of fame, she would do it. In the process she might find something she'd lost four years ago with the death of her parents. The one thing celebrity could never give her. The one thing worth chasing.

Meaning.

Zack Dylan held a steaming mug of black coffee in one
hand and his Bible in the other. He stood on the wrap-
around wooden porch of his parents' farmhouse and watched a
pair of Arabian horses run through the Kentucky bluegrass. The
hundred-acre horse farm had been in the family for six gener-
ations.

He breathed deep the sweet July air and set his things down
on the old wooden table. Four metal-back chairs made up the
seating. Zack took the one with a view of the horses. This had
been his routine lately. Taking his coffee out here and reading his
Bible. He loved Jesus more than his next breath. He could feel
Him close as skin. But these days he needed all the wisdom he
could get. His girlfriend, Reese Weatherly, would be here in half
an hour.

Their last chance to hang out before he left for Atlanta.

The Arabians stopped as if they could sense something

changing, something big about to happen. Then, like the wind they took off again, flying through the grass, a song in motion. Zack leaned his forearms on the old table and watched them run. His great-great-grandfather had raised thoroughbreds, and in 1934 the Dylans' horse farm had produced the winner of the Kentucky Derby. A sketch of the champion with a bouquet of roses formed the farm's logo.

Dylan Champion Horse Farm.

A farm doomed to foreclosure if something didn't change.

Zack let the history hit him again. Sometime in the 1950s the family stopped raising costly thoroughbreds and switched to Arabians. Now dressage riders boarded their horses here and rented time in one of the three arenas. Faith, family, and Southern horse farming. Danville, Kentucky, born and bred. The problem wasn't the business. It was the tornado that had come through and damaged the barns and stables in January.

The damage didn't touch the house, but the insurance didn't cover the barns and stables. Liability, yes. Storm damage, no. The operation was too tight to justify that sort of insurance. Especially when six years ago a different tornado had done similar damage. Back then the family's insurance had been comprehensive. After the claim, covering the outbuildings against storms wasn't possible.

From the moment the storm passed, Zack and Duke, his fifteen-year-old brother, had worked alongside their dad to fix the damage. They needed additional lumber to replace the roofs on the outbuildings. Tens of thousands of dollars in supplies. Without that, the buildings had stayed in disrepair and most people had moved their horses to other facilities. The Dylans spent more money than they made and the tension around the kitchen table grew every day.

On top of that Zack's sister, AJ, had been sick. She had Down syndrome and juvenile arthritis, an especially severe kind. A host of other complications had left doctors convinced she wouldn't live another ten years.

Zack exhaled, feeling the weight of his family's troubles. Regardless of the broken buildings and dwindling bank accounts, this was his family's horse farm. Sure, Zack had other dreams, songwriting, even singing. Those were tangents, really. Hobbies. More than anything he wanted to see the farm up and running, wanted to bring in new Arabians and even Derby contenders. Put the Dylan Champion Horse Farm on the map once more. Horse farming was supposed to be his and Duke's legacy. The fabric of their past, the lure of their future.

A creaking sound made him look over his shoulder. The door opened and Grandpa Dan stepped out, most of his weight on his black cane. "Zack."

"Sir." He pushed his chair back and stood.

His grandpa's steps were slow, Parkinson's disease stealing a little more of his freedom every week. A smile lifted his weathered face. "Beautiful morning."

"Like a painting." Zack waited.

The porch boards protested with each step. His grandpa reached him and put a shaky hand on his shoulder. The old man had lived in the guest house out by the largest arena before the tornado hit. Now he stayed in the guest room on the main floor. He spent most of his time here, on the porch overlooking the farm, staring out at images from decades gone by.

The old man struggled to his seat, exhaled slowly and leveled his gaze at Zack. "You're leaving. Is that what I hear?"

"I am. Yes, sir." Zack leaned closer, took his grandfather's black cane and rested it against the porch railing. He sat back down. Neither of them said anything for a while, the morning breeze warm and easy between them.

Zack broke the silence first. "How are you?"

"Wonderful. Never better." The old man's eyes looked deep and full. "Good Lord gave me another day. Got nothing to complain about." His look grew serious. "AJ's coughing more. I'm worried about her."

"Me, too." Zack studied his grandfather. Stoic, strong. A throwback from another era. Complaining wasn't an option. He could be drawing his last breath and he'd be more concerned with those around him.

"I hate when she's sick. She can't get on a horse coughing like that."

Zack patted the man's leathery hand. "She needs a different doctor, someone from Louisville."

"Yes." The old man eyed him, sizing him up for a long moment. "You have some time?"

"Yes, sir." Zack had expected this. Dreaded it.

His grandfather looked deep into his eyes, right through him. "The audition. *Fifteen Minutes.*"

"Yes?"

"You know how I feel about it."

"I do. Daddy told me." Zack took a swig of coffee. His father's words rang in his heart constantly this past week. *I believe in you, son. No harm in trying out. But you know your grandfather. Dylan men don't chase fame . . . they tend the farm and keep up tradition. They get a second job and buy the wood and fix the buildings. They find a way.*

Zack forced his dad's words from his mind. He respected his father, but still he was going to Atlanta. He couldn't be afraid of success. The idea was ridiculous. He sipped his drink more slowly.

His grandfather gazed back at the front door, his eyes a steely reflection of some yesteryear. Gradually he found Zack again. "Why are you going?"

"What if I'm supposed to go?" Zack felt his heartbeat quicken. He set down his coffee and leaned back in the chair. His words came measured, unrushed. "Maybe God could use me better on a stage somewhere." He tried to smile. "I could pay off the farm. Daddy wouldn't have to work so hard." Zack paused, feeling the weight of the situation. His father had looked older lately, constantly worried. He thought of something else. "We could get better doctors for AJ. Duke could go to college like he wants to."

"A lot of good men get lost on a stage."

"Not me." Zack folded his hands on the table and studied his grandfather's eyes. "You know me, Grandpa. If I make it . . . I won't get lost. Not ever. God loves me too much for that." Nothing stood more certain in Zack's mind. He watched the Arabians flying across the Kentucky grass. Why was his grandpa so worried? He would go with God's blessing, sing for His glory, and one audition to the next he would walk only through the doors that the Lord Himself opened. If singing on *Fifteen Minutes* got in the way of him and God, he'd pray to be sent home.

It was that simple.

His grandpa watched him. "You're a Dylan, and you're a good boy." The old man searched his eyes, processing. "But if they keep you, it'll change things, Zack. Fame always does." He hesitated, his tone kind. "God-fearing men . . . we live a quiet life."

Zack didn't argue. He respected his grandfather's opinion, but nothing would change his mind. He had prayed for God's will and he was going to Atlanta. Besides, was he supposed to go his whole life untested? What good was his faith if it couldn't see him through whatever lay ahead?

"What troubles me"—the old man drew a shaky breath, and for the first time a flicker of fear showed in the lines on his forehead—"is your motive, son. What do you hope to gain?" He waved his hand around. "Yes, you want to pay off the farm. Rescue your tired father. I admire that, Zack, I do." He let the moment breathe. "When I was your age I worked two jobs. Three, even. You could do that, son. Why the show?"

"I need an answer." Zack didn't blink, didn't waver. He breathed deep, the certainty of a lifetime filling his heart. "God gave me my voice, Grandpa. I have to at least try."

"You sing at church." Sincerity softened his eyes. "With the teens. They love you."

"Yes." Zack stared out at the far reaches of the field, at the Arabians standing alert now in a tight herd. "It's just . . ." He turned to the old man. "What if I could shine brighter for God on a bigger stage? In front of the whole world?" A growing passion filled his tone. "Country music, Grandpa. That's as big as it gets. People will *see* my faith and they'll want Jesus. They will."

His grandfather stayed quiet, his eyes never leaving Zack's. "God doesn't measure big the way people measure big. Jesus had just twelve followers." He blinked a few times. "Fame is a demanding mistress."

Zack hesitated out of respect. Most people he knew were excited for him, wishing him well. But his family hadn't gotten behind him. He swallowed his frustration. "I'm twenty-three. I've waited a long time to try this."

"Just remember the Derby days." His grandpa's eyes narrowed, more serious. "Some people never find their way back home."

Zack had heard the story often. One of his great-grandfather's friends had owned Kentucky Derby winners also. Only the guy had gotten caught up in a party crowd from New Jersey and lost his life to a heroin addiction. It was the only brush with fame Zack's grandpa knew about and it hadn't ended well. Which explained his warning. But that didn't apply to Zack. He patted his grandpa's hand. "You're assuming I'll make it." A slow, nervous laugh slipped through his lips. "A hundred thousand people will try out for the show." He paused. "I could be home by Monday. If so, I'll get another job. I promise."

His grandpa studied Zack and a certain knowing filled his expression. "You really believe that?"

Zack thought about the hours he'd prayed, the conversations he'd had with Reese and his parents. The people who had heard the EP he made last year and told him he should get a manager or move to Nashville. He was the next Keith Urban, everyone said so. Year after year he had resisted the desire to audition. Now he could almost hear the clock ticking, almost feel his chances slipping away. Here when his family was facing financial ruin, it was as if God Himself were telling him to go for it.

His grandpa was waiting. "You believe you'll be home by Monday."

Zack didn't think he'd win. But he had a chance. He had to believe that. He shook his head. "No, sir. I guess I don't really believe that."

"Me either." The man angled his head slightly. He took his time with the next part. "You're the best country singer I ever heard."

Zack felt the compliment to the depths of his heart. "Thank you." He took another drink of coffee and felt himself relax. His grandpa wasn't here to talk him out of leaving. "What you said . . . it means a lot."

"It's true." Concern darkened his eyes. "That's why we're

talking. The family needs you here, son. You make it on that stage and . . ." He looked out across the farm. The Arabians were running again, the sun warming the bluegrass. "You could lose all this."

Reese's car appeared on the horizon. Zack weighed his words. "I have to try. It might be the answer for all of us. God's plan."

Together they watched her pull in to the long, winding drive and head slowly for the house. "Remember this, son." Grandpa stared at Zack, like he was willing him to understand. "If it gets crazy, come home. While you still can."

"Yes, sir." Zack put his hand over Grandpa's. "Thank you." His family was worried over nothing. No matter what happened, Zack wasn't going to change. He had his faith, the promise that God was with him. Jesus was his helper; what could man do to him? That was right out of the Bible, after all.

The old man watched Reese climb out of the car. "She loves you."

"I love her." Zack caught her look from across the way; her dark brown hair swished around her pretty face. "I'm going to marry her. As soon as we get the farm on its feet."

"She'll always be special to me. You know that."

"Yes." Zack and Reese's journey was intertwined in a love story that came with the most beautiful history, as if all their lives had led to the single moment in time when their eyes first met. Zack wouldn't do anything to hurt what he and Reese shared.

His grandpa looked concerned. "How does she feel about this?"

"She believes in me." Zack looked at his grandpa, deep into his eyes. "Same as you." He moved to the spot beside the old man and crouched low as he put his arm around his grandpa's thin shoulders. "It'll be okay. You know me."

"I'll pray." In a move that told Zack the depths of his concerns, his grandpa rested his head against Zack's. Reese walked up the porch steps slowly, her eyes on the two of them. Zack remained where he was, his arm still around his grandpa. "I'll be fine." He gave the man his black cane and helped him up. They walked together back to the house.

His grandpa stopped at Reese and took both her hands in his. "I prayed for you today."

"I count on that." She smiled at him, her eyes shining.

The two of them hugged and Zack's grandpa looked from Reese to Zack. His eyes said what his words did not as he nodded, turned, and headed back in the house. When the door shut behind him, Zack turned and faced Reese, looked deep into her pale blue eyes. If for some reason he became crazy successful on *Fifteen Minutes,* that would be fine. God's will. Because nothing—absolutely nothing—would ever get in the way of what he had here. The farm, his family. And the girl standing in front of him.

The one he loved with all his life.

ZACK TOOK THE spot next to her, the two of them leaning on the porch rail. Her eyes shone with a trust he didn't take for granted. But something was different. As if already she were protecting herself from the imagined storms ahead.

"Let's walk." He held out his hand. "When do you go to work?"

"I have an hour." They walked down the steps toward a path that wound through the estate to the barns and beyond. "How's AJ?"

"Sick." Zack eased his fingers between hers. The closeness of her, the touch of her skin against his, the familiarity of it—the sensation was always special. Today he felt more aware of her, the gift of her in his life. Of course he did. He was leaving tomorrow. He stopped when they were out of sight from the front windows.

"We miss her at the center." Reese was an equine therapist. For the last three years AJ had been one of her students.

"She can't wait to get better. She misses you and the horses." He stopped and took her other hand, facing her. She was the most beautiful girl he'd ever seen. Her beauty worked its way out from her heart, through her eyes. But today her joy didn't shine as brightly. "Hey . . ." He studied her, reading her. "You're sad."

"No." She worked one of her hands free and ran it over her hair. "Nervous, maybe. Not sad." She smiled, and their connection felt stronger than ever. "I'm proud of you, Zack."

"Why are you nervous?" He searched her eyes.

"I don't know. Everything feels . . . up in the air." She squinted in the sun. "Unsure, I guess."

"Baby." Zack took a step closer, breathing in her perfume, the nearness of her. "Nothing's going to change. You and my family . . . Give me more credit. Even if something crazy happens and I make it through, nothing will shake me. Nothing ever could."

"How do you know? You've never done anything like this." She smiled. "And you will make it through. You're the best." The sweetness of her tone told him more than her words could. No one believed in him more.

Zack pulled her close, swaying with her beneath the summer sun. When he drew back he found her eyes again. "You said you wanted to talk?"

She slid her hands in the pockets of her dark shorts. "It's

nothing bad." A hint of nervousness flashed in her expression. "I got a call today. From a woman in London."

"London?"

"Yes." She looked to the distant parts of the property and then back to him. "She runs a horse farm. She wants me to help bring equine therapy to her center. Maybe get the program established in the UK. She talked about teaching it to three of their instructors. Which could take a while."

Zack's mind raced. "You mean like . . . move there?"

"For a year, maybe. Yes." She hesitated. "Eight students and their families have already signed up. They can't find a program without a several-year waiting list."

"Wow! That's amazing." The sun shone higher in the sky, the heat and humidity heavy around them. Reese moving to London? What was happening? This talk was supposed to be about the show, about his audition. He should be assuring her that he'd be home soon and nothing would change. He blinked a few times and tried to clear his head. "How . . . how did they hear about you?"

She started to explain. Something about the woman knowing Reese's boss here in Kentucky, and how Reese came highly recommended, one of the best therapeutic horse instructors in the South. And how the London stable wanted someone with experience, someone from Kentucky with a history of horse sense. Her sentences ran together and Zack found himself stuck back at the beginning.

She's moving to London?

They'd been dating since their freshmen year at University of Kentucky. Zack had been an animal science major and Reese competed on the Wildcats dressage team. Double major—special education and equine therapy. Only one thing in all the world was

more beautiful than seeing Reese ride. Seeing her help special-needs kids find their way on a horse. Kids like his sister AJ.

Zack used to tease her that if he could ever get her off the
back of a horse, he'd marry her. Four years had flown by, and a
month ago they graduated. Zack had never loved her more. Their
beautiful history—the history they didn't realize until after they
started dating—the way she made him laugh, the very deep beauty
of her heart. Her love for special-needs kids and horses and him.

They hadn't talked about an exact date. But he'd figured that
if the farm were solid again by Christmas, he'd buy her a ring.
This was the year he'd been waiting for.

"Zack?" She moved closer. "Did you hear me?"

"You're moving to London?" His mouth was cotton balls and
sawdust. He led her into the shade against the side of the house so
he could see her eyes. Straight through them. "For a year?"

"I'm thinking about it."

"Why?"

She allowed a single laugh, one that held her usual grace.
"I'm good at it."

"I didn't mean it like that." Zack's mind raced as fast as his
heart. "No one's better at what you do." His mouth felt dry. "I
mean . . . why now?"

"They need me. The kids there . . . they have no one." She
stared at the spot between their feet for a moment before looking
at him again. "Maybe it's God's timing. You know, with you auditioning."

"A whole year?" Zack brushed his hand against the side of her
face. If only they could stay in this moment. Without the audition
or this crazy London idea. He looked deep into her, all the way to
her heart. "You can be good at it right here in Danville."

"So can you."

Her tone remained kind, but her words took his breath away. "Okay. So you're serious."

Her smile was tinged with sadness. "It'll be hard to be apart. But right now, I don't know. Our dreams are maybe taking us in different directions."

"London?" He released his hold on her and took a slight step back. "Sure. I mean, I'm happy for you. If your dream is to live in Europe for a year." The feeling that he'd been hit by a truck lingered. The news had him dazed and off-balance. "I guess . . . I didn't know."

"Right. Like I didn't know you were going to try out for *Fifteen Minutes*." She folded her arms tight in front of her, almost as if she were cold despite the morning heat. "Look, I want you to go. I'll be your biggest fan, Zack. But you'll be busy with the show. The whole thing, the audition, the process . . . the tour. It could take a year." She reached up and touched his cheek. "Maybe then we'll know what's next."

"The tour, Reese? Really? I haven't even made it past the first round."

"Maybe the timing is part of God's plan." Her words didn't come all at once. She took hold of his hand. "It sort of seems that way."

He tried to keep control of his frustration. "What?"

"Don't get mad." Her smile softened things for a few seconds. "Just . . . you know, sometimes being apart is good. So we can be sure who we are. Before . . ."

He ran his fingers through her windblown hair. "Before I marry you." He brought his face closer to hers. "That's what you mean, right?"

"Yes." Her voice was barely a whisper. Her smile touched his soul. "Maybe that."

"Baby . . ." He wanted her so badly. "I'd marry you today if I could. You know that." He stepped back and searched her eyes. "I have to audition. It could mean . . . saving this farm. It could change life for my family."

"I know." Her smile touched his soul. "If I move to London it could change things for those kids."

"Look." He kept his voice steady and worked to control his warring emotions. "I need you. Whether I make it or not. Please . . . don't move to London."

His words seemed to hit their mark. A few seconds passed and she took his hands. "I haven't said yes. It's just an option."

"Crazy girl." He put his hands around her waist and drew her close. "London's not your dream. And New York's not mine."

"No?" Gradually the shine returned to her eyes.

"No." He could breathe again. They had found their way back to normal. He eased his hands from hers and gently framed her face. Then he kissed her the way he'd wanted to since she arrived. "This is your dream, remember?" His voice fell a notch.

"You?" She giggled, brushing her cheek against his. "Zack Dylan? You're my dream?"

"Not me." He kissed her again and when he pulled back, he felt the humor leave his expression. "Us." He searched her eyes, making sure his place in her heart remained. Untouched. Like before he'd made his decision to audition for *Fifteen Minutes*. "We're the dream. Okay?"

"Is that right?" The corners of her lips lifted and she rested her head on his chest, the two of them swaying in the warm summer morning air.

"Yes, baby. That's right. This is the dream." The words he'd said to his grandfather came back and he repeated them. "I want to marry you, Reese. I'll audition and then I'll come home. Please don't go. Not for a year, anyway."

"It is a long time." She smiled up at him as they started walking. "Hey, Toby's doing better. He's talking in sentences."

His pride for her work welled up inside him. "I love that boy."

"He loves you."

Zack listened, loving her heart, the way she cared for her students. They checked the one small stable that hadn't been destroyed in the storm and walked back to her car. The show didn't come up until he took her in his arms again.

"Zack, I've known you since you were eighteen." She allowed some space between the two of them. For a long while she said nothing, only looked out at the land, at the horses. Finally she drew a deep breath and stared at the sky. "You said singing at church was enough. You were never going to try out."

"We need the money. You know that. Singing's the only other thing I can do and—"

"Let me finish." She put her hand on his shoulder, a fresh depth in her eyes. "Please, Zack."

"Sorry." He shifted, waiting.

She paused as if having this part of the conversation with her own conscience. "You were going to be a songwriter. You'd spend your life here and continue with your family's farm." Her words came slowly again, like the passing white clouds. "That's the Zack I fell in love with. You said the fame thing, singing on a stage, it wasn't for you."

"Reese . . ." He raked his fingers through his thick dark hair. They'd been over this.

"That's what you said." She turned her eyes to his again. The defeat in her tone turned to sadness. "Remember?"

"Try to understand." He searched her eyes. "The music, the songs . . . they live in me. I have to try. Sure I want to write, but if I can sing, if I can do something I love and help my family, shouldn't I try?"

"I know." She nodded, never breaking eye contact. Her fight was gone. The finality in her tone told him she had accepted his decision. Even if she had doubts. She took a step toward her car door, her eyes still on his. "I want you to go, Zack. You're amazing. I think you could win the whole thing." Her smile didn't hide the hurt in her eyes. "But you have to know . . . if you win, that could change things. It could change us."

"Not in a million years." He was sick of this, of the doubts from people who should've known him best. "Not ever."

"Okay." She smiled despite the shadow of sadness in her eyes. "As long as you've thought it through."

He didn't respond. Couldn't say anything in light of her heartfelt reminder. Whether he liked it or not, she was right. If he went far, if he won, there might be no way back to the life they shared here. Now.

"You need answers." Her tone was kind. "Your family needs money. I get it." She kissed him more quickly than before. "I need to go. We'll talk tonight."

"What about your song? You haven't heard it."

She giggled. "Later. You're busy."

"But you want to hear it, right?"

"Of course." She placed her hands alongside his face. "I can't wait."

He felt the minutes slipping away. He planned to leave at sunup. "I'll play it tomorrow. Before I go."

"Okay." She tilted her head, like she couldn't say exactly what she was feeling.

"I'll be home soon."

She shook her head. "You won't."

"Reese." He wouldn't argue with her. He was grateful she believed in him. He said the only words that mattered. "I love you."

"I love you, too."

She took a few steps back, her eyes still lost in his. But then she turned around, climbed into her car, and drove off. He watched her go. She was worried over nothing. If his parents were about to lose the farm that had been in the family for over a hundred years, then he needed to find a way to make money. Other than working with horses, singing was all he knew.

That and the saving power and love of Jesus Christ.

God would see him through wherever the ride took him. Of course he had to audition, had to pray for a chance. If by some miracle he made it, he would have a platform to share his faith and the money to pay off the farm. Then he would marry Reese—the way they'd planned all along—and Grandpa Dan could die happy.

As he walked up the stairs to the old farmhouse peace spread from deep inside him. Whatever happened next he would be home soon. Reese would stay in Kentucky and they'd be engaged by Christmas. He was sure.

Before he turned in that night he found his guitar and played her song, the one he'd written for her. He called it "Her Blue Eyes" and the verses talked about a girl who saw beauty in the life of a handicapped child and joy behind the counter of a homeless shelter. As he fell asleep, the chorus stayed with him.

Of all I see through her blue eyes
What gives me my direction

Is always seeing my reflection
There in her blue eyes.
I always want to see me there
Under a Kentucky sky
There in her blue eyes.
Lost in her blue eyes.

Reese Weatherly had pictured many things for her and Zack after college, but she never imagined this. Zack trying his hand at fame. Now the day was here and she needed to handle it with grace. She loved him. He deserved her support, especially this morning when he was on his way over to say good-bye. They'd share a few words, a hug and a kiss as he drove off for the Atlanta audition.

And then what?

She sat in the dark on her parents' front porch steps and tried not to shiver. The uncertainty of tomorrow was colder than the early morning. She hugged her ribs and stared at the stars blanketing the sky. *He's going to make it, right, God? This is going to change everything.*

She waited. Sometimes she could almost hear the voice of God when she talked to Him. But not here, not now.

Maybe because she didn't need an answer from heaven. If

he survived the audition process and made it to the televised show, Zack could win the whole thing. He *would* win it. He looked like a young James Dean or Elvis, and his smooth voice captivated people. The struggle was this—Zack had never talked about being a singer. Like his dad and grandfather, Zack always planned to take over the horse farm. He'd stay in Danville, bring on a few thoroughbreds, maybe raise a Derby champion like his ancestors. Sure he'd write songs in his spare time, and maybe that would bring in a second income someday. But auditioning for *Fifteen Minutes*?

It was the financial crisis that had forced his decision. And that had led to his curiosity that maybe God had created him for the stage.

A shiver ran down Reese's arms. If he won, he would need to live in L.A. or New York or Nashville, caught up in the madness of whatever that life looked like. *And I'll be here.* She blinked back the sting of tears. *Teaching special-needs kids to ride horses. Working with Zack's sister.*

Gradually, with the soft steps of sock feet and Sunday mornings, their beginning came back, the first time she met Zack Dylan. As a freshman, she had won a spot on the university dressage team. A week after classes began she was about to compete in her first event. She remembered the way her heart pounded as she walked with the team to the arena, how nervous she was to compete in her first collegiate competition.

As she'd reached the gates, Reese had felt her heart sink. She'd forgotten her gear bag back at the stable. She told the coach and then ran as fast as she could back to the school's horse center. Darting through the door and down a dimly lit path covered in sawdust, she found the bag at the edge of the covered arena. But before she could turn back for the door, she heard a guy's voice. Someone singing. Even out of breath and in a hurry to get back, she could do nothing but stop and listen. The voice came from one of the stalls. He was brushing down a horse, with sunlight streaming in from one of the windows.

Slowly she set her gear bag down. She couldn't take her eyes off him. The fractured sunlight on his handsome tanned face, the silhouette of his muscled arms in the shadows, the sure way he had with the horse. The beautiful voice. Reese had gripped the wooden post. If he worked with the UK horses, how had she missed him?

He must've heard her; barely half a minute passed before he stopped and looked up. Their eyes met, and across the stable the connection was immediate. Like they'd known each other all their lives.

"Hey." He set the brush on a shelf and dusted his hands off on his jeans. Then he walked over to her slowly. Curious. "You on the dressage team?"

His question jolted her from the moment. "I have to go." She grabbed her gear bag and flung it over her shoulder. "Loved the song."

"Thanks. Nice to meet you." He chuckled. "I'm Zack."

Already she was running toward the door. She was going to be late, and then the coach would bench her or kick her off the team.

"Hey," he called after her. "What's your name?"

She didn't have time to turn around. Instead she raised her hand without looking back. "Later."

That afternoon Reese had the best ride of her life. Halfway through the competition she caught a glimpse of the stands and there, near the top of the bleachers was the dark-haired boy. Sitting by himself and watching her. He waited for her after the competition and they walked together back to the stable. "You didn't tell me your name." He grinned at her.

She could barely think. The combination of the win and the guy beside her. "Reese."

He nodded, thoughtful. "It fits you."

"Thanks." She allowed a light bit of laughter. "I think."

"Yeah, it's a good thing." He narrowed his eyes. "Well, Reese. That was beautiful."

"What?" She felt his eyes on her, felt the warmth of his gaze all the way to her soul.

"How you ride." He shoved his hands in his jeans pockets. "I've been around horses all my life." He stared at her. "The way you ride . . . that's how it's supposed to look."

"Thank you." She hoped he couldn't see the heat in her cheeks. "And you? You're a singer?"

"Nah." He laughed and looked up at the sky. "Only for God and my horses."

They reached the barn and he waited while she changed out of her dressage clothes. Afterward they walked to the far side of the university where the view of the hills was prettiest. They talked the whole time. She learned about his family's horse farm and she told him about her dream of helping handicapped kids. They both were single. No time to date with the newness of college and the demands of the horses. Zack worked eighteen hours a week grooming, required for his major. She spent about that much time practicing dressage.

"Looks like we'll see a lot of each other," he told her as they walked back to the dorms.

"Yeah." She grinned at him. "I know how to find you."

"How's that?" They'd reached her dorm and he faced her.

"Your voice. As long as you're singing, I'll find you. You're amazing."

"Thanks." His eyes held hers. "It'll be easy to find you, too."

Reese liked the easy banter. "Do tell."

"Simple." His eyes sparkled. "I'll look for the prettiest girl on campus." He put his hands in his pockets again and smiled. "See you around, Reese."

The memory dissolved in the early-morning quiet. Reese hugged her knees to her chest. She and Zack had seen each other the next day at the stable and after that they were inseparable. On their first date he'd told her something that stayed with her still. "I feel like I was born for this, for knowing you."

She remembered his words because she had felt the same way. Then, and as their friendship turned to dating a few months later, and a year after that when the story of their grandparents came to light. Craziest story ever. Like something from a movie.

How could she not feel destined to love Zack Dylan?

At least before today.

Other memories swirled and danced in her mind. The first time she visited Zack's church and watched him lead music at the beginning of the service. It wasn't just his beautiful voice that captured her that day.

That afternoon they had gone to her house for dinner and afterward they walked through her neighborhood. "Have you thought about *American Idol* or *Fifteen Minutes*? You're so good, Zack." She wasn't testing him. She only wanted to know.

His response had found a permanent place in her soul. "I could be a songwriter. But I don't want a crazy life." His smile had faded as he seemed to grasp for the right words. "I sing like I breathe, because it's in me. I feel closest to God when I'm on that stage at church singing for Him." He shrugged slightly. "I don't need to win a reality show to be a singer." He grinned. "I'm already one."

She had liked his answer, not so much because it protected what they had but because it suited him. Year after year his answer remained. People would suggest he try out for one of the singing shows, but he would smile and shake his head. The fame thing wasn't for him.

It didn't matter whether deep down Zack's money trouble or his curiosity led him to his decision to audition. Whatever had changed his mind, she was at peace.

Headlights appeared around the bend in the road. Reese shivered again and wondered—what if this were the last time they shared a morning like this? She had loved Zack for so many years, had felt herself destined to a future with him. The guy whose grandpa had been praying for her specifically since she was born. What if Zack left this morning and never came home? *Enough,* she told herself. She stood as he pulled up and parked. If God wanted Zack to audition for *Fifteen Minutes* so be it. He needed her support and belief, her encouragement.

She could break down later.

REESE FELT WARM the moment he embraced her. For a long time they didn't say anything. It was enough, standing there wrapped in each other's arms. Reese could feel the way their hearts beat faster than usual, the impending good-bye making even their bodies aware of the little time they had left.

"You're cold." He drew back and looked at her. "Were you waiting long?"

"Not really. I wanted to be out here." She forced a smile. "I'm excited for you, Zack."

"Know what I want?"

"What?"

He brushed her cheek with his thumb. "I want to jump on your horse with you and ride together till the sun comes up. Just forget the whole singing thing."

"Hmmm." She gazed off toward the horizon, already growing lighter. "Sounds beautiful." She met his eyes again. "Why haven't we ever done that?"

"We will." He smoothed a piece of her hair blowing in the breeze. "Next week when I get back."

Crickets played softly somewhere in the distance. She narrowed her eyes, seeing to the deepest part of him. "You really don't believe it, do you?"

"Believe what?" His words came slowly, a whisper wrapped in the newness of the morning.

"That you'll make it." She refused her gathering tears. "That you'll win."

"It's not humility. I'm realistic." His grin came easily. "Guys who can sing are a dime a dozen." He kissed her and their faces remained close. "Now, guys who sing to horses, maybe not."

She was enjoying the moment more than she'd expected. "You know what *I* think?"

"What?" He swayed with her, the rest of the world forgotten.

"I think your days of singing to horses are numbered."

"Speaking of which." He walked back to his car and returned with his guitar. "I owe you a song."

She felt tears in her eyes, but her smile remained. He pulled his guitar from the case and perched himself on the porch railing.

She had to admit to the possibility that she was hearing it for the first and last time. If things changed . . . if Zack never came back.

She focused on the words and the way Zack looked straight at her as he sang. The song was beautiful, every line a message from his heart to hers. She would never love anyone the way she loved Zack Dylan. By the time he reached the last chorus she had tears on her cheeks.

> *Of all I see through her blue eyes*
> *What gives me my direction*
> *Is always seeing my reflection*
> *There in her blue eyes*

He smiled at her, his own eyes shining with the good-bye ahead. The song played out, the words moving easily from his soul to hers.

> *I always want to see me there*
> *Under a Kentucky sky*
> *There in her blue eyes.*
> *Lost in her blue eyes.*

When it ended they didn't move or speak. Finally he slipped the guitar back in its case and took it to his car. When he returned, his eyes locked on hers.

"After this you'll have your answers." She reminded herself to smile. "Maybe we both will."

He took half a step back. "Both?" He searched her eyes. "What are your questions?"

"Come on, Zack." She willed him to understand. "If God gives you answers, He'll give them to me, too."

"Like . . . ?"

"Not about you." This was a slippery slope. She chose her words with great care. "About the future . . . London. That sort of thing."

"I thought we were finished with London." He took her hands in his, clearly troubled. "Please, Reese. I want to marry you. Don't decide anything until I get back." Fear flickered in his expression. "Okay?"

She searched his eyes. He didn't understand. Once he was on the show he'd be busy. Too busy to come back to Danville until the ride ended. Whenever that might be. Of course she had questions. About London . . . about the two of them. About all of it. Again, she didn't want to send him off worried or troubled. They'd have their answers soon enough.

She closed the distance between them, letting his body warm hers again. "Go audition. You have to. You're the best." She memorized the feel of his arms around her. "Go find your answers, Zack. Do it for your family and for God."

Her words seemed to ease his anxieties. She felt him relax against her. "Remember what I told you?"

"It's going to be okay." She felt the compassion in her eyes.

"Exactly." He released her hands and brought his lips to hers. And for the sweetest seconds they forgot everything except what it felt like to be together, to be in love. The kiss led to another, and the desperation built.

Finally he pulled himself away. "I'll call you when I get there."

She pressed her head to his chest, and he wrapped his arms around her. "Make me a deal?"

"The pre-dawn horseback ride?"

She giggled despite her sadness. "That, too."

"Mmm, baby, I mean it. That'll be us the first morning I'm back."

She smiled, and hope waved a flag in her heart. If only she could hold on to that picture. "I like that."

He chuckled. "What was your deal?"

She felt her eyes grow watery. When she was sure she wouldn't cry, she looked up at him. "Prove them wrong, okay? Please . . ."

"Who?" He held her face in his hands and searched her heart, her soul.

"The world says fame changes everyone." She found her smile. "Prove them wrong."

Strength gathered in his eyes. "I will." He kissed her again. "If I get that far, I absolutely will."

She nodded and felt her heart fall in line. "I believe you." No matter what lay ahead nothing could change Zack Dylan.

His lips met hers and the kiss lingered. "See you soon."

"I love you." She willed herself to remember the look in his eyes, the kindness and humility that set him apart. "I always will."

"Whatever tomorrow holds, you're a part of it. God made us for each other."

She wanted to believe it. With all her heart she wanted to. She held his gaze, lost in his soul. "Go win it."

"I'll call you."

He kissed her one final time, seeing to the places in her heart that belonged to him alone. He held his hand up in a frozen sort of wave. Then he turned and jogged to his pickup truck. He looked back at her as he drove away, as she stood there, watching until his taillights faded into the distance.

By then the morning sun had splashed light onto the day and Reese felt a peace that hadn't been there before. Zack would survive the weekend auditions. His voice would catch the attention of the judges and the nation. He would win their hearts with a single song.

The way he had won hers four years ago.

He really could win it all, but even then she knew Zack. He wouldn't change. Nothing could sway the feelings he had for God, who had given him the gift of song. He would make this competition about glorifying the Lord and helping his family.

And then he'd come back for her.

chapter 3

Downtown Atlanta was bedlam.

Cars with license plates representing half the U.S. jammed the streets around the Georgia Dome. Everywhere Zack looked, streams of people headed for the stadium. There were groups of teens and whole families with handmade signs and scattered through the mix, too many bearded, bespectacled hipsters to count. There was the occasional soccer or basketball team come to support one of its own. And of course the random person dressed in a chicken or cow costume. Three guys had their shirts off and the words "Anything for *Fifteen Minutes*" painted on their chests. Some had guitars slung over their backs; most carried duffel bags and overfilled backpacks.

The electricity in the summer air was palpable. According to the news, *Fifteen Minutes* producers had seen nearly forty thousand singers at the earlier auditions. This was the last one. The last chance for season ten. They were expecting a far bigger turn-out than in any of the previous cities.

Zack tried not to think about it. He needed a parking place. That was all that mattered for now. Cars were grid-locked all around him. Five minutes passed, then ten. No movement. Zack looked in his rearview mirror. How hard would it be to turn around? Find his way to the freeway and never look back?

He meant what he'd told Reese. He probably wouldn't make it past a few rounds at best—too many people, too much confusion for a single voice to stand out. Everything he'd read told him that at this level the producers scanned the crowds for a certain look, something different—red hair or a unique body type or ethnicity. Getting through the first round was as random as it was difficult.

The mirror still had his attention. Why bother? He could spend the weekend with Reese, write a few songs and work with the horses. Take his girl for that early-morning ride tomorrow. Maybe go to the mall and look at wedding rings. Come Sunday he could sing for half an hour at church and life would be good.

Except for one thing. He wouldn't have the answers.

A trio of police officers strode into sight and began directing traffic. Another joined them and another. Someone must've opened additional lots, and with the help of the officers, the traffic began to inch forward. By the time Zack found parking and pushed into the river of people heading for the stadium, it was nearly nine-thirty. The back of the line was ten blocks out. Ten long blocks.

Zack hadn't brought a guitar. Most of the people who made it through did so without an instrument. Less to carry. Less to worry about if he wound up sleeping on the sidewalk. His back-pack held a camping pillow and blanket, protein bars and a six-pack of water. Cough drops and garlic pills. So he could keep his immune system strong if he had to wait till early tomorrow morning to audition.

In front of him a group of teenage girls bounced and squealed and waved at cars still searching for a parking spot. "I'm gonna win!" one of the girls shouted. She waved her hands and rallied her friends. "Let's do a cheer." And like that the girls burst into a chant. "Bang bang, choo choo train, wind us up and we'll do our thing!"

A few nearby cars honked their approval. One of the girls, a lanky blonde, spun around and batted her eyes at Zack. "Hey! You're new!" She waved her girls closer. "We're from South Carolina. Medford High cheer squad." Without waiting for his response, she pointed at him. "Who are you?"

"Zack Dylan. Danville, Kentucky."

The blonde gasped. "Zack Dylan." She looked at her fellow cheerleaders and then quickly back at him. "That's like a famous name." A hurried clap of her hands. "Sing for us, Zack."

Instantly the other girls chimed in. "Yes, sing for us, Zack. Come on!"

"It's too crazy out here." Zack had to yell to be heard. All around them, people were singing and playing guitars, shouting at passing cars.

"It's perfect, come on!" The blonde pointed to herself amid a series of giggles. "I'm Zoey. I'm the captain, so what I say goes. Right, girls?"

"Right!" Their singsong voices were in perfect pitch. "Sing for us, Zack! Come on!"

"Plus your names are cute together, right?" One of the brunettes put her arm around the blonde. "Zoey and Zack. It has a ring."

"Yeah, you're way cuter than her boyfriend." The shortest in the group covered her mouth to stifle her laughter. The other girls nodded along. "Yes, way cuter. Totally cuter."

"I don't know. He looks young but . . ." Zoey put her hands on her hips. "How old are you, Zack?"

"Twenty-three." Zack enjoyed their enthusiasm. He wasn't crossing lines, just soaking in the experience. The show he'd watched all these years had come to life and he was smack in the midst of it. "What about you?"

"Eighteen." She lowered her chin and gave him a look that defined flirty. "Old enough for twenty-three."

Coming up the line Zack spotted a *Fifteen Minutes* camera crew. They had explained on the show's website that they'd be shooting B-roll all day, looking for footage to capture the circus-like atmosphere and excitement of the contestants.

"So you have to sing for us." Zoey clapped her hands again and bounced back in line. "Please!"

Zack saw an opportunity. The cheerleaders wore the same T-shirts and shorts, all of them bubbly and beautiful. If Zack sang now, the cameras were sure to catch the moment. Which meant maybe they'd tell the producers about him and maybe he'd be through to the next round.

Just like that.

He cleared his voice and started in with an old classic. "My eyes adored you . . . though I never laid a hand on you, my eyes adored you . . ."

Sure enough the camera crew moved in close. Zack hammed up the song, stretching his hand out toward the girls as they formed a tight cluster of what looked like starstruck fans. The

Fifteen Minutes crew loved it. Zack could feel them grinning and nodding their approval.

Zoey apparently wasn't about to miss the opportunity. She stretched her hand toward Zack and responded with another classic. "The first time . . . ever I saw your face . . ."

After a few lines, the cameraman made a cut sign and called Zack and the girls over. "I need names and cities. That was perfect."

The girls squealed and stopped long enough to give the information and wait while Zack did the same. "Hey." Zoey bounced a few times. "We should do a cheer."

"Can you cheer, Zack?" The guy with the clipboard raised his brows. "That would make the show for sure."

"I can try." Zack fell into the middle of their group and the girls filled in around him, their arms around his shoulders, patting his head and showering him with attention. "Way to go, Zack! Way to go!"

They formed two lines with Zack front and center and did the cheer the girls had performed earlier. "Bang bang, choo choo train, wind me up and I'll do my thing . . ." When the cheer ended, the girls pumped their fists in the air and kicked one foot high over their heads, the way cheerleaders do. Then they gathered around Zack and started another chant. "Zack, Zack, he's our man. If he can't do it, no one can!" The group of them high-fived Zack and hugged him, hamming it up for the cameras.

It wasn't until the production crew had moved on that Zack felt sick. What had he just done? He hadn't come here to get camera time. Being here was about singing for God and helping his family. He'd pictured himself standing alone, taking in the craziness around him. Now he hadn't been in line half an hour and already he'd fallen in with an entire cheer squad.

All so the cameras might feature him on the show.

He stepped away from the girls, and most of them picked up a conversation with a man in full Native American headdress. But Zoey hung back, standing with Zack and catching her breath. He could feel her shaking off the high-energy silliness as she exhaled. "That was wild."

"Yeah. The camera guys loved it." Zack leaned against a stop sign. The line hadn't moved in a few minutes.

"I'm only like that around them." She smiled. "I guess it's good to act crazy once in a while."

"Pretty harmless." They were talking like old friends. It was a strange sensation. Zack didn't have time to think about what to say next.

"So Zack, you're too cute to be single." She flipped her long hair over her shoulder, looking straight at him. "You have a girl-friend?"

"I do." Zack could feel his ship righting itself. These were waters he could navigate. "We've been together four years."

"Hmmm." She looked unfazed. "I have a boyfriend. Four months." She grinned and held up her left hand. "No ring, though. I can do what I want."

Her meaning was unmistakable. Zack took a step away from her and looked back at the line of contestants winding along the sidewalk as far as he could see. Behind him were six black gospel singers, and behind them was a trio of kids dressed as vampires. The gospel singers might be interesting. He'd have time to get to know them in the next few hours. But he had no way to escape the girl beside him. Their places in line were set.

"So your girlfriend." Zoey batted her eyelashes. "Do you love her?"

"Absolutely. I'm proposing to her this fall."

"Really?" Zoey's eyes grew wide. "You're young to get married."

"She's amazing." He kept his gaze steady. "I want to spend my life with her. I'm old enough to know that."

Zoey fell quiet as the line moved forward. They could see the gates seven or eight blocks ahead. Her arm brushed against his as they walked. His frustration grew. How could he be any clearer? Once more he took a step to the side and peered at the line ahead. When he turned back to her he kept his distance. "It'll be another few hours at least." Why had he jumped at the chance to play to the cameras? He should've stayed quiet as the crew passed by, or watched while the cheer squad entertained them. Hopefully Reese would understand. He was caught up in the moment—nothing more, right?

"Zack . . . are you listening?" The crowd noise was crazy loud. Zoey moved closer so their arms touched again.

"Sorry." He chuckled, trying to keep things light. "I was thinking about my girlfriend."

"No you weren't." She elbowed him lightly in the ribs. "You were thinking about this forever-long line. I said, 'Don't worry. At least we have each other.' " She held her hand out and waited until he shook it. "Deal?"

Zack hesitated. "Deal." He tried to imagine what sort of deal he was making, but again his words came without thinking. As if they were playing parts in a movie and his lines had already been written.

"Yes, sir." Zoey grinned. "I think you and I are going to be good friends before this day is over."

He had no response. He could only hope the day would fly by. So he could get away from the madness in downtown Atlanta, away from the cheer squad and Zoey.

And back home to Reese where he belonged.

IT WAS ALMOST Zack's turn.

He and the cheerleaders and gospel singers and vampires had reached the Georgia Dome gates sometime after noon. They'd been sitting in section 8B ever since. Sitting and singing and laughing and talking. Zack had gotten to know most of them, and he had found a true friend in one of the gospel singers. Now it was midnight and after a few more groups they'd be up.

Fifteen Minutes staged auditions a little differently. They took contestants in groups of fifty to a tent and had them sing a cappella all at the same time. A dozen judges with clipboards would walk around and through the group, making their way from one singer to the next, taking notes. When three minutes had passed, the group had to stop singing. A couple contestants' numbers might be called for the next round. Or not. The singers chosen to go through to tomorrow's auditions were flashed on the Jumbotron whenever a group left the tent. No one had gone through from either of the last two groups.

"I'm freaking out." Zoey briefly leaned her head on his shoulder. "How can I sing when I'm so tired?"

Zack shifted away from her. Maybe if he turned the conversation to her, she'd forget about him. "Why'd you decide to audition, anyway? You never said."

"Me?" Zoey seemed to sense that he wanted space. She turned in her seat and faced him. "All us senior cheerleaders decided at the same time. Like, we can all sing. So yeah . . ."

Fifteen Minutes encouraged contestants to try out in groups. Once in a while, a group actually made it through, sort of like the TV show *X Factor*. But coming in a group was only one way of capturing the judges' attention. Zack took his time. They had thirty minutes at least. "Not your *group,* Zoey. You. Why did *you* audition?"

She looked at her squad, chatting with a group of guys a few rows down. "It's my dream." She lowered her voice. "The girls don't know that. They think it's all sort of a joke. You know, just to get on TV or whatever." She blinked a few times. "Truthfully? It's all that matters."

Zack had heard her sing earlier. She had the skill to pull off a show like *Fifteen Minutes*. Maybe not the maturity but definitely the talent. "This?" He looked around the packed stadium. "This can't be all that matters."

"It is." She uttered a sad laugh, and in the stadium lights he saw her eyes well up. "My boyfriend's cheating on me. He thinks I don't know." She looked down, her trembling fingers proof of her uneasiness. "I didn't want to say that earlier."

"High school guys aren't real loyal. Most of them, anyway."

"I know." She tilted her head, opening her heart to him whether he wanted it or not. "I need an older guy. That's what my mom always says."

Zack ignored that. He glanced at the screen. A countdown clock told him the current group had thirty seconds. Already ushers were approaching their section. "This is it." Zack stood. "Hit it or go home."

"I'm so scared." Zoey stood and followed him. She seemed to lose her balance as they headed for the aisle and caught herself on Zack's shoulder. "Sorry." A smile tugged at her lips. "Clumsy."

He put his hands in his pockets and looked straight ahead.

He was grateful when she removed her hand from his arm. The girl was very pretty, but her flirting had gotten on his nerves all day; he was in love with Reese. But somehow against his will he caught himself starting to think about Zoey. Sixteen hours together could do that. He would have to sort out his thoughts later. "You're close to your mom?"

"Sort of. She's in rehab. I live with my grandparents." Her eyes darkened, as if maybe she'd said too much. "See what I mean? This show, making it. That's all I have. It's all that matters."

He wanted to tell her about his faith, about the God of hope who had helped his family survive the last year. But as they shuffled to the aisle and down the stadium stairs, the timing seemed off. He would tell her after this first round.

If her mom was in rehab, she had to be lonely. Zack thought of the hours his mother spent with AJ, the conversations about horses and school and the farm. Zoey had none of those moments with her mother. Maybe she hadn't been exaggerating. He felt sick. All day he'd worked to avoid her, to discourage her advances. But the girl was in trouble. Maybe he'd figure out a way to introduce her to Jesus. Maybe pray for her.

He focused on the outer flap of the enormous striped tent. Suddenly everything faded. The crowd and the noise, the conversations and random bursts of singing. This was his single moment. The chance to see if this was how he could help his family. And if God wanted him to sing professionally.

If I make it, I make it for You, Lord. I'll be the brightest light this show has ever seen. I promise.

Stay with me, son . . . I have the words of life. The quiet whisper silenced every sound around him.

Yes, Lord . . . You have the words of life. I believe that.

The thought filled his heart and soul. If he stayed close to God, he could get through this. He would either go home at the end of this audition or shine from the *Fifteen Minutes* stage. It wasn't enough to go through a day simply existing, the way he'd been doing since he arrived in Atlanta. Hamming it up for a camera, not seeing the pain and loneliness in a teenage girl. He felt his determination double. If he made it through in the next few moments, he would absolutely shine for God.

The way he'd failed to do so far today.

I t was time.

In a blur of anxious conversations and shuffling feet, Zack and his group moved into the tent. The instructions were nothing new. All of it was on the show's website. Still, the fifty singers stayed silent while a man with a megaphone explained. "We will announce a start time." The man's accent was distinctly British. "At that point you will sing your best song to the best of your ability." The man seemed bothered, looking down at them from his place on a small platform at the front of the tent. "You will have three minutes. If your number isn't announced at the end of the round, you will go home. No questions. Thank you for trying out. If your number is called, wait inside the tent for further instructions."

Around Zack, people moved their feet and cleared their throats and tried to separate themselves from the crowd. Nervous energy sucked the air from the tent. Zack had seen TV footage of this part of the audition, fifty people singing every sort of song from every genre, trying to push their voices above the noise, desperate for their fifteen minutes of fame. But nothing he had seen prepared him for this, how it felt to have just one shot, one chance to impress the judges.

He glanced at the people in black shirts standing around the perimeter of the tent. None of them looked glad to be there. It had been a long day for everyone, and by now chances were Atlanta had given them what they were looking for. A few of them whispered to each other, and another checked his watch. The man in charge was talking to another group. The contestants began to whisper. A few squeezed in vocal exercises.

Here I go. Help me, God . . . He was going to sing "Wind Beneath My Wings," an old country classic, something familiar that would showcase his tenor voice. According to a forum of past contestants, the more familiar the song the better. It helped the singer stand out.

"I'm gonna be sick." Zoey leaned toward him. She had been quiet since they entered the tent.

"You'll be fine."

The man in charge returned to the platform and glared at them. "Silence!" He nodded to a woman who was clearly his assistant. "Timer ready?"

"Ready."

"Okay. Set . . ." He turned to the contestants. "Go!"

All around him people began singing, creating a noise that shook the tent and took Zack by surprise. The decibels must've been near that of a jet engine or a cheering stadium. If he didn't focus quickly he would lose himself and his song in the mass confusion. *Help me, God . . . I can't do this without You.* He closed his eyes and began to sing. After a few seconds something miraculous happened.

He couldn't hear any voice but his own. Instead of worrying about who was walking past or evaluating him or crossing his name off a list, he forgot about everyone else in the tent. He hit the first chorus singing for a familiar audience of One.

God alone.

By the time he reached the second verse, Zack opened his eyes. Never mind the vampires bopping out to some fifties tune a few feet away or the pop song Zoey was belting or any other sound or song around him. He could hear only his. A spot on the tent wall caught his attention, but instead of red and white canvas, in his mind's eye he was looking across a serene and distant ocean, the presence of God like a breeze against his face. He was able to get through the second chorus and halfway through the bridge before the man waved his hands. "Time. Everyone silent."

Like that the contestants stopped. Several were breathless and a few had tears spilling down their cheeks. Zoey was one of those. She hung her head, her shoulders shaking. Though he'd tried to keep his distance all day, here she needed his support. He put his arm around her while they waited.

"This was one of the best groups we've seen." The man looked surprised. "Most of you look more suited for a Halloween party than a hit reality show." He took a piece of paper from his assistant. "That said, we've chosen four of you to move on to the next round. Here are those contestants."

The man read a number and across the tent one of the gospel singers screamed. He grabbed the necks of his friends one at a time. "Praise Jesus . . . hallelujah!"

"Quiet, please." The man waved his paper at the guy. "No celebrating until I've read all four numbers."

"Yes, sir." The gospel singer whipped back around, breathless. "Sorry, sir."

The next number caused a vampire to drop to the ground, her hand across her mouth. Her companions looked more disappointed than happy for her. Zoey's number was called third and she was immediately engulfed by her cheer squad.

Zack could already feel himself walking back to his truck. What had he expected from a situation like this? Instant success? No, he would go home with his future and his answers firmly in hand. And he would work three jobs if that's what it took to save the—

"Our last contestant from this round is . . ." The man rattled off the number.

CHANDRA OLSON COULDN'T take her eyes off the television monitor.

This was the first day of Atlanta auditions, and for the most part—since this was the last weekend of city stops—Chandra knew the routine. She hadn't paid much attention to today's tent singing. She and the other judges weren't needed until tomorrow afternoon, and in the meantime the show's producers kept them busy with local media.

The judges had suites at the downtown Hilton, but they also had custom trailers in the back lot of the Georgia Dome, each with a live feed to the mass performances happening in the tent. Chandra had done interviews here all day and spent dinner with local network executives, so she hadn't made it back to her hotel room.

She had just wrapped up a phone call with her manager and was about to grab her bag and have her driver take her to the Hilton when something caught her attention. The group of contestants filing into the tent. Six of them looked like gospel singers from a high school or college. She could sense something different about them even through the satellite feed.

Chandra turned up the volume and sank slowly into the trailer's leather sofa. She watched the hodgepodge mix of singers, some who looked barely out of middle school and others who might be seizing their last chance at fame. William Gaines, the show's contestant coordinator, led the audition process. Chandra smiled to herself as he barked at the contestants. She remembered this, the first step. How it felt to be crammed into a tent ready to sing alongside so many others.

After a few minutes of instructions, the singing began. Several sweet voices stood out among the chaos. Chandra focused on the gospel group. It was tough to pick out which of their voices sang so beautifully above the rest.

She watched them, suddenly aware.

Could it be one of them? Was this why she was a judge? So she could warn one of the innocent-eyed kids in that group about the perils of winning?

The trap of having the whole world idolize them?

Chandra stayed till the singers stopped and waited, watching William tally the results. Four of them had survived—more than any other group. Chandra slid to the edge of her seat. How could they know what lay ahead? That every perceived victory was only a step closer to losing themselves, losing life the way they'd known it. There would be no going back, but none of them knew that now. The choir group linked arms, waiting. They were dressed for church, nice and respectful. Not crazy like most of the contestants around them.

William took the podium and made his announcement. One of the gospel guys was in. Chandra gasped softly. She moved to the small screen anchored to the wall of the trailer. Her fingers brushed the surface, the spot where the choir guy celebrated. *Sweet boy. You're just like me.* Chandra wanted to shout at him, warn him not to celebrate. *Fifteen Minutes* swallowed up church kids like this, like Chandra had been back then. Innocent, regular people with light in their eyes. The show loved that kind of singer. Who of them ever counted the cost?

"Boy, you have so much to learn," she whispered to the screen even as William announced the other names. A vampire, a cheerleader, and then . . .

Chandra squinted at the white boy whose number was called last. Slowly she stepped back from the screen, scrutinizing him, his dark hair, his fine features. He looked like a young Elvis. Better, maybe. Taller, more fit. But there was something else about him, a charisma and energy. He looked like top-ten material. The gospel guy could probably sing, and the same had to be true for this guy. But this one had that intangible quality a person couldn't fake or learn. Like he was destined for fame.

The feeling remained strong, so strong Chandra didn't have to wonder if she'd have a chance to talk to him during the audition process. She was convinced. As she turned off the TV monitor and the lights and left the trailer, she did something she hadn't done in a long time. She prayed. For the handsome black singer and every other contestant who'd made it to tomorrow's round.

And for the guy who looked like Elvis. Especially him. Because if her hunch was right, the boy would need it.

Maybe more than all the others combined.

IT TOOK ZACK three full seconds to realize why the cheerleaders had shifted their celebration to him. Since the man was finished, the contestants were free to talk again. The cheers and screams were almost as loud as the singing had been earlier.

"Zack, we both made it!" Zoey yelled to him from across the tent where she was receiving congratulatory hugs from a dozen singers. "Way to go, Zack!"

The news was still trying to find a place in his mind. He'd made it through? He was one of the contestants chosen for the next round? Clarence Brown, the gospel singer who'd become Zack's friend, hadn't made it through. Now he smacked Zack on the shoulder and hugged him. "You got a gift, man. Keep singing for Jesus."

"I will." Their eyes met. For the first time that day Zack felt like himself, those two words summing up his word and his promise to God. "You, too. Keep singing. This isn't the only stage."

"I know it." Clarence pointed up. "God's got a plan." He tapped his finger at Zack's chest. "Go shine for the rest of us."

The tent began to clear and the four contestants made their way to the front platform. Again the guy running things seemed impatient. "You'll meet at the stadium gates at nine tomorrow morning. Once you enter we'll usher you into a large room where you'll wait your turn. You'll have one round with our producers. Eighty of you will survive that. Tomorrow afternoon those eighty will go before the TV judges." He nodded toward the tent flap. "Thank you."

Zack and the others headed out as the next group filed in. The vampire girl was hitting on the gospel singer before they reached the bleachers. Zack did the only thing he wanted to do—he silently thanked God, promised to sing for Him always. No matter what.

That done, he couldn't wait to tell Reese. He pulled out his phone, turned it on and was about to call her when a producer with a camera crew motioned the group closer. "Winners over here. We need an interview."

The questions weren't easy. This was the part of the process where the show executives figured out who was in their midst, what set them apart and what aspect of their lives might be featured on the live show if they made it that far. The questions went on for half an hour and after that an escort took the four of them to an office near the players' locker rooms. There they were given a packet of paperwork to fill out.

The show's producers had booked hotel rooms for the winners but it was nearly three in the morning before Zack checked in. He shot out a single tweet on his Twitter account. *I made it through! Someone tell me this is really my life! Thank you, Jesus!* His roommate was the gospel guy, but both of them were too tired to talk. Not until he hit the pillow did Zack realize he hadn't called Reese. Frustration dampened the elation of the evening, the excitement of surviving the first round. He honestly hadn't had a single minute, and now he'd have to call her in the morning. He checked Twitter. Forty-three new followers. More than he'd had all year. A strange thrill passed through him. This could be huge. The stage, the platform, the chance to shine for God.

Zack's whole body buzzed with adrenaline. He could still feel the nervousness and hear the songs from those few crazy minutes in the tent. How had he gotten through? He must've projected better than at any time in all his life. He blinked a few times in the dark, picturing the moment. Then the truth hit him. God had gotten him through the tent audition. Not his own ability. How had he lost sight of that? He let the moment pass. God had given him his voice, so whether he got through on his own or by some miracle, God got the credit.

And now . . . now he would sing his heart out tomorrow and who knew? All those years of leading worship in Danville, and now this.

Suddenly anything was possible.

He closed his eyes and settled into the pillow. A certainty filled him and helped him fall asleep. Reese would understand why he didn't call tonight.

No one believed in him more than her.

chapter 5

Kelly Morgan had never been more thankful for Botox. Especially after six straight weeks of judging these crazy auditions.

She looked in her dressing room mirror and smiled. Her plastic surgeon had flown in yesterday and administered it himself. No one knew the landscape of her face, the curves and slipping ground the way he did. She looked a little closer, pressing her fingertips to her forehead. Not a fraction of give. She didn't look a day over twenty-five. Never mind that she was knocking at thirty-seven. Her face and body said otherwise.

"Ms. Morgan, your trainer called. He'll meet you here at nine tonight." The production assistant looked barely out of college. She handed Kelly a small folded piece of paper. "He found a gym willing to stay open for a private session."

"Good." Kelly didn't make eye contact. She opened the piece of paper and read what her trainer had written. *Glutes. Nine o'clock. Private car will be waiting. Five minutes from the stadium. Be ready.*

Kelly could already feel the burn. The sensation that reminded her she was still in the fight, still winning the war against the clock. She would do what it took to beat the hands of time. Even when she lived out of a suitcase the way she had since *Fifteen Minutes* auditions began.

Makeup and hair hurried into her dressing room at the same time. "Ms. Morgan." The stylist stood at her side, confident. "Same as we discussed?"

"Go bolder. I want to make a statement for Atlanta. It's the last city."

"If anyone can make a statement, you can." The woman opened her box of brushes and curling irons and started working. Both women were part of Kelly's staff. Her regulars. She wouldn't think about being a judge on *Fifteen Minutes* without them. Another ten staffers buzzed about, prepping her wardrobe, organizing a table of organic kale and celery and ginger and green apples—the ingredients of Kelly's mandatory power juice. Kelly credited her looks to the juicing almost as much as the Botox.

The room was in full swing, everyone doing his or her job so that in an hour Kelly Morgan could take her place as one of the premier judges on America's hottest vocal reality show.

Kelly loved the energy in the room. She closed her eyes and breathed it in as her stylist worked a brush through her famous blond hair. The hair that had helped make a name for her twenty years ago when she starred in her own hit TV show. Back then she was America's sexiest sweetheart. Every day Kelly worked so America wouldn't forget.

The phone in her hand vibrated. A quick glance and she frowned. Her manager shouldn't be calling now. Makeup was already poised over her, analyzing the shades and colors and choices that would make Kelly look best under the studio lights. Kelly held up her hand and the makeup artist stepped back. Rudy Smith had been with her since the beginning so she took the call. "Rudy." Her impatience was part of the routine. "We roll cameras in less than an hour. What's up?"

"I know your schedule. I booked you, remember?" He sounded tired.

"Fine. What's wrong? Tell me this is urgent. Otherwise you wouldn't call me till tonight, right?"

Rudy sighed. "It can't wait." His words seemed slower than usual, as if he dreaded what was coming. His hesitation drove her crazy. "We presented Cal with the divorce papers today. Like you asked. Kelly . . . he won't sign. He absolutely refuses."

"What?" She didn't mean to shriek. She couldn't help it. She waved her team off and hurried from the chair to the hallway. Where no one could watch her or quote her or snap a picture of her with an expression that would damage her reputation. She dropped her voice. "He *has* to sign the papers. He said he would."

"He doesn't have to do anything."

"Isn't that what he said?" She paced a few feet away from the dressing room door and back. "I have a boyfriend, for heaven's sake. I've moved on. Of course he has to sign." She felt her heartbeat quicken, felt the heat in her face. She wanted to hit something. "What game is he playing? We've been over this."

"He's changed his mind. Says he wants to work things out." Rudy sounded baffled. "He doesn't believe in divorce. That's what he's saying now. He won't sign even if you never talk to him again. His words."

He didn't believe in divorce? Kelly laughed, but it sounded more bitter than funny. "This is what people like us do. They get divorced. What do you mean he doesn't believe in it?"

"You'd have to ask him." She could almost see Rudy slumped in his big leather chair.

Kelly paced again for several seconds. She stopped and closed her eyes. The past grabbed at her and for a few seconds she could see Cal Whittaker III on the day they married, feel his arms around her, hear him whispering to her as they danced in front of their family and friends. "I'm never leaving you, Kelly . . . never." They were just twenty-two.

"Kelly?" Rudy was waiting for her orders.

The image in her mind disappeared. Who were they back then? Time had changed them into different people. Cal had been photographed with Europe's hottest print model, and Kelly was dating the nation's most-loved singer, a guy ten years younger than her, an *American Idol* finalist from a few seasons ago. As for Cal, there was no way back to the people they used to be.

She let her forehead rest against the wall. "I'm tired, Rudy. Tell Cal to quit playing games. Give him two months to sign the papers. I don't want our lawyers involved. The press will make it the story of the year."

"Okay. Two months." Doubt crept into Rudy's tone. "I don't think it'll work, but I'll tell him."

"Fine. Update me tomorrow."

The call ended, but Kelly stayed unmoving. Her dad's face

filled her mind, the words of his last e-mail pushing in on her. *It's time, baby . . . you need to make things right. With me and your mom . . . with Cal. Your kids need you.*

The memory of his voice sounded so clear he might as well have been standing beside her. The man she once admired, the one she hadn't spoken to in a year. Not since her first affair became public and her dad pulled the God card. His advice never changed. She needed to repent and seek forgiveness and make things right with Cal. Blah, blah, blah.

Kelly breathed in deep through her nose and adjusted her posture. She didn't need this, didn't need Cal making life difficult for her, didn't need the memory of her father's e-mail. This was the biggest gig she'd had in five years. She was making $5 million for her role as judge this season, and the pre-show publicity had shot her last three albums back to the top of the charts.

Calm. Everything's okay, Kelly. It'll be fine. She exhaled and thought about her stylist and makeup artist waiting in the other room. She would go back to her chair and they would transform her, peel away the years so she was even more beautiful than she'd been in her twenties. In an hour she'd be in front of the cameras. Where she belonged. Where she had always belonged. *I don't need Cal's games. I'm on top of the world. I'm Kelly Morgan.*

What does it profit you to gain the whole world and lose your soul?

Kelly jerked back as if she'd been struck by a bullet, straight to her very soul. Had someone said the words or was she only hearing them in her heart? And who was talking to her? She thought for a moment. The words were from . . . They were from the Bible, right? A message from her childhood. Scripture verses meant to make her feel guilty. Why would the words scrape against her anxious heart now, when she didn't believe any of them?

Her father's e-mail. That had to be it. Stirring up ancient reminders of guilt and recrimination. The list of things she shouldn't do. The choices that would send her to hell. She clenched her fists and released them. *Peace . . . take hold of peace, Kelly.* Her therapist had taught her the trick. *Clench and release. Clench and release. Peace is there for the taking.*

She could hear the therapist's voice from the tapes she had bought a month ago. She'd dropped three thousand dollars on them. The woman's voice soothed her soul. "You have it all. You have goodness and health and beauty and wealth. Peace is yours. Take it. Own it. You define your truth. Choose positivity and energy. You are always master of your own destiny . . ." On and on and on.

Truth. Okay. Kelly clenched her fists and released them. Truth helped. She remained master of her own destiny. Yes, that was truth. Anything to get her mind off the Bible verse about losing her soul. She tapped her high-heeled toe in a rapid beat. The therapist's truth . . . truth, truth, truth.

What else was true? She was in perfect health, fitter than she'd been at any time in her life. That was truth. That and the fact that her boyfriend was crazy about her. There . . . that was a start. Michael Manning was the hottest guy in music and he was completely in love with her. What else? She racked her brain. *People* magazine! Of course! She'd been voted one of *People* magazine's most beautiful women the week after her role on *Fifteen Minutes* was announced. Next year she'd be on the cover. That was the sort of truth she needed to fill her mind with.

Peace began to wash over her.

Before she could return to the dressing room her phone rang again and the tension returned with a vengeance. Why couldn't people leave her alone? Before she could throw it across the room a photo appeared on the home screen. She and Michael Manning locked in a passionate kiss. *Michael.* The guy had her heart. She took the call, silently chiding herself. *Peace is yours. Take it. Own it.* She found her most intimate tone. "Hey, sexy."

"Hey, pretty girl." Michael chuckled. "I'm higher than a kite, and you're not here."

"Mmmm." Kelly closed her eyes and let her shoulder lean against the cool wall. The hallway was still empty, the moment hers and Michael's. No one listening, no one taking pictures. "Where are you?"

"Morocco. Plushest hotel room ever. Just finished a meet and greet." His voice was deep and slurred, the way he sounded when he first woke up. "A fan gave me the weed. It's amazing."

Kelly considered what else the fan might have given him. The fan was a girl, no doubt, like all of Michael's followers. But how old? And had she followed him back to his hotel room?

"You there?"

"Hmm?" Kelly forced the thoughts from her mind. *He loves me only. Truth. Stay with the truth.* "Sorry. Just picturing you there . . . the room." Her tone changed as she imagined him. "The bed."

Michael groaned. "Don't do that to me. Two weeks till I see you."

"Then you're home for a while."

"In Nashville, yes. Unless you have a better idea." He breathed deep. "Seriously, this is the greatest pot."

Kelly was stuck back at the Nashville part. "I'll be in New York City for the show."

"I don't have a place in the city." His throaty chuckle filled her senses. "But if the most beautiful girl in the world lives there, then maybe I should look."

She giggled. There was no way to measure the joy he brought her. Around him she felt young and beautiful and on top of the world. Like she always would be. "I might have a spare bedroom."

"Mmmm. You asking me to move in with you?"

"Maybe."

Before he could answer, the sound of other voices crowded the line. "Hold on, boo." Frustration replaced the sleepiness in his voice.

"Is . . . someone there?"

"No. It's housekeeping." He was either nervous or much more sober. He cursed under his breath. "I have a privacy sign on the door." He hesitated. "Hey, I like the live-in idea." The calm in his tone returned but not the happy high. "I gotta go, okay? Get these people out of my room. I'll call you later."

She was about to explain that she'd be on camera for the next several hours, but he ended the call. A wave of uncertainty ran through her. Michael's reputation had been scandalous before they started dating. He wouldn't have fans in his room, right? Not when someone could catch him smoking, take a picture, and sell it to TMZ in an hour.

Either way she couldn't say anything—it was one of his ground rules. Implicit trust. Michael loved his fans and he loved smoking. Two nonnegotiable aspects of their relationship. Kelly closed her eyes again. What had he told her? He wouldn't touch another girl as long as they were together. *When one of us is ready to move on, we say so. Love is freedom. No chains. When it ends, it ends. Until then, we trust.*

Yes, that was truth. They had to trust each other. If he said the voices were housekeeping, then that's what they were. She only wished she could be with him, with the good weed and the great room and the view of Morocco.

At first she worried about how much pot Michael smoked. But not anymore. Kelly had come to love it as much as he did, though she smoked only a couple times a month. Everyone in the industry smoked, but there was a cardinal rule for people in the brightest light, people like the two of them.

Don't get caught.

Not in bed with her much younger boyfriend and not intoxicated. Not looking too fat or too thin or too old. Nothing that could be plastered in the tabloids and harm her contract with *Fifteen Minutes.*

Who were the voices in his room?

Breathe, Kelly. She gave herself the order, but she struggled with the reality. *If I had some of that weed, maybe.*

Your body is the temple of the Holy Spirit . . . honor God with your body.

What was this? She stood straighter, looking over her shoulder and down the hall as if she expected to see someone. Enough. The voices in Michael's hotel room, the voice taunting her with outdated Bible verses. She took a deep breath. *You are successful and young and beautiful and famous.* There. That was the truth. She opened the door to the dressing room and swept back to the chair, a smile on her face. For the rest of the day only one set of voices mattered.

The voices of the contestants.

REESE WEATHERLY WANTED to turn off her phone and bury it out back behind the stable. Zack's tweets were that frustrating. But she couldn't. Other than one rushed conversation and a few short texts, Zack hadn't talked to her. Very busy and all. Lots of demands. But somehow he'd had time for Twitter, time to update his followers and answer people who tweeted him.

People like this Zoey girl, whoever she was.

Reese took her phone out back, walked to the far fence and leaned against the worn wooden slats. She stared at the cloudy sky as if the answers might be there. Zack didn't mean anything by the tweets. She knew that. He couldn't help what other people said about him. Still, her heart hurt. It ached even while another part of her celebrated the fact that he'd made it through. She had seen this coming. The fact that Zack had made it this far was no surprise. Sometime in the next few hours he'd sing for the celebrity judges.

But Zack's tweets were making Reese feel something she hated, something she had never felt around him. Jealousy. Reese pulled up the Twitter app on her phone and checked it once more. Zack had updated again.

In line waiting. Jesus, shine through me in front of the judges!

Reese could hear his voice, picture him standing in line, praying and telling the world about his faith. Despite the tension, her heart relaxed. He was keeping his promise, making the journey about Jesus. She went to her saved searches and clicked @ZackDylan. That brought up a host of tweets aimed at Zack—most of them from Zoey, @songleader. She was relentless.

> In line behind @ZackDylan. Oh. My. Word. Girls you're gonna wanna know this guy!

Reese read down the list of the others from Zoey.

> How am I supposed to sing with @ZackDylan warming up in front of me? The guy's voice is as gorgeous as he is!

> Hey everyone! Follow @ZackDylan. I'll be home in no time. He's gonna be famous. Longer than #FifteenMinutes!!

> Conversation with @ZackDylan. Zack: "I have a girlfriend." Me: "I don't see a ring on your finger." #allisfairinlove

Reese stared at the tweets, confused. Was the girl serious? She didn't care that Zack had a girlfriend? Of course Zack had told Zoey he had a girlfriend. The girl was either obsessed or immature. Maybe both. Reese clicked Zoey's profile for the sixth time. Long blond hair, cheerleader. Another few clicks and Reese could read everything Zoey's friends tweeted to her in response. Most of them gushed about how they agreed with Zoey, how Zack was "so hot" and how they couldn't wait to hear him sing.

All of them loved Zoey's tweet from earlier today. The one where she had attached a photo of her and Zack. Reese tapped the app a few more times and saw the tweet again.

Here we are, me and the next #FifteenMinutes winner. That's right, @ZackDylan. #BeJealous

Reese clicked open the photo and stared at it the way she had ten minutes ago. If she squinted at it long enough, she could convince herself that Zack looked uncomfortable. Disinterested. She stared at the photo until she couldn't stand it another moment. She clicked out of the tweet. Zack was doing the girl a favor, taking a photo with his first new fan. Nothing more. Reese checked his Twitter profile. Zoey might've been the first, but she wasn't alone. Zack had gone from two hundred followers to nearly a thousand in a few days.

Word was getting out.

Knots twisted at Reese's stomach. She had to stop looking, had to stop thinking about Zack at the auditions with girls like Zoey squealing over him. It wasn't that she was worried. Not at all. Zack loved her and no one else. A few days away weren't going to change that.

But could they change him? If he made it far enough, would he be the same Zack? The one who loved watching her help little Toby find confidence on the back of a horse? The guy who cared about the progress his sister was making and who worried every day about his family's horse farm? Would that Zack still exist?

She stared at her phone as another of Zack's tweets came across. *I'm next. Pray for me! Here goes . . .*

Reese looked at the words. Slowly, methodically, she turned off the phone and slipped it into the back pocket of her jeans. Zack wanted everyone to pray that he'd sing his heart out for the judges. Reese stared at the sky and did what Zack had asked her to do.

She prayed for him.

Not that he'd be the best singer or that this would be his brightest stage moment ever. She prayed for something else, something that mattered more.

For God's will, whatever it was.

That above all else.

chapter 6

Chandra Olson sat back in her seat while her makeup artist worked a brush full of loose powder over her cheeks and forehead. Auditions were under way. Touch-ups for the camera happened after every ten singers or if any of the judges needed a break. This one was called by Kelly Morgan. Her recent Botox injections were making her shinier than usual. At least that's what she said.

Chandra kept quiet, taking in the moment. Analyzing it.

The judges on the panel for the tenth season of *Fifteen Minutes* had been handpicked by the show's infamous producer, Samuel J. Meier. Over the past decade, national singing competitions had come and international contests had gone. But *Fifteen Minutes* remained. The show had topped the ratings chart every year since its inception and after ten seasons everyone knew the reason for the show's success.

The reason was Samuel J. Meier.

Tan, blond, and fit, Meier was in his late thirties, a machine with a net worth in the hefty nine figures. Everything Meier touched turned to gold. He had produced five successful pop artists, all of whom had multiple records with platinum sales. Meier hadn't only produced the artists, he'd written most of their music.

His talent was world-renowned, his name synonymous with pop music success. When the first singing competition show came around, Meier quit working with artists and started *Fifteen Minutes*. The show debuted the next year. In an interview Meier once explained why he created a singing competition when one already existed. Simple. He could do better. *Fifteen Minutes* drew the best talent and the best production, delivering polished emotional pieces on the contestants' lives and making America feel personally connected to everyone in the top twenty.

Meier had explained a number of times that success was an intangible. There was no way to figure out the formula for what worked and what didn't. But this Meier knew . . . He needed to stay ahead of the curve. Over the last decade a number of singing shows had come along and tried to knock *Fifteen Minutes* off its platform. Meier managed to keep the edge. One way, he had told reporters, was through the judges he chose. They had to be as likable as the finalists. No one scandalous or scantily dressed. The panel would never have someone whose reputation was in any way tarnished, no one who had ever been labeled by paparazzi as a failure or a joke or a has-been. *Fifteen Minutes* paid its judges well and expected articulate commentary and feedback. Meier kept certain judges, but he also liked bringing in newcomers.

Chandra closed her eyes while the artist dusted her brows. She and Kelly Morgan were new this year and after six weeks on the road they were friends. As far as that was possible. The panel was rounded out this year by longtime judge Cullen Caldwell, a colorful Australian-born hit songwriter whose expertise and talent analysis were unprecedented. Cullen added a level of credibility and eccentricity. He used Down Under slang and spoke with a charming Australian accent. He kept his head shaved and owned an entirely white wardrobe with accessories in bold colors. His spot color today was a red sweatband that accentuated his white jeans and V-neck. The combo would've looked ridiculous on anyone else. Somehow Cullen pulled it off. Women were crazy about him.

The judges were expected to bring something to the table. Cullen brought expertise and sarcasm. Not the sort of sarcasm that demeaned contestants but the sort that drew a laugh from the home audience and even the other judges. Cullen was funny, no question.

Kelly Morgan brought her famed history, musical flair and her ability to spot talent. She could be hard-hitting, but over the last five weeks she'd found her stride with the contestants. Once the show aired, people would hate Kelly at times for her biting remarks. Meier would be fine with that. Kelly was pretty enough to pull it off. America would love her either way.

The compassion this season would come from Chandra. Meier had made that clear from the beginning. Chandra wouldn't have done it any other way. In the last seven cities she'd been moved to tears a handful of times. She, more than anyone, understood the depth of the dream, the impossibility of it. The cost.

Kelly sat in the middle, and now she leaned in close to Chandra. "I'm not impressed with this group. That last girl was pathetic. She'd be laughed out of a karaoke bar."

"The next ten might be better." Chandra had to agree about the first several groups. No one really stood out. She'd done her part, done it as easily as she breathed, giving the contestants a sad smile and the suggestion that maybe there was another dream they could follow. Painting or writing. That sort of thing.

But as each dejected or devastated singer walked out of the room Chandra silently celebrated. They could go home unchanged, unharmed. Whatever life they'd left behind would be waiting for them. Nothing lost. No psycho fans waiting on the front porch for their unsuspecting parents.

Kelly pulled out a compact and checked her look. "Love that Botox." She glanced at Chandra. "You use it?"

"No." Chandra allowed a confused laugh. "How old do you think I am?"

The question seemed to catch Kelly off guard. She turned and stared at Chandra. "You could be twenty-five or forty-five." The compact caught her attention again. "You know what they say. Black don't crack."

"True." Chandra laughed. Inside she felt sorry for Kelly. The girl was a piece of work. So totally consumed with herself that she barely noticed anything about her surroundings or the people who made up her world. At least that's what Chandra thought so far. "Twenty-five. I'm twenty-five."

"Well, good for you." Kelly added a fresh layer of lip-gloss, her eyes glued to her image. "You'll be just as stunning in twenty years. Botox or not." She stopped and looked at Chandra. "How many Twitter followers?"

The question felt jarring. "I don't know. Ten million or so."

Kelly shrugged and smacked her lips, her eyes back on the compact. "Me, too. That'll double once the show airs."

"Yeah." Chandra wanted to think of something clever to say, something about how it didn't matter how many followers they had as long as they were true to themselves. Nothing came to mind. Besides, Kelly wouldn't hear her, anyway. She was going on about how her boyfriend didn't know about the Botox and how she felt flabby if she didn't work out twice a day. Chandra tuned her out. The sky behind them was brilliant blue. The judges' table was set up in front of an expansive window that gave a stunning view of downtown Atlanta and an expanse of the day's cloudless sky. The room was airy and spacious, and the table was made of chunky hundred-year-old wood planks from some local teardown. The feel of the set was warm and inviting, vintage and high-end.

Cullen was talking to Samuel J. Meier, who was nodding and frowning appropriately. The producer made a point of being at every taped audition. Like a consummate director, Meier would give the judges praise and pointers, check the lighting and angles caught by the cameramen, and talk with the sound guys about music and production. Meier prided himself for being a hands-on producer, and today was no exception.

Whatever was being said, Cullen was upset. Chandra tried to hear the conversation.

"I thought we were looking for different stories this year. Something new." Cullen snapped a document with his hand and slapped it on the table. "The best we can do in the next ten singers is three waitresses and two Christians? That's not different. We can't lose ratings, not if we want to stay on top. You know that."

"Trust me." Meier's tone was respectful, clearly concerned about his top judge's opinion. But he hardly looked worried. "The Bible series broke records on the History Channel. America will love these contestants." He smiled, patience marking his expression. "You know the drill. It worked last year. It'll work again."

"I don't know, mate. Have you checked the *Fifteen Minutes* hashtags on Twitter?" Cullen sat back hard, his red headband wrinkling with his brow. "More Jesus talk than ever."

"Jesus talk brings in viewers, Cullen. Nothing new there."

"Yeah, well, I want different. Rodeo blokes and strippers. Hot-air balloonists and medical students. That sort of thing."

"We'll have those. Don't worry."

Chandra could hear every word and she felt uncomfortable. Something about the way Samuel Meier spoke about his strategy troubled her. She held a finger up to Kelly, who was still talking to her compact. "Hold on." She sat a little straighter. "Mr. Meier, excuse me. What's this? A strategy?"

Meier stopped cold. He wore a tailored charcoal suit jacket over a pale aqua V-neck and expensive dark skinny jeans. His blond hair couldn't have been more perfectly styled. "Strategy?" He hesitated, then found his smile again. "Oh. That." He clearly hadn't intended for Chandra to hear him. "It's nothing."

"Something about Christians?" Chandra didn't want to create tension, but she needed to know. She had her reasons.

"Just that after the first few weeks, the candidates with the more outspoken faith are asked to tone it down." His smile grew bigger. "So we can get to know other sides of their life and personality."

"Hmm." She paused. "Got it." Chandra nodded and hid the fact that her world had just tilted off its axis. Of course there was a strategy. Now it all made sense. Six years ago she had been asked by the contestant coordinator to limit her comments about God, find other ways to make a name for herself. At the time

Chandra had been more than willing to cooperate. *Fifteen Minutes* was a singing show, after all. No need to preach to people.

It creeped her out to think of Meier himself making a strategy to quiet people of faith. Was there a strategy to keep people from talking about their sports obsession or city or whatever else defined them? Of course not. Meier left the judges and busied himself near the cameramen. She studied the document in front of her, the same one Cullen and Kelly had. It gave the names of the contestants and a few lines about them. Cullen was right— at least two were known for their strong faith.

Chandra breathed deep. Were the walls closing in or was it just her imagination? The sense of meaninglessness came over her again. What was the point of any of this? *Fifteen Minutes* was a machine, churning out new talent for a public whose appetite for celebrities was never satisfied. Meier wasn't the only one with issues. If faith was so important to certain contestants, then why were they here? Shouldn't they be leading Bible studies or taking the gospel to villages in Africa? Did they really think being on *Fifteen Minutes* would give glory to their God, like she once thought it would? Or was this the easiest way to justify their very human desire for fame? Chandra stared at the blue sky and tried to remember herself back then, her own first week of auditions. Her motives had been sincere, right?

"Ready on the set?" one of the grips shouted from the side stage. The makeup artists finished in a hurry and disappeared to the wings. Someone snapped a slate. "Camera up. Roll sound."

"How do I look?" Kelly turned to Chandra, the compact hidden away.

Chandra wanted to laugh. But Kelly was serious, her insecurities as much a part of her as her voice and her beauty. "Perfect."

"Really? Not shiny?" Kelly smacked her lips again.

"Not at all."

Kelly found her red-carpet smile and turned toward the door at the back of the room. Auditions were taped in their entirety, though only the strongest clips would be used when the show aired. Even so, Kelly never allowed a less than perfect moment.

Back when Chandra was more of a praying person, she would've felt compelled to talk to God about Kelly. But the cameras were rolling and the next contestant was entering the room. A waitress from Mississippi, early twenties, Harvard dropout. Chandra forced herself to listen to the girl's introduction.

She was still trying to remember why she'd agreed to this gig in the first place.

KELLY MORGAN LEANED forward, elbows on the table, and watched the waitress begin to sing. Like so many of the girls, this one sang an Adele song, which created two problems. First, no one could sing exactly like Adele. Second, Adele's style was so distinct that if contestants covered Adele correctly it became impossible to hear their own style. But the girls sang Adele anyway.

The waitress wasn't bad. Her tone was nice, but halfway through her song a fly buzzed up near the girl's mouth and she freaked. She screamed an obscenity and waved at the insect, spitting a little and shaking her head. "He . . . he flew in my mouth!"

With the cameras rolling, Kelly was certain the segment would make the show. Cullen was the first to comment. "Didn't we pay that little bugger to come on earlier?"

Kelly laughed out loud and then—in a mock show of kindness for the struggling contestant—she covered her mouth with the papers in front of her. On her other side, Chandra stared helplessly at the table.

After an awkward few seconds, Kelly giggled again and gave her fellow judge a light rap with the papers. "Cullen! That's terrible!" She motioned to one of the grips. "Can we kill that fly? Please? Somebody?" Kelly looked at the waitress. "Is the fly gone, dear?"

"Yes." The girl gulped. "I think so." She stood perfectly still, terrified and blank-faced. "Do . . . you want me to start again?"

"Let's not." Cullen held up his hand. "Tell me, dear, why'd you leave Harvard?"

"I wanted to sing." She shifted to her other foot. "You know, full-time. Like a professional."

"Okay," Kelly chimed in. If she wasn't careful Cullen would steal the show. She had to make her mark to be asked back next year. "What were you studying at Harvard?"

"Law." The waitress's cheeks were red. She would no doubt remember this horrifying moment the rest of her life. She cleared her throat. "Medical law, actually."

"Is it too late to get back in?" Cullen adjusted his red headband. "Because something tells me you'd make an excellent medical attorney." He shifted his gaze. "Chandra? What do you think? Is she through to New York?"

Chandra clearly felt for the girl. "Hi, honey, you doing okay?"

"Yes, ma'am." The waitress relaxed a little. "Sorry about the fly."

"It wasn't your fault." She hesitated, struggling to find the kindest words. "As for your voice . . . I think Cullen's right. You have a nice sound, but maybe not original enough for *Fifteen Minutes*."

"It's a no for me." Kelly sat back in her chair, ready for the next contestant.

"Yes, sorry. I'll have to say no this time." Chandra hesitated. "Maybe Harvard again, or voice lessons. Something."

"Yes, ma'am." The waitress was already taking a few steps backward. "Thank you."

"Next!" Kelly straightened her papers and folded her arms, ready to move on. The middle seat at the table suited her. She felt in charge, sort of like the head judge. She looked at the next name on the list. *Zack Dylan. Worship leader at his church. Grandfather raised a Kentucky Derby winner. Strong Christian.*

Kelly rolled her eyes. *Just what we need. Another believer.* Cullen was right.

Daughter, don't harden your heart . . . I am here. I am calling out to you and—

No! She closed her eyes and gave a slight shake of her head. *Not now!* She smiled at the door, ready for Zack Dylan. Maybe the fly would stick around for one more contestant.

Kelly could only hope.

chapter 7

Zack hadn't stopped praying since he entered the holding area. He and nine other contestants sat in a small room not far where Kit Barker stood conducting interviews with contestants before and after their time with the judges.

Zoey sat next to him, one of the ten. Something Zack was beginning to see as less of a coincidence. He'd texted Reese while he was waiting, but no response. Did she even know that he'd made it through the morning round?

"Texting your girlfriend?" Zoey leaned over his shoulder.

Part of him liked the girl's attention, if he was honest with himself. Which couldn't be right. But his patience with her was waning. "Yeah."

"Is she excited for you?"

Zack held his breath. "She's praying. I know that."

"That's cool." Zoey smiled at him, her eyes more guarded than before. "You and her, your faith being so strong and all."

"Yeah. It's important to us."

"Clearly." She sat back and pulled one knee up to her chest. She wore a pink T-shirt and pale blue jeans. Anyone would've thought she looked very pretty. The judges were going to love her. She tried to catch a look at Zack's phone. "What's her name?"

Zack had told her before. "Reese."

"Reese. Right." Another pinched smile. "Lucky girl."

Around them others were humming quietly, pacing the small floor or stone-still, eyes closed, focusing. "Hey, I need to get ready." He stood and stepped away. "Sorry."

"No, yeah. Go ahead. Me, too." She leaned her head back and launched into a vocal exercise that jarred the entire room.

Zack moved to the window and stared at the busy street below. *God, is this You? This opportunity? If it is . . . please, help me stay true to You. You alone.* He blinked and thought about the people of Atlanta, busy people going about their business, working their jobs, climbing their ladders. If Atlanta were like any other city in the U.S., lots of the people on the street below watched *Fifteen Minutes.* Could his faith touch their hearts? Could something he said or did on the show cause one of them to think differently about God or to believe for the first time? He searched his heart. *Check my motives, Lord. Keep me on the straight path.*

"Zack Dylan?" A perky young assistant with a clipboard appeared at the door. They'd seen her before, but then, lots of people worked for the show.

Zack stood. "That's me."

She smiled at him. "This way."

"Hey." Zoey reached out and caught his hand as he walked by. "You'll make it. I know you will."

"Thanks. You, too." He turned and followed the well-dressed assistant. If he and Zoey both made it through, he would have to be very careful. She was attractive and crazy about him. That was bound to be flattering, no matter how much he loved Reese. He wasn't interested, but the girl was relentless.

Out in the hallway, the assistant turned to him. "She might be right."

"Ma'am?" Zack walked alongside her, confused.

"That girl. She said you'd make it through." The assistant gave him a quick once-over. "If you can sing, you're in. They need to find two hot guys in Atlanta. From what I've seen, you're the hottest." She tossed her hair and looked straight ahead as they walked. "Just saying."

"Thanks, I guess." Zack laughed, surprised. He would've expected an employee of the show to be more professional. They rounded a corner and the assistant's demeanor changed. She lost her smile and nodded at the show's famous host, Kip Barker. "Zack Dylan, sir."

"Thank you." Kip held out his hand. "Zack. Nice to meet you."

"Nice to meet you." Zack was shaking the host's hand when he caught a sly wink from the assistant as she headed back down the hallway. Zack kept his focus on Kip. "Is there anything I should know?"

"We'll do a little interview out here, and then, well"—he shrugged—"you know the rest. Go in and sing your socks off." Kip motioned to the cameraman and the guy came closer. Kip smiled at Zack. "Ready?"

Zack exhaled, searching for the calm he'd felt that morning in his hotel room. "Ready."

Zack wasn't worried about Kip Barker. The guy had been

with the show from the beginning. He was a former baseball star from the Dominican Republic, half-Hispanic and half-Irish with an uncanny ability to put contestants at ease and connect with America.

Zack's interview turned out to be one of the few exceptions.

"Your faith is important to you, so does that mean you were praying in the holding room?" Kip talked fast and almost always smiled.

"Yes." Zack grinned. "One of the biggest days of my life. I've been praying all day."

"All day. Right. So does that mean like . . ." Kip dropped to one knee, planted his elbow on the other knee and bowed his head. Just as quickly he looked back up at Zack. "Sort of like this? Tebowing in the back room? 'Cause I've always wanted to see someone Tebow in person."

Zack laughed, which was the expected response. "Tebow's a great guy, but I pray my own way."

"Why don't you show us? Can you show us, Zack? Like a demonstration?" Kip was back on his feet, his likable smile aimed at the camera. "Maybe you've got the Zack Dylan drop. Flat on your face." He spread his arms like an umpire making a safe call.

Again Zack laughed. "Nothing that crazy."

Kip gave him a friendly shove in the arm. "Just teasing you, Zack. It's okay. So who'd you bring to the audition? Good-looking guy like you? Girlfriend or wife? Both?" He laughed at his own joke.

"Not married." The guy was bugging Zack. "Here by myself, actually."

"That'll be great news to the ladies out there. So are you nervous?"

Zack hadn't meant to leave Reese out of the equation, but the questions were coming too fast. The interview ended and Kip settled into his usual chill personality. "Sorry about the Tebow comment." He chuckled, his microphone relaxed at his side. "No harm intended."

"No worries. I get it." Zack stuck his hands in his jeans. He thought about asking Kip if he believed in God, then changed his mind. No time for that kind of conversation. He would be singing in front of the judges in a few minutes. Kip excused himself and moved into a meeting with what looked like part of the production staff.

Father, it's almost my turn. Shine through me. I'm Yours alone. I'm ready. If it's Your will, please let me go through to New York.

The female assistant was back. She gently touched Zack's elbow. "It's time." She led him through the door to the audition room. "Break a leg," she whispered.

"Thanks." He looked at the panel of judges. They were all watching him, the cameras trained on his every move. Immediately Zack found his comfort zone. Like the athlete he'd been in high school, he walked confidently to a small X on the floor in front of the old wood table.

The moment felt surreal. This season's judges looked back at him. Chandra Olson, Kelly Morgan, and Cullen Caldwell. Some of the most famous names in pop music right here in person. Kelly raised her eyebrows and muttered something under her breath to Cullen.

"Hey." Cullen turned to Zack. "She says you look like her boyfriend." He laughed as he looked down at his notes and back at Zack. "Just so there're no secrets between us."

Kelly grinned like a high school girl caught crushing on the guy in her biology class. She gave Cullen a lighthearted punch. "Thanks a lot."

"No problem." Cullen chuckled and shook his head at the camera. "What I put up with."

Chandra's eyes were kind and deep. "You're Zack Dylan?"

"Yes, ma'am." Zack squared his shoulders.

"Okay, Zack." Kelly rebounded. "Where're you from?"

"Nowhere near New York." Cullen patted Kelly's shoulder, a smirk on his face. "Settle down, you little Sheila. Give the bloke a listen."

"Yes, tell us about yourself, Zack." Chandra leaned forward, the only one who was serious.

"Okay." He chuckled, going along with the situation as best he could. "I'm a worship leader from Danville, Kentucky. My family owns a horse farm and one day I'd like the chance to raise a Kentucky Derby champion."

"Your great-grandfather did that, correct?" Cullen reined himself in.

"He did. Yes, sir."

"Well, good on you, Zack. You look a little like a young Elvis Presley. Anyone ever tell you that?" Cullen stroked his chin, surveying Zack.

"Once in a while." Zack shrugged, his smile in place.

"Better-looking than Elvis." Kelly seemed to speak under her breath but her words remained loud enough for the camera to catch. She seemed to gather herself. "Okay, Zack. Let's be serious here. What're you going to sing for us?"

" 'Dream Like New York' by Tyrone Wells."

"Mmmm." Cullen nodded. "Nice song. Strong artist." He waved a pencil in Zack's direction. "All right, mate. Let's hear it."

Between his earlier audition and this one Zack had practiced almost constantly. The song was one of his favorites. He'd sung it a thousand times at least, and as he opened his mouth his voice wrapped itself around the notes and words with hardly any effort at all.

The song had a rhythmic feel, like ocean waves on a summer afternoon. It didn't push his range, but the chorus was high enough to let him shine. Zack looked beyond the judges while he sang, through the window and toward the deep blue over Atlanta. *Dream like New York, as high as a skyline, aim for the stars . . . above those city lights . . .*

Something happened while he sang, while the song played out. The judges began to smile. No one made a move to stop him or cut him off, and when he sang the last note, all three judges were clapping and Kelly Morgan was on her feet, bowing toward him.

"What in the world?" She laughed and did a little dance standing in place. She put her hands on the shoulders of her fellow judges. "Did you hear that boy?" She did a celebration shout and then pointed at the closest camera. "Listen up, America! You just met Zack Dylan! You can say you saw him here first."

Zack's heart raced. This was beyond what he had hoped or imagined. Kelly sat back down, but still the judges were laughing and shaking their heads. "Okay . . . all right." Cullen slapped the table. "Bring it in. What are we going to do with Zack Dylan? Is he through to New York?"

"I'll say yes." Something in Chandra's smile held a familiar depth. "You have a beautiful voice, Zack. If you're careful, I think you can go far in this competition."

"Yes, ma'am." *Is this really happening?* The floor beneath Zack's feet felt suddenly liquid. He tried to stay focused. "Thank you."

"It's a yes for me." Cullen leaned back hard in his seat. "I'll make the prediction right now. You'll be one of the finalists. The ladies will love you."

"Thank you, sir."

"Zack Dylan." Kelly grinned at him. She stood again and threw her hands in the air. "You're through to New York!"

"Thank you." Zack clasped his hands and looked up for a few seconds. "Thank you, very much."

"Listen, bloke, I think someone wants a hug." Cullen folded his arms, leaned back in his chair and chuckled.

Kelly ran carefully around the table. She was wearing what looked like five-inch heels. "Let all the girls know I was the first to get a hug from Zack Dylan!"

Zack hadn't expected this. He had no choice but to go along with it, so he laughed and held open his arms as the two of them came together. Kelly pressed in close and whispered near his ear. "You're a good sport. Don't worry, I won't do this every week."

The hug ended before Zack could respond. Kelly pranced back to her spot. Zack waved once more and then collected the famous red invitation to New York from Samuel J. Meier. "Congratulations, Zack."

"Thank you. I'll do my best."

"I'm sure you will." The show's producer hesitated. "You're a team player, right?"

A team player? Zack's heart was racing, the floor still mostly liquid. "Yeah, definitely. Of course."

Samuel Meier smiled. "Good. I thought so." He nodded. "I think you'll go far this season. I'm happy for you." He pointed toward the back door. "Kip'll talk to you out there."

Zack was almost there when an older man with an air of importance and a fancy headset stepped out from the shadows. "Hold on!" He put his hand up, clearly listening to direction through the headset. "Kip says they're not ready for you yet."

Zack's breathing came fast, and he could feel a fine layer of sweat at the top of his forehead. "Yes, sir."

The man listened again and nodded slightly. "I'm on it." He took a step closer to Zack, his voice low. "This is what you need to do. You'll burst through the door holding the red ticket, hands raised." He seemed rushed. "You'll let out a shout or some victory cry. Then you'll drop down and do your best Tebow-type prayer."

A strange feeling came over him, starting at the back of his neck and working its way down his spine. "What?"

"Tebow." Impatience marked the man's features. "You know, drop to your knee. That thing."

"That's not how I pray."

The man raised his eyebrows half an inch. "I don't care how you pray, kid. That's what we want for the show."

Zack had seconds to make a decision. He hated when movie stars like Alec Baldwin mocked the pro football player. Zack respected Tim and everything he stood for. But to drop to one knee and do the Tebow just wasn't him.

"Look, kid, praying is praying." The man pointed at the door. "You believers want people to know you're religious. So do the Tebow. You might have a few extra weeks to talk about God."

There was no telling whether his anger or shock was greater in the moment, but Zack had to make a decision. And in the time it took for his heart to rattle off another few rapid beats, he decided. If Tebowing was how he could make a name for himself, the contestant with the strong faith, the Tim Tebow of *Fifteen Minutes,* then fine. That's what he would do.

He'd act like it was his idea, and he'd win the favor of the show's producers.

God, let people see this in the right light. Please . . . give me the chance to say how I feel about you. Thank you, Lord . . . thank you.

"They're waiting." The man stepped back, a scowl etched onto his cheeks. "Go!"

Zack stared at the door, held his breath and rushed for the other side. He did just as he was asked, milking the moment, the red ticket, the hands raised, the victory shout. Then he dropped to one knee and did the Tebow. He barely held the pose, and once he was back on his feet he hurried to Kip and the microphone.

"It's official!" Kip patted Zack on the back, congratulating him. "Our first Tebowing contestant! Zack, you're on to New York . . . just like Tebow, by the way! So how did it go in there?"

"God gets all the credit. I can't believe I made it through!"

Kip motioned to the cameraman to cut. "Hey, so thanks, Zack. Way to go." He took a clipboard from another assistant. He didn't look up. "You'll receive a packet from a table at the end of the hall. Your flight to LaGuardia will take off first thing in the morning."

"Wow . . . so fast."

"It's always like that for the last group." Kip smiled at him again. Already he was moving toward the hallway; the female assistant was walking toward them.

Zoey was at the girl's side, long blond hair spilling over her shoulders. She looked ahead and spotted him. "Zack!" Her eyes lit up and she pointed at his red ticket. "You're in! I knew it!" She ran to him and threw herself into his arms. Just as quickly she drew back and clapped her hands. A squeal came from her. "I'm so happy for you!"

"Thanks." He could see Kip watching from his place near the cameramen. He whispered something to one of them. Zack wanted to get out of there, but he couldn't be rude. Not now. He turned to Zoey. "You'll be perfect. The judges are great."

She linked her arm through his and raked her free hand through her hair. "I'm so scared."

"Don't be." With everyone watching, Zack couldn't remember ever feeling more uncomfortable. He sidestepped her clutches and faced her, placing his hands on her shoulders. "You belong here."

Out of the corner of his eye he saw Kip come closer, his radar clearly up. "You two know each other?"

"Just from auditions." Zack's response came quickly. Already he felt like it had been a year since he said good-bye to Reese, since he held her in his arms. "We were in line together."

"Hmm." Kip stood between them. "I sense a little chemistry, am I right?"

"No." Zack laughed and watched how his comment made Zoey's face fall. "I mean, I have a girlfriend. Zoey and I . . . we're friends. That's it."

"Yeah." Zoey found her winning smile. She leaned in and kissed Zack on the cheek. "What he means is, if he didn't have a girlfriend he'd be madly in love with me."

Zack laughed and took a step back. "Crazy girl." He fist-pumped her. How had he lost control? He pointed to the door. "Go kill it." Only as he was leaving did he notice something that dropped his heart to the floor.

The cameras had been rolling the whole time. He had signed up for this, of course. He knew he was giving up his privacy when he drove to Atlanta yesterday. He had no control over what the cameramen caught and how they might play it on the show. Still, of all the scenarios he had imagined, if by God's grace he made it through to New York, getting kissed on camera wasn't one of them. He needed to be more aware, ready for whatever came next.

Especially if Zoey made it through.

Kelly Morgan didn't feel like herself through the next few auditions. She added a comment here and there, but she wasn't on her game. Something about Zack Dylan stayed with her. It wasn't his looks. That act had been for the show, for the ratings. It was something deeper. Something in his eyes.

At the next break, she poured a cup of coffee and took it outside on the terrace just off the audition room. There, with a view of downtown Atlanta and the summer breeze blowing in her hair, she tried to figure out what she was feeling. For the first time in years she stopped reciting good thoughts and actually allowed herself to think.

It was Zack's genuine smile, the kindness in his eyes. He reminded her of Cal when the two of them were in high school. Yes, that was it. Cal back when their lives revolved around her father's church and youth group every Wednesday night.

She'd been rebellious even then, whispering during the

message and sometimes ditching the group meeting for a trip to the river with the wilder kids. She'd had her first beer at the river and on one particularly daring night, her first kiss with a kid three years older. She hadn't even known his name. Yes, she had given her parents fits, intent on breaking rules and pushing limits.

Not Cal. He was strong and tall, a baseball player, with a wristband that read *I can do all things through Christ who gives me strength.* She used to tease him for being so good, for caring so much. For meaning every word of the faith that somehow came up in every conversation. She kidded him about how he should've been the PK, the pastor's kid. Not her.

Zack had the same look in his eyes, the one that had defined Cal. As if the windows to his heart were wide open and he really believed that all people, all situations were a part of God's story. Cal had the look back then and it had drawn Kelly like a moth to a flame. She would've done anything to get Cal's attention. His character and kindness were what turned her around and made her stop acting crazy.

She remembered one Wednesday night after youth group. Cal pulled her aside and looked at her. Straight through her. "You try too hard to be bad."

Her heart had pounded, her breath shaky from standing so close to him. But she wouldn't let him see that. She laughed. "What do you mean?

"I mean your dad's the pastor. You think you have something to prove, running with those other kids and missing group." He put his hand on her shoulder, his eyes locked on hers. "But that's not really you, Kelly. One day I hope you figure out who you are." He grinned before walking away. "You might like yourself."

Now Kelly took a long drink of her coffee and turned her

face to the sun. How long had it been since she'd thought about that conversation? She blinked and stared at the street below. More to impress Cal than anything else, Kelly changed. She stopped trying to fit in with the kids who saw church as a joke, and allowed herself to listen to the messages, to learn and care and grow up. Cal was right. The way so often he had been right. Kelly began to like herself. Her last two years of high school, she and Cal were never apart. He was her best friend and his eyes were exactly like Zack Dylan's. They shone with hope and a joy nothing could touch, and they told the world he was ready for to-morrow, excited about it.

The look in Cal's eyes didn't change until they moved to L.A., until she got an agent and started finding opportunities to sing and perform. Cal had great intentions. He would get a job at one of the studios and develop wholesome programming, a goal he reached. Even now—despite the scandal of the paparazzi photos—Cal was widely recognized as the go-to guy for all things faith and family in the movie industry.

But his eyes were different. He wasn't the same, and there was no going back.

She breathed in deep and finished her coffee. Then she tossed the cup in a nearby trash can, pulled out her cell phone and brought up Cal's contact information. His photo was still the one she'd set many years ago. Her favorite from back in high school—the two of them sitting side by side in the back of his truck, tailgate down, tanned legs hanging off the edge, blue sky overhead.

She willed herself to remember the truth, everything that had led to where they were today. There was no way to do that without going back to the beginning. Back when she thought she'd love Cal Whittaker till the day she died.

* * *

THE MOVE TO L.A. came when she and Cal were just twenty-three, a year into their marriage. At first their California life seemed magical. Within a year she found a manager and a record deal and a spot on a hit Disney musical show playing one of a trio of girls who made up a fictitious teenage singing act.

The other girls were legit teens, so the producers didn't want anyone to know Kelly was twenty-four and married. She looked seventeen, after all. And so she removed her wedding ring and hid the fact while Cal took a job in marketing at one of the top moviemaking machines in Hollywood.

Marriage was their secret, and that made it fun. They no longer had time for church, and the messages of youth group felt like part of another life. Quickly Kelly Morgan became the most-liked, best-known singer of the trio, a household name across the country. In addition to the show's ratings, her music took over the charts. A poster of her from the show hung in the rooms of teenage boys everywhere.

Cal liked to tease her when they were at home. "Every guy wants to be me." He'd put his arms around her waist and hold her close, swaying with her in the kitchen. "We're Hollywood's best-kept secret," he would tease her. "As long as you stay with me."

She would smile and kiss him, passionate and full-bodied. "There could never be anyone for me but you."

Sometimes rumors arose that Kelly was dating Cal—and people would question their age difference. But her publicity team worked to never reveal her age. If people assumed she was in her teens, so be it. Those were the days before Internet and instant access into the lives of celebrities. Secrets could be kept.

Even so, the news came out when the show was in its last

season. By then Kelly and Cal were in their late twenties and Cal had worked his way onto the marketing team for some of the biggest movies being made. Kelly's publicist drafted a release that read simply, *Teen star Kelly Morgan announces marriage to studio executive Cal Whittaker III.* Details—including Kelly's age—were sketchy and the public never knew that while Kelly was playing the part of a high school girl, she was actually married and in her twenties.

After a few years of mediocrity and lackluster performances, Kelly decided to take a break from the world of entertainment. When she turned thirty she was pregnant with Kai, and two years later little Kinley joined them. Meanwhile Cal was finding success in the faith-and-family film industry. Kelly had a housekeeper for the laundry, chores, and cooking, but she took care of the kids. Until Kinley turned three the domestic life was enough for Kelly.

But one day she looked in the mirror and no longer recognized her image. The media still talked about her as if she were a teenage star, but she clearly had aged far beyond that. One week the paparazzi snapped a photo of her pushing Kinley's stroller while Kai walked alongside. She and her son held ice cream cones, and the picture showed Kelly mid-lick. Her face looked fat, a few chins marking the fact that she'd let twenty extra pounds creep onto her small frame.

And that was that. She hired a nanny and a trainer and a dietician. Six months later, she looked a decade younger and made headlines by publicly daring the paparazzi to capture an unflattering picture of her. They never did.

The memories stopped for a moment. Yoga and strength training were a regular part of her life now, the weight long gone. She was in better shape than she'd been in high school. Definitely better than when she'd been her most famous, during the run of the hit show.

A year later Kelly knew her marriage was in trouble. By then Cal regularly criticized her for the changes she'd made. "You're not the same person," he would tell her. "I don't recognize you." He preferred the happy, domestic Kelly over the glamour girl she'd become.

Her father felt the same way. "You're selling out, Kelly. Don't let fame become an addiction."

Kelly would only laugh at their concerns. Of course Cal and her father preferred the old her. Back when she had been a homebody, playing with the kids and having dinner on the table when Cal came home. Even if she didn't cook it. That Kelly lived for the moment when he walked through the door. The changes had turned her into an in-demand actress, one associated with a different leading man every few months.

Another year passed before a story ran in *People* magazine and *USA Today*, declaring that Kelly couldn't act. "But she looks like a million bucks," the reporter wrote. "Even if she's playing scenes that are a little scandalous, she's still America's sweetheart."

The article also questioned whether Cal Whittaker III—America's premier faith-and-family filmmaker—could be happy about his wife's choices. Maybe to silence the critics or to keep an eye on her, Cal had asked her to be in one of his bigger films. Kelly turned down the offer. Another decision questioned by the media.

She remembered the night she tried to explain her decision to him. "I don't need your audience scrutinizing me. Church people will hang me up and throw darts at me." She kissed him. "Try to understand, okay?"

What he did next would forever stand as the first blow, the first battle in a war they'd eventually lose.

To pay her back—at least it seemed that way at the time—Cal hired an actress who had publicly hit on him. The woman made a spectacle of herself by talking with reporters about the crush she had on Cal Whittaker. "Star Actress Hot for Kelly Morgan's Guy," the headlines read in that week's tabloids. Kelly was asked about her husband's decision in a dozen interviews over the next few months, especially when she landed her biggest role of all—the lead in a movie about a singer trying to hold on to her fame.

That year the paparazzi were ruthless. "Is Cal having an affair?" they would shout at her as she left the studio. "Has he walked away from his faith?"

Kelly ignored them, but she and Cal fought about the situation constantly. He swore that the executive producers had made the decision to hire the actress, but she believed he had a hand in the matter. "You wanted to get back at me," she would insist.

Around and around the argument went. Kai and Kinley spent more time with their nanny, and Kelly took parts in three films back to back, each of which took her away from L.A. for months at a time.

It was while she was on the set of the third movie that she first saw pictures of Cal and the European model. The girl was stunning, just twenty-four years old. In the photo Cal had his arm around her as they ran from a Hollywood restaurant to a cab in the pouring rain.

More fighting and unhappiness followed. More insistence from Cal that nothing was happening, that there was an explanation for the photo. He was a producer. Of course he spent time with possible leading ladies, looking for the right fit for his next film. Kelly quickly grew tired of the fighting. She had always resisted the sort of roles that put her in bed with her costar. But in light of Cal's public antics and the way he had humiliated her in front of the world, she took a guest role on a racy hit vampire show. Her role recurred for three weeks and over that time she had several steamy sex scenes.

The show filmed in North Carolina, and a couple times local photographers caught her with her costar at a café or coffee shop. She had barely flown home when Michael Manning direct-messaged her on Twitter. She remembered the tweet word for word. *Heard about the steamy vampire scenes, love. You still married? I'm next in line.* She didn't respond but his message did strange things to her heart and made her feel twenty again. Every girl was in love with Michael Manning. He couldn't be serious, right? She was a decade older than him. But the situation presented a possibility Kelly hadn't really considered since her wedding day.

The possibility of being single.

Six rocky months passed, and one day over backyard coffee with Cal she brought up the idea of divorce. He panicked at first and swore he and the model had met only to discuss her interest in family-friendly films. "Not all things are in my control," he told her. "We need counseling, Kelly. We made a promise before God." Tears filled his eyes. "I didn't cheat on you. I never would."

"Come on, Cal. You don't talk to me or text me. You're sharing your life with someone else. Whoever she is." She clenched her fists, equally frustrated. "It's like we're strangers."

"You're never home." Cal waved his hand in her direction. "How can I share my life with you when every few months you're on to the next big thing? Where do I rate on your list of priorities?"

"You have plenty of women in your life. You don't need me."

Cal studied her, his face a mask of pain and suspicion. "Is there someone else? Because if there is, I want to hear it from you. Not the tabloids."

"There's no one, Cal." The words came easily and felt like truth. At that point she hadn't responded to Michael's tweet. She kept her tone controlled. They didn't need to give her house-keeper a reason to think they were fighting. "This isn't about other people. It's about us."

He reached for her hands, but the gesture somehow lacked the passion they once shared. "Kelly, please. Don't do this."

"It's the only way."

His voice fell to a whisper. "How did we get here?"

Kelly had no answers. That night she finally responded to Michael Manning's private tweet.

Hey Michael . . . I finally found time to get back to you. I'd love to get coffee some time.

At the end of the message she included her cell phone number. She said nothing about her marriage. That week two things happened that prompted Kelly to call her lawyer and have the papers drawn up. First, the tabloids had new pictures of Cal and the model, along with a whole slew of photographs of Kelly and her vampire costar.

Second, Michael Manning called her.

From that first conversation Kelly knew there would be no turning back. She fell for him in a way she'd never fallen before. Cal had been the only guy she'd ever loved, but her feelings for

Michael made her wonder if she and Cal had simply been too young, the influence of her pastor father and church friends too overbearing.

One night with the kids and their nanny upstairs, Kelly and Cal had it out in a heated fight. "It isn't working," she yelled at him. "I want out."

"Of course it's not working. You're taking roles that make you a joke. I mean really, Kelly? That vampire show? So the whole world has to see my wife—the pastor's daughter—in bed with some other guy? Body parts fully visible?"

"It's art. The show won six awards last year, okay?" Rage heated her face. "And don't tell me nothing happened with you and that . . . that girl. We both want out. Quit lying to yourself. You have to see it." She paused for a long minute. Then she blinked and in a tone more controlled than she'd felt in weeks delivered the final blow. "Cal." She sighed. "There's someone else."

And like that something snapped. The fight left his body and his expression went flat. He hesitated for a long minute and then exhaled. "Who?"

"Michael Manning." She felt a thrill just saying his name.

"The singer?" Cal's shock was immediate. "He's got a different girl every other week. He's a decade younger than you."

She shrugged one shoulder. "He's crazy about me." She went on to assure Cal that she and Michael were only friends. "But it could get serious."

Cal's eyes—the eyes that once were so like Zack's—grew dark and distant. "Fine." He stood and headed for the bedroom door, looking back just once. "Have your lawyer send me the paperwork."

She had stayed with Michael at the Ritz-Carlton in Laguna

Beach that weekend, leaving the kids with their nanny. When her father called three times that week, Kelly refused his call. Michael had that sort of power over her. The offer from *Fifteen Minutes* came the next week, and since then she and her singer boyfriend had been very careful. She was still married, after all.

Which was why she needed to make this call.

KELLY TURNED HER back on the city of Atlanta and leaned against the railing. She stared at her phone again, at Cal's profile and the picture from another lifetime. *Why haven't I deleted that?* She looked long at the photo, at the people they used to be. *Enough.* She tapped the call button, held it to her ear and waited. One ring . . . two. On the third ring he answered.

"Hi." His voice sounded different, defeated and kinder at the same time. "You really called."

"You gave me no choice." Kelly faced the city. The people down below were too small to see clearly, but there were lots. She wondered if any of them were trying to navigate a messy divorce. "How are the kids?"

"They're great. We went to the park today. Kinley learned how to roller-skate." This was something new for Cal, the time he was spending with the kids. Usually they were with Kelly or the nanny; Cal was simply too busy. But between her contract with *Fifteen Minutes* and the divorce, Cal had changed. Kelly was glad—both for him and the kids. But it didn't change the reasons why they were separating.

She breathed in deep. "Cal, look. I don't want to drag this out. Rudy called. He gave me your message." She paused, frustrated. "What do you want me to do, take a personal day and fly there? Have it out face-to-face?"

"None of that. I want—"

"Stop. You're playing games, Cal. We both want this divorce." She found a calmer voice. "I have Michael now."

"That's your choice. Mine is simple." His voice held no trace of anger. "I want to stay married to you."

One of the assistants opened the door and leaned out. "Two minutes."

"I'm on set. This shouldn't be so hard." Kelly motioned to the assistant that she was nearly finished with the call. "You want to stay married? Really, Cal? What's that mean, exactly? We don't have a marriage. We have a legal document."

"We have two kids. And we have a past." He hesitated. When he spoke again there was no denying the pain in his voice. "Yes, the world knows you're having an affair. And yes, that hurts. But you're my wife and I won't let go of us. Even like this. Don't forget that."

She felt her heart start to respond, but her common sense was louder. Who was he kidding? This wasn't going anywhere. "My lawyer will be in touch." She kept her tone kind. "Cal . . . if this gets ugly we both lose."

He started to say something and stopped himself. "I'm sorry for everything. When you're ready to talk, I'm here."

The last thing she'd expected was an apology. It caught her off guard and took the edge off her anger. "I need to go. Good-bye, Cal."

"Good-bye."

If he was going to say something else, she didn't give him a chance. The phone call had gotten her nowhere. She looked at Cal's contact and with a few swipes of her finger she deleted the photo. She had it in a frame in some box back home. Something their kids would want one day. For now she didn't need reminders of a past better forgotten.

A sad thought hit her as she headed back inside. She could delete the photo and have her lawyer contact his. She could make plans with Michael Manning for the coming weeks and believe that life would be wonderful once Cal signed the divorce papers. She could box up yesterday and dream of new tomorrows. She could publicly disclaim the faith she was raised with and cut her father out of her life. She could walk further away from everything she had once been.

But there was one thing she couldn't stop.

The way Zack Dylan's eyes made her remember.

chapter 9

Chandra was at the airport the next morning when she spotted Zack. He was with a couple of the guys who had made it through, the three of them buying water bottles at a Hudson News stand. Kelly and Cullen had taken the private flight on the *Fifteen Minutes* jet the night before. Chandra had an early meeting with her manager, so she'd opted for a commercial flight. The same one as the contestants.

She hadn't stopped thinking of Zack since his audition. He had it all, Zack Dylan. The voice, the look, the rare and intangible charisma that set stars apart from everyone else. Chandra had hoped for the chance to talk to him. She was partway out of her seat before she stopped herself.

There was no rush. They would be holed up in the same Lower West Side château in the Village. Besides, she couldn't talk to him here, with so many other contestants gathered near the gate. For now it was enough to watch him, to imagine what the world would do with him once he was discovered. *Poor boy,* she thought as she settled back into the hard airport seat. *He has no idea what he's headed for. No idea that his days of wandering casually unnoticed through a busy airport are about to be cut short.* Zack and the guys headed for a section of seats not far from Chandra. She glanced in that direction and saw several other contestants including the blond cheerleader, the one who had been in the tent auditions with Zack.

Chandra stared straight ahead. Last night's meeting with Samuel Meier and the rest of the judges and production staff had been jarring. It was the first of its kind. Until now they'd been focused on the cities and finding the right kinds of contestants. That alone had been strange. Samuel Meier kept a list. There needed to be a racial mix, a gender mix, and a diversity of stories. Especially that.

But yesterday's meeting had taken another slant altogether. The team sat in chairs gathered in a circle on the set with Meier standing in the middle. "We have a few new policies. Strategies, I guess." He glanced at Cullen. "They've always been a part of the show, but now they're going to be in writing. Legal wants it that way." He wandered to a nearby open chair and sat down. His looked at the faces in the circle. "First, we are not a show that endorses any one religion." He moved on quickly. "We've been fairly lenient with our contestants. But from here out we have to be more careful." He held up a piece of paper. "Legal has crafted a release that every contestant will have to sign. Basically saying they won't talk about their faith on the show once we're at the New York rounds."

Chandra had felt ice in her veins. She wasn't a spokesperson for her parents' faith. But no one should be silenced about something that defined them. Whatever it was. She raised her hand.

"Yes." Samuel's expression told her to be careful; better to go along than to push back. "Chandra. You have a comment?"

"I do." She slid to the edge of her seat, staring at the expressions around her. "Does that seem a little weird to anyone else?" Her eyes turned back to Samuel. "What if they like knitting or ballet or watercolors? Will they have to be careful how much they talk about those things?"

"Chandra." The warning note was there again. "Religion is different. You were a contestant. You should know that."

"Okay." Chandra crossed her arms. "I have another question." She didn't wait for his approval. "Why are contestants allowed to talk about God at all? They have to put it on their application, right? Religious preference? Are you outspoken about your faith? That sort of thing. So why not tell them upfront that they can't talk about it?"

"Because." Cullen chuckled. "Christians bring in viewers." He winked at Samuel. "Right, bloke?"

"True." Samuel smiled. "Nothing wrong with that. At first the show belongs to the contestants. But once we get to New York, contestants belong to the show."

Chandra blinked and the memory of the meeting dissolved. But his words still troubled her soul. She looked over her shoulder at Zack again. He was sitting between two contestants—the black gospel singer and the blond cheerleader, Zoey. No question the blonde had it bad for Zack. Chandra studied the guy, the innocence in his eyes. When would he be presented with the release? Told that he couldn't talk about the God he believed in?

She remembered something else. She'd heard Kip say that Zack and Zoey were an item.

"I like it. The alliteration. Their good looks." Samuel nodded and signed something on Kip's clipboard. "Let's run with it."

Chandra had wanted to scream. Run with what? The insinuation of a relationship that wasn't there? She shifted in her seat so she could see them better. America would love Zack and Zoey. But what if he didn't want to be paired up with her? Chandra pictured the handsome face of her own former fiancé, the one she'd lost during the run of the show. What if Zack had a life before he auditioned? The way Chandra had.

Sadness came over her. The young man from Kentucky stood out in the group of contestants. The show would make him a star, she had no doubt. But she worried about him. What if the show changed him? What if it cost him something he held dear from his former life? The truth was, if Zack wound up being a finalist, the unsuspecting young man waiting for his flight to New York City would never go back to Kentucky. Not exactly like this.

She thought about her parents and how much she missed them. *Can you see me, Mama? Is there a hole in the floor of heaven where you're watching me? You'd be so proud. Your girl, a judge on* Fifteen Minutes. She closed her eyes. Her mother should've been sitting beside her. Her mom loved Manhattan. Her father would've given them a long list of dos and don'ts, how they had to be careful around the taxis and wait for the green light when they crossed the street. He would've told them not to stay out too late and to be aware of who was around them.

Her daddy had loved her so much. But her mom had been her friend. Her best friend. Winning this show had cost Chandra so much.

Already she could feel tears welling in her eyes. She couldn't cry. Not in public. Even with her head down, a number of people had already recognized her—though thankfully none of them had come up for her autograph. She was pretty sure a few cell phones were aimed at her from across the concourse. People who would put up YouTube clips of Chandra Olson sitting at the airport. No, she couldn't cry. People would always associate her with the tragic death of her parents. If someone snapped a shot of her wiping tears, the picture would make the front page of tabloids. "Chandra Olson Missing Her Parents."

If she were going to move on, then she needed to grieve in private.

There were two reasons why she'd agreed to be a judge. Because maybe in walking through a season from behind the judge's table, she would see again the girl she'd been. She would find her past.

The second reason was to make a difference for someone else. She called up a photo on her phone—the one taken minutes before she left home for her *Fifteen Minutes* audition. Her parents and her fiancé were gathered around her, believing in her. She looked deep into her mother's eyes.

His name is Zack, Mama . . . I know you're up there with Jesus. So if you could help out this young singer, that'd be great. Ask God to give me the chance to talk to him. Maybe even to warn him. She pictured her mother, her soft brown skin and shining eyes. *I miss you. So much I can hardly breathe sometimes. Only you know the real me, the one I can't show the world. The girl who just wants to go home and have her mama and daddy waiting for her. I'm still that girl, Mama. I am. I still cry every night missing you.*

Chandra switched gears. She couldn't stay in the past, not for more than a few minutes. She checked her boarding pass, anything to bring her back to the present. The truth was something no one knew. Something no camera would ever capture.

Just the way Chandra wanted it.

* * *

HE COULDN'T FIND a minute alone. Even here at the airport. That was the problem, and Zack knew he had to do something about it. Ever since his few minutes in front of the judges, since the whole Tebowing circus, he'd been moved from one event or interview or meeting to another.

His roommate—Jackson Blackwell, from the gospel choir—sat next to him, humming. "You like that, Zack?" Jackson's smile was contagious.

"Don't know it."

"Really? Come on! That's 'Souled Out' by Hezekiah Walker." Jackson rolled his eyes. "Man, everyone knows that jam. We sing it every Sunday."

Zack laughed. "Not at my church."

"Well." He slapped his knee. "When this madness is over I'm paying a visit to Kentucky and we'll fix that right up."

"Deal." Zack nodded.

"I wanna be there for that." Zoey sat on his other side, her eyes bright. "Okay, Zack? You gotta tell me."

Zack checked the time on his phone. At this rate he wouldn't find a single moment to talk to Reese.

"Attention," a voice came from the airport loudspeaker. "We will begin boarding in a few minutes. Please have your boarding pass ready."

During the interruption Zoey hurried over to the gospel singer to listen to more Hezekiah music off Jackson's phone. Today she seemed intent on flirting with other guys, maybe to prove to Zack she had options. Whatever her deal, Zack didn't care. He was grateful for a few seconds alone.

Last night the contestants didn't get back to the hotel until well after midnight, the first free time all day. Jackson had gotten on the phone with a buddy from back home, and Zack had sent a series of texts. He read them again now.

I can talk now if you're up. Crazy day around here. Don't know if you've been following everything on Twitter, but I made it through! I'm headed to New York! And yeah, the producers gave us times when we were supposed to update Twitter, but we had no other time until this minute. Anyway, I wanted to call you sooner, baby. Can you talk?

He figured she would be up late, waiting to hear from him. But five minutes became ten, so he sent her another text. *Please don't be mad at me. I haven't talked to my parents or anyone. I couldn't even use my phone till now. Except for Twitter. I thought about you all day. I hoped you were reading my tweets.*

There was no response until early this morning when he was in the shower. *Headed to the stable. Didn't see your texts till now. Congrats on making it through . . . praying for you.*

He had texted her three times since then. *Good morning, beautiful. On my way to the airport.* No response. *Through security, baby. Text me.* Nothing. *At the gate. I have almost an hour before we board. Are you there?* Still nothing. Her silence was louder than the few lines she'd jotted off this morning. He had a feeling she was upset, but he couldn't be sure. They needed to talk. He swallowed hard and looked out the window at a plane taking off. If she was upset now, wait till she saw the audition. He would explain it all before the show aired. That was his only hope.

"What're you doing?" Zoey was back beside him. She leaned in, pressing her cheek against his arm and peering down at his phone. "Texting the girlfriend?"

"Yeah." He clicked the screen off. "She's super happy for me."

"Is she on Twitter?"

"Not a lot." He didn't want this conversation. Didn't want to smell Zoey's perfume. He edged away from her and smiled. "I gotta make a few phone calls. I'll be back."

He walked to the corner of the waiting area and dropped to the floor. With one hand shading his eyes he searched his phone's Twitter account. How would Reese take the things he'd tweeted yesterday? He'd talked about the show. Done the hashtag *#FifteenMinutes* thing the way the producers had asked. But he'd also mentioned his faith in almost every tweet.

Then he checked something he hadn't before. His @s. The tweets that had been directed to him in the last few days. What he saw shocked him. Zoey must've known a hundred high school girls, and all of them were now following Zack. Most of the tweets were from Zoey. Including one she'd shot off ten minutes ago.

Headed to NY for next round of #FifteenMinutes. Sitting next to @ZackDylan. Yaaa, baby! Whatever cologne he's wearing it's perfect. #Winning

Zack felt his heart sink. If Reese had checked these tweets, no telling what she was thinking. Actually, he knew her well enough to know. She would trust him. She had no reason not to. But the comments could have bugged her enough that she might've turned off her phone. Or stopped checking Twitter altogether.

He needed to call her. He clicked her number and waited. Three rings, four . . . on the fifth her voice came on the line. "I'm out with Zack or the horses. You know how it goes. Leave a message and God bless!"

He waited for the beep. "Hey, baby, I'm at the airport. Not sure if you're getting my texts. Just wanted you to know I miss you. I can't believe I made it through. I'll be in New York in a few hours. Call me and I'll tell you what happens next." He paused. "I love you. Please call."

Zack felt the frustration in every cell of his body. The producers had told them that when they landed in New York their lives would get crazy. "You thought you were busy here?" one of the assistants had told the group headed to Manhattan. "Wait till you reach the city. You won't have time to turn around."

Call me, Reese . . . come on.

He could feel Zoey looking at him every minute or so. Zack ignored her. He had another call to make: to his father. Other than a few texts he hadn't checked in with his family. His dad answered on the first ring. "Son! Congratulations! We're all so proud of you."

Zack pictured himself Tebowing in the minutes after getting his red ticket. How would he explain that to his parents when the show aired? He squeezed his eyes shut. "Thanks, Dad. It's crazy out here. I can only imagine New York."

"You'll be fine. You know who you are." Joy rang in his father's tone, the kind he had always had for Zack and his efforts.

"Did you and Mom talk to the guy at the bank?"

"Listen." His dad's voice fell. "Please. Don't worry about that now. Just focus on singing for God."

"I have to think about it." Zack laughed a little. "Saving the farm . . . that's one of the reasons I'm here. You know that."

"We'll figure it out. If we have to sell it, then the Lord has a different plan."

"I don't want to sell it." He gritted his teeth. "I want to raise my kids there, Dad." He stopped himself. This wasn't the place.

"Talk to the guy at the bank. Get the loan. Tell him we'll pay him back as soon as we can."

After they hung up, Zack pictured Reese, working at the stable, her long dark hair pulled back while she helped one of the kids. He missed her so much. *Call me, Reese. Please.* He kept his eyes from the others so he wouldn't give Zoey a reason to join him. Instead he stared at his phone, willing it to ring. Then he remembered something. There'd been no time to read the Bible since he arrived in Atlanta. He opened the NIV app on his phone and read Colossians 4. Whenever he couldn't quite see north, he pulled out Colossians 4.

Devote yourselves to prayer, being watchful and thankful . . . Be wise in the way you act toward outsiders; make the most of every opportunity.

For now, though, he needed to live out the verses. Pray constantly, watch for pitfalls, and thank God with every step. That way he could make the most of every opportunity. He looked at Zoey again. *God, help me be wise in the way I treat her and the other contestants. I'm not wise on my own. I'll mess it up. But with You . . . God, with You I can do this. I know it. I feel it. Please let my dad get the short-term loan, let us keep the farm. And let Reese know I'm still me. I miss her. Thank you, Father. I'm thankful. Truly, I am. Stay with me, Lord. In Jesus's name, amen.*

As he finished praying, he felt someone watching him. He scanned the boarding area and saw Chandra Olson sitting in a row twenty feet from the contestants. Their eyes met and Chandra gave a slight nod. Then she smiled and looked back down at her phone. There was something deep in her eyes. It had been there yesterday during his audition and it was there again now. Like she wanted to talk. She was the only one who knew what it was like to go through the audition process. Maybe she would be helpful in the days ahead. He wanted to talk to her.

But he'd rather talk to Reese.

He remained consumed with the thought until they boarded, constantly checking to see if she had texted him or if he'd somehow missed her call. He even checked Twitter, in case she had chosen to talk to him that way. But there was nothing. He waited until the last possible moment, and then he did what he was asked without talking to Reese. He turned off his phone.

When he turned it on again he would be in New York.

chapter 10

The hot piercing sun sliced through the wooden siding
of the barn at the Lowell Therapeutic Equestrian Center.
Ten in the morning and already temperatures were well past
ninety degrees. Reese's attention was taken entirely by six-
year-old Toby, the little boy in the saddle. Which meant for the
first time all week she was thinking about someone other than
Zack.

Twenty minutes later, the lesson ended. For the first time
since Toby arrived she checked her phone. Zack had been in
New York for a week and they'd only talked once. His reason remained the same. Too busy. Always too busy. Reese tried to understand. What choice did she have?

Now, though, there were three texts from Zack. The first
only told her hello and that he was thinking about her, praying
for her. She smiled and clicked on the next one. It was much
longer.

Baby, I know this is crazy but I'm leaving New York on a flight in two
hours. I'm headed to the airport now. A film crew connected with some
people at church got the okay to come tonight and film me leading
worship. See? Crazy, right? Talk about last-minute.

Reese closed her eyes and imagined his arms around her. He
was coming home! He'd be here today! She felt like she was
dreaming. *Thank you, God . . . You know how much we miss each
other. Thank you.* She found her place and kept reading.

Anyway, we're going to my parents' house first. They know I'm
coming—but just for an hour. The producers know about the farm
being broke. Long story. My parents and Grandpa Dan are okay with
it. Then we'll go straight to church. I can only stay for worship and the
interviews. We have a ten o'clock flight out tonight. Just wanted you to
know. I love you. Can't wait to see you—even for a few minutes.

Reese moved around the barn to the back where she could
be alone. Then she clicked Zack's number and waited while it
rang. He answered it immediately. "Yes! I caught you!"

"This is amazing!" She closed her eyes and leaned against the
barn wall. "I can't believe you're coming home!"

"I know. I'm flying out on their private jet. A few other contestants, too."

"So you can't stay overnight?" She hated the thought of him
leaving so quickly.

"No. They'll take off from Kentucky around ten and head to
Nashville for the crew who's going there. Every minute is
planned. Seriously."

"It's fine." Her tone was soft, the sun on her shoulders. It was the most tender moment between them in too long. "I wish you could've seen Toby today. He's doing great."

"What about AJ?"

"She hasn't been by. She's still sick."

"I'm worried about her." Zack sounded tired. "My parents are dealing with a lot."

"They are. I'm sorry." She moved to a more shaded area. The signal between them was breaking up. She wiped the back of her hand over her forehead. "Zack . . . are you there?"

"I am. I can hear you now."

She held the phone a little tighter. "I miss you."

"I miss you, too. So much. I can't wait to see you. We need to catch up. I . . . I haven't had any time." His words cut out again.

"Zack?" She moved again. "What'd you say?"

"I'll tell you later."

The sound of his voice made its way through, soothing the anxious places in her heart and calming her doubts. "I'm proud of you. Really."

"Thank you." Relief flooded his tone. "Baby, I gotta go. I'll text you when I land."

"Should I be at your parents' house?" She held on, waiting for his answer. Instead three beeps sounded. She checked the screen. Call failed. She breathed in slowly and smiled. Communication was bad, but it would get better. Today or a month from now. Nothing would change Zack Dylan. She knew that in the core of her being. If they couldn't talk much now, so be it. One day soon Zack would tell her every detail, all the moments she'd missed. But today she was off work at three in the afternoon. If there was one moment she wasn't going to miss, it was this.

Being at his parents' house when Zack arrived that afternoon.

THE FLIGHT FELT wonderful, every minute of it. It was the first time Zack had sat still since he arrived in New York City. There were times in the last week when he wondered if he'd feel dizzy forever. Not that he was complaining. The experience was a constant rush of highs; the old château where they were staying in New York City was a palace of granite and marble and soaring ceilings, the sort Zack had only imagined. But the pace was beyond anything he'd known. And during the downtime he was constantly with the talented, compelling team of twenty contestants. A team that included Zoey. There were four groups of twenty at this stage of the competition. They were preparing to perform in groups of five, fully aware that only two groups from each team would survive the weekend.

When eighty contestants would quickly become forty.

Everyone talked about who was going to make it through the next round and who would struggle. In theory everyone had the same chance, but the producers clearly knew something the contestants did not. Because only a fourth of them had been asked to shoot a produced piece on their lives. Those headed out today and tomorrow were the favorites—there was no getting around that. What gave the other contestants hope was that there were favorites in every one of the sixteen groups of five. When a group went through, everyone passed to the next level. So in that sense they all had a chance. At least for one more week.

Zack sat by himself, another first in the past several days. The two other contestants on his flight were from Tennessee and had stories among the best this season. William Gaines had moved back a few rows and now took the empty seat beside Zack. He wasn't smiling.

Gaines was a tall, thin black man in his forties with a neatly trimmed goatee and an air of perpetual scorn. He didn't only look nervous. He walked nervous and talked nervous and sounded nervous as he directed the contestants into groups and practice sessions. He had a way of making everyone around him nervous, too. Zack was no exception. He sat straighter, wide awake.

"Hi, Zack."

"Sir." He turned so he could make eye contact with the man.

Gaines looked forward, in no hurry. Something was coming. Something big. Zack clenched his fists and waited. After a week in Manhattan, Zack had figured out that though Samuel J. Meier was the producer, the judges were the talent, and Kip Barker was the recognizable host, the success of the show landed squarely on the shoulders of William Gaines. The contestant coordinator. His work took place behind the scenes, and if he did not organize a dramatic, heartfelt, talented show backstage where no one was looking, the acts who took the stage wouldn't keep the ratings. In many ways, William Gaines was the show.

Finally the man faced him. "We like you, Zack." He stroked his goatee. "America is going to like you." He smiled, proof that he was able to do so. "You're very good."

"Thank you, sir." Zack waited. There was more. He was sure.

"The thing is you have two stories. Two ways America can relate to you. Understand?"

"Uh, well . . ." Zack felt heat in his cheeks. "I guess I see it as one."

"The horse farm." Gaines loosened his tie and held up one

finger. "Your great-grandfather raised a Kentucky Derby winner. The farm's been in your family for over a century. Now it's facing closure. You're trying to save it. Willing to walk away from your private life on the farm, willing to travel the world using your gift of song so that no one would ever think of closing it. Willing to make enough money to help your sister with Down syndrome."

"What?" Zack felt his stomach slide to his boots. "How do you know that?"

"I know everything about my contestants." Gaines's tone was condescending. "That's my job. The farm and your sister . . . that's a great story. You become America's next Keith Urban, a young Elvis. Your dad can go on working the farm, and one day when the music runs out you'll take over. All that land paid off and owned by the Dylan family." He paused, searching Zack's eyes. "You follow me? That's the story we like."

Zack tried to look confident. "My faith. That's what you don't like, right?"

"See, it's not your faith that bothers me." Gaines waggled his finger at Zack, his eyes narrowed. "It's just that I have too many contestants with the *same* faith. It's not interesting."

"Huh. Okay." Zack paused. He wasn't going to make it easy for the man. "So what do you want from me?"

"I want you to focus on the horse thing. Talk about your sister. Your family. That sort of story." He didn't blink. "Talking about Jesus . . . that's cliché, you know? America is looking for something sincere. Something tangible they can get behind."

Zack leaned over his knees. He clasped his fingers at the back of his neck and rubbed his thumbs into the knotted muscles there. Was this really happening? The contestant coordinator for *Fifteen Minutes* was telling him his faith wasn't interesting? He breathed deep and held it. Then he sat up and stared at Gaines. "Here's the problem. My life on the farm . . . it's linked to my faith. I can't separate them."

Frustration deepened the lines at the corners of Gaines's eyes. "I'll make it more clear. Once we move past this weekend we'll assign new Twitter accounts to everyone who remains. Just before the show goes live a week later. That goes for everyone." He sounded suddenly weary. "We'll ask you to suspend your personal account and we'll assign you one with *Fifteen Minutes* as a part of your name. Our legal department is drafting a document everyone will have to sign. A promise that you won't use the Twitter name we give you for issues of religion or politics." He leveled his gaze at Zack. "It's not optional."

This was news to Zack. He felt the hair on the back of his neck rise. First the fact that Gaines knew about AJ, and now this. "What if we keep our old Twitter accounts?"

"Not possible if you make it through this weekend." His tone left no room for negotiation. "We want everyone on board. It's easier for the viewers that way." He settled back in the seat. "We have nothing against religion. We just want to avoid topics that divide."

Zack nodded and after a few seconds he turned his gaze out the window. Was this really happening? Could they do this? A rush of questions cornered him, but they were nothing compared to the next thought. How could he sign the document? He could turn to Gaines and tell him to forget it. *Don't film the piece in Danville, don't meet my family, don't ask the kids at church tonight how much they love me.* He could get off the plane and never get on it again.

Zack gritted his teeth, but before he could open his mouth, Gaines leaned closer. "You'll sign it. You can't quit." He leaned back in his seat, his eyes locked on Zack's. "You want your chance. Same as everyone else."

His words slapped at Zack's face. Not because they were intended to mock him or offend him, but because they were true. If his Twitter account were censored, monitored, could he stay on the show and be a light? He might win a recording contract and help the farm. But could he be true to the God who meant everything to him?

Gaines was waiting for a response. Zack turned to the window for a long time and then back to the contestant coordinator. "Thank you. For making me aware."

"Do I have your word? You'll do things our way?"

"I'll try. I can't promise anything. My words are my own." Zack didn't want to sound disrespectful. But they really couldn't tell him what to say or not say on Twitter, right? "It helps. Knowing what you expect. Knowing the rules."

Gaines studied him. "I'll be watching, Zack. Don't hurt your chances." He smiled and patted Zack's knee. "You could win the whole thing."

With that the man stood and returned to his seat at the front of the plane. Zack watched him go. Surely he didn't mean for Zack to cut God out of his story. He meant he wanted Zack not to go overboard, not to preach at people or polarize them. Zack had talked about his faith from the beginning, after all.

If he toned things down now was that a compromise?

Lord, I want to represent You. People need to see You when they see me singing on that stage. Help me know what that looks like.

My son, stand firm. Always be prepared to give an answer for the hope that you have. Speak all things with gentleness and respect.

The words sounded as clearly to him as those Gaines had

uttered a few minutes earlier. Zack looked around and felt his heart fill with a peace he hadn't known in the last week. He hadn't heard God speak to him like this before, but that's what just happened. It had to be. He'd read that section from 1 Peter earlier today. Now it was coming back like a direct message from God.

If he was going to shine brightly in his *Fifteen Minutes* run, it was a message he would have to hold on to with every breath, every fiber of his being. Starting tonight. He wasn't letting anyone film or interview AJ. She didn't deserve that. And Zack wouldn't be ashamed of the Gospel. His faith was everything to him. He couldn't hide it from others. And when it came to Twitter, no one could tell him what to say.

Not even William Gaines.

R eese got the text from Zack as soon as he landed. They had
to get the crew's camera bags and then they'd be at his parents' house in an hour. *Can't wait to see you. Sorry we won't have
time alone.* Reese smiled at his words. She would've liked time
alone.

She received an alert that a tweet from Zack had gone out. A
few clicks and she could see it.

> Back home in Kentucky! Seeing my family and leading worship at my
> church tonight. #homesick #finally

Reese checked his @s and sure enough. Almost the moment
Zack had tweeted, Zoey had responded.

> Can I just say I miss @ZackDylan already? Hurry back to New York.
> The team's not the same without you.

There was no mention of Reese. She examined herself to see if that bothered her. It didn't. Not really. Zack hadn't talked about her on Twitter since going to Atlanta. But that wasn't so unusual. He used Twitter as a way of sharing his faith with the teens at church, not to give a public window to their relationship. Now there were simply more people paying attention.

She breathed deep. *God, help me shake this feeling. I don't want to wonder or be jealous. Zack will be here in less than an hour.*

Feeling his arms around her would lighten her heart. She would look in his eyes and know nothing had changed, not even a little. And he could see how much she supported his journey with *Fifteen Minutes*. Maybe they could steal away for a brief moment and she could ask him if he was okay. Really okay.

She cleaned up her section of the stable at the Lowell center and clocked out. The heat had left her weary today, but the improvements in four of her kids convinced her she was right where God wanted her. She could hardly wait to tell Zack. Reese drove to his house and found his mom in the kitchen.

"I thought you might come by." Dara Dylan was slicing cheese, making a platter of snacks for Zack and the crew. She crossed the room and hugged Reese. Then she looked up. "AJ's awake. She's in her room. The doctor said her lungs are breaking down. He switched her to a new medicine." A sad smile lifted the corners of her lips. "She'd love to see you. She doesn't know about Zack coming home."

Reese nodded. She struggled to understand AJ's troubles. One setback after another made it hard. Wasn't it enough that the girl had Down syndrome? Reese tried to stay positive as she jogged up the stairs and found AJ in her room. The girl had

Zack's dark hair, but it was flat and unkempt, especially since she'd been sick. "AJ . . . it's me." She stepped into the room.

AJ was lying on her side, facing the wall. She rolled over at the sound of Reese's voice. "Hi." She sat up and hung her head. A few coughs and she looked up. "How are the horses?"

Reese smiled. "They're good." She moved closer and sat on the edge of the bed facing AJ. "Better question . . . how are *you*?"

"Oh, you know." AJ shrugged. She was very small, not a hundred pounds if Reese had to guess. Her character remained childlike, a quality that made her endearing to anyone who met her. "I wanna ride horses later."

"I want that, too." Reese tilted her head. "Your mom says you're on a new medicine."

"Sure." She looked a little bewildered, not certain of the details surrounding her health. She squinted at Reese. "Have you seen my brother? He's been missing for a long time."

"I have exciting news for you." Reese took gentle hold of AJ's hand.

AJ smiled. "I love that kind."

"Zack's coming home today! Just for a few hours, but he can't wait to see you."

The girl sat straight up and stared openmouthed at Reese. "My big brother's coming home?"

"Just for today. He'll be here soon."

"Yay!" AJ raised her hands over her head like an Olympian. "Yay, yay, yay!" She stopped to cough a few times, but nothing could dim her excitement. Finally, breathless, she dropped back on her pillow. "I hate when he's gone."

"Me, too."

"I think I'll rest. So I'll be all better when Zack gets here."

"Perfect." Reese touched AJ's shoulder. "I'll tell him to come up when he gets here."

Exhaustion was clearly having its way with the girl. She nodded, but already her eyes were closed. Reese crept out, not wanting to wake her. Back in the kitchen she found Zack's mom again. "She's sleeping. She can't wait to see Zack."

"She talks about him constantly." His mom adjusted a few platters on the kitchen island near a pitcher of iced tea and set a stack of plates and napkins nearby. Then she brushed her hands on her jeans and slid a plate of lemons toward Reese. "You know how Zack likes his sweet tea."

"Yes." Reese squeezed three lemons into the large pitcher and found the sugar canister across the kitchen. "They've kept him so busy."

"That's what he says."

"I told him this would happen." Reese smiled, but she could feel a sadness in her heart. "I knew he'd make it. This is only the beginning."

"I guess I never . . . I mean, nearly a hundred thousand contestants tried out."

"It's down to eighty." Reese sprinkled extra sugar in the tea, the way Zack liked it. "He could win the whole thing."

His mom kept slicing, slower than before, as if her heart were distracted. "Does that worry you?"

"Sometimes." Reese stirred the tea and then leaned against the counter. "Fame and recognition take a lot of time. Things could change."

Grandpa Dan walked in, heavy on his cane. He saw Reese and his face lit up. "Young lady! I didn't know you were here."

"Zack's coming home." She ran lightly over to him and hugged him. "Just for a few hours, but still."

"How wonderful." A smile filled his face. "I miss that boy." He raised an eyebrow. "Probably worse for you, huh?"

Reese laughed. "Feels like a month."

"Glad you could be here." Grandpa Dan nodded toward the porch. "You have a minute?"

"Sure." Reese turned to Zack's mother. "Can I do anything else?"

"Go talk." His mom waved her off. "He loves you. You know that."

Reese hadn't chatted with Grandpa Dan in too long. She followed him outside and sat across from him at the small table. "How are you?"

"Everyone wants to know about me." He chuckled and set his cane down against the table. "I want to know about you and Zack."

"We're good. I miss him." The sun splashed across the porch. Reese smiled at the old man. "It's hard to be apart—especially in the summer."

"That's right. It's July." His eyes sparkled. "You know what that means."

"The story." She hadn't forgotten.

"Yes. Every July I get to tell you again."

"Every year." Reese smiled. "Start at the beginning."

"I will." He leaned back slowly in his chair. "Lucy and I were friends in high school. Close friends." Grandpa Dan took his time. "A lot of people thought we were sweethearts, but we never were. She didn't see me that way." His eyes grew distant, far-off yesterdays alive again. "After high school, we lost touch. I joined the service and she became a nurse."

Reese knew the story well. She could've recited any section of it. But there was nothing like hearing Grandpa Dan tell it. He had a way of bringing the details to life again, making Reese feel like she'd been there. Grandpa Dan continued: He had come home from the war to find everything changed for his friend Lucy. She had taken up with a young soldier and the two had gotten married. The man was killed a month after their daughter was born.

By then Grandpa Dan had met the love of his life, Jean, and the two of them were engaged. "We had a conversation once, Lucy and I. I took her flowers and met her baby. She wasn't a year old." A twinkle shone from Grandpa Dan's eyes. "Beautiful child."

The conversation Dan and Lucy had that day was the first and last time they ever talked about their feelings for each other. "Lucy told me she loved me. She said she always would. I had no idea, of course." Grandpa Dan's voice was heavy with emotion. "It was too late. Life had moved past us. And I was in love with Jean."

For a season, life was easier for the two families. Lucy re-married a doctor. They raised the little girl and had three more children before the doctor ran off with a woman in California when the kids were teenagers. Lucy grew close once more with Dan and Jean, and the three spent a great deal of time together raising their kids and riding horses at the Dylans' farm.

But the day after Lucy's first grandchild was born, her doctor gave her the diagnosis. "Cancer. There was nothing they could do."

Grandpa Dan smiled at Reese. "Lucy loved that little grand-daughter of hers. Loved her with all her heart."

Reese felt her heart grow heavy. This was always the most touching part of the story. Because four months later Lucy died. "The day she died, Jean and I were with her." Tears welled in

Dan's eyes. He looked to the distant horizon. "Lucy made us promise something. She asked us to love her granddaughter. She wanted us to pray for that baby every day. And one day when the child was older, she wanted us to tell her about her grandma Lucy."

Dan and Jean kept their promise. They were the only grandparents the little girl ever knew. Even after Jean died ten years later, Dan kept the promise. The little girl's mother moved the family to northern Kentucky, but still Dan loved her and prayed for her and sent her Christmas presents. And every year he called her on the phone and told her the story.

"I always want you to know." Grandpa Dan smiled at Reese. "Your grandma Lucy loved you so much."

The impossibility of the story, the enormity of it swept over Reese the way it did whenever Grandpa Dan remembered the connection they all shared. The idea that she would meet Dan's grandson her first year in college; that when Zack had brought her home the first time to the horse farm, she would recognize it from when she was a little girl and Grandpa Dan would immediately know the girl Zack had fallen in love with.

"I prayed for both of you every day since you were both born. But I had no idea what God had planned for you."

The story always made Reese smile, but this time around it also made her a little sick. What if she and Zack didn't stay together? The woman from London had called again. Somehow, though, Reese hadn't wanted to think about giving her an answer. What if Zack's time on *Fifteen Minutes* took him far from her, and what if she went to Europe to train people in equine therapy?

The sense that she and Zack were destined for each other, that as Lucy's beloved granddaughter she belonged with Dan and

Jean's grandson, had always been comforting. But now she wasn't sure.

"What are you thinking?"

"Mmm." Reese met his wrinkled eyes. "You know me well."

He smiled. "I should." Again he was in no hurry. "You want to tell me?"

"Just thinking about Zack."

"I understand." Grandpa Dan slowly reached for her hand. Once his weathered fingers were around hers, he squeezed softly. "Don't you worry, Reese. No one knows if you and Zack will stay together. That's up to God and the two of you."

She nodded, fresh tears spilling from her troubled heart. "Yes."

"But no matter what . . . no matter where life takes you . . . I'll pray for you and tell you the story of Lucy. I'll do that as long as I live. I gave her my word."

How did he know exactly what to say? She wiped discreetly at her eyes. "Thank you. That . . . means a lot."

As they headed back in the house, as the *Fifteen Minutes* crew in their rented van appeared on the horizon and drove up to the Dylan horse farm, Reese felt more peace than she'd felt all week. Not because she had clearer answers about Zack and her but because she had the love and prayers of her parents and Zack and Grandpa Dan.

And somewhere in heaven, her sweet grandma Lucy.

THE VISIT FELT rushed from the moment Zack walked through his parents' front door. He saw Reese first, standing in the doorway to the kitchen, waiting, her eyes full of a love he'd missed more than he knew. "Reese." He rushed to her and drew her into a full embrace, the kind usually reserved for people returning from war.

Behind him the *Fifteen Minutes* crew filed into the house and past Zack and Reese into the kitchen. They didn't seem in a rush to catch footage of the two of them, and Zack was glad. Reese was a private person. What they shared was private, too.

Zack took Reese's hands, breathless at the feel of her in his arms. They heard the film crew making introductions to the rest of Zack's family. But before Zack and Reese could join them, he had to know about AJ. "How is she?"

"Not great. She's coughing a lot," Reese whispered, instinctively knowing that it wasn't her place to tip off the film crew to the existence or condition of Zack's handicapped sister. "I told her you'd find her upstairs."

Zack put his hands on either side of Reese's face and kissed her hard and fast. "Thank you." It was all he needed to say. He led Reese up a back staircase to AJ's room and when they walked in, his sister opened her eyes.

"Zack! You're here!" She flew out of bed to him. "My brother is home!"

He picked her up, twirled her around, kissed the top of her head and set her back down. She looked thinner, her face pale. Zack still had her hands in his. "You need to get better."

"I'm trying." Her grin took up her whole face. "I will now that you're home."

They talked for a few minutes, and then Zack and Reese had to join the others in the kitchen. He didn't want William Gaines overseeing a line of questions to his parents or grandfather without being in the room. Already Gaines's agenda felt shady.

On the way downstairs, Reese whispered, "How are you? Really?"

He stopped on the landing, the dark lighting perfect for the moment. He kissed her again, slower than before. As he pulled back, he breathed his answer against her cheek. "Perfect now."

"Mmmm. Me, too." She looped her arms around his neck. "I wish we had more time."

"Maybe tonight." He kissed her once more. "After church." He took her hand and they finished the rest of the stairs and moved into the kitchen.

From that moment on the night passed in a blur. Gaines oversaw the filming while one of the on-air correspondents asked the questions. He was a young guy just out of college and excellent at getting responses.

Zack stood next to Reese and watched from across the kitchen. The correspondent was interviewing Zack's younger brother, Duke. Their parents stood next to each other, clearly proud of the way Duke was handling the spotlight.

After Duke the questions were aimed at Zack's mom and dad and then Grandpa Dan. The only one not interviewed was Reese. Zack pulled Gaines aside as the crew packed up and readied for the move to the church. "Did they forget about Reese? She knows a lot about my love for the farm. She works with horses."

"Yeah, I know about that. She does equine therapy." Gaines patted him on the back and smiled. "They'll probably get her over at the church. She's going, right?"

It was too weird how much Gaines knew about his life. Not that it would've taken a detective. Facebook and Twitter were enough to connect the dots. Still . . . Zack wondered as the group headed to the church just how much Gaines knew. There could be only one reason why he wasn't in a hurry to get Reese on camera. She was the girlfriend. If Zack were single, more people might tune in to the show. Chandra Olson had warned him about that.

Of all the people connected with the show, Chandra was easily the kindest, the most genuine. Everyone knew her story, the tragedy of it. If she had a faith in God, she didn't talk about it. But she seemed concerned for Zack.

Yesterday when Chandra heard that he had a girlfriend, she warned him. "They won't want you to talk about her. Just be aware. It's easy to feel single when the producers are treating you that way." Chandra told him something else, too. "They're talking about you and Zoey. It's a better story if a relationship develops from the show. Coming in with a girlfriend doesn't do anything for ratings. Unless she's sick or famous." She smiled. "You get it?"

Zack got it. Proof played out through the night when Zack suggested twice that it might be a good time to interview Reese. The moment never happened. Reese stayed in the background while the on-air talent arranged camera time with five of the youth group kids and the pastor. They filmed the worship session, though Zack doubted they would use it. If they didn't want him talking about his beliefs, they wouldn't highlight that.

Either way, he used the chance to sing his heart out for the Lord, something he hadn't felt the freedom to do since he left for Atlanta. He sang "Ten Thousand Reasons" by Matt Redmond and then Chris Tomlin's "Your Grace Is Enough". The moment spoke to his soul and a hundred teens sang along, many of them with hands raised.

The song hit a musical break and Zack looked over the beautiful sea of teens to the *Fifteen Minutes* crew. He wondered if they had ever seen anything like this. And then it hit him. Of course they had. They'd seen worship at every *Fifteen Minutes* finale. At every concert for one of the pop icons on the show. Zack

looked across the room. Yes, there was something weirdly familiar about the scene.

Zack wondered if the film crew saw the difference. Here the
object of worship was not a celebrity. People were frail and broken and never meant to be worshipped. Here the adoration was
geared toward the only One who deserved it. The One who
would never leave or change or forsake His people, even those
who denied Him. The One who had breathed life into the world
and then sent His son to save it. Zack sang with all his heart.

"Bless the Lord, oh my soul . . . Oh my soul . . . worship His
Holy Name . . ." The melody of the piano, the full chords from
the guitars filled the building. Zack raised both hands to heaven.
"You, Lord . . . You are the only One . . . the One who was and is
and is to come."

The teens cheered in response. Zack smiled. He needed
this, needed to remember it. This was true worship. Centered on
and directed at the only Holy One. God Almighty, Creator of the
Universe, Savior and Lord.

The only frustrating part came when Gaines and the production team decided to pack up ten minutes early. Zack and Reese
slipped out a back door with the crew and he pulled her off to
the side so they'd have at least some privacy. "I'm not ready to
leave." He put his hands around her waist and searched her eyes.
"I miss you."

"Me, too." Her eyes held an undeniable sadness. But she
smiled all the same. "Just keep being a light. God's in control."

"It won't be easy." He looked over his shoulder at Gaines. "I'll
tell you later. Just keep praying."

"I won't stop." Tears gathered in her eyes. "They're waiting."
She brought her hand up and touched his hair, his cheek. "Don't
forget your promise."

Zack looked deep into her eyes, through her. "Never."

That was it, all the time they had. He caught the back of her head and leaned in to kiss her. "I'll text you."

She nodded and smiled again. The tears spilling down her face left her without words. She raised her hand and he did the same, taking backward steps away from her and then finally turning and jogging to catch up to the crew.

As they pulled away, he saw her standing there, watching him. The way she would watch him that week when his *Fifteen Minutes* audition aired. The van drove out of the church parking lot and Zack could no longer see her. He looked straight ahead and thought about the pace that awaited him in New York, the dynamics and skills and personalities of his team and his performing group.

He closed his eyes and sleep came in a rush. Next thing he knew they were at the airport, boarding the *Fifteen Minutes* private jet. He was exhausted, but he had no time for feeling tired.

Group rehearsals would start again first thing in the morning.

chapter 12

Kelly Morgan stepped off the private jet at LaGuardia and hurried through the muggy August night air to the waiting Escalade. The whole six-hour flight back from L.A. she couldn't wait to talk to Michael. They hadn't had a conversation in three days. Not that worry consumed her. But her heart was anxious about her boyfriend's tour schedule and crazy fans and the foreign countries where he was spending his time. Tonight his show was somewhere on the coast of South Africa.

Maybe the concerns were a by-product of her exhaustion. She and her fellow judges had just finished a crazy three-day media blitz in anticipation of the first *Fifteen Minutes* episode, airing this week. The heat on both coasts only made her more tired. It was almost ten o'clock at night and still a humid ninety-six degrees. Kelly realized she'd have to pace herself. The demands on her time would be crazy from here out.

Which was why she wanted a Skype date with her boyfriend. Now.

She thought about her *Fifteen Minutes* schedule on the drive through the Lincoln Tunnel to midtown Manhattan. The previously taped and produced first-round auditions from eight cities would air alongside the ongoing auditions in New York. Over three weeks the episodes would catch up to the live auditions at which point the final twenty contestants would compete for the win. The Atlanta and Chicago auditions would air first—the strongest of the city stops, according to Samuel Meier. After three weeks there would be another nine weeks of audience voting and at the end of October the next *Fifteen Minutes* winner would be crowned.

Twelve weeks from now.

Kelly sat in the backseat in silence. Her driver was an Irish guy who'd been in New York for two years. He knew to keep to himself. She stared at the stopped traffic ahead of them and felt her frustration double. Twelve weeks? Three months of Michael touring the world and Cal leaving her messages and her father e-mailing her? This morning she'd found another e-mail from her dad. Cal and her father. Two reasons why she would fall asleep tonight with the tapes. A positive inner voice. That's what she needed. Something to take her back to the way she felt when she was young and love was new and all was right with life. That life no longer existed. With the tapes she could at least feel that way. That was the plan.

Kelly's driver took her bags to the entrance of her bedroom and quietly left. Finally silence. Kelly let it wash over her. Her rented flat was four thousand square feet with a private entrance for the live-in help. Kelly wouldn't see them today. They knew her schedule. When she returned from a trip she liked a clean house, a fridge full of fresh kale and chard, blueberries and almond milk. Fresh Atlantic sockeye salmon, baby organic spinach, and bottled organic egg whites. Special soy candles lit. And quiet. Perfect quiet. She checked the fridge and spotted the candles. She breathed in and closed her eyes for a few seconds. Everything would be fine with Michael. They just needed to talk.

She breezed through the entryway down the expansive hall to the kitchen. The air-conditioned spaces felt wonderful. On the way she checked her look in the mirror. She resisted the urge to frown. Travel aged her. She hated that. She pressed lightly at the top of her cheekbones. More Botox, sooner than later. More yoga. She looked herself up and down. At least her body looked young—mid-twenties for sure—thanks to the two training sessions every day, even on the road.

She stared at her image a little longer. Every week someone younger came onto the scene. A twenty-two-year-old Oscar winner, a fifteen-year-old *American Idol* winner. Some blond singer-songwriter who would take the nation by storm and win a roomful of Grammys before she was twenty.

Meanwhile, every day Kelly Morgan grew older, another day away from her prime. Relentless, ruthless age. Her opponent in the battle to stay at the top. She breathed in deep again. Amber and sage. The candles she'd chosen for her Manhattan home. The smell of peace. If things went well with *Fifteen Minutes,* she might be asked back. In that case, she and Michael might buy this place. They'd talked about it. The scent would stay.

Peace in the midst of the crazy city.

She poured herself a glass of cabernet and dropped to her spot in front of the kitchen computer. The screen was the size of most televisions, Apple's biggest and best. Before turning it on, she tapped a button on the nearest wall. Instantly Michael's music sang to her from a dozen hidden speakers in the kitchen. Another deep breath. There. That was better. She checked the time and her heart fell. After eleven at night in New York meant five in the morning in South Africa. Michael partied hard after a show, staying awake into the wee hours of the morning. But even he would be asleep now.

She thought for a moment. She would text him. Just in case he was up.

Home sweet home. Finished shooting Leno this morning and flew straight back to New York. Miss you, baby. You awake?

Without waiting for a response, she set down her phone and brought the computer to life. Another e-mail from her father. Two from Rudy Smith, probably about Cal and his refusal to sign the papers. Another few from the *Fifteen Minutes* production team. She would read them later. First she wanted to see how the media was handling the recent L.A. interviews, specifically how they were playing up her part in the show. Her fingers moved over the keyboard and she called up yahoo.com. Sure enough—the launch of this season's *Fifteen Minutes* was the top story. The headline was favorable. "Kelly Morgan, Chandra Olson Set to Spice Up *Fifteen Minutes*."

Kelly smiled. But before she opened the story, the one next to it caught her attention. A piece about Michael Manning. Her smile died. At first the words didn't make sense, didn't connect. They shouted at her and made her head spin, made her dizzy and breathless. Seconds passed before she could get the slightest grip on her panic, enough so she could read the story.

No, she told herself. *No! This isn't happening. It couldn't be! He would've told me if . . .*

Her heart nearly pounded out of her chest and she struggled

to grab a full breath. *Open the story. You have to open the story.* The headline over the full-page piece was the same as the teaser. "Michael Manning Hooks Up with South African Star." In case there was any doubt, the photo showed her boyfriend in two separate moments with a stunning blonde. In the first, they were walking down a busy street, holding hands and smiling into each other's eyes. The second, they were in what looked like a dark-lit nightclub, locked in a passionate kiss.

Kelly could feel her stomach twisting, the nausea grabbing at her, suffocating her. This couldn't be happening. They had promised each other. If they felt the need to move on, they'd say so. He wouldn't have an affair without breaking things off with her first. That was his promise.

She stood and paced across the kitchen and then back. Her eyes found the headline again and for the first time she saw the second, smaller headline. *"Fifteen Minutes* Judge Kelly Morgan Jilted for Younger Woman." Anger ripped through her veins making her head hurt. How could he? On the very week the *Fifteen Minutes* season debuted? Michael knew how important the show was, and how hyper-sensitive the media would be to any story dealing with Kelly Morgan.

She took her seat and despite the panic and pain welling up inside her, despite her racing heart, she read the story. The facts jumped out at her in jarring detail. Michael Manning planned to spend a few extra days in South Africa with his latest love—Saphira Sanders. At just nineteen, Saphira was that country's hottest pop star. Manning had been in town for a series of concerts, and he and Saphira had been inseparable. On and on it went. The last paragraph etched itself in Kelly's heart.

"Manning has previously been linked to a number of high-profile celebrities, including most recently this season's *Fif-*

teen Minutes judge Kelly Morgan, a decade his senior. Good thing Kelly has the hit show. Otherwise she'd have a lot of time on her hands to handle her heartache. Then again, Kelly shouldn't be surprised. Michael Manning has a track record, after all."

Shouldn't be surprised? Kelly felt sicker than before, her heart racing ahead of her. She ran to the nearest bathroom and dropped to her knees at the toilet's edge. She couldn't believe a word of it. He wouldn't do this to her, not publicly. Her dinner sat perilously close to the back of her throat and she held her hair in one hand. Michael was her muse, her love, her life. The one she planned to share her future with. But if the article was flawed, the photos were not. The evidence was there for all the world to see.

Michael Manning had moved on.

Tears streamed down her face. How had this happened? Hadn't she been enough for him? He had chosen a girl almost two decades younger—a princess in the one area where Kelly could no longer compete.

Age.

Kelly's body convulsed at the reality, emptying her stomach and heart, her mind and soul of all things Michael. When it was over, when she had nothing left inside her, she struggled to her feet and with shaking hands she gripped the sink. For a long time she stared at herself.

She hated this, hated the feeling of her broken heart. Hated being alone. She breathed in, filling her body with the strength to survive another minute. At least that long, while she tried to think of what to do next. Maybe she didn't need Michael. She was Kelly Morgan, star for two decades running. An American icon. But what about tomorrow? What about the photos of her boyfriend and his new love? The press would be unbearable. People would ask her about the broken relationship, and then what? She stared at herself awhile longer grasping for control, any control.

An idea began to take root. She could tell them the truth of her choosing. Not that she was jilted, definitely not. She thought another minute. Michael was a diversion, a hobby, that's what she could say. The two of them were never really in a formal relationship. The possibility grew. She would tell the press the split had been mutual. Yes, that was it. She blinked, letting this version of the truth sink in. Mutual. Maybe that would stop the press.

Even if it didn't stop her heart from breaking.

Kelly rinsed her mouth and dried the tears and water from her face. She would survive. Michael Manning wouldn't dictate how the public viewed her or how her life was defined. He wouldn't turn her into a victim. She was strong. Like every other hard time in her life, she would get through this.

Her feet moved slowly, her new reality taking shape around her as she made her way to the kitchen. She no longer wanted the wine. From the distance of the kitchen bar she stared at the computer screen, the image of Michael and Saphira remained, shouting at her. Confirming the truth. Whatever she'd had with the singer, it was over.

Anger added to her barrage of emotions. She hurried to the computer, sat down, and closed Safari. The screen saver was a stunning shot of New York City, one she'd snapped from the Top of the Rock. The observatory on the sixty-ninth floor of Rockefeller Center. She'd been on a date with Michael. She stared at the view and remembered the possibilities she'd felt that day.

With a few quick clicks she changed the photo. Something

from a beach trip she'd taken with a few of her girlfriends two years ago. Blue skies, pale green waters and white sandy beaches. There. She leaned back and looked at the image. That was better. She exhaled. What did her counselor's tapes tell her? With every out-breath a negative thought left her body. Yes, that was it. She could picture them leaving her heart and mind and soul.

Breathe, Kelly. Breathe out. Kelly exhaled and pictured Michael Manning leaving her. After four breaths her heart still hurt. She leaned back in her chair and closed her eyes. She should sleep. The camera would pick up every missed hour of rest when filming began in the morning. But she wasn't tired. Nothing the tapes could tell her would change the fact.

She would survive, but tonight her heart was breaking. Not just for the loss of Michael Manning; for all the losses of a lifetime. For the dreams she and Cal had shared and the hope that had been at the center of their lives. She'd lost at love long before tonight.

Her eyes opened and without too much thought she checked her e-mail again.

She had two new letters from her dad and several from her manager. Nothing from Cal. Lately he seemed intent on going through Rudy Smith in his quest for reconciliation.

There were requests for donations and appearances and endorsements. Communication that should've gone through Rudy's office. But people found her. If they could bypass her manager, they figured they'd be that much closer to getting what they wanted. Kelly forwarded them all to Rudy without opening a single one.

Next she opened the oldest one from her manager—dated three days ago, the morning Kelly and the other judges boarded a plane for L.A. Back when she thought her life was perfect. The first two were requests. Rudy passed on only the ones that stood a chance of getting her attention. A celebrity golf tournament in Palm Springs a year out. The event organizer was willing to pay her half a million dollars to be the spokesperson. And a request to sing on the Grammys. Both an easy yes, and Kelly quickly tapped out her response.

Rudy's final e-mail was longer. *We've been over this,* he wrote. *Cal wants to talk to you. He says you made a promise all those years ago before God. He won't sign the papers. At this point I have to recommend the two of you meet to talk. Otherwise things are at a standstill.*

Kelly closed the e-mail and gripped the countertop. Were the walls closing in or did the room just feel that way? Michael might be out of her life, but she wasn't going back to Cal. He'd made a mockery of her and their marriage. She'd done the same to him. There was no going back.

Finally she opened the e-mails from her father. The oldest one first. Her defenses stood a mile high as she started to read.

My darling Kelly, the letter began. She blinked. His words wouldn't trick her. The man was critical and judgmental. He never took her side when life got tough. She kept reading.

I haven't been well lately. Lots of doctor appointments. But even so, with every breath I pray for you. The person you are—the one you really are inside—is lost right now. But God is chasing you, Kelly. I've prayed that the world you're choosing will let you down. And once it does that you will see that God never has.

Tears fell on Kelly's jeans. What was this? Why was she crying? She dabbed lightly beneath her eyes and blinked so she could see more clearly. *Be strong,* she told herself. *Daddy is narrow-minded. He doesn't understand.* But no matter how she steeled herself against his words, her dad's voice echoed in her mind. She kept reading.

> My daughter, fame is a demanding lover. But fame is an illusion. Come back home, baby girl. Where you belong. We can sit next to each other in the front room and talk about you. The real you. I love you. Cal loves you, too. We've had the kids at our house this week. They know you're busy, but they talk about you all the time. I tell them to pray for you. That's what we'll keep doing until you come back around. Your mother may write to you in the next day or so.
>
> Love you lots,
> Daddy

More tears slid down her cheeks. Kelly didn't bother wiping them away. Her father didn't understand her life, her situation. But she couldn't deny the fact that he still loved her. She moved on to the other e-mail from her father, sent a day after the first one. As soon as she opened it, she saw it wasn't from her daddy. It was from her mother. Her heart rate quickened.

> Dear Kelly, it's been a long time.

Kelly glanced out the darkened window, guarding herself against the guilt trip certainly coming. Her mother hadn't talked to her since she and Cal split up. Her dad kept trying, but not her mom. The two had gotten into a fight the last time her mom called, and that was it. Kelly might not agree with her father, but here in the quiet of her own heartbreak she could at least acknowledge his effort. Since her breakup she could feel her mother's disapproval in the silence and now in the opening words of her e-mail. Kelly exhaled slowly. *My mother's rejection is leaving my body. It can't hurt me.* The pain remained. She kept reading.

Your father is sick, Kelly. Very sick.

Kelly slid to the edge of her seat. What was this? How come no one had said anything sooner? Her mouth felt dry as she continued.

Your daddy was diagnosed with cancer of the liver a year ago. He didn't want you to know. If you came back around he wanted it to be by your own choice, not because he was sick. Besides, you know your father. He thought he could fight it. The doctor saw him yesterday, and the truth is he doesn't have much time. Six months maybe. He didn't want me to tell you, but I insisted. You need to come home, Kelly. Before it's too late. I love you even when I don't say so.

Mom

Kelly's hands began to tremble. She pushed back from the computer and crossed her arms in front of her, doubling over against the pressure of her fists in her gut. Her father was dying? It was impossible. Her daddy was bigger than life. The strongest man she had ever known. She'd been angry with him, of course. He was old-fashioned, stuck on his beliefs of the Bible. But he was still young and full of life. The way she would always see him. What had happened? How had he gotten sick? And how could she have just six months to make things right?

The events of the night swirled together, pressing in on her, sucking the air from the room. First Michael, then this. The tapes would be useless tonight. Tears filled her eyes again and became rivers running down either side of her face. Never mind how she looked in the morning. Her daddy was dying.

Suddenly everything about her life these last few years felt shallow and flat. What was she doing, running around with a twenty-seven-year-old womanizer? Regardless of her views on right and wrong, she'd made a public fool of herself and her family.

Her marriage was finished, her faith was a thing of the past, and her place on the celebrity A-list was always a photo away from extinction. But the little girl who lived inside still ached for her daddy's arms. Deep inside she ached to be that sixteen-year-old nobody, in love with Cal and sure of Almighty God.

Tomorrow she would look terrible, but she no longer cared. She couldn't go to sleep until she did the more important thing.

She pulled up her father's e-mail and hit reply. For a few seconds she stared at the blank screen. Then gradually her fingers began to move.

Dear Daddy,

I read your letter and Mom's, and I'm devastated by your news. How could you be so sick? There must be something we can do, some doctor who can help you.

She thought about her schedule. The soonest she could take a trip home would be midweek. Never mind their differences, she needed to go. She began typing again.

We're taping *Fifteen Minutes* over the next few days, but then I'll come
see you. I'm sorry it's taken this to make me come home. We can
disagree about a lot of things, but not about family. I've been away too
long. I'm sorry. I'll call you this weekend and we'll make a plan. We'll
find the right doctor. I love you, Daddy.

Kelly

A weight she couldn't see or touch settled on her shoulders.
She stood and trudged to her bedroom. There was no need to
mess with the tapes tonight. Yahoo and a handful of e-mails had
said all there was to say. If she'd had any remaining threads of
belief in God, they were severed now. Michael was gone and her
dad was dying. Her dad, the best man she knew. The kind of
man the world needed more of.

If God were real, He never would've allowed that.

Zack wished they had another day to rehearse. The producers had them busier than ever, filming a Jeep commercial all day Monday and hosting a number of reporters on Tuesday in anticipation of the show's debut next week. Every remaining hour was spent in rehearsals, but even that didn't feel like enough.

On top of everything, Zack had exchanged only a few texts with Reese and his parents. The pressure was intense. Reese had assured him that she understood. His parents, too. Zack needed to put everything into making it through to the next round. And that meant he had to focus on his group's number.

Zack sat eight rows from the front, next to Zoey. Like always. The girl was like glue. No matter how much he talked about Reese, Zoey found her way beside him. It could've been his imagination, but it seemed whenever Zoey leaned in to talk to him, one of the cameras caught the move. Kip had asked earlier today for an update on the budding romance.

"There's no romance." Zack had tried not to sound angry. Last thing he wanted to do was get on Kip's bad side. Still, he was tired of the talk about him and Zoey. "She's a friend. Nothing more."

"Sure." Kip had winked at him.

Now Zack looked to the wings and saw Kip talking to one of the production assistants. Standing beside them was a cameraman and sure enough his lens was aimed straight at Zack and Zoey. He looked at the stage and tried to block from his mind whatever story the producers were creating.

The rest of their group sat nearby.

"We're up in three acts." Zoey leaned in and whispered near his ear. "I'm scared to death."

"We know the song." He smiled at her. The sort of smile reserved for his sister. "We'll do great."

"I wish we had more time. We need it. You said so yourself."

"Everyone needs more time. We're good." Regardless of what he thought, he needed Zoey to be calm. "You'll be great."

"But Zack"—she brought one knee up to her chest—"aren't you a little scared? I mean, we're at Carnegie Hall."

"Zoey." Zack forced a smile. "You need to focus. No more questions."

"What?" She looked like a child who hadn't gotten her way. "Are you serious?"

"Yes." He cast her a side glance. "Carnegie Hall or not, you can sing. You'll be fine." He looked straight ahead. "Just give it a rest for a minute." He drew a deep breath. Why did she have to be a part of every waking moment of his *Fifteen Minutes* experience? There were other guys. Single guys. He felt bad for her, for her insecurities, so he tolerated her. That was all.

Even when he could feel the cameras on them.

She folded her arms. "I was just saying. I mean, Carnegie Hall. I still can't believe it." Zoey leaned back in her seat and looked around the hallowed white ornate walls. "Think of all the people who've performed here."

She wasn't going to be quiet. Clearly. Zack kept his eyes straight ahead and thought about her last statement. She had a point. They knew their song, and in most ways this audition was only a means to an end. William Gaines had told their group that morning they'd have to forget most of the words or fall off the stage to be sent home at this point. Zack and the others were pretty much through to the top forty. A troubling thought came to Zack. He hadn't prayed about their upcoming performance since first thing this morning. The realization felt strangely foreign. He couldn't be too busy to pray, couldn't rush past this moment without taking it in, without thanking God for getting him this far. *Lord, use me today . . . use our group. Let me shine for You. Thanks for letting me be here at all.*

Zoey leaned in close to his arm. "What do you think of them?" She nodded to the stage. The group was mostly country singers, and the sound attempted to be something close to Lady Antebellum. It fell short, but Zack didn't want to say so. "They're all right."

"I think we're better."

Zack shifted so there were a few inches between him and Zoey again. "No guarantees today. We'll need to bring it."

"You're right." Zoey leaned in again. "But you think we're ready, right?"

Zack didn't say a word. He looked at her and then at the stage again. He couldn't make her be quiet. He scanned the front of the auditorium. Production assistants were everywhere, bringing meals and water, connecting contestants with instruc-

tors brought in for wardrobe expertise, vocal training, and movement design. Whatever that meant. All of them talked. The
consensus seemed to be that Zack's group was one of the strongest. The gospel singer from the first round back in the tent was
one of their five. Each of them could sing.

Zack definitely believed his group was one of the best. Certainly better than the country singers onstage. He felt a surge of
competitiveness mix with an ugly kind of pride. The sort he
barely recognized in himself. The feeling didn't sit well and Zack
closed his eyes. What was wrong with him? If God allowed him
to make it through to the next round it would be to glorify Him.
Not because he had sized up his competition and decided he
was a better singer or a stronger performer. He had to keep himself in check on so many levels.

He blinked his eyes open as one of the singers onstage forgot
several seconds of the lyric. Zack felt for the guy. The next singer
forgot words, too, and the youngest girl in the group began to cry
midsong. Long before the country group finished, Cullen Caldwell waved them off. "Stop!" He stood and scowled at the five
singers. "Are you blokes serious?" His Australian accent was
sharper than usual. "You're trying to make the top forty with that?
You don't even know the words." Cullen wore all white as usual,
this time with a fluorescent green knit cap. He motioned them
off the stage once more. "Someone get the next group out here.
The five of you are done. Go home!"

Just like that their time on *Fifteen Minutes* was finished.
Theirs was the first group eliminated, even though according to
show tradition, no group was officially eliminated until tomorrow, after everyone had competed. Zack pressed his back to the
hard pew and winced at Cullen's harsh tone. The singers hung
their heads, all but one. A woman in her late twenties. "Please."

She walked to the edge of the stage, her eyes scanning the judges. "This is my last chance. I mean, I have two kids at home and this is my dream. Can we try it again? We didn't even finish."

"No." Cullen was still standing. He pointed her off the stage. "You sounded like cats locked in a freezer." He sat down and stared at his notes. "Next group!"

Zoey looked at Zack, her eyes wide. "Intense," she mouthed. "Now I'm really scared."

"Pray."

"I don't know how."

Zack held his finger to his lips. If they got caught talking, they could be the next ones kicked out. Especially with the tension in the room.

Zoey pressed. "Let's talk later, okay? I want to know how to pray. I need it. I'm so nervous."

Zack nodded, more so she wouldn't keep talking to him. Did she really want to learn how to pray? Was that what she hoped to talk about? Zack wanted to believe her. Maybe if he talked to her about God she would understand him better, how he was only here because of his faith in Christ, how that and his family and Reese were what kept him going.

The next group took the stage, this one full of hipsters singing a whiny folk song from the sixties. Zack watched, wondering what Cullen would say or if he'd let them finish. The trouble with Zoey's flirting, the way he missed Reese, the conversation he'd had with his father last night—all of it weighed on him. The farm was in worse shape than any of them thought. It wasn't just the mortgage that was behind. They owed back taxes, too. His father didn't share many of the details, even when Zack pressed. But yesterday he could hear the despair in his father's voice.

"Don't worry about us. God has a plan," he had told Zack. "You'll stay as long as He wants you there."

Zack had felt his emotions get the better of him as the call ended. "I love you, Dad. Tell Mom the same." If it weren't for the fact that he'd made it this far, he would've climbed in a cab, headed for LaGuardia and caught the next flight home. He couldn't, though, because the Lord had allowed him to make it this far. He would see where the next round might take him.

The hipsters were allowed to finish, but watching Cullen mutter in Kelly Morgan's direction told the rest of them that the group didn't have long. They'd almost certainly be cut the next day. Zack and Zoey and their group filed to the side stage, and Zack motioned for them to hold hands. "Is it okay if we pray?" He looked at Zoey and the gospel singer and the other two. The group nodded, all of them clearly nervous. William Gaines and Samuel Meier had made it clear they weren't to overtly involve faith in their time on the show. Zack didn't care. If he didn't pray now he might as well go home. Besides, they were in a room where they couldn't be heard from the main stage and auditorium.

Zoey took his hand first, and the others followed suit. Zack didn't hesitate. "Dear God, we know that Your purposes are greater than ours. Help us shine for You on that stage. Make it clear what Your plans are for us. In the name of Jesus, amen."

A TV monitor showed a group of pop singers on the stage, one of the strongest of the day. Chandra Olson gave them a standing ovation, which made Cullen laugh out loud. "They were good, Chandra, not great. Save the standing O for perfection."

Whether it was an act for ratings or Cullen was having a rough day, Zack wasn't sure. But the judge's harsh intensity made him question his earlier confidence about his own group number. Maybe they weren't as ready as he thought. Either way their turn had come. Zack led the five of them onto the stage and tried not to notice the multiple layers of balconies in the storied auditorium. A set had been built at the base of the stage, a place for the judges. The remainder of the show would be filmed at Carnegie Hall, the first time *Fifteen Minutes* had been broadcast from here. The buzz was that ratings might be higher than ever.

As they took their places, Zack smiled and nodded at Kelly, then Chandra, and finally, Cullen.

"G'day, Zack. You look awfully happy." Cullen gave Zack a smirk. He nodded in Zoey's direction. "And look at you, Zoey girl. You look cheery, too. Something going on you wanna share with the viewers?"

Zack had hoped this wouldn't come up, but he was ready. He chuckled, keeping his demeanor and tone easy. Beside him, he could feel Zoey blushing, shifting uncomfortably. "We're a tight group." Zack held out both arms and, as if on cue, the other four singers filled in around him. "We're all happy, right?"

The others nodded. Definitely happy.

"Zoey, you look happier than everyone else." Cullen raised his brow. "Doesn't she look happy, Kelly? Chandra?"

Kelly laughed and shook her head, but Chandra gave Cullen a teasing shove on his shoulder. "Leave them alone."

"Just saying . . . I think we've got ourselves a couple of lovebirds." He shrugged, feigning innocence.

"Zoey and Zack." Kelly grinned. "Has a good ring to it. Cutest couple we've seen on the show for sure."

Chandra leveled her gaze at Zack. "You have a girlfriend, right?"

"Yes, ma'am, I do. Her name's Reese."

"See!" She shoved Cullen again. "Leave them alone."

"Play your cards right, Zack." Kelly gave the two of them a sly smile. "Sometimes you have to let go of the old and grab on to something new."

"*Someone* new," Cullen added. He and Kelly shared another laugh.

Zack figured the comment had something to do with Kelly's boyfriend hooking up with some South African singer. The story was all over the media.

But still . . . he wished the producers would quit assuming some kind of affair between him and Zoey.

Deep breath, Zack. You can do this. Clear my mind, God . . . Please, clear it.

"All right, enough." Cullen waved his hand, his face still lit up in a grin. "What are you singing this afternoon?" He leaned his elbows on the table and studied the group. He looked more relaxed than he had all day.

Zack leaned in to the microphone. " 'I Can Only Imagine.' The Wynonna Judd version."

"Keeping it country, huh?" Cullen raised his brow. His expression said the group had a lot to prove.

"Yes, sir."

"Well, good on ya'll, then." Cullen crossed his arms, focused. "Give it a go."

Zack took a step back and looked at his group. Then he cued the music and they began. The song was a hit from Christian group MercyMe, and it spoke of the first moments in heaven, the glory of meeting Jesus face-to-face. Wynonna's version added folk flair and a fiddle, but the ballad soared just the same.

The lead vocal went to Zack. He watched the red light come to life on the camera just behind the judges' table and he sang straight into the lens. As if he could see his parents and Grandpa

Dan and AJ and Duke. As if Reese were sitting across from him, cheering him on.

" 'I can only imagine, what it will be like . . . when I walk by your side . . .' "

Zoey stepped up. " 'I can only imagine . . .' "

They each took a part and on the chorus they harmonized in a way that made Carnegie Hall sound like heaven. Midsong Zack saw Chandra rub her arms and say something to Cullen, as if she had chills at the beauty of the music. At least that's what Zack hoped was happening.

When the song ended, the audience of contestants erupted into applause and shouts. Kelly and Chandra jumped to their feet, and Kelly pulled Cullen out of his chair. "Get up! You said we could give a standing ovation for perfection." Kelly shouted above the cheering contestants. "*That* . . . was perfection."

Cullen looked reluctant, but even he rose to his feet. He clapped slowly at first and then more powerfully. "Okay, okay," he quieted the crowd. "Yes. That was impressive, Zack. Your group sounds ready for the stage. Maybe you should stick together when this is all done."

"We might just do that." Zack motioned for the others to join him again, arms around one another. "We liked group week."

Chandra waved off the cheering crowd again. "That was easily the most beautiful rendition of that song I've ever heard." She shook her head, clearly amazed. "Where did that come from, that sound?"

Zack didn't hesitate. He leaned in toward the mic. "I think it only could've come from God. We asked Him to shine through us." He smiled at the others. "I think He did that today."

"I guess so." Kelly Morgan chuckled, though something about her expression looked off. She looked at her peers and

held out her hands in a grand shrug. "You sing a song about
God, that's what you get." She spun around and pointed at the
remaining contestants. "It's not too late. You can sing a song
about the Father, too. Everyone can use a little divine help,
right?"

She was making light of the situation, but Zack didn't care.
The song, the moment, the glory to God—all of it had been captured by the cameras. Never mind the romance they were trying
to conjure up between him and Zoey. This was the real story.
And now all the watching world would see it. Never mind the
limitations Meier and Gaines wanted to put on him. The judges
had asked and he had answered. Nothing wrong with that.

As they filed off the stage, each of them swapped hugs. Zoey
held on a little longer and spoke close to his face. "I was serious
about talking later. I want to hear more about God, okay?"

Zack pulled back and met her eyes. "Yes." He couldn't tell if
she meant it or if this was just another ploy to spend time with
him. "After dinner."

Her eyes lit up. "Perfect. I can't wait."

They headed back to their seats to watch the final groups.
Seventy-five contestants remained in the room, all eighty minus
the country group Cullen had sent home. As the performances
played out, Zack allowed for the fact that maybe one of them—
and not him—would be better suited to win this year. *Whatever
You want, God . . . whatever You want.* Throughout the afternoon,
Zack prayed and watched and wondered. Every few minutes he
fielded another question or arm touch by Zoey. Finally three
hours later they broke for dinner.

By then Zack wasn't hungry.

Not when all he could think about was his looming talk with
the relentless girl beside him.

* * *

THE STORY ABOUT Michael Manning ditching Kelly was all over the Internet, no surprise. With all eyes on her, she had stopped at a clinic on the Upper West Side early that morning before the office opened. A doctor she knew had given her eyes and cheeks a treatment, a mix of mild Botox and glycolic acid intended to remove any proof of her tears.

On top of that, her fellow judges had been nothing but kind since they arrived early that morning. Cullen had pulled her aside before the taping began. "The guy's a jerk, Kelly. You're rich and beautiful and famous. You deserve better." He pointed to the *Fifteen Minutes* logo atop the famous microphone. "Your star is rising. He's an idiot." He hugged her neck and pinched her cheek. "When the bloke figures that out, don't take him back, you hear me?"

"I won't." Kelly appreciated Cullen's support.

All day her tight skin reminded her to keep smiling. She wasn't a victim. She wasn't. As the groups paraded in front of them, Kelly reminded herself to call her parents that night. Samuel Meier had said she could take off three days for a trip back to Greenville, South Carolina. Kelly figured she could take care of the visit in two.

Now that it was time for dinner, Kelly was about to leave the auditorium when Chandra tapped her on the shoulder. Kelly turned around, surprised.

"You have a minute?" Chandra didn't look happy.

"Sure." Kelly never knew what to expect from Chandra. The woman was young and beautiful, but she had a past full of heartache and lately she seemed distant. Kelly had no idea what to expect.

When they were alone, Chandra put her hands on her hips. "I don't want to talk about Michael." Her eyes looked deep, concerned. "I heard you on the phone with your manager when we were at lunch in L.A. Your husband wants reconciliation, right? He doesn't want the divorce?"

"Wow." Kelly bristled. "That's none of your business."

"I know that." The singer's tone was sharp. "But you're going to hear me out."

No one talked to Kelly Morgan like this. She opened her eyes wider, too surprised to do anything but listen.

"You and Cal had one of the most beautiful marriages in Hollywood." Chandra spoke with all the diva attitude she was known for. "That's right. I followed your story. It was a fairy tale right up until a few years ago."

"You don't know—"

"Wait!" Chandra pointed at the ceiling. "I'm not finished. I know this is your breakup day and your heart's all in a knot and I'm sorry about that. But let me tell you something, Kelly Morgan. You looked like a fool dating that boy. And right now you're gonna listen. At this point in my life I have nothing to lose."

Again Kelly could only hold her breath and listen, curiosity winning over her outrage.

"All right." Chandra smoothed the wrinkles in her red silk top and found a new level of composure. "The way I see it, *you* changed. Not Cal. You." She jerked her thumb toward the stage. "All that fame crap got to your pretty head and you started believing it. Next thing you know you're talking about your trainer this and your Botox that. Your husband ain't good enough and you're too busy for your kids. Your family, your home, everything that used to matter fell to the idol of fame." She looked Kelly up and down. "Why? Because you decided you're all that. When you're not." She lowered her voice. "No one is."

Kelly rolled her eyes. Her stomach felt bunched up and she needed a restroom. A lecture was the last thing she'd expected from Chandra today. "I don't need this."

"Listen to me." Chandra leaned closer and pointed at her. "You call that husband of yours and figure it out." She settled back a few inches. "My parents were a beautiful example. They loved each other and took care of each other. They'd be here right now cheering me on if . . . if they had the chance."

A light dawned in Kelly's heart. This was about Chandra's parents, not her and Cal. She folded her arms and let the woman finish.

"Marriage is beautiful. Fame is ugly. Your boyfriend's out of the picture, fine." Chandra's words were rich with passion. "Call your husband. Before it's too late." She raised both hands in the air and shook her head. "That's all. I had to say it."

Chandra started to leave, the tension between the two of them still thick. Kelly called after her. "Wait."

The singer stopped, her eyes flashing with emotion. "What?"

"You're as famous as I am. Don't tell me it doesn't matter."

"It's a prison." Chandra took a step closer, her tone seething. "I'd give it up right now." Her voice settled into a deep sorrow. "To be back at home with my parents, the day before my *Fifteen Minutes* audition. All of it!" She said the words "fifteen minutes" as if they were poison. Chandra pointed at Kelly again. "There's no escape. I'm here this season so I can whisper the truth to a few people about fame. Maybe you." She held up her hands again and headed for the door. She looked back at Kelly once more. "Call your husband."

Chandra left the room and Kelly leaned against the wall, exhausted and trembling. What was all that? The diatribe was misplaced and uncalled for. How had she felt the right to say those things? Kelly shouldn't have to deal with this. If Samuel Meier asked Kelly back next season, she would tell him how Chandra felt. Then the black queen of pop music could be cut from the panel. Kelly's problem wasn't fame or her refusal to call Cal or even Michael Manning. Her problem was Chandra Olson. One of them would have to go next year.

The show had room for only one diva.

chapter 14

Monday's premiere of *Fifteen Minutes,* season ten, took forever to arrive.

Finally, Reese was headed over to Zack's house to watch the show, to gain a window on his world, the new life he was living. Her nerves had been on edge all day. Halfway to Zack's house, her phone rang. She pulled over and looked at the starry Kentucky sky. No clouds tonight. Reese took the call. "Hello?"

"Reese. It's Maggie Coltrain from London. Do you have a minute?"

"Absolutely. Sure." Reese did the math. It had to be early in London. Before sunup.

"Very well, let me explain where we're at in the process of hiring." Maggie had talked to her a few times already, though Reese had been careful not to commit. The London woman had explained that Reese was her first choice, but she had a few other equine therapists she was looking at. Now, though, she sounded almost desperate. "Our committee checked out the other options. None of them matches your experience, Reese. You said you needed time, but we'd like to offer you a one-year position starting in a month. The sooner you can get here for training, the better. We really hope you'll say yes."

Reese's head began to spin. She gripped the steering wheel while Maggie explained that there was a small house on the horse farm where Reese could live, and all her expenses would be covered. On top of that they would pay her twice what she made now.

"We have so many kids who need help." Maggie hesitated. "You're our first choice. Consider our offer and get back to us, okay?"

"Thank you." Reese was breathless. "I'm honored, Ms. Coltrain. Really."

"Why don't you take the next few days? Get back to us on Monday. How would that be?"

Monday. Reese squeezed her eyes shut. Five days from now. Five days to decide if she should leave Kentucky for a year and whether this would be what she and Zack needed or the final act that could separate them forever. "Yes, ma'am. Monday would be fine."

"Very well." A smile filled the woman's voice. "I have a feeling you'll say yes. You're exactly what we need over here."

The call ended and Reese realized her hands were shaking. She needed to talk to Zack, needed to hear his voice and know his heart. He was still sailing through with *Fifteen Minutes*. His group had survived last weekend's eliminations. They would have another round of group performances this weekend, where some contestants would move on and others would be kept. Groups would be broken up and pared down to ten guys, ten girls. By Monday Reese would know whether Zack had made that cut or not.

Even if he did, would he want her gone for a year? Before he drove off for Atlanta, he had told her he couldn't stand the thought of her leaving. Now though so much had changed. He was constantly tweeting about the show and the sponsors and what God was doing in his life. When it came to her, he barely had time to text. Could there be a better year to spend in Europe?

Suddenly the thrill of being in a foreign country, training instructors, making a lasting difference for kids without hope, even the doubled salary—all of it was too much to ignore. If God didn't want her to take the position, then why did Maggie Coltrain call? Maybe this was His way of getting her out of Kentucky, out of the path of Zack Dylan. For now, anyway.

She pulled her car back onto the road and a few minutes later she was in the Dylans' living room with the rest of the family. Duke took the spot next to AJ and across the room Zack's parents sat together. Grandpa Dan hunkered down in his favorite recliner and Reese slipped in beside AJ.

"I'm nervous." Dara Dylan slid closer to her husband.

He put his arm around her shoulders. "He'll do great. We already know that."

Even though Atlanta was the last big-city audition, the producers of *Fifteen Minutes* had chosen to air it first. Zack had explained the situation to Reese during one of their rare phone calls. "They pick the audition with the best stories, the most drama. Anything to hook the audience."

"How many cities will they cover today?" Duke looked

around the room. He seemed nervous, too, wringing his hands as he sat at the edge of the sofa.

"Two today and two tomorrow." Reese had studied the format. "Then four more next week. After that they'll start showing the group auditions."

"Then what?" Zack's dad shrugged. "None of us are really sure."

Reese did her best to explain. *Fifteen Minutes* would air one episode a week starting with week three. After six weeks, they would be down to twenty contestants and the shows would air live, two a week, one show for the competition and another for the elimination of two singers.

If Zack survived the cuts, he would get busier and more in demand with each passing week. Reese kept that part to herself. The show was about to start and all eyes were on the television.

The music began, the production slick and professional. Reese folded her hands and tried to relax. No need to be nervous. They all knew how this was going to play out. Zack would sing and he would make it. No surprises in this episode. But this was the premiere, so all of America was going to see Zack Dylan for the first time. They were going to see the amazing man he was. The guy Reese had fallen in love with.

Ten minutes into the show Kip Barker's voice-over began talking about Zack Dylan. "Every year a number of heartthrobs find their place in line with the masses." A camera zoomed in on Zack, standing with what looked like a group of high school cheerleaders. "But it's not every year that a heartthrob can actually sing." The camera cut to Zack partway through a beautiful solo, which he was clearly singing to the group of girls while they fawned over him.

What was this? Reese felt her heart skip a beat and the room started to tilt. The others were glancing at her, checking her reaction. Everyone in the room seemed uncomfortable. Why hadn't Zack told her about this? She settled back against the sofa and tried to slow her racing pulse.

Kip was still talking. "Girls were crazy about Zack Dylan from the moment he stepped foot in line at Atlanta." While his voice-over provided commentary, a pretty blonde stood closest to Zack, barely containing herself. As Zack finished the song, the girl threw her arms around his neck. A quick cut and Zack was walking into the audition room.

"Well, hello, hunky young thing." Kelly Morgan whispered the words to Chandra Olson but the camera caught every syllable.

Cullen Caldwell heard the exchange and chuckled. "Try to control yourself," he whispered to her.

Kelly gave him a light punch in the arm. "I am trying."

"Really?" Cullen laughed again. "What I put up with."

Down the sofa from Reese, Duke broke the awkward tension in the room. "Wow." He looked at Reese and then at the others. "People are crazy."

"Definitely." Zack's dad cleared his throat. He leaned his forearms on his knees and studied the screen. "I didn't expect this."

"Inappropriate." That was all Grandpa Dan said.

Reese stayed quiet. She felt a strange pit in the center of her stomach. Not once as she looked forward to the season opener had she imagined this. Zack was this season's heartthrob? And even Kelly Morgan seemed to be falling for him? Reese clenched her fingers and kept watching.

Chandra Olson looked stunning, the picture of professionalism. She was the one who took control of the moment. She asked Zack's name and then Kelly asked where he was from.

Cullen elbowed Kelly. "Nowhere near New York." He patted her shoulder. "Settle down and give the bloke a listen."

"Why can't they let him sing?" Grandpa Dan rarely sounded angry, but this was one of those moments.

Again Chandra stopped the insanity. She asked Zack to talk about himself. He mentioned that he was a worship leader at church and he told the story of the horse farm. The Kentucky Derby winner came to light and the judges all seemed impressed. Reese sensed a collective sigh of relief in the Dylan's living room.

Cullen mentioned that Zack looked a little like a young Elvis Presley and Kelly couldn't seem to resist adding that Zack was even better-looking. Finally Zack was able to sing. Reese knew the song. He had practiced it for her the week before he drove to Atlanta. Tyrone Wells's "Dream Like New York" came off better than Zack had ever sung it.

All three judges clapped for him and Kelly Morgan was on her feet. "Did you hear that boy?" She danced around and pointed at the camera. "Listen up, America! You just met Zack Dylan! You can say you saw him here first!"

Reese struggled to stay in her seat. Something inside her wanted to run, wanted to chase down yesterday and find herself back on the front porch of her house before sunrise the morning he left for Atlanta. Before he belonged to *Fifteen Minutes*.

Zack made it through to New York, as they knew he would. His mom and sister clapped when the judges announced their decision. Kelly jumped up from the judges' table and ran around to the other side to hug Zack before he left. She said something about being the first to get a hug from Zack Dylan. All of it began to blur in Reese's mind. She'd never pictured the guy she loved being elevated to heartthrob status right before her eyes.

After the hug, Zack left the room and the judges commented once more about how handsome he was, how well he could sing. How he was going to take America by storm and how music needed a face like Zack's. A quick camera cut showed Zack rushing through the doors to the lobby where Kip Barker waited. Zack clutched the red ticket to New York, both hands raised over his head as he whooped and hollered.

Then before Kip could speak, Zack dropped to the floor in the Tebow pose—one knee to the floor, elbow anchored on the other, head in his hands.

Reese felt sick to her stomach. What was happening? Zack would never do this.

"I'm confused." Dara stood and paced a few steps toward the TV. "Why's he doing that?"

"No idea." Zack's dad looked concerned, his eyes on the images playing out on the screen.

"This is ridiculous. Completely staged." Grandpa Dan waved his hand at the television in disgust.

AJ and Duke squirmed on the sofa. "That isn't Zack," Duke whispered.

Reese said nothing, waiting, watching as Kip joked about Zack being the first contestant to Tebow. Zack popped up and grinned, and the music changed to Taylor Swift's song "Love Story." At the same time the shot cut to Zack entering the room of contestants and holding up his red ticket. Everyone shouted and screamed and ran toward him. "And so the heartthrob who looks like Elvis and sings like a dream is through," Kip's voiceover confirmed. "Of course . . . some people were more excited than others."

While Taylor Swift sang on, the shot switched one more time. This time Zack was in the hallway as the blond cheerleader spotted him and his red ticket. Her face lit up and they slowed the footage as she ran to Zack and threw her arms around his neck. "Who knows?" Kip's voice continued. "We might have our own *Fifteen Minutes* love story this season. We'll keep you posted."

The show cut to a commercial, and Zack's father muted the sound. His sigh filled the room. "Reese . . . I'm sorry. None of us knew what was coming."

"It's okay." She smiled even as tears gathered in her eyes. "He probably didn't know they were going to play it like that." She was trying, but her voice sounded shaky. She wanted to run in the worst way. "It's all for the ratings. That's what Zack told me."

Everyone was quiet except AJ. "He had to know about the Tebow thing." She looked at Reese. "Did he tell you?"

Her question was valid. He would've known about that and about singing to the cheerleaders in line and about Kelly Morgan hugging him. Certainly he would've known that they'd show the hug between him and the blonde. So why hadn't he said anything? Why hadn't he warned her?

"I'd like to know why he didn't give credit to God." Grandpa Dan took his baseball cap from his head and slapped it on his knee. "I thought that was the whole point."

"He may have." Zack's father sounded tired, not exactly anxious to defend Zack but not sure they should gang up against him either. "They'll use what they want to use."

Reese's phone was in the pocket of her jean shorts. She felt it vibrate and in a hurry she pulled it out. "It's Zack." She held up her finger and the room fell silent. "Hello?"

It sounded like a party in the background, but after a second or two she heard his voice. "Reese? I can barely hear you."

"Hi." Her heart pounded so loudly she could barely hear her own voice let alone his.

"I have to explain." He was shouting and still the background noise made it almost impossible to understand him. "They . . . everything . . . God."

"What?"

"You're breaking up." She pressed her finger into her free ear, desperate to hear what he was saying, how he felt about the episode.

". . . sorry. I'll . . . back in a few hours."

"You'll call me back?"

The phone went dead.

Everyone was looking at her. "He . . . It was loud wherever he was. They must've had a party for the debut."

"What did he say?" Zack's mother sat back down, her eyes concerned.

"Something about explaining things. He mentioned God and the girl. But it was too loud. I couldn't really understand him."

The commercial break ended. The blond cheerleader was up next. A montage of footage showed her with Zack in line and then sitting together in the stadium before their tent audition. "Eighteen-year-old cheerleader Zoey Davis came to Atlanta looking for a shot at *Fifteen Minutes*," Kip's voice explained. "She didn't expect to find the perfect guy."

More footage of Zack and Zoey talking, laughing, making their way into the tent audition, hugging as their names were called and they were sent through. The shot cut to an interview with Zoey. "Zack's amazing. I don't think I would've gotten this far without him. He doesn't know how good he is."

"Now," Kip continued, "the question remains. How good is Zoey Davis?"

The camera cut to Zoey walking into the room with the judges. This time it was Cullen's turn to act goofy over the looks of a contestant. "You're a pretty little Sheila, aren't you?" He grinned at Zoey. "And I hear you and young Elvis have a thing going on, is that right?" Cullen raised his eyebrows at her, grinning. "Or do I still have a chance?"

Zoey giggled. "I'm single."

Kelly rolled her eyes and quickly brought matters back to the audition. After a few seconds, the girl sang "Wind Beneath My Wings." The song was beautiful, her voice like that of any top pop singer. She made it through and again there was a commercial break.

"It's okay." Reese blinked back tears. This wasn't the place to break down. Besides, she hated how everyone in the room was looking at her, feeling sorry for her. Even if they didn't say so, their expressions did. She stood and hugged Grandpa Dan. "Zack will explain everything. As soon as he has a good signal."

But she was struggling with the truth. He was at a party and by the sounds in the background, he was having a great time. The connection was bad, but he was in Manhattan, right? Couldn't he move somewhere across a hallway or into another room? Couldn't he step outside if it meant talking to her?

Grandpa Dan excused himself, but Reese and the others watched the rest of the episode. The whole time Reese held her phone, watching for his call, waiting for it. When the show was nearly over a thought occurred to her. She called up Twitter and found Zack's profile. What she saw made her quietly gasp out loud.

"What is it?" Dara was in tune with Reese. "Is it Zack?"

"He has a new Twitter account. He told me about it yesterday." Reese stared at the screen, shocked. "He already has over a hundred thousand followers."

His dad looked confused. "Is that a lot?"

"Yes." Dara kept her eyes on Reese, the two of them more aware than the others. "He had just a couple hundred before the show aired."

And like that Reese felt the earth shift, felt her reality changing. She tapped the screen a few times and checked the things people were saying to him. After a minute she changed the screen back to Zack's profile. The girls were relentless, offering themselves in every possible way. Totally shameless. She checked his recent tweets. His latest tweet read, *How bout season 10 #FifteenMinutes? Best season ever, right? The beautiful @songleader just killed it! Follow us! The ride's just begun.*

"Beautiful"? "The ride's just begun"? That didn't sound like Zack. The tweet sent Reese over the edge. She clicked out of Twitter, stood and grabbed a deep breath. "I have to go. The stalls at home need cleaning."

"Want help?" Duke was on his feet. "I'm finished here."

"That's okay." She smiled at the boy. He was growing up, so much like Zack. No, that was wrong. So much like Zack a month ago. The way he'd been before he auditioned.

Dara came to Reese and hugged her. "We'll figure everything out. I'm sure there's an explanation."

"Yes." She smiled again. Anything to keep the tears at bay. "I'll call you if I hear from him."

"I'll do the same. He may only have a few minutes to talk."

Her smile felt sad. "Usually."

Reese hugged AJ and the rest of the family and thanked them for having her over. She was halfway to the car when it occurred to her that the show had been over for ten minutes and Zack hadn't called. By the time she was behind the wheel and heading down the driveway, she realized that she wasn't thinking so much about his phone call as the one she'd gotten earlier that day.

The one inviting her to London for a year.

chapter 15

Zack was furious. His Twitter account had been hacked. He had no idea who had sent out the last tweet, but he'd had nothing to do with it. He slipped his phone in his back pocket and found William Gaines near the bowl of punch in the party room they'd rented for the season opener.

"Hey, man, listen." Zack tried to control his anger. "Someone just sent out a tweet under my name. But it wasn't me."

William leaned against the wall and laughed. "What are you trying to say, Zack? You think *I* did that? Hardly." He nodded to Zoey, surrounded by four other girls at the center of the room. "Did you ask her?"

"Zoey?" He shook his head. "She didn't have my—"

That was when it hit him. Gaines might be right. Five minutes before the show started, Zoey had squeezed into the spot beside him. The room had been packed with cameras and cozy, overstuffed leather sofas. Pillows were everywhere. Not until the show was over did Zack find his phone between the cracks of the sofa. He figured it had fallen out of his pocket during the show, with all the bodies packed onto the cushions. But maybe Zoey—

Gaines laughed at him. "The girl has it bad for you. Don't put anything past her." He raised an eyebrow in Zoey's direction. "She's got her mind made up. Whether you like it or not."

Zack's anger doubled. He gritted his teeth and headed over to Zoey. She looked up when she saw him coming her way. He had to yell over the music. "Can we talk?"

"Sure!" She gave the girls around her a look that said maybe this was her lucky day. The others giggled and Zoey bounced up, ready to follow him. "Where are we going?"

"Out in the hall." He could feel the cameras on him, so he kept his smile in place. Everything they did was fair game for future shows. "Hurry, okay?"

She stayed close as they darted out of sight of the cameras. The hallway was dark and finally the two of them were alone. Only then did Zack let his frustration show. "Did you tweet from my phone?"

Her flirty expression became indignant. "Someone had to. You added a hundred thousand followers tonight." She grinned. "Which, by the way, so did I."

Zack was stuck back at her first response. "You really did that? You tweeted like you were me?" Zack wanted to shout at her. He raked his fingers through his hair. "I can't believe this."

"I didn't think you'd be mad." She lowered her chin, pressing her shoulder to the wall, defeated. Her eyes met his. "I'm sorry, okay?"

"Zoey. Never do that again." He exhaled, struggling for control. "That's not your place."

"I said I was sorry." She blinked a few times, and in the silence between them he watched tears fill her eyes. "Nothing ever goes the way I plan."

Zack's anger dissolved. "What do you mean?"

"You don't think I'm pretty, do you?"

"Oh, man." He slumped against the wall, facing her. She was easily the most beautiful girl this season. It was way after ten o'clock, and the hallway was mostly dark. Just a thin stream of light from the city flooded in from the windows at the far end of the building. Zack felt his guard slip. All this time he had looked at her with disdain, frustrated by her advances, certain of his convictions. But right now, with her crying and questioning her beauty, for the first time he could feel himself responding to her. He swallowed, praying for his world to right itself. "You're . . . very beautiful, Zoey. You know that."

"But not to you." She ran her fingertips beneath her eyes. "I annoy you, right? That's how it seems."

"I have a girlfriend."

"You should at least be open to new things. New people." She sniffed and lifted her pretty face to him. "You told me we'd talk that night after group auditions. But we didn't." She put her hand on his shoulder. "How come?"

He could smell her perfume and a faint bit of mint from her breath. They needed to get back in the room with the others. This was crazy, being out here in the dark hallway with her so close, so emotional. With him suddenly racked by uncertainty. He swallowed discreetly, searching for control. "I . . . I still want to talk."

"It doesn't seem like it."

His heart went out to her. She had been at his side for nearly two weeks and here, against all reason, Zack could admit the reality of the situation only now. He liked her spunk and her energy. He really did. Maybe his frustration with her was only his way of protecting himself from feeling something more.

Zack drew a deep breath and tried to make sense of it all.

She seemed to melt, her tears coming harder than before. She closed the gap between them and slowly her arms came up around his neck. She seemed weary, exhausted as she pressed her face against his chest. "Hold me, Zack. Please. Just hold me."

He had no choice. He wanted to be there for her. That was the right thing to do. But what started as his way of showing concern, of being the big brother she needed, gradually became something Zack struggled to deny. With her body pressed against his, he found himself running his hand along her back. "It's okay. Zoey, I'm here. It's okay."

"I need you."

Step back . . . you need distance between you, his conscience shouted at him. But all at once the pressures of the competition, the strange feeling of seeing himself on television, the sudden onslaught of Twitter followers, all got in the way. Suddenly it seemed like only Zoey could understand what he was going through, the same way only he could understand her. Kip Barker had called them the Romeo and Juliet of *Fifteen Minutes* season ten. And right now that was exactly how it felt.

"Zack." She pulled back just enough so she could see his eyes. "Do you think I'm pretty?"

"Yes." His mouth was dry. What was he doing? "Everyone knows you're pretty. I have eyes, Zoey."

"What if . . . what if we were meant to be? And we met too late?"

This wasn't happening. Zack needed air, needed to breathe

somewhere far away from Zoey Davis. "What if we were meant to be friends?"

She ran her fingers lightly down his arms and pressed in close again. "You want to kiss me," she whispered. "I know you do."

Zack shook his head. He didn't want that. He wanted to get away from her and call Reese before he lost himself in this dark hallway, somewhere in a rented party space in the heart of New York City. He shook his head. "I want—" That was as far as he got.

Her lips were on his and like that her kiss hijacked his senses. His arms were around her and the connection he'd been avoiding since they met was actually happening. But after a few seconds, control found him. He pushed away from her and wiped his mouth with the back of his hand. "No! I can't."

"You did." For the first time since he'd known her, she looked angry. "Don't lie to yourself, Zack. You felt something just now." She took a step back and adjusted her tank top. In the shadows he could see goose bumps on her tan arms. "Remember this . . . when you lie to yourself about your girl back home."

With that she turned and left him standing alone in the hall. Zack's heart pounded in his chest. Slowly, he sank to the floor, his back against the wall in every possible way. What had he done?

He pressed his fists to his eyes, furious with himself. She was pretty, yes. But he was in love with Reese. How could he have let that happen? And how could he call Reese now and tell her about his night? *Father, I failed her and I failed You. I failed my family and everyone pulling for me back home. How can I even stand after this?* The prayer felt strangely foreign and he realized something else. He hadn't talked to God all night. Not once until now. He thought about his next move. Maybe he should go back in the room, find William Gaines and quit. Tell him the show officially had one less contestant. It wasn't worth losing himself.

Lord, help me . . . I don't know what to do.

Fear—pure, unfiltered fear—ran through his veins. They still had more than two months before the winner would be crowned. If this could happen in two weeks, who would he be when the season ended? For ten minutes Zack stayed there, his head pressed against his fists, trying to find the courage to quit.

But gradually an answer took shape in his heart.

He'd messed up, yes. But everyone messed up at one time or another. He couldn't be so hard on himself. He'd kissed Zoey, but only for a few seconds. It wouldn't happen again. He would apologize to her the next time they were alone and then he'd do what he should've done from the beginning. He would have that talk he'd promised her. The one about Jesus.

And when he talked to Reese in person next, he'd tell her what happened. She deserved to know. He would apologize and explain how the moment had gotten away from him, how he hadn't kept boundaries in place and how he'd learned from the situation. Yes, that's what he would do. That way he could stay on the show. He would just be more careful with his heart and emotions. His promise to Reese and Grandpa Dan would remain intact.

Everything would be okay.

CHANDRA OLSON PRIDED herself on watching, studying people. Even trapped by fame, she remained a student of life and love. She saw things other people missed. So when Zack and Zoey slipped into the hallway a few minutes after the season premiere ended, Chandra noticed.

She saw them leave and she saw something else—something neither Zoey nor Zack could have noticed. The cameraman who followed them through a distant door at the back of the room.

When Zoey came back alone and angry, Chandra had an idea of what might've gone down. She waited until the cameraman slipped back into the room before she made her exit. By then everyone was in full party mode.

Spirits were sky-high. Music blared and rays of neon light added to what had become a dance floor in front of the big-screen TV. The room was dark and more than a few of the contestants seemed to be coupling up. Not that any of them mattered to Chandra the way Zoey and Zack mattered.

The producers had already told the judges. They had made their decision. They loved the Romeo and Juliet story, and if they had it their way, Zoey and Zack would be the last two contestants standing. By then they intended to have plenty of footage showing the reality of the denied romance, the heartache of the forgotten girlfriend back home. At a meeting last week Samuel Meier had put it simply. "America's going to fall in love with Zack and Zoey. It'll be the biggest finale ever."

With everyone caught up in the moment and the cameraman getting a drink at the bar, Chandra slipped into the hallway. Sure enough, Zack was ten yards down sitting on the floor, his back to the wall, one knee pulled up. Head in his hands. Whatever had happened, he looked crushed.

Chandra made her way quietly to him and when she reached the spot where he sat, she dropped down cross-legged and faced him. Only then did he notice her. He looked alarmed at first, but then his face fell and he brought his fists to his eyes again. Whatever had happened, he was struggling.

Chandra remembered the moment in her trailer before the

season began, after Zack had made it through the tent round. She wondered then if he was the reason she was here. Maybe she could offer insight to this young man and in the process find a meaning that had evaded her since the death of her parents.

"Hey." She realized it probably seemed strange to Zack, one of the celebrity judges sitting on the floor of a dark hallway across from him. Especially this early in the show run, when the contestants felt a chasm between themselves and the judges. But that didn't change the fact that Zack clearly needed help. Chandra kept her voice gentle. "You wanna talk?"

"It's okay." He lowered his hands and stared down the hallway toward the door. "I need to think."

Chandra searched his face, saw the muscles in his shoulders. He was one of the best-looking contestants the show had ever seen. But she felt nothing but pity for him.

"Well." She drew a slow breath. "If you don't want to talk, I do." She leaned her elbows on her knees, only a few feet separating them. From the distant party room, the noise grew, the music louder than before. "What happened?"

He gave a frustrated shake of his head. "We kissed. Me and Zoey." He looked defeated as he moved his eyes from her to a spot on the floor. "Was it obvious?"

"No. I had a feeling." There was no judgment in her tone.

"It was a stupid mistake. I . . . It happened before I could stop it."

"I get it." She slid back and leaned against the wall, her eyes locked on his. "Living together like this, it isn't natural. Things happen."

For the shortest moment she remembered her own secrets. How she had done the same thing when she was a contestant. She had been engaged back then. The affair was another part of her story—the part she rarely thought about anymore. That season the producers constantly placed her with Broadway singer Demetri Johnson, a beautiful brown-skinned dancer with a silky tenor voice and an ocean of charisma. The two of them had done more than make out in their weeks housed together.

She refused the memories. "Tell me about your girlfriend."

"My . . ." He shook his head. "She's amazing. She . . ." His voice trailed off. "The two of us, we need to talk."

"Zack." Chandra held up her hand. "Just tell me about her."

"Okay." His eyes welled up. "She's . . . she's perfect. Our grandparents were friends decades ago. It's like . . . like we were destined to be together."

"Mmm." Chandra nodded. "Is she in school?"

"We graduated. She teaches equine therapy." He ran his fingers through his hair, his eyes strained from the stress of the night. "Her work . . . it's changing lives."

"Have you talked with her? Since the show aired?"

"I tried to call her. The signal was bad."

"Yes . . . convenient." She leaned her head back and surveyed him for a long time. "Zack, can I tell you something?"

"Yes, ma'am."

"Don't 'yes, ma'am' me. I'm your age. Don't look at me and see Chandra Olson, celebrity. Okay? Can you do that?"

Zack looked slightly baffled. He sat up straighter and nodded. "I can try."

"Before *Fifteen Minutes,* I was just another girl. I was in college and I was engaged to my high school sweetheart. I was close to my parents and all of life was real and alive and perfect." She raised her eyebrows, her gaze intent on his. "Can you see that?"

The question seemed to hit a mark with Zack. He nodded slowly and exhaled, settling down some. "I think so."

"Okay." She lifted her chin, wanting him to see the changes as clearly as she could see them. "What did I want when I auditioned for *Fifteen Minutes*? What was I trying to do?"

He shrugged. "Make it as a singer."

"Yes. I wanted people to know I could sing." She smiled, but the feeling didn't reach her soul. "You know what happened instead? I stepped on a speeding train, and there was nothing I could do to stop it. Overnight, Zack. Overnight people knew my name. I couldn't go shopping or stop at Starbucks for a latte. My Twitter blew up and so did my Facebook. I couldn't tell my friends from the people who stalked me."

His eyes grew a little wider.

"You feeling me?"

"I think so."

"How many Twitter followers did you add tonight?"

"A hundred thousand." He picked up his phone beside him and shoved it in his pocket. "I haven't really looked."

"Oh"—she pointed at him—"but they're looking, aren't they? And by next week it'll be twice that. All those girls wanting a piece of your look and your voice and your body. You ready for that, Zack Dylan?"

He looked at the ground again. "I guess . . . I didn't think about it."

"You're thinking about faith, right? How you can give God the glory through the platform of *Fifteen Minutes*." Her tone didn't quite mock him, but it came close. "We had your type the year I won. It's the same every year. But you know what?" She leaned close again, bent over her lap so she could see his face through the shadows. "Your God doesn't shine in this environment. It's like you have to pick who you're gonna serve. God or fame." She sat back and stared at him. "Really, Zack. That's how it is."

"I've seen people . . ." He didn't sound convincing. "You know, make a stand for Jesus on shows like this."

"No." Her answer was quick and sharp. "You see what the cameras show. Behind the scenes there's always compromise. Always."

"What about—"

"*The Voice* last year? Sure, okay. He came out alive. But he hurried over to a Christian stage, didn't he? Country music? Pop rock? Those worlds would've destroyed him. He knew better than to go that route. You remember how he left, right?"

"I do." Zack narrowed his eyes.

"On his knees. He left on his knees, Zack. Singing to God, because he had to choose. God or fame." She felt herself getting worked up. The last thing she wanted was anyone from *Fifteen Minutes* looking for her. This conversation was for her sanity. Her purposes. Not theirs. She forced herself to be quieter. "You know about my parents?"

Zack shook his head. "They were killed. I don't know a lot more than that."

"My fame killed them." She waved her hand at demons she couldn't see. "Some crazy stalker hunted them down and killed them when they came home one afternoon."

He looked down. "I'm sorry."

"You see it better now, Zack?" Her tone softened. "This show, shows like it, they suck people in and spit them out. They build them up and make them famous. For *their* purposes alone." She leaned close again. "Hear me, Zack. When normal people become famous overnight they can never, ever go back. Not for any amount of money."

Zack was listening now, no question. His look was more intent, deeper than before. "Back to the girl you were the day before you auditioned. Is that what you mean?"

"Exactly." She sat back, drained. "If I could give you any ounce of advice, if I could make the decisions for you, know what I'd tell you?" The question was rhetorical. She didn't wait for a response. She pointed to the doorway at the end of the hall. "Run, Zack. Take your life and your family farm and the girlfriend you love so much and run like your life depends on it." She grabbed a quick breath and lowered her voice again. "Know why?"

"Why?"

"Because your life does depend on it, Zack." She pointed her thumb at the party happening in the adjacent room. "Zoey Davis? Girls like her hamming it up for the camera? That's not life. This isn't life. And every day you stay, you're one day closer to losing everything you had. Fame's a prison. Celebrity is a life sentence. You need to know." She stood and seemed to force herself to soften. "That's all."

"Thanks." Zack rose to his feet and brushed off his jeans. For a long time he looked at Chandra. Just looked at her. The warning was intense and personal. Even in light of his actions tonight it was hard to imagine being as famous as Chandra. But what if she was right? What if his actions today, the conflicts, the distance he felt from the people he loved—what if it were all just the beginning?

"You need to get back. I'll stay out here. Step outside for some air." She raised one eyebrow. "With my bodyguards, of course. Two of them waiting for me at the street entrance. See, Zack? You can't go back."

"I . . . needed to hear that."

"Okay." She smiled, the first time since she'd spotted him sitting alone in the hallway. She reached out and took his hands in hers. "About the kiss, don't beat yourself up. If you find a way back home sooner than later, that mistake will be worth it. Might even save your life."

"Hmm. Maybe." He squeezed her hands. "What you said . . . it means a lot."

"I hope so." She released his hands and nodded back to the party. "Be careful. They're watching. They want America to fall in love with you and Zoey."

He squinted, not sure he understood. "Like, you mean they *talk* about it?"

Chandra laughed, but it sounded bitter. "Absolutely. Now go. Before they find you out here with me."

Zack felt sick again. He stuck his hands in his pockets and nodded. Then he turned and walked down the hallway and into the party. Chandra waited till he was gone, then she did what she'd told him she would do. She pressed a button on her phone and waited until a guy picked up. "Ms. Olson?"

"I'm coming down."

"Yes, ma'am. Someone will meet you at the top of the stairs." His voice was gruff. This was serious business, guarding the life of Chandra Olson.

Chandra liked to think of herself as beyond tears. She'd already lost everything that mattered. What reason would her heart have to get involved now? But as she made her way to the stairs, as she watched for her bodyguard so she could step outside and get a few minutes of fresh air, she thought about Zack and a horse farm somewhere in Kentucky and a family who loved him. Parents and a brother and sister. She thought about the girl he loved waiting for him, and then she noticed something.

She was crying.

Crying for all that Zack stood to lose. And for the girl she'd been the day before her *Fifteen Minutes* audition.

A girl she could never be again.

chapter 16

The insanity of the next week was marked by rare quiet moments, usually in black Escalades or Hummer limos, when
all Zack could think about were the words of Chandra Olson. Her
story and her warning.

Her insistence that fame was a prison.

Zoey had cooled toward him, but only because she was hurt.
That much was obvious to Zack, but apparently not to the producers. They placed the two of them in the same group for every
activity, every red-carpet moment and photo shoot. Every rehearsal. By the time Thursday came, when it was time for a Disney movie premiere at Radio City Music Hall, neither of them
was surprised when the production assistants asked them to
walk the red carpet together. "Hold his arm," one of them told
Zoey. "Make it look good."

She followed instructions, but along the way she whispered
through her smile. "Sorry. This wasn't my idea."

"Don't be sorry. This isn't your fault." He spoke without moving his smiling lips as cameras took a thousand pictures. Against his will, something inside him enjoyed her nearness, the fact that they were talking again.

He hadn't exactly been kind to her. He had no reason to be angry with her. When he thought about it, the kiss in the hallway wasn't totally her fault. Guilt crept into his heart as they found their way into the theater. Zack was aware of her every move and comment, and he realized something else. In a way he couldn't explain, this past week he had missed her. They sat together when the movie started, and halfway through, under the veil of darkness, he reached for her hand. "I'm not mad at you," he whispered. "There's so much pressure. Everything's crazy."

She worked her fingers between his and for a few seconds she leaned her head on his shoulder. "Thank you." Her voice was loud enough only for him. "I needed to hear that. I never . . . I never planned to kiss you."

"Me, either." He gave her hand a gentle squeeze and then released it. The friendship they shared was real. No one else could understand what they were going through.

Zack settled back in his seat and remembered what he could about the week. Every time he tried to speak to Reese since the show premiered things had been strained. He wasn't sure what to say, how to bridge the gap. He told her how his words of praise to God had been cut from his post-audition interview, and how they'd forced him to do the Tebow. How he and Zoey were only friends.

What he didn't tell Reese was how it bugged him this week when Zoey kept her distance. Now he felt her arm against his, and this time he didn't move away. Friends could be close and not cross lines. This was one of those situations.

He blinked and tried to focus on the movie. But his life kept interfering. Whatever the situation with Zoey, Reese believed him, which only made it worse. Zack tried to convince himself that there was truth to his statement. There was no romance with Zoey, nothing Reese had to worry about. When all this insanity was over, Reese would still have his heart. His love would be hers alone. Zack had no doubt. But then what was he feeling for Zoey here in the shadows of the theater?

Deep compassion, maybe. Friendship, certainly.

Whatever it was, the words he said to Reese—and those he didn't say—felt bitter on his tongue, acid on his heart and soul. He still believed that whenever he came home, he would explain it all to her, even the kiss. But that talk needed to happen in person. He wanted to look into her eyes and pray she would understand. As for whatever this was with Zoey, well, he couldn't even explain that to himself.

All he knew was that life was suddenly insane for all of them. But especially for him and Zoey. There was a sense that the two of them would glide through the second round of auditions and well beyond. Like Chandra said, their Twitter accounts continued to blow up. After Monday's show someone started #ZackandZoey, and for a few hours yesterday it was trending in the top twenty.

Who else but Zoey could understand how different life had become, how surreal? He felt the warmth of her beside him. She was pretty, but what he felt for her wasn't a typical attraction. She understood. Maybe that was all. At a time when there was no way Reese or anyone else back home could begin to understand, Zoey did. With a glance she could relate to the pressure and the changes in their schedule and the loss of privacy. And most of all the giant called fame beating down their doors.

Chandra was right. Zack still found ways to mention God, but each time Gaines told him to cool it. People were looking for success and star quality. Not preaching. Zack wanted to be both a light and a team player. So for a few days he hadn't talked at all about his faith or his family. He could justify the decision. They had too many other things to talk about. Besides, maybe Gaines was right about overdoing it. No one was questioning Zack's faith just because he'd cooled his references to it. His number of followers was growing faster than ever, which could only be good. Because one day when he was off the show he could reach even more people with the truth about Jesus.

The movie played on, but Zack didn't catch a single word. Outside of a car ride, this was the first time any of them had been able to sit all week. Just sit for more than a couple minutes and think about what was happening. Here in the dark, no one was shoving a microphone in his face or taking his picture, no production assistants were prompting him to give the cameras his best smile or response or angle. Zack breathed out and felt himself relax. Chandra Olson came to mind again. Her advice had been simple.

Run.

Leave the show, go back home, and never look back. Zack pictured the passion in her face that night in the dark hallway. Chandra hated fame—no question. The crazy thing was the world had no idea how she felt. Chandra played the part of a celebrity with grace and poise, smiling for the cameras and answering questions with thoughtful consideration. She signed autographs and stayed safely between her bodyguards wherever she went. She'd taken cameo roles in movies, endorsed a cosmetic line, and had a perfume named after her. Every song she sang found its way to the top of the charts.

Chandra Olson was as A-list as she could get, and yet she hated the fame, every single second of it.

Zack thought he understood Chandra's strategy. Better to ride out the fame, own it. Zack shuddered. Was that what he wanted? He had wrestled with the question every possible moment since Chandra had talked to him. At this pace, he was headed fast toward fame, and yet the ride never felt as awful as Chandra described it. Sure, it was crazy, but most of the time he was having fun, and after coming this far, he couldn't leave. Couldn't consider walking away now. He had a list of reasons and a signed contract, promising he wouldn't leave until he was kicked off, unless he got sick or had a family emergency.

He shifted in his theater seat. His family. Yes, that was another reason. There were still the matters of saving the farm, getting better doctors for AJ, making a life for Reese. He couldn't let them down.

But all of it was happening too fast to consider the impact, whether down the road he would long for these days and the chance to walk away. Before fame became a prison for him, too. He believed Chandra that it could happen. She wasn't the only one talking about it. Last night Gaines had patted him on the back while he ate. "The other teen heartthrobs keep messing up. Lucky for you."

"What?" Zack turned to look at the contestant coordinator. "Who?"

"The big names. Their reputations are sinking like the *Ti-*

tanic." Gaines gave Zack another hearty pat. "It's your turn, my boy. Watch and see. You're gonna be one of the biggest stars this show has ever created."

Zack was glad none of the other contestants had heard him. No one but Zoey, who was sitting across from him. Their eyes met and what she had said stayed with him. "Ever get the feeling our lives are scripted? Whether we like it or not?"

Now a chase scene played out on the big screen, and Zoey leaned in closer. "Chandra talked to you the other night. I've been wanting to ask you about it, but people are always around."

"Yeah." He didn't try to pull away. "She told me fame is a prison. After this week, I can sort of see what she means."

"Hmm." Zoey let that sink in and nodded slowly. "I feel you. It's like . . . we never had a life before the show."

She was right, even if the thought terrified him. Their routines had been lost. The usual communication with family and friends was gone.

For a long moment Zack wondered about Reese. In the few minutes they'd had to talk, he hadn't done more than ask how she was. Her answer was always the same. "I'm great, Zack. Everything's fine."

Their lack of communication created a distance that again only Zoey could understand. The scene in the theater remained loud. He spoke near the side of her face. "How nice is this?"

"The quiet? I love it."

He thought about the way she'd chased him the first two weeks and how she'd backed off. She understood that he was serious about Reese. "I mean, it's been fun. But the craziness has to stop sometime."

"Exactly." She stole a glance at him. The shine was back in her eyes. "You still have to teach me to pray."

"It's easy. You just talk to God like He's there beside you." Zack smiled at her. "Because He is."

"There's more to it than that." Her eyes held his. "We need to find time alone. So you can tell me what you believe and why. Deal?"

"Deal." Zack felt a pang of guilt. How come he hadn't already told her about his faith? She'd asked a number of times. Yes, they were busy, but what could be more important than telling a girl like Zoey about Jesus? Not that he could do that here in a theater. And with Gaines watching him so closely he would have to be quiet about it. He'd signed the agreement. But there had to be time, right? "Maybe later this week."

Suddenly he realized how much he loved being able to talk without anyone taking their picture. Nights were for rehearsals and after that curfew was strictly enforced. *Fifteen Minutes* had leased an entire floor of hotel rooms at the Benjamin, not far from Times Square. But production assistants did a pretty good job of making sure contestants stayed in their rooms.

"You know what?" She took his hand again, but this time held it only for a few seconds. "This is the most like me I've felt all week."

"Same." He smiled at her. "I'm glad you're my friend. No one else understands."

That truth should've terrified him, should've sent him running for Gaines and the permission to leave. Family emergency or not. Chandra had warned him, right? There would be no going back to life the way it had been. Instead, Zack wished the movie would last another hour. Reese didn't know the insanity of what they were going through. She didn't have to worry about people constantly taking her picture or making up stories about her. Only Zoey understood that. Which was why he wished they had more time. Because here, safe and unrushed, comfortable with Zoey at his side he felt something they had already left behind.

The feeling of being normal.

chapter 17

Kelly Morgan took the *Fifteen Minutes* private jet into Green-ville. The plane gave her time to think—about the show and Michael and Cal. About the fact that her father was so sick. All of it stayed heavy on her heart.

She settled into the leather seat and stared out the window. Michael had called her on the way to the airport, spewing apologies and excuses. He would've called sooner, but the time difference was too great. The couple days with the South African singer hadn't meant anything. The media exaggerated the facts. He didn't plan to see her again.

Kelly had waited until he ran out of words. "Is that all?"

"Baby, come on. Don't be like that. You're the only one I love."

His words poked pins at her, but the surface of her heart was too tough for him to pierce. "I'm boarding a plane, Michael. It's over. Call the girl. Maybe she feels like talking."

"Are you serious? I never took you as the jealous type." He sounded desperate.

"I'm hardly jealous." Kelly had found a very natural laugh. "You were good for a time, Michael. I've moved on."

"It hasn't been a week."

"Good-bye." As she had tapped the end button she knew it was true. They were finished. She blinked back the tears and put him out of her mind. Michael Manning was a part of her past—where he would stay.

She dismissed the memory of the call and closed her eyes. As she did, a conversation from earlier in the week came back. One she'd had with Cullen and Chandra about celebrity energy. Which of the contestants had it and which never would. They all agreed Zack Dylan and Zoey Davis had it. But then Chandra had said something that surprised Kelly and Cullen. "That boy should walk away from all this. If he knows what's good for him he'll head home to Kentucky and never look back."

Cullen had looked at her like she'd sprouted an extra set of eyeballs. "Zack is about to own the world. How could you wish him back on the horse farm?"

Chandra could have a sharp tongue when the cameras weren't rolling. Like the way she called Kelly out about Cal. In that moment, Chandra's response had been much softer. "Really, Cullen? You like being famous?"

"Of course." He looked smug.

"No you don't." She stared at him. "You can't walk out your front door without people taking your picture."

"Oh, please." Cullen laced his fingers behind his head and leaned back in his chair. "Everyone wants to be us. Look at your life, Chandra."

Kelly winced a little. In light of Chandra's parents, Cullen hadn't exactly been sensitive.

Chandra's voice grew icy. "You know why they want to be us? Because they're *not* us. You and you." She pointed at Kelly. "You're addicted to all this and you tell yourselves you're happy." She gathered her long ironed hair. "But look at us. Our personal lives are a mess. We can't do what we want or wear what we want or go where we want." She lowered her voice again. "I wish the boy a ticket back to Danville, that's what."

Kelly opened her eyes and looked at the green rolling hills twenty thousand feet below. Did the pop singer have a point? Fame had cost them much. The murder of Chandra's parents and a broken engagement. Her own marriage to Cal failed, and for Cullen, at least four publicly failed relationships in the last two years. The man stuck to his dramatic all-white getup. So had fame become an addiction for him? Had it become that way for her?

The plane landed and a sedan met her. Now she was ten minutes from her parents' home in the country. She would stay today and leave tomorrow afternoon. Hopefully in that time she and her dad could find common ground. She hadn't processed that he was dying. Her memory of him would always be bigger than life, no matter what cancer might do to him.

The driver passed the church where her dad had been pastor for nearly four decades. *Don't bring up Jesus, Daddy. Don't do it. Not this time.* She looked away from the church. Too much history, Kelly and Cal. Wednesday nights. Rides to the lake in his pickup truck. She looked straight ahead. Chandra Olson's rant had stayed with her. Kelly had no intention of taking Chandra's advice about Cal. The singer's verbal attack last weekend was completely out of line. If Chandra tried to corner her with a dose of relationship advice, she would tell her where she could take it. Kelly had been caught off guard, nothing more.

It wouldn't happen again.

She narrowed her eyes, trying to see farther ahead. The road never changed. Pale gray asphalt lined with fading yellow dashes. Two stoplights a mile apart and then the turn. Right on Bentonville, another three miles on a road that was more one lane than two. A few more minutes, then a left on Sandy Creek, and there it was. The house she had grown up in. Kelly pulled her compact from her purse and checked her look.

All this travel wasn't good for her skin, but she was holding up.

The breakup, the news about her father, the constant pressure from Rudy for her to meet up with Cal. All of it took a toll on her face. She pressed lightly on her cheekbones. As long as she looked okay on the outside she could keep it together. Play the tapes in her head. Life was good. She was young and successful. Everything would be okay.

She touched up her lipstick and returned the compact to her purse, a subtle Marc Jacobs number. The last mile felt like ten, but finally they pulled into her parents' gravel driveway and up to the front door. The driver helped move her bags to the front porch while Kelly put the conversation with her fellow judges out of her mind. She hadn't reached the door when she heard the voices of her children.

Kelly's heart sank. What was this? No one had told her the kids would be here. She hadn't seen them in two weeks, not since the last time their nanny had brought them from Cal's house in New Jersey to her flat for a few days. They had planned for the kids to stay mainly with Cal while the *Fifteen Minutes* season played out.

Now as she opened the door, as she watched them run to her, she realized how much she missed them. How could two weeks have gone by without the three of them being together?

"Mommy! You're here!" Kai was six, a miniature of Cal with blond hair and beautiful blue eyes.

"I am." Kelly dropped low and held out her hands. Kai ran at her full force, wrapping his tanned arms around her neck and holding on as if his next breath depended on it.

Kinley was four, right behind her brother. "Mommy! You were gone for so long!" She worked her way into the hug and all three stayed that way for a long time.

"I'm sorry!" Kelly whispered into her daughter's long pale blond hair. "Mommy's been so busy."

Kinley leaned back and smoothed her hand over Kelly's head. "Grandma says mommies should never be too busy for their kids."

Kelly bit her lip. She would have to thank her mother later. "Grandma's right. Maybe your nanny can bring you over one day next week."

"And we can spend the night." Kai put his hand on her cheek, his expression deep and earnest. "Okay, Mommy? Can we spend the night?'

Something about his words or the way he said them exposed in her heart a blind ambition, a cancerous complacency that had found its way there. She ran her hand over his small back. "That would be nice, Kai. I'd like that."

"Me, too!" Kinley jumped around, her eyes big. "We could finger-paint, okay, Mommy? Could we finger-paint?"

"We could." The sting of tears was back, and Kelly wasn't sure what to say or think or feel. Sorrow was rising within her like storm waters. These were the faces she'd spent every waking moment with until Kinley was one. The year she began answering more to the mirror and her manager than Cal and the kids. None of what she was feeling would make sense to Kai and Kinley. So she stayed there, on her knees. Hugging them and quietly saying the only thing she could say. "I love you both. I do."

She saw something in the corner of her eye and when she looked up her mother was standing in the hallway watching. Kelly kissed Kai's cheek and then Kinley's. "I'm here for two days. We can bake cookies for Grandpa, okay?"

"Yay!" Their voices made a single chorus that rang through the house. The sound was more beautiful than Kelly remembered.

As she stood, Kai hugged her waist. His eyes lifted to hers. "We'll be outside, okay? We're making a fort."

"Perfect. I'll come see it in a little while." She ran her hand over his head and smiled. "You're more handsome all the time."

He grinned in response. Then he took hold of Kinley's hand and the two ran back outside. When they were out of earshot, Kelly looked at her mother. "Mommies should never be too busy for their kids?"

Her mom gave the slightest shrug, her expression unforgiving. "They shouldn't."

"Thanks." Kelly pulled her bags into the house and glanced at her mom. "Nice to see you, too."

"Kelly." Her mom's face changed. Instead of anger and indifference, a desperate hurt filled her eyes. "I don't want things to be like this. You're . . . you're so different." She looked over her shoulder toward the backyard and then at Kelly again. "Sometimes I wonder if you remember any of us. Me and your dad . . . Cal." Her voice fell away. "Even your babies."

The comment settled like gravel in Kelly's gut. "Fine. You

can think that." She sighed as she walked past her mother to the kitchen. She helped herself to a glass of water. Through the window she could see Kai and Kinley chasing each other around a couple of the biggest backyard trees. She took a few long sips and turned to her mother. "It's a busy life. I can't help that."

Her mom only stared at her, as if trying to see past the makeup and hair and designer clothes to the girl Kelly used to be. At least it felt that way. She thought about closing the distance between them and hugging her mother, but the timing felt off. "Where's Dad?"

"In his room. He's . . . thinner." Her mom's eyes grew damp. "Very thin. He'll be glad you came."

"That makes one of you." Kelly set her glass on the counter and walked down the hallway to her parents' bedroom. Her heart skittered into a strange rhythm and fear shouted at her. She had never seen her father anything but strong and vibrant and bigger than life. Able to take on anything and anyone who came against him. She opened his door and one thing was immediately evident.

Those days were behind him.

"Daddy?" She walked quietly to where he lay on the left side of the bed. If she hadn't known this man was her father, she might not have recognized him. He'd lost half his size at least. His frame seemed smaller, too, as if the battle with cancer had even cost him his great height.

She sat on the edge of the bed and put her hand on his bony shoulder. "Daddy . . . it's me. Kelly."

"Mmmm." The muscles in his eyelids flickered and after a few seconds—with a great struggle—he squinted at her. "Kelly! You're here!"

Why was everyone so surprised? Was that really how her

family saw her? Too busy to visit or call or care about them? She wasn't willing to wrestle with the possibility now. Not yet. She found her smile. "I would've come sooner if you'd told me." She touched her fingers to his cheek. "You're still so stubborn, Daddy."

"I wanted to beat it first." The corners of his lips lifted just a little. "So you wouldn't see me like . . . like this."

"Aww, Daddy." She bent down and kissed his cheek. It felt hot and dry. She watched him try to keep his eyes open. Again she put her hand on his shoulder. "Does it hurt?"

"Not really." Despite the cancer ravaging his body, the familiar shine in his eyes remained. "Not as much as missing you."

There it was. Another reminder of how she had failed him. Failed all of them. "Daddy, please . . ."

"I know you . . . you don't want to talk about . . . the past." He paced himself, his energy clearly gone. "But the thing is . . . we don't have much time, baby girl. I have to tell you the truth."

"The truth?" She was confused. Did he mean about her life or about his disease? Were things even worse than she'd thought?

"You have walked away from everything . . . everyone who once mattered to you." Compassion softened his expression. Despite his wasting body he suddenly looked like the father she remembered. Ready to pull her up onto his knee, always kind. Always merciful.

"My life . . . it's my choice, Daddy. I've told you that." She wasn't going to fight with him now. But she wasn't going to budge, either. "I don't believe the same things I used to."

"I understand." He struggled to lift his arm from the bed, and slowly he reached for her free hand. "But God . . . still believes in you, Kelly. He . . . loves you."

She had expected this. *Be patient. You don't have long with him,* she reminded herself. "I need to spend more time with the kids. With you and Mom. I know that."

"Good." He smiled, and a fresh sense of peace seemed to ease the lines around his eyes. He squeezed her hand. "That's a starting place." He squinted, seeing straight to the place in her soul where the girl she used to be once lived. "Have you talked to Cal?"

"Daddy . . ." She exhaled long and hard. Was there nothing else they could talk about? "Cal's been seeing someone else."

"No." Her father's expression grew serious. "That's not true. We had a long talk a few . . . weeks ago. He still . . . He loves you, Kelly. He'll do whatever . . . it takes."

She needed air, needed to escape this moment and her dying father and his insistence that she find her way back to Cal.

"I can still see you two . . . sitting together at youth group every Wednesday night." He ran his thumb over her hand. "God . . . brought you together. You have a family with that man." He shook his head, and the effort seemed to exhaust him. "Please . . . don't throw it all away."

The conversation created in Kelly a series of worsening knots. She didn't believe in marriage the way she used to because she didn't believe in God the way she used to. Without that foundation, she saw no reason to stay with Cal, no reason to call him. But her faith, her feelings about marriage, her decision to stay in the fight in Hollywood, none of it could be sorted out here. On her father's deathbed.

"Daddy." She smiled at him and ran her knuckles gently over his cheek. "Let's talk about something else. I'd like to get another opinion on your cancer. Maybe someone somewhere has a cure." She angled her head, remembering a thousand moments when the two of them had talked like this. Back before every conversation turned into an argument. "I want you here. Alive and well."

He grinned, even while the sorrow remained in his eyes. "I've never been more alive. The apostle Paul said to live is Christ. To die is gain. Either way I get to live."

"Yes." She nodded, amazed. He still believed. Even in the face of a cancer that would likely kill him, he believed. He had lived in this house and served at that church and stayed married to Kelly's mother and never once for a single moment had he doubted God along the way.

Her father looked tired again. His eyes closed for several seconds and then opened. "Thank you . . . for coming."

"We're going to get you better, Daddy. We are." The sting of tears again. This was where she wanted their conversation anchored. On the hope of healing. "You get some sleep."

One more kiss on his cheek and she slipped out of the room. She could hear her mother in the kitchen, so she took a different route to the backyard. The minute she opened the door she was surrounded by Kai and Kinley's laughter. She breathed in deep and felt herself relax a little. This was where she needed to be. Outdoors where the air was fresh and she could laugh like a child and play with her kids. Where questions about her faith and her fame and her family didn't weigh heavy on every heartbeat. But even as she ran to meet Kai and Kinley she couldn't entirely block out the truth.

Those questions would be there when she went back in the house. And sometime over the next few days she would have to make herself clear. She wasn't ever going to believe again and she certainly wasn't making amends with Cal.

Even if those things were her father's dying wish.

chapter 18

C handra wasn't sure she could finish out the season.
Everywhere she looked contestants were falling apart, giving in to the pressures around them and losing the people they used to be. Even Zack Dylan. Sometimes she wanted to grab the mic stand on the judges' table and scream at them all. Couldn't they see what was happening? How they were being used by the producers to create a product? A hit show whose ratings and profit were the end-all?

It was mid-Saturday, the second round of group auditions, and already half the contestants had competed. Tomorrow half the singers would be sent home. Chandra couldn't be happier for them.

"Your panties in a wad?" Cullen gave her a critical look as his makeup artist applied powder to his shiny forehead. "You haven't said two words off-camera all day."

"My panties are just fine." Chandra stared at the table, at

the names of the contestants yet to perform. Zack and Zoey were on the list. She glanced through the open door at the stage wings. Kelly was out there somewhere on what seemed like a critical phone call. So just Chandra and Cullen sat at the table for now.

"Look, Chandra. You're not happy here. We can see that."

"I'm fine." She lifted her chin. No matter what she felt, she had a reputation to uphold. If she had to be famous, she would do it with grace. She would never give the producers and paparazzi a reason to smear her name.

"You haven't said much since last week. When you wanted to send Zack Dylan running home to his horses."

She looked straight at him. "That's where he belongs."

"You're wrong." Cullen shifted his face so the makeup artist had a better angle. He pointed at the stage. "Zack Dylan belongs on that stage. For the rest of his life."

"I can't think of anything worse." Chandra spun her chair around and searched the auditorium. Zack and Zoey were sitting beside each other near the back, laughing about something, their heads bowed close to each other. *Be careful, Zack . . . you have so much to lose.* Last night the judges had watched a segment on Zack and Zoey that the producers had put together. It was set to run the first week the show went live.

"We'll air it if the two of them make it that far," William Gaines had told the judges.

Chandra rolled her eyes again at the memory of his statement. As if anyone would dare kick Barbie and Ken off *Fifteen Minutes*. "Romeo and Juliet," the piece was titled. The footage was compelling, the production perfect. By all accounts Zack and Zoey seemed to have found love on the journey to *Fifteen Minutes* of fame. The kiss in the hallway that night provided the most dramatic moment in the piece. The producers positioned it right after Zack's earnest statement that he had a serious girl-friend back home.

"So negative, Chandra." Cullen's makeup artist was gone. He took the seat beside Chandra and turned the chair so that he, too, could watch the contestants interact during the break. "This show made you who you are." He raised his eyebrows at her. "You could be a little more thankful." His eyes scanned the room. "One of them will win it all. And when he does, you need to be part of the celebration."

Chandra considered her attitude. Cullen had a point. Nothing would change her views on the sudden fame that a show like *Fifteen Minutes* cast upon its finalists. But she had to remember the reason she'd agreed to this. Not because she believed in fame. No, it was so she could remember the girl she'd once been and maybe warn a few contestants along the way. Not only from the pitfalls that awaited them when the show placed them forever in the public eye. But from desiring that life in the first place.

She glanced at Zack again. If only she could get him to believe her. She had thought he was different, that he would hear her story and want nothing more than to tread carefully through the landscape of escalating fame. But maybe she was wrong. Maybe he was just like every other contestant.

Including herself.

Chandra sighed and slowly turned her chair back around to the table. The next group would take the stage in two minutes. Kelly returned to her spot, and a minute later Cullen joined them. Chandra shot Kelly a quick look and she felt a hint of re-morse. She'd been rough on Kelly. Truthful but rough. Chandra leaned closer to her. "Everything okay?"

Kelly's eyebrows raised ever so slightly. "What's this? You have a heart?"

"I do." Chandra faced her fellow judge. "I'm sorry. About the other day." She looked down at her painted nails, her glittery jeans and high heels. She found Kelly's eyes again. Maybe it was time to let her walls down a little. "Sometimes . . . I kind of panic."

Suspicion colored Kelly's expression. "Panic?"

"Yeah." She hesitated. "Being Chandra Olson, it's cost me everything. So then I see you and I want to say, Kelly baby, if you can save your marriage, save it. Don't let this"—she motioned toward the table and the contestants and the vast, hallowed walls of Carnegie Hall—"all of this . . . don't let it take one more thing."

For a long time Kelly only stared at her, studied her as if she wanted to be sure Chandra was being sincere. Finally she nodded. "Thank you. But some things you give up willingly." Her slight smile looked plastic. "No one's taking my marriage from me. It was over a long time ago."

Chandra nodded slowly. Kelly still didn't get it. Maybe before the season ended. "Okay. Well . . . I *am* sorry about the other day."

"We're all under a lot of pressure." This time Kelly's smile seemed almost genuine. "And with your past and all."

"Sixty seconds!" a voice shouted. "Places everyone."

Chandra held still while an assistant ran onto the set and adjusted a few strands of her hair. *Here we go,* she thought.

Zack's group was up next.

ZACK DYLAN WAS killing it.

Despite everything Chandra knew about the changes ahead

for Zack Dylan, the heartache and compromise sure to come, she couldn't help but enjoy his performance. He really was that good. Zoey, too. Most days, they were easily the strongest singers remaining in the competition.

As the song played out, Zack and Zoey commanded the stage, so that it was impossible to watch anyone else. They sang a Lady Antebellum ballad, and the number showed the difference between Zack and Zoey's talent and that of the others in the group. When they finished, this time Cullen was first on his feet. "Zack Dylan!" he shouted above the roar of applause from the other contestants. "Good onya, bloke. You can saaang!"

"Thank you!" Zack was out of breath. He had his arm loosely around Zoey's shoulders. The rest of the group stood close by. All of them were beaming.

Cullen stayed on his feet, over the top about Zack. "I mean, look at Zack Dylan, will you, America?" He raised his arms toward the audience of contestants, and another roar of applause and whistles followed. When they settled down, Cullen turned to Zack. "You ever get the feeling you were born for this?"

Zack laughed, his humility very much part of his charm. "I don't know about that." He grinned at Zoey and the others, then back at Cullen. "Singing . . . well, it's a gift. I can't really take credit."

Chandra's heart dropped. Usually this was where Zack would've given credit to God. He would've talked about prayer or Jesus or faith or all of it. Not today. She noticed the change even if no one else did.

Cullen was still gushing. "Today the whole group was better

because of Zack. Zack and Zoey." He turned to Zoey. "You love singing, don't you?"

"I do." Her cheeks were tanned from an afternoon performance at Central Park the day before. "It's all I've ever wanted to do."

Cullen looked at Kelly. "I don't think singing is all she loves."

Chandra cut in before the conversation could turn to Zack and Zoey. "I agree with Cullen." Chandra looked straight at him, through him. As if to keep him on track. This was about singing, not dating. Chandra held her hands in Zack's direction and clapped a few times. "That was easily one of the best performances we've seen this season."

"Maybe *the* best." Kelly clapped, too. She smiled at Zack. "I still have a crush on you. But even more than that, Zack Dylan, Cullen's right. You can saaang." She looked at Chandra and then Cullen. "I'll make the prediction right now. Unless someone steps up, you're looking at the next winner of *Fifteen Minutes*."

Cullen chuckled. "Get it together, Kelly. You're forgetting Juliet over there." He winked at Zoey. "Darling, if anyone can give Zack a run for his money on this show, you can."

"Thank you." Zoey grinned at the others in their group. "We all loved that song."

"How's the romance going, by the way?" Cullen straightened a stack of papers on the table before him and raised his eyebrows at Zack. "I heard people are hashtagging the two of you on Twitter."

Chandra watched, her frustration simmering. Why couldn't Cullen leave them alone? *Hold your ground, Zack . . . don't give in.*

"It hasn't changed with us." Zack reached out and took Zoey's hand. "We're good friends."

"Yep, just friends." Zoey smiled at Zack and then back at the judges. "No matter how it looks."

Cullen's laugh took on a sarcastic tone. "That's what Romeo and Juliet told people, too." He looked at Kelly. "What about Zoey Davis?"

"She's stunning, of course." Kelly turned her attention to Zoey. "Your tone was a little flat that time around. But I still see you in the top ten."

"Thank you." Zoey's face grew red, probably a mix of nervousness and embarrassment.

"We'll see about that." Cullen picked up the contestant lists in front of him and straightened them. "America's going to love you two."

Zack leaned toward the mic. "The way we feel"—he looked at Zoey—"we're just happy to be here. Our whole group feels that way."

Chandra wanted to roll her eyes. No one was just happy to be here, no matter how often contestants repeated the phrase. She sat back in her seat and let her smile fade. Zack and Zoey were falling straight into the trap. They'd be a "couple" at the end of this season whether they wanted that or not. Reality wasn't reality for the famous. Reality was whatever segment producers chose to air and whatever stories and photos were featured in magazines. It was whatever people chose to believe.

The judges made the obligatory comments about the other contestants, how they couldn't compare to Zack and Zoey, how they needed to work on their diction or their style or their projection if they wanted to compete at the highest level of *Fifteen*

Minutes. The mostly discouraged group left the stage. Zack kept his arm around Zoey as they walked off, and again the camera followed every step.

Later there were no surprises when Zack's group was called back onstage and three of the members were sent home. Only he and Zoey remained. The two of them hugged each of the departing singers and then Zack welcomed Zoey into his arms, swinging her around in what seemed like the most beautiful celebration.

As if Chandra had never warned him at all.

REESE COULDN'T TAKE her eyes off Twitter.

That was how she knew before hearing from Zack that he'd made it through. He and Zoey. He must've sent out the tweet moments after hearing the news.

Fifteen Minutes wasn't like *American Idol* or other singing competitions, where they kept the news about who made it through a secret. The producers welcomed the masses to jump on social media and find out before the show aired who'd made the top twenty. There would still be millions surprised by the results, people who didn't follow the show on Twitter or Facebook.

The contestants were free to talk about the results, though this show wouldn't air for a few weeks. Zack had tweeted earlier about his group's win.

> Sad 2 say bye 2 some of the greatest singers ever. No group like ours! Congrats to @songleader!! Gotta represent! #TopTwenty #FifteenMinutes

And of course Zoey's tweet in response.

Still breathless. Can't believe me and @ZackDylan are through!! This
is going to be fun! #TopTwenty #FifteenMinutes

Reese read the tweets three times over that Sunday afternoon before closing out of Twitter. That was that, right? Zack
had been busier than ever and his photo showed up every day on
Yahoo!. The camera loved him, that's what reporters said. Everyone had him pegged as one of the top two finishers. The guy
with the Elvis good looks. The other half of Zack and Zoey—as if
they were a couple.

Her Zack, the guy who had only wanted to live out his
faith raising horses and helping his family and marrying her
one day. The things Zack never talked about anymore. Reese
had stopped by to visit Zack's mother yesterday. The woman
was worried, seeing the same changes in Zack that Reese was
seeing.

"Sometimes I don't feel like I know him anymore." She sat
across from Reese at the table on the family's front porch. "I
don't know, maybe it's going to his head."

"I don't think it's that." Reese defended him because she
knew him. Even now she knew him. "He's having fun. It's a
whirlwind, one public appearance after another. There's barely
any time to call home or even think about the people back in
Kentucky. That's all it is."

Now Reese was in her parents' barn, sitting at the top of
a stack of hay bales. The only place far enough from the curious eyes of her parents. Everyone knew today was the day.
Now that Zack had made it through, she had a decision to
make.

The biggest one of her life.

She was about to call Ms. Coltrain when a text flashed on

her phone's screen. Like always lately, Zack tweeted his three hundred thousand followers before reaching out to her. That was okay. The producers expected that from him. Reese had to understand. She had promised to support him. Whether he noticed or not.

A quick tap on her phone and his text appeared on the screen. *Baby, I made it! I'm in the top twenty! Can you believe it?*

She held the phone with both hands and let her thumbs fly over the virtual keys. *I saw your tweet! Congratulations, Zack. I knew you'd make it. I'm so proud of you! You and Zoey from your group. And who else made it?* This wasn't the time to talk about London or her own feelings. She had to make that decision apart from his success. She realized that now.

A minute passed and then two. Reese checked the *Fifteen Minutes* Facebook page. Sure enough, Zack had posted the news and already hundreds of girls had commented their approval. She checked the clock on her phone. Ten minutes. Wherever he was, whatever was happening around him, he was no longer able to text.

She would have to understand that, too. What choice did she have? This was what Zack had prayed for, what he wanted. The show had become his all-consuming passion. She could tell from his tone and see it in his eyes during interviews. *God, give me wisdom. I feel like You're leading me to London, like that's where You want me to be. Where I can make a difference.*

Even as she prayed she felt the Lord approving, giving her the green light. A thrill of excitement began to build in her. Moving to London for a year wouldn't be the end of her and Zack. He'd be busy touring and working on his album, after all. A year was nothing. Maybe when she came back home he'd have time to talk. Maybe they'd still have something between them.

She checked the time. It was nearly nine o'clock at night in London. Reasonable enough. She dialed Ms. Coltrain's number and waited as the phone began to ring.

"Hello?" The connection was clearer than before. "Reese?" The woman sounded enthusiastic. It was a good sign.

"Yes, ma'am." Reese realized she was smiling. For the first time in a long time she was smiling from the inside out. "I've made up my mind about your offer. I'd love to move to London and work with your instructors."

On the other end of the line, Ms. Coltrain shrieked. "Really? You don't know what this means to us!"

Reese's heart swelled. She was good at what she did. She would go to London and make a difference, and along the way she'd be too busy to think about Zack and his run on *Fifteen Minutes* and the hundreds of thousands of girls who followed his every move. Too busy to worry about what Zoey was saying on Twitter. The break would be good for her.

Ms. Coltrain was talking about how the dates had been changed some. "The best time to come would actually be September. Say the first or second week."

That would give her more time to wrap things up with her current students. "That'll be perfect."

They discussed a few more details, and in very little time the plan was set. Reese hung up and slid down the stack of hay bales. Tears blurred her vision, and she blinked them back. This wasn't how she had imagined the year. The plans she and Zack used to have were so different from the ones playing out.

She stared at her phone. Nothing. No response. She clicked her phone off. *No crying,* she told herself. Not for herself or for how much she missed Zack or for how uncertain things were between them. She had no time for tears. A year in London lay just ahead. She could hardly wait to tell her parents the news. Never mind what Zack was doing right now or why he was too busy for her. Her future was suddenly filled with adventure and excitement.

She was moving to London!

chapter 19

Something inside Kelly Morgan was changing. She could feel it deep inside.

Somewhere at the center of her heart a softening was happening, whether she liked it or not. She noticed it in quiet times as she watched the top twenty practice their choreography for group numbers or when she and the other judges sorted through music for the live shows.

Usually it started with a memory.

She would see herself at seven years, playing catch with her dad in the backyard. Other girls played with dolls; Kelly played catch. Back then she thought she would pitch for the Yankees one day. Her dad humored her, telling her she could do whatever she set her mind to. Then the image would change. She would be twelve, pigtails and braces and sitting in the front row at church while her dad practiced his sermon. *He's the greatest man in the world,* she would tell herself. And when he finished he would take her by the hand and they'd go to Della's Diner for chocolate shakes. "Extra sprinkles," he'd tell the guy behind the counter. "Give my girl extra sprinkles."

Sometimes she'd be older when the memory started up out of nowhere. Seventeen and behind the wheel for the first time, her dad there beside her. "You can do it, baby girl. You're gonna be the best driver in Greenville."

When she took out the family's mailbox that year, her dad only blinked a few times and smiled at her. "We needed a new one, anyway." The memory would put down roots and she'd close her eyes for a few seconds, feigning weariness so the other judges wouldn't ask what she was thinking about. In the darkness another image sometimes took shape. She and Cal, holding hands and singing songs to God by Steven Curtis Chapman and Amy Grant and Michael W. Smith. Songs that still played in her mind if she let them.

Kelly tried to stay busy so she could find shelter from her memories.

She talked more to the contestants. They were a mess by now. A few of them had marriages in trouble and others were starting to crack under the pressure. They cried more often. Forgot to eat. Kelly found herself wanting to be there for them. But the contestant she talked to most often was Zack Dylan. The guy always seemed to be around, and every time their eyes met Kelly was struck by him. Yes, he was good-looking—though her early infatuation over him was more of a joke. Her way of making an impact as a judge. Now, though, she knew Zack. She had talked to him about his family and the horse farm, his sick sister and his longing for Kentucky. His love for God and his girlfriend. At this point in the show, Kelly could no longer lie to herself about what drew her to Zack Dylan.

It was his clear-eyed, full-hearted faith. A faith he talked about less than before, but one she recognized all the same. Because she'd seen it all her life growing up.

The faith of her father.

The cast and crew of *Fifteen Minutes* was in the midst of the quiet period, a time for learning group numbers and preparing for the debut of the live shows. The feeling was a little like summer camp. She and Cal used to go every summer with their church group. Like camp, the break allowed camaraderie to run deep and spirits to run high. Everyone was on equal footing and anything was possible. On the days when the top twenty weren't busy perfecting the live show, they made appearances around New York City. The *Today* show had them perform two group numbers and they appeared on Letterman and Leno. The publicity was at an all-time high, and Kelly loved the distraction.

But when they were back at the leased studio across the street from Carnegie Hall, when she had time to sit and actually think about her life and her father and the little time they had left, the memories came. Kelly couldn't stop them. And gradually, one day at a time, they were changing her.

It was late Monday night, eight days into the most intense rehearsals. The contestants were on the makeshift warehouse stage—all twenty of them. Carnegie Hall had only been reserved for the group auditions and live shows. Rehearsals were here. The choreographer was one of the best in the world, responsible for Beyoncé's last Super Bowl and Katy Perry's world tour. Kelly sat watching with Chandra and Cullen.

The choreographer, Demetrius Davidson, clapped, clearly in a hurry. "Okay, come on. Everyone in your lines. That's two lines, people." Demetrius put his hands on his hips. "And . . ." He pointed at three guys sitting at a soundboard. "Music!" Over the blare of the song, the choreographer shouted again. "Five, six, seven, eight." He clapped to the beat as all twenty contestants launched into the moves.

Cullen leaned near Kelly and Chandra. He spoke loud enough so they could hear him. "We need two more weeks."

"They'll be fine." Chandra nodded at the stage. "I see enough dancers out there to carry the left feet."

"Maybe." Cullen stroked his chin as he settled back into the long leather sofa. The producers had rented comfortable furniture for the judges and enough sofas for the contestants to use during breaks. It felt like a glorified clubhouse.

Even the lighting was conducive to what would eventually be the polished live show.

"Cut . . . cut it!" The instructor waved off the music and moved onto the stage to two girls. They looked terrified. "Have you *never* seen a pivot turn?"

One of the girls bravely spoke first. "Not before tonight."

"Really?" Demetrius looked at her, then back at the three judges. He raised his voice. "Really?"

Cullen laughed out loud. "You're the magician. Make it happen."

The music stayed off while those who understood the dance helped those who didn't have a clue. Kelly let her eyes settle on Zack. He was helping one of the guys in the back row, a big farm boy from Iowa with a voice as deep as a storm cellar. *Good luck.* Kelly covered her mouth, careful to keep her laughter hidden. The farm boy wasn't going to be a dancer. But the kids were trying, she had to give them that.

Especially Zack. Kelly still watched him. How different would he be at the end of the season? And what if he won? Maybe Chandra was right that the fame and celebrity would change him. As Kelly pondered that from the comfort of her corner on the couch, a lead production assistant stormed up to Zack. Whatever the guy said, he pointed at Zack and then motioned him over to Zoey.

A hush fell over the room and the cameramen took a break. The judges weren't sitting close enough to hear every word, but whatever had been exchanged, Zack looked surprised. He said something in response and nodded to the farmer. This time the assistant took a step closer, clearly upset. "Look, Zack, you'll do it our way or you can sit this one out."

Chandra and Cullen were also drawn to the drama onstage. The assistant stormed back to his place at the side of the stage and cued the cameras. When the music resumed, Zack danced next to Zoey. Someone else had been assigned to the farmer.

Kelly blinked a few times. "Did that just happen?"

"I believe it did." Cullen crossed one leg over his knee. He chuckled. "Better bloke than me, letting some bludge assistant tell him what to do."

"Wow. I guess I didn't know they were that serious about the Romeo and Juliet thing." Kelly stood and walked slowly to the edge of the stage. She stayed in the shadows so the contestants wouldn't notice her, as close as possible to the spot where Zack and Zoey danced together.

The music stopped and Zoey looked up at Zack. She mouthed the words "I'm sorry." Her expression showed her helplessness. In response, he put his arm around her and gave her a brief hug.

Kelly couldn't hear what he said but she didn't have to. She was suddenly angry. She marched over to the side stage where the production assistants were clustered. The lead guy turned to her as she approached. "Kelly, what's up?"

"Them." She pointed at Zack and Zoey. "Are we that desperate for ratings?"

"It's not coming from me." The guy looked tight-lipped. "Boss says they're a couple. America will love 'em. Nothing this adorable since Justin and Kelly on *Idol*."

"That's crazy. They're not a couple."

"The kiss says otherwise." He shrugged. "Anything these contestants say or do will be on the show."

"That's lousy." She turned her attention to the stage. The group was running through the number again. Zack and Zoey were still together. She glared at the PA. "Things happen on a show like this. It's all fantasy, you know that."

"Exactly." He chuckled, clearly unconcerned. "And the fantasy this time around is Zack and Zoey."

Kelly stared at him, not sure what to say. How could Samuel Meier feel good about manipulating people? Was this what celebrity had come to? *Fifteen Minutes* creating situations and relationships for ratings? The producers would present whatever picture they wanted, and the public would eat it up. The show turned people into stars for the sake of ratings and profit. Something about that was plain old ugly.

"I'll talk to Samuel." She crossed her arms and looked from the PA to the dance floor and back. She searched his face. Then she took a step closer. "It isn't *real*."

"Well, Ms. Morgan"—he took a step closer, obviously not threatened by her—"the cameras say it *is*. For a show like *Fifteen Minutes* that's all that matters."

chapter 20

They had ten minutes before dance rehearsal started up again, and Zack had just one way he wanted to use the time. If he didn't call Reese soon she was bound to worry. Especially with all the talk on the Internet about him and Zoey. Tweets from the other contestants, hints on the show's website that a romance was budding. He needed to talk to Reese tonight. Right now. He slipped out the main entrance into the dark of the night, intent on heading to the coffee shop across the street.

But blocking his way were eight bodyguards.

"Hey, guys." He hesitated.

"Zack. How's it going?" The group nodded and greeted him.

He pointed to the Starbucks across the street. "Anyone want coffee?"

"Hold up." The biggest in the group took a step closer, concerned. "You're not going anywhere. The public's figured it out. They know y'all are rehearsing here."

"Oh." Zack hadn't considered that. "Okay, then. I'll be right back." He raised his brow, looking for approval. "Is that all right?"

"Definitely not." The first bodyguard lowered his eyebrows. "One fan spots you and it's a madhouse. Bedlam. We don't wanna mess with that."

The other bodyguards muttered their agreement.

"If you absolutely must go, one of us goes with you." It was the biggest guy again. "Either that or you stay here. One of us can get the coffee."

"I'll do it." The shortest of the group slipped his hands in his pockets and moved a step toward the street. "What do you want?"

"Uh . . ." Zack's head was spinning. *Time alone. Time away from Zoey Davis. The chance to think. Reese Weatherly.* He didn't voice his thoughts. The bodyguard was waiting. Zack cleared his throat. "Uh . . . how about a grande black tea with an inch of cream? Is that okay?"

"Definitely. Got it." The man jogged to the intersection and crossed at the green light.

Like being hit by a gust of hurricane-force wind, the truth took his breath. He could no longer cross the street for a cup of hot tea in New York City. People might see him, recognize him. They could even mob him. Even as he processed this, a crowd of people headed in their direction. The big guard pointed to the door well. "Stay there. We've got you covered."

Zack did as he was told. He hunkered in against the inset brick door while the guys formed a wall around the entrance. They were an intimidating presence, for sure. They looked like the starting offensive line for the New York Jets. Four of them were assigned to Chandra; the other four split time between protecting Kelly and Cullen and the contestants. Together they provided a force no one dared think about crossing. True professionals, they kept their posture casual, talking among themselves so they wouldn't draw attention to Zack.

The crowd walked closer—some sort of tour group wearing the same blue stickers on their shirts. As they neared, many of them peered at the building, trying to see what was behind the line of bodyguards. But the door was set far enough back from the sidewalk that Zack remained shrouded in shadows. He watched, eyes wide. This was crazy. Did he actually need protection from strangers? Did that mean he'd somehow made it?

He wasn't sure whether to be scared or excited.

"Hey! I think *Fifteen Minutes* rehearses there! I saw it on Twitter!" A teenage girl's shrill voice rose above the others and the group slowed. She jumped around, pointing at the bodyguards. "We should ask if they'll let us in."

An older woman—the girl's mother maybe—pushed her way through the throng. She tapped one of the bodyguards on the shoulder. Until then they had seemed unaware, but now they faced the crowd, shoulders touching.

"Hi." The woman smiled. "Is this where *Fifteen Minutes* rehearses? My daughter saw something about it."

"This is a private business, ma'am." He didn't smile. "I'm afraid I can't answer questions."

The girl squealed and covered her mouth. "It is! It has to be!" She put both hands in the air and gave a short scream. "I wanna meet Zack Dylan, please! Can we go in just for half a minute? I'm in love with him. Please?"

"We won't be long." The mother took a step closer, trying to see between two of the bodyguards. "We'll stay in the back and watch for a minute. No longer."

"Ma'am." The bodyguard's tone was stern. He crossed his arms, his chest puffed out. "No one may enter the building without clearance."

"There has to be another way in." The girl wasn't taking no for an answer. She pulled her phone from her purse and began snapping photos of the bodyguards.

Watching from the doorwell, Zack pressed himself into the far corner. His heart pounded as the moment played out. He stayed quiet while the bodyguards dashed the girl's hopes of getting into the building. Finally—reluctantly—the group moved on. "They'll be back." The tallest bodyguard shook his head. "People are crazy."

"Girls are craziest." Another of the guards laughed. "Always amazes me."

One of the guys turned around and pointed at Zack. "See that? You stay close to the building. No getting coffee on your own, understand?"

"Yes, sir." Zack felt adrenaline work through his veins. He exhaled and slumped against the warm brick. His break was half over. If he called Reese now, he wouldn't have time to talk. Not the sort of conversation the two of them needed. He took a deep breath and made a decision. In a hurry he dialed his parents' number.

"Hello?" Grandpa Dan answered.

"Hi! This is Zack." He felt his throat tighten. What was he doing standing in a dirty door well in New York City behind a bunch of bodyguards? Why wasn't he back in Kentucky with the people he loved? He swallowed hard, searching for his voice. "How . . . are you, Grandpa?"

"Worried." A pause followed. "Son, what's this about some other girl?"

"It's nothing." Zack wondered if he'd responded too quickly. "She's on the show with me. We're friends. That's all."

More hesitation. "Son . . . have you thought about how Reese might feel?"

"Yes." He stopped there, defeated. He couldn't defend himself. The show had taken all his time, and the insanity had thrown him and Zoey together constantly. She needed him. He tried to find the right words. "They're keeping us very busy. Please . . . tell Reese I'm sorry. I'll . . . I'll make things right when this is all over."

"Be careful." Grandpa Dan sounded sad. Like he could cry. "This show, don't let it change who you are." His voice was scratchy. "What you believe."

Zack squeezed his eyes shut and shook his head. "I won't. I'm trying, Grandpa. Please pray for me, okay?" He needed to know his grandpa was praying. His own time spent praying was a fraction of what it had been. He hadn't found time to talk about his faith after the last group performance, and lately he could go all day and not think about praying until his head hit the pillow.

"I'll pray, Zack. I will." A spark of hope sounded in his grandpa's voice.

Zack turned his back to the city street. More people passed by, shouting about *Fifteen Minutes* rehearsing there and talking to the bodyguards. Zack struggled to hear his own voice. "Some days . . . nothing makes sense."

They talked another few minutes, all of it a struggle with the noise from the city. Zack would've stepped back inside but the cell reception was terrible. Besides, he wanted a moment away from the other contestants. His grandpa told him that AJ was still sick, still spending most of her time in her bedroom. "She has something wrong with her kidneys. They're trying to get a diagnosis."

Zack drew a deep breath and exhaled slowly. "Should I come home?"

"Well . . ." His grandpa was quiet. "The situation with AJ isn't an emergency." He hesitated. "Whatever God tells you . . . just do that, son."

Tension tightened its grip on Zack's soul. "I'm trying. He keeps moving me on to the next round."

"Sometimes God's voice is hard to hear over the world."

"Yes." The city was louder now. Zack had to yell to be heard. The noise drove home his grandpa's point. "Thank you. For reminding me."

The call ended and the bodyguard returned with Zack's hot tea. He thanked the guy, and the others, too. Then he slipped his phone in his pocket and hurried back inside. The next dance rehearsal was about to begin.

Grandpa Dan's words spoke to him. *Sometimes God's voice is hard to hear over the world.* He let the reminder play again in his mind. Once he reached the open rehearsal space, Zoey spotted him before anyone else. She walked to him, her eyes never leaving his.

Zack searched his motives as he waited by the doorway. He wasn't falling for her, right? She needed him, that was all. Or maybe they needed each other. She was still the only one who understood this crazy ride. As she reached him, he stuck his hands in his pockets. "Called home."

"Mmmm . . . me, too. There's cell reception in the restroom." She came a step closer. "How's your family?"

"They miss me." He smiled, searching her eyes. What was it about her? She seemed different somehow, bolder, the way she'd been when they first met. He dismissed the possibility. "My sister's still sick. She needs prayer."

"I'm sorry." She ran her hand over her arm. "I really do need to learn how to pray."

"I told you." His voice grew softer. He didn't need a lecture from William Gaines before rehearsal. But he wanted Zoey to understand. "You just talk to God. That's all."

"Show me?" She tilted her head. "Later? Please, Zack."

"I'm not sure when we'll be done here." He looked to the stage. The other contestants were already in place. "Come on." He started to lead her toward the stage.

"Zack." She hesitated.

He looked back at her. "Zoey, we have to go."

"Did you call her? Did you call Reese?"

For a long beat he didn't say anything. He could feel his shoulders fall a bit as defeat slithered alongside him again. "There wasn't time."

The slightest smile tugged at her lips. "Just wondering." She fell in easily beside him as they walked to the stage. "I'm sure she'll understand. We're so busy."

As they walked Zack suddenly realized he was still holding Zoey's hand. Not only that, but the camera in the corner of the room was trained straight on them. He let go in a hurry and shoved his hands once more in his pockets. She hesitated. "Everything okay?"

"Perfect." He jogged the last few steps and shouted Demetrius. "Here. Sorry."

The guy ignored Zack. He checked his watch, then looked at the group. "Places."

And like that Zack began doing the one thing he needed to do for the next hour. Dancing with Zoey. Reese would understand. But whenever the two of them did talk later that night, Zack would be lying if he said he wasn't having fun. God kept letting him stay on the show, so there must be a reason. It was okay to enjoy the process, right?

Zoey was a very good dancer. In Zack's arms and at his side he couldn't help but notice, couldn't help but feel something. The electricity of her skin against his or the smell of her faded perfume. The sound of her laugh. One hour became two, and that became a night of dancing and breaks and instruction that took them way past midnight. One of his and Zoey's best nights as a team. When he finally crawled exhausted into his bed, he couldn't stop thinking about the dance and the music and the girl who had been beside him. It was too late to call Reese. Which was probably a good thing. Because he didn't fall asleep thinking about God or his family or even Reese. Instead he was consumed by one thing.

The way Zoey Davis had felt in his arms.

chapter 21

Just after midnight, when the rehearsal was finally over, Kelly gathered her things and headed out the front entrance. She was the first to leave and as she opened the door, she was struck by the scene. They'd been found out. A crowd had gathered on either side of the sidewalk, smothering the doorway and spilling into the street. The bodyguards had set up ropes and stanchions, and they had positioned themselves along the boundaries to keep stray fans from blocking the path from the door to the waiting cars. Kelly paused and took a deep breath. Two guards were immediately at her side.

"Kelly! Look, it's Kelly Morgan!" one of the women screamed, and the others in the crowd followed suit. Cell phones appeared from every angle, snapping pictures and casting a series of flashes in her direction. For a brief moment she felt good about the scene. Michael Manning gone from the picture and still she drew this kind of attention.

But just as quickly another scene flashed in her mind, even as her bodyguards escorted her between the ropes to the waiting Escalade. The image of her father running alongside her as she learned to ride her bike. "You can do it, baby. I'm right here." His tanned face full of life, his pride for her shining in his eyes. "I'll always be right here."

But he wouldn't always be here. Not anymore.

The crowd was shouting louder, screaming as the body-guards helped her into the SUV. She blinked twice and the image of her father cleared. Two days had passed since she'd heard from either of her parents. She needed to call them in the morning before reporting for rehearsal.

The bodyguards followed her home and didn't leave until she'd been safely inside for an hour. The staff would take over safety duties from that point until the morning, when the body-guards would escort her to the SUV once again. William Gaines called to say another six guards had been hired.

Once inside her apartment she grabbed her laptop and set-tled into the sofa. The silence was heavenly. For a long time she stared at the dark screen, not ready to check e-mail or Yahoo! or do anything but sit and think. The Romeo and Juliet piece had shaken her. It was wrong what Samuel was doing to those kids.

But Chandra had talked to her before they left that night and the two of them had a suspicion. What if Zoey were in on the whole ruse? Kelly thought about Zack's sincerity, the way his eyes shone with the faith he barely talked about anymore. He had no idea how obsessed his fans would be once he finished the run of *Fifteen Minutes*.

She thought about the look in Zack's eyes when the produc-tion assistant forced him to dance with Zoey. Chemistry, yes. They definitely had chemistry. But what contestants didn't, after this insane experience? Their lives were upside down and on display. Nothing was the way they'd known it before their auditions.

Once the piece on Zack and Zoey aired, there would likely be no girlfriend to go home to and no way to undo the damage. The two *Fifteen Minutes* singers would be linked forever, whether there was any truth to the segment or not. The coming storm would probably send them running into each other's arms. Then the producers would have what they wanted.

Her heart kept time with the antique clock on her mantel. She had never questioned fame, never imagined it to be anything other than a dream come true. Something everyone wanted and only a few people found.

Now she began to wonder.

Certainly Chandra had paid the ultimate price, losing her parents to a psycho fan. She'd said something tonight that stayed with Kelly. They were talking about the changes in the contestants and how there was no going back to the life they once lived. Kelly commented that the world would be shocked to know how Chandra Olson really felt about being a celebrity. "You're so self-possessed, everywhere we go. Every interview. Complete control."

"It's my secret. It's how I keep my prison cell bigger." A slight, sad smile graced her face. "Look at me, Kelly. The only guy I ever loved moved on years ago. I have no real friends. I'm constantly on tour. If I flip out and start drinking, doing drugs . . . hiding from the press and throwing things at the paparazzi, then the cell gets smaller. The walls close in. I'm getting through it the only way that makes sense." Her smile fell off. "But if all my money could buy me back the day before my *Fifteen Minutes* audition, I would do it now. Right now."

Kelly brought her computer screen to life. So sad. Living like that, hating the fame and being reminded of it every waking hour. She mindlessly began typing in names of former *Fifteen Minutes* winners. A country singer whose good looks had gotten him a fair amount of attention a few years ago. The guy was married with a two-year-old when he appeared on the show. In one of the final rounds, he sang so well people still talked about his performance. When the applause and screaming died down, Cullen had chuckled the way Cullen often did. "Too bad you're married," he muttered into the microphone. "I can only imagine how big a star you'd be if you were single."

Kelly remembered the guy's response. He laughed along with Cullen, but he held up his wedding ring. "This guy's proud of his wife." He received another standing ovation for the comment.

For the most part the public seemed shocked by Cullen's callous remark, even if the judge was right. The situation had bugged Kelly back then. Marriage was tough enough without Cullen Caldwell making it more difficult.

Now in the quiet of her apartment, Kelly typed the guy's name into the Google search bar. His songs were played on the radio, and he toured with the biggest country acts. But what about his family?

The singer's Wikipedia page came up at the top of the search. Kelly clicked it. Sure enough he was selling records like crazy, reaching gold on a few singles. She scanned down to the section about his personal life. Her heart sank as she read the news. A year ago the singer's divorce was final. He was dating one of country music's up-and-coming new artists.

She remembered another entertainer, a beautiful dark-skinned actress and singer who had starred on a show that took over after Kelly's show finished its run. The girl had been full of light and innocence. Over the show's five-year run, the public had a front-row seat to watching the actress change. Her clothing became more risqué, her makeup more severe. She was photographed in the arms of a number of leading men, partying at various A-list nightclubs. Her sitcom ended and she tried to make her mark in movies. But no one took her seriously. Kelly almost didn't want to run a check on the girl, but she did.

A sick feeling started in the pit of her stomach. The actress had been dropped by her label and cut off from her studio deal. Today she was in rehab, hoping to find her life again. Reports said she was addicted to painkillers and heroin.

What about the celebs at the top of today's pop music? One young pop artist had started off talking about purity and faith, but after a few years she was singing songs that shocked the world at the time—songs that seemed to change teen culture overnight. At the last Grammy Awards the singer wore a dress that caused Ryan Seacrest to blush. People in Kelly's circle liked to joke that the young artist might single-handedly be responsible for loosening the morals of a generation.

But was that funny? Really?

Sure, Kelly no longer believed in her father's faith. But she felt deeply uneasy at the examples most singers set for their fans.

What about the young boy bands and teen heartthrobs? Most of them started out genuine and down-to-earth. Not much older than kids. Documentaries had been done about a number of them, their love for music and how the sudden fame changed them.

In one documentary, a few of the singers from a boy band could be seen praying with their crew, being patient with fans and almost oblivious to the celebrity status closing in around them. Wide-eyed and innocent. Then for each of them something began to change, or at least it seemed that way. The paparazzi would become relentless; dangerously so. At one point a photographer attempting to catch a photo of one of the teen singers ran across a busy street intent on a picture. He never made it. A car hit him as he closed in for the picture. He died at the scene.

All for the possibility of a photograph.

Kelly squirmed. A few clicks and her computer screen filled with recent stories about a couple of young heartthrobs. Some were into drugs, others had been caught drunk in public. None of them seemed unscathed.

She scanned a series of Google images on a few of the singers and her heart hurt. They looked angry, not that Kelly blamed them. Everywhere they went someone wanted a piece of them. They hit the scene as kids and a year later some of them were at the top of the charts. One of them headlined his own tour and was the most Googled celebrity in the world.

Kelly sighed. The prison cell of fame was very small indeed for teenage singers. How were they supposed to handle that sort of pressure? Jaded by the time they were nineteen years old.

There were others. Elvis and Michael and Whitney. Kelly tried to think of a celebrity who had come through the madness of A-list attention without changing, without losing the people they loved or their very lives. Where were the shining examples of fame? Those stars had to be out there somewhere, though Kelly couldn't think of a single one.

Even the successful celebrities had lost marriages or kids or some level of sanity.

Slowly, Kelly shut her laptop and set it down beside her. As if she were seeing blue skies after a storm, a new reality began to take shape before her eyes. What about her own life? At one point she had been close to her parents, in love with Cal, and content to live in South Carolina. But she could sing. Everyone said so, and deep inside Kelly knew they were right. So she convinced Cal to move to L.A. They packed up their few belongings and went on a quest for fame and fortune.

Oh, sure, they didn't talk about it that way back then. On the unknown side of fame there was only one thing to talk about. Finding it. But now? What did it all mean? Why were a hundred thousand unknown singers willing to audition for a show like *Fifteen Minutes*? Was it all just one big popularity contest? Wanting to be idolized and sought after, craving the attention and insanity of celebrity? Was it about the money?

For the first time in her life she actually thought about it. Since booking the hit teen show she'd been consumed by one aspect of celebrity. Keeping it. Holding on to it. Staying young and thin and current. Being A-list. But sitting here in the quiet of her living room she saw it all from another angle.

She remembered something from her high school days.

Cal had sketched a staircase in pencil. Each step included a landing. At first glance the drawing appeared to be the top of a set of stairs, looking down. But look at it long enough, and the entire image flipped. The view seemed to be from underneath the stairs, looking up.

"That's weird." She had jumped back, struck by the sudden flip-flop.

"It's an optical illusion." Cal had grinned at her reaction. "The guys on the football team showed me. There's more than one way to see it."

An optical illusion. Like the quest for fame. Like Kelly's entire life.

Suddenly she knew without a doubt there were people who pitied her. They'd watched her change from the wide-eyed innocent girl on the hit TV show to the Hollywood diva in the midst of a divorce. Her parents were probably part of that group.

One time after her early success reached epic levels, she called her mom and asked her a burning question. "You knew I could sing. Why didn't you take me to Hollywood sooner?"

Her mom's answer burned in her mind now. "Why would I do that?"

"Why?" Kelly had been outraged. "So I could've found all this sooner."

"Kelly . . . hear me. I knew you could sing. I believed producers would fall in love with you." Her voice held a lifetime of emotion. "But you only get one childhood. I wasn't willing to trade it so you could be famous."

Chills ran down Kelly's arms at the memory. What if her parents had taken her to L.A. sooner? Would she be another starlet statistic, in and out of rehab? Would she be dead?

The questions began to surround her, the new view of fame taking clear shape in her mind. What could she do about it? She couldn't undo the attention, the celebrity. Chandra was right. The thing Kelly worked day and night to keep, to make perfect, carried a hefty price tag. All along she had really believed that those things would make her happier. Tighter skin would make her prettier. More Twitter followers would make her popular. More money for every gig and she would be successful. But the effort exhausted her and what did she have to show for it? Her all-consuming pursuit of those things was the reason she and Cal had fallen apart, the cause for the break in her relationship with her dad.

It was the reason that tonight she sat alone in her multi-million-dollar New York flat while her kids took their baths and shared bedtime reading with Cal two hours away. What would become of them? Her mother was right about childhood. The time didn't last. One day all too soon her kids would be teenagers, and then what? Paparazzi would catch them slipping into bars with other celebrity kids, sleeping with people they barely knew, probably far older than them. They would spend their lives chasing the same stardom that had always defined their mother.

Was that what the future held for her kids?

Kelly had barely eaten dinner that night, and now she felt sick to her stomach. Kai and Kinley, her babies. They would probably reach high school age and give interviews to *People* magazine about how they hated their mother, how she had chosen fame over playing with them.

Tears fell onto Kelly's cheeks and a series of quiet sobs began to build. From this view she didn't feel like the luckiest girl in America. She didn't want to spend another hour with her trainer or get up early for another shot of Botox. She couldn't see an end to her fame. But she could feel something she hadn't felt before tonight.

The prison walls.

More tears poured down her face, and she did nothing to stop them. Chandra had said she didn't really have friends. Wasn't the same true for her? Tonight she should've been reading to Kai and Kinley, helping them get ready for bed. Talking to her husband about how they'd fallen so far from the people they used to be.

Kelly could barely breathe for the sobs that choked her. She realized as she wept that for the first time since she could remember she wasn't worried about whether her eyes would be swollen in the morning.

She was lonely and broken and worried about her heart. Her kids. Worried about her future. Her life.

How terrible that she hadn't talked to her parents in forty-eight hours. Her dad's situation wasn't stable. She was about to open her computer again and check her e-mail, see if her parents had updated her on her father's condition, when her cell phone rang.

The sound made Kelly jump. As she answered it she caught a glimpse of the caller ID. It was her mother. "Mom!" She sounded awful, her nose stuffy. "I was just thinking about all of you. How's Dad?"

"Honey . . ." Her mom clearly had been crying, too. "He's worse. He has an infection." She paused. "His fever is very high."

Panic pulsed through Kelly. She was on her feet, pacing, pushing her fingernails through her hair. "What . . . what happened?"

"We don't know. The ambulance came." Her voice broke. "I can't lose him. Please . . . can you come? He's . . . he's in trouble."

"Dear God, no." She whispered the words as more tears blurred her eyes. She wasn't ready for this, wasn't ready to say good-bye to her daddy. Not yet.

"Kelly?"

"I'm sorry." She fought through her sorrow. "Yes, I can come. Of course. I'll find a way. I'll see if the show's private jet can get me there before sunrise."

Her mom told her the details, which hospital, which room. "Cal's already here. He has the kids."

"Right." The kids! Kelly felt dazed. She finished the call and dropped to her knees at the edge of the sofa. Kelly had completely forgotten about Kai and Kinley going with Cal to Greenville this weekend. Cal had arranged the visit through Kelly's manager. Rudy had shot a quick e-mail to Kelly explaining that Cal wanted the kids to have as much time as possible with their grandparents. Kelly felt horrified. Until her mother's call she had completely forgotten where they were. What sort of mother did that make her?

The tears came harder and she collapsed over the edge of the sofa. For the first time in too many years, more than her next heartbeat she cared about just one thing.

"Dear God. Jesus . . ." she prayed out loud. Spoke His name out loud. And though the words sounded foreign, a peace fell like rain around her. "I need to get home. I . . . I have to be with my family. Please . . . help my dad. Help me get there in time." She was shaking, overcome by the strangest mix of emotions. A peace like she'd never known and a fear big enough to consume her.

"Is it too late for me, God?" The sobs kept coming. "I turned my back on You." She squeezed her eyes shut, her fists pressed to her face. "Stubborn pride." Anger strangled her voice. Who had she become? Celebrity was nothing but a snare. Running after a body and Botox and a boyfriend barely out of college. What had she been thinking? "Plain old stupid. That's all it was, God." Sadness and frustration came in waves, fury at her years of selfishness.

All of it consumed her until she had no more tears to cry.

The urgency of her father's situation drew her back to her feet. She found her phone and called Samuel Meier. "There's been an emergency."

And like that pieces fell into place. An hour later Kelly flew out of LaGuardia on the *Fifteen Minutes* private jet. Three hours after that she rushed through the front door of the hospital, up the elevator to the seventh-floor intensive care unit. She found the waiting room and there they were.

Kai and Kinley and Cal.

The kids looked sad and tired but mostly confused. When they saw her they ran to her, their eyes flooded with relief. Mommy was here. All was right with their world. Kelly stooped down and hugged both of them. What was she thinking, missing so much time with them? She had no answers for herself. As she stood, empty and exhausted, Cal came to her. Their eyes met and in a single heartbeat there was no broken relationship, no affairs or unkind words, no years of estrangement.

"Kelly . . . I'm sorry." His eyes were red, his cheeks tearstained. He loved her dad as much as she did.

"No. It's my fault." She stared at the floor, struggling. When she looked up, his eyes held a love she'd forgotten. She took a step closer. "I'm so sorry, Cal."

They came together in a hug that only a husband and wife could share, close, connected in body, heart, mind, and soul. Never mind what had happened or where things might go from here. She had no real answers, and whatever they decided none of it would be easy. But here and now with their kids sitting nearby, the hug was the most right thing in the world. They stayed that way for a full minute, not speaking.

Because for the first time in a long time, no words were needed.

chapter 22

A strange uneasiness had become part of Reese's existence. The feeling woke her up each morning and breathed fear against her while she showered and curled her hair. It was something she couldn't shake even in the happy moments each morning with her parents. The uneasiness sat strangely next to her in the car on the way to work and shared a saddle with her while she helped Toby and AJ at the Lowell Therapeutic Equestrian Center. AJ was feeling better, her serious symptoms gone for the time being.

But even that didn't help the way Reese felt.

Especially today when the first live performance of *Fifteen Minutes* would air in a little over an hour. She parked in front of Zack's house and skipped up the stairs. She wore white shorts and a light blue T-shirt. Her face and arms were tanned from being on her horse, and humidity made the back of her neck damp. Still, despite the smoldering heat something cold ran through her blood. She hesitated before knocking, leaning her forehead against the Dylans' front door. Her heart pounded in her chest.

Please, God . . . I don't want to feel this way. If something's going on with Zack, if You're trying to warn me, then make it clear. Otherwise, please give me peace.

As she started to knock, Grandpa Dan opened the door. "Well, hello." He leaned on his cane, his smile kind, gentle. "It's the big night."

"Yes." She stepped in and hugged him. "You excited?"

Grandpa Dan looked as troubled as Reese felt. "I'm not sure." He put his hand on her shoulder. "What about you?"

"Nervous." She tried to smile. "I can't figure it out. I just . . . I don't feel right about things."

The old man put his free arm around her and together they walked into the family room. For now the TV was off. Zack's mom was at the computer, but as they walked in she stood and came to Reese. "It gets serious starting tonight."

"Hmm. Very serious." Again Reese had to remind herself to smile. "You checking the website?"

"I was about to. I haven't looked in a few days." His mother shared the same concerned look. "I can be obsessed with all the media attention."

Reese allowed a sad laugh. "It's overwhelming." Between Twitter and the updates on Yahoo and other gossip sites, someone posted a different story or photo shoot or event involving the top twenty from *Fifteen Minutes* every few hours.

When they had moved into the kitchen to work on dinner and she was alone, Reese finished typing in the web address for *Fifteen Minutes*. The site opened immediately, as flashy and polished as any Reese had ever seen. The home page had changed him, with Zack and Zoey clearly featured. "Watch a real-life Romeo and Juliet story that includes more drama than we've had any other season."

A quick cut showed Zack singing his heart out and then the judges asking if he was single. "No," he told them, "I have a girl-friend back home." Just as quickly the image changed and Zack was onstage finishing a group number, his arm around Zoey. "Every season involves some kind of heartbreak," Kip said in the voice-over. "But this season it gets personal." Video snapshots from half a dozen photo shoots showed Zack and Zoey constantly together. "What happens," Kip said, "when the pressure gets too great, when circumstances throw two unsuspecting people to-gether." The shot became dimly lit, Zack and Zoey sitting in an empty, darkened hallway, lost in what looked like some serious conversation.

Reese wanted to shut off the computer or look away, scream for time to stop, but it was too late. The next shot showed Zack facing Zoey in the same hallway, his hand along-side her face as he moved closer for what absolutely looked like a kiss.

The video cut back to Kip in front of the rehearsing con-testants. "Find out what's happening to this real-life Romeo and Juliet"—Kip sounded deeply dramatic—"tonight . . . when the live shows begin . . . on *Fifteen Minutes*."

Reese stared at the screen, and for several seconds she couldn't breathe or cry or scream. Had he really kissed her? Zack, the guy she'd loved all these years? She could see him sit-ting beside her in the pre-dawn light the morning he left for au-ditions. *Nothing will change, I promise . . .*

The memory of his words stabbed at her. Why hadn't she seen this coming? The signs were all there. The answer—the only answer—was that she had trusted him. Implicitly. Perfectly. Other people might let success change them, but not Zack. Not her guy.

Reese stood and black spots danced before her eyes. *I'm going to faint. Please, God, don't let me faint.* She had to leave, had to get out of Zack's house before she threw something or fell on the ground in a heap and never got up. She wanted to run to the other side of the world, as far away as she could from the *Fifteen Minutes* craze and the fact that in just a few hours everyone would be buzzing about Zack and Zoey. And people who didn't know her from Texas to Tacoma to Tampa would feel sorry for the girl back home.

She closed her eyes for a moment. This couldn't be happening. She grabbed her keys and started for the door, but then she stopped. None of this was Zack's family's fault. She was about to turn back and make a quick explanation about her departure to Mrs. Dylan and Grandpa Dan, when Zack's father and brother entered the house. They looked hot and worn out, but they must've seen something in her face that made them stop cold.

"Reese?" Zack's dad took a step closer. "You okay?"

She shook her head. "No, sir." Her tone remained kind, gentle. The go-to voice for any good Southern girl. "I need to get home."

"What happened?" Duke came to her and touched her arm. "Something with your family?"

"The show." She pointed back at the computer. Words wouldn't come. The shock was too great. "They're showing something tonight . . . with Zack and that girl."

Grandpa Dan and Zack's mom joined the others in the room and seemed to sense immediately that something was wrong.

"Honey, what?" Grandpa Dan came to her, his brow furrowed. "What happened?"

Zack's father took control of the moment. "Reese said there's going to be something on tonight's show about Zack and some girl." He looked to her. " A girl from the show?"

"Yes." Reese needed to leave. She had to make this quick. "Her name's Zoey. Zoey Davis?"

The other four nodded, all of them holding tight to every word. "Go on." Grandpa Dan still stood beside her.

"I watched a preview . . . on the computer. They're calling Zack and Zoey this season's Romeo and Juliet."

Grandpa Dan sighed and looked out the window. "That's not right."

"Is there any proof?" Dara moved to the spot next to her husband, her troubled eyes on Reese. "About the two of them?"

"Sort of. " Reese grabbed a partial breath. If she didn't leave soon she'd start crying. "The preview only showed part of the video. But they look . . . very close." She didn't want to talk about it. She couldn't. "I'm sorry. I don't want to see the rest." The right thing to do might've been to walk around and give hugs, bid everyone a proper good-bye. But she didn't have time for that. "I need to go."

"Okay." Dara hugged her. Together the family walked her to the front door. "You're going home?"

"I'm not sure." Reese could feel tears welling in her eyes again. The sadness was gaining ground. "I'm sorry. I'll talk to you soon." She looked at Grandpa Dan and over her shoulder at Zack's dad and brother. "All of you."

Grandpa Dan gave her a side hug as she headed out. "We'll

watch the show. And then I'll call Zack myself." He held Reese's gaze. "Whatever this is, there has to be a reason. That boy loves you."

Reese couldn't talk. She nodded and smiled and hurried down the steps to her car. She felt like she'd fallen into a dark hole, a nightmare. Was she really leaving before the show even began? Had that video really happened? And had Zack really kissed her?

"No," she whispered the word out loud as she reached her car. "He wouldn't do that. He wouldn't."

Tears fell down her face again. *How could you, Zack?* The question drilled itself into her mind. She missed him so much. Missed walking with him and riding beside him and laughing late into the night. The real Zack, the one the world knew nothing about. That Zack consumed her heart and mind. The same wasn't true for him. Clearly. Whatever was happening behind closed doors on the *Fifteen Minutes* set, one thing was obvious. Zack and Zoey shared something special.

Once she was out of Zack's driveway, she turned left. She had no idea where she wanted to go, just that she needed to get there. Away from Zack's house and Grandpa Dan and his family who felt so much like her own. Away from a TV set. Without meaning to, she headed toward the Lowell Therapeutic Equestrian Center. She drove through the pitch-dark parking lot to the spot closest to the stables. The groundskeepers had seen her come at this hour before. No one would bother her.

Reese killed the engine and climbed out. The air smelled sweeter here, and she breathed deep. The fence called to her. She walked to it and swung herself up onto the top rail. This was her spot, the place she sat between students, when she wanted only to watch the horses and dream about making a difference for hurting kids.

On those sunny afternoons, the view from this part of the fence was like a painting, and over time it had come to represent the future for her. A future that would be built around horses and horse farms and beautiful rolling green open spaces. The future she had pictured with Zack. It was appropriate that now, through the muggy summer night, she could see nothing but darkness.

"Why, Zack? How come?" Her broken voice pierced the silence. She wiped her tears with the backs of her hands. She covered her eyes with her fingers and let the tears come. She should've seen this coming, with all the tweets between the two of them. With the pictures coming out of their photo shoots and staged events.

But this was Zack Dylan. No matter what her eyes had told her along the way, she had listened to her heart, to the past and everything she had known to be true about the guy she loved. Zack hadn't given her any hint that he was falling for Zoey. Maybe Reese was going crazy, blinded by devotion. Whatever the reason, she hadn't seen this coming.

She leaned on the fence post and stared into the black sky. The stars were alive here and with each breath, with each hard-hitting heartbeat she came to grips with reality. Her tears slowed and then stopped. *God . . . You're with me. I feel You here.*

I am with you always, my daughter. I love you too much to leave you alone.

The response whispered at her from all sides, in a way that could only be divine. Reese breathed in deep again. She couldn't change the situation. The video had told the story.

Zack was caught up in some sort of relationship with Zoey Davis. Whatever their story, they were absolutely connected.

The next move was hers.

As this truth settled in around the edges of her soul, Reese felt her world right itself. Her body ached from the impact of the video, but she would get through this. Somehow she would get through it. With that in mind, she had no question about what to do next. She pulled her cell phone from the pocket of her shorts and called up Zack's number. His profile appeared with a photo taken in May, at the beginning of summer. Reese and Zack in swimsuits and shorts, sitting on the edge of a dock at Cumberland Lake. They'd gone with the high school kids from church for a day of boating and tubing, and during lunch they'd found a quiet place to talk.

"I'm going to marry you, Reese Weatherly." He had looked deep into her heart. "As soon as my family figures things out with the farm, it'll be you and me. Forever."

She had smiled and they talked about having a big wedding or a small gathering with just family and a few friends. Church hall reception or catered dinner and a dance in a ballroom. But here beneath the August night sky, that day felt like a million years ago. Like it never happened at all. Zack had become someone she no longer knew. At the beginning of his *Fifteen Minutes* run—when their biggest problem was a lack of communication—she had refused to feel anything but happy for him. Somehow things would work out. Sure the tweets from Zoey bugged her. But she never saw the girl getting in the way of what she shared with Zack. The connection with their grandparents, their shared faith and love of horses, the magic of how it felt to be in his arms . . .

Enough. She gripped the fence until she felt the wood splintering against her fingers. The call had to be made. She couldn't wait another minute. She stared at the screen of her cell phone and tapped his number. Then she looked back at the sky and waited. She'd called him only a handful of times since he left, and never once had he answered. The producers made them keep their phones off—that's what Zack had said. They were busy. Every minute booked.

Once, twice, three times it rang, keeping beat with her broken heart. She didn't want to leave a voice mail, but she had no choice. "Zack . . . it's me." She kept her tone neutral. "Can you call me? We need to talk."

She clicked the end button and realized she hadn't breathed. A quick breath and she tucked her phone back in her pocket. There. She had done it. Whatever real or manufactured drama was playing out on *Fifteen Minutes,* Reese was no longer going to be part of it.

The last thing she wanted to do was drive home and watch *Fifteen Minutes,* but she couldn't stop herself. Her parents were out, so she drove home to an empty house and turned on the TV. The light from the screen pierced the darkness.

She had captured the show on DVR, and now she forwarded it past Zack's performance to the end of the show and the segment with him and Zoey. Reese slid to the floor and pulled her tanned legs up close to her chin. Her long dark hair hung over her knees as she watched the reality of her life play out for all of America.

The segment ended as the teaser had promised it would. With the two kissing. Zack really kissed her. Reese held up the remote and cut the power. The screen went dark and the room followed. There were no tears on her face and none in her eyes.

Just the cold, consuming shock. Because for all the ways she had pictured life with Zack, for all the happy moments they had shared and the ones she had absolutely seen coming . . . the engagement, the future, their life together, there was one thing she hadn't imagined.

That it might end like this.

chapter 23

The high was like some crazy drug, different than anything Zack had experienced in his life. That's all he could think as he stepped off stage with the other nineteen remaining contestants after the first live show. Carnegie Hall was packed with screaming fans, and when Zack sang the Dierks Bentley song he'd practiced all week the audience stayed on its feet and screamed the entire time. After weeks of buildup, the show had definitely delivered.

Zack couldn't wait to talk to Reese, see how she felt about his performance and ask how she was doing. He hadn't been on a computer in days, and he hadn't talked to Reese in that much time at least. A few texts but nothing more. Their distance was beginning to worry him and tonight he felt desperate to hear her voice.

When the show ended, the group of contestants moved to a small room backstage. Zack tried to catch his breath. Adrenaline flooded his body, making his heart race and sustaining the feeling he'd had onstage. Backstage Zack's group hugged and talked and laughed all at once. Congratulations flew from one singer to another. The judges had made sweeping comments about how theirs was easily the best group.

Zack wondered if Reese had watched the show with his family the way she had planned. He had no cell service in Carnegie Hall and it could be hours before he would have a chance to call her. Like always, there was no time to rest. In the next few minutes William Gaines was supposed to meet them with an update.

"That was unreal." Zoey worked her way to the spot beside him, as breathless as he was. Without hesitating she threw her arms around his neck and stayed that way, swaying in the kind of hug usually reserved for long-lost lovers. "You were amazing, Zack," she whispered, her eyes wide with clear admiration. She stepped back, her face bright and full of life as she looked at him. "I swear, you're gonna win the whole thing."

"Not me . . . you." He put his hands casually on her shoulders. After all they'd been through on the show, Zoey meant a lot to him. But there had been no more clandestine hallway moments, no temptations like there had been the night they kissed. When this was all over, his heart would belong to Reese.

"I felt shaky on the belting notes."

"Not at all. Did you see the judges?" He grinned at her. "You started singing that Kelly Clarkson song and they were on their feet before the first chorus."

One of the married guys—also a finalist—overheard their conversation. He walked up. "It'll come down to you two. No one else is close." He nodded at the rest of the group. "We all know it."

Zack wasn't sure, but the guy's words only added to the headiness. "Thanks, man. Seriously."

"It's true." The guy gave Zack a hearty fist pump. "One day I can tell my kids I sang on the same stage as you."

The possibility existed, Zack could see that now. But he believed it existed more for Zoey. Tonight for the first time Zack could see Zoey winning. Her voice was as pure as Carrie Underwood's and as strong as Chandra Olson's. All wrapped up inside a blond, blue-eyed high school cheerleader. The perfect all-American girl. Viewers were going to love her.

William Gaines entered the room with two assistant producers, and in a flurry of motion he took the spot at the front of the room. The contestants fell silent. "Well done, people. That was one of the greatest live shows since we started ten years ago." Gaines beamed, making eye contact around the room. "Now." He clapped a few times, clearly in a hurry. "We have a very tight schedule."

The list was daunting. Wardrobe needed everyone immediately for a fitting. They would wear three different outfits for tomorrow's kickoff show and no one could leave until the decisions were made. Production had brought in a few pairs of pricey jeans for Zack. He could hardly wait to sort through them.

"While that's happening," Gaines continued, "you will return to this room one at a time for your exit interviews. Remember, ten of you will go home tomorrow."

A strange feeling came over Zack. He desperately didn't want to go home. Just a few months ago if he'd been cut he easily could've climbed in his truck and driven back to Kentucky. No regrets. But now . . . now that he had come this far

he wanted to keep winning, keep singing in front of that audience with cameras aimed at him from every part of the
venue.

The next two hours passed in a blur, with production assistants whisking them from wardrobe to the interview room until
everyone finished taping. Only then did Zack turn on his phone
and see the missed call from Reese. His heart soared. He
couldn't wait to talk to her, couldn't wait to hear what she
thought of his performance. Other than short teasers on the *Fifteen Minutes* website, she hadn't seen him compete until tonight.

Zack picked most of what he needed for his three outfits for
the kickoff show and then filmed his exit interview. His emotions
were raw; so much had happened that day already. As he talked
about leaving the show, putting the adventure behind him, he
felt his eyes grow damp. He chuckled and shook his head. "No
one ever wants the ride to end."

When the interview wrapped, he felt sick to his stomach.
All the way back to the wardrobe room, he assured himself
that they wouldn't cut him. Not this round. He could already
feel himself singing again next week, moved by their applause
and shining for God. Because that's what all this was about.
He'd make the cut, right? God knew he needed to stay on the
show to save the farm and help his sister. Zack stared at his
phone. He also needed to talk to Reese. As he reached wardrobe, he hesitated and then slipped into the men's room down
the hall. He took the last stall and locked the door. Leaning
against it, he quickly turned on his phone. The screen came
to life slowly. *Come on . . . work!* He stared at the dark screen,
willing it to come to life. As soon as it did, he called her. Today

more than ever he felt out of touch with her and his family, everything about his life back home. He hadn't led worship or been to church in two months.

On the fourth ring the call went to voice mail. "Hey, it's me." He could hear the urgency in his whisper.

In the distance he heard William Gaines's voice over what seemed to be a megaphone. "Buses are here! Everyone finish what you're doing. We leave in three minutes."

Zack groaned. "Baby, I'm sorry. I can't talk. I promise I'll call you as soon as we have a break." He didn't know what else to say. His words felt stiff and unnatural. Even leaving a message for her felt different now. He heard Gaines's voice again. "Sorry . . . gotta go. Love you."

Using cell phones was against the rules except during breaks. Zack turned his off and hurried back to wardrobe where Gaines was directing contestants toward the exit. "If you haven't picked your wardrobe for tomorrow, you'll have to find time in the morning." He spotted Zack. "You finished in here?"

"Yes, sir, almost. Did the interview. I'll get my shoes figured out tomorrow."

"Good." Gaines would've made a successful drill sergeant. "Get on the bus. Seats are assigned."

Zack's place by the window next to Zoey didn't surprise him. Clearly the producers were fans of what they perceived to be happening between the two of them. As long as Reese knew the truth.

"They're filming a music video tonight—a promo piece or something." Zoey leaned in close to him. "You know what I hated?"

"What?" He was aware of her knees against his legs. The seats had barely any legroom.

She settled her shoulder into the seat back and faced him. "Filming the exit video." Her eyes held his for a long moment. "I don't want this to end."

He smiled and felt himself relax. "Me, either." He could be himself around her, so he closed his eyes and for a few heart-beats he stayed that way. They hadn't stopped moving since hours before the show.

Gaines stood at the front of the bus as it pulled away. He rat-tled off their itinerary for the night. They would be bused to a media party at a club on Manhattan's Upper West Side to a cele-bration at Cullen Caldwell's house and finally to a photo shoot at the Hard Rock Cafe. No surprise that the whole thing would be videotaped.

At every stop, the *Fifteen Minutes* producers had bodyguards and roped-off pathways. Somehow people had found out their itinerary and hordes of fans greeted them wherever they went. Again the feeling was heady for Zack. Like he'd become some-one else. Or like it was all some crazy dream. A couple of girls outside the Hard Rock were in such a frenzy over seeing him that they started shaking and crying, screaming his name. Gaines came up alongside Zack. "They love you, man. It's a whole new life."

Zack could picture being greeted this way everywhere he went. For years, maybe. Reese would be there, too, in time. And when he was finished with the show, when no one could tell him what to do, he would get back to talking about his faith. He grinned at Gaines. "I could get used to it. Definitely." The crowd was too loud to say anything else.

By the time they returned to the hotel it was after midnight. The group moved to a private lobby, where the contestants could hang out away from the public eye. Zoey took his hand and tried to lead him to a quiet corner. "Let's talk." Her eyes spoke to him in a personal way, as if he'd known her forever. "Come on. So much happened today."

"I can't." Zack eased his hand free. He smiled at her, but he could only think about Reese, how much he had to tell her. "I need to call her."

Zoey nodded, her eyes sad. "Reese?"

"Yes." He gave her a puzzled look. Why would that surprise Zoey? "She and I, we haven't had a real conversation in a week."

"Hmm. Okay." She hesitated, her eyes holding tight to his. "If you can't reach her, call me. I'm not tired."

"Zoey . . ." A momentary gust of desire came over him. He waited till it passed. "It's late. I'll see you tomorrow."

"Okay." Her shoulder lifted in a girlish shrug. She waved as he walked away and he could feel her eyes follow him.

No matter how much he loved Reese, he had to be careful. Part of him wanted to stay back and hang out with Zoey. They'd been together all night, but there hadn't been any time to talk. Not really. He forced himself to keep walking. Nothing good would come from hanging out with Zoey tonight. She looked stunning from the moment she took the stage, and she made him laugh in the midst of the madness. No, he couldn't spend time with her. Not when he was still so high from his performance and hers. Yes, Zoey was a part of his life today. But Reese was his future. He needed to talk to her, hear her voice so he could find gravity again.

My son, no temptation has seized you except what is common to man . . . I will always give you a way out.

What was this? Scripture now? Zack kept walking toward his room. He didn't need a way out, not when he wasn't doing anything wrong. He was singing better than ever. It was okay to enjoy the ride, have a little fun in the process. God had let him make it this far; He would hardly want Zack to sit on the sidelines pining for home. That feeling came at night when he turned off the lights. But the days belonged to *Fifteen Minutes,* and yes, he was having a blast. Life was crazy, but it wouldn't always be like this. He knew what he did and didn't want. He turned on his phone in the elevator and the moment he closed his hotel room door behind him, he called her. "Be awake . . . come on, Reese."

He checked the time as the phone rang. His heart sank. Two-forty. Way past midnight and so much later than he had thought. Again her phone went to voice mail. Of course it did. Why in the world would she be awake at this hour? He pictured her, probably hopeful that he would call, keeping her phone nearby, maybe spending time with his parents and Grandpa Dan. But when one hour had led to another and his call had never come what was she supposed to do?

Zack sighed and slumped over his knees. He had to be more intentional about calling her, had to find time regardless of their schedule. Otherwise this strange feeling would continue to plague him. Already too much silence had passed between them.

He paced the length of his room. His whole body buzzed from the rush of the night. Like Zoey, he was hardly tired. Breakfast was set for ten tomorrow morning and then they were supposed to wear pajamas to a room with sofas and plush chairs, where they would watch last night's show for the first time.

Zack's new roommate was Hank, a married guy. But even he had stayed in the private lobby with most of the other contestants. The twenty of them had so much to talk about, so much that only the others in the competition could understand. They had become a family, a team whose existence pushed out everything and everyone who had been so important just a few months ago. Zack knew of a few marriages on the rocks, though not Hank's, and two serious couples had broken up since the competition began.

Reese and Zack were the success story, the ones who would survive.

Sure, they were struggling to find time to talk. But when this was all over they would make their way back to good again. When Zoey was out of the picture. He stopped pacing and sat on the edge of the bed. And when there weren't so many people scrutinizing him, when he wasn't so busy, he would use all this for God. He definitely would.

His mind was spinning. Had he prayed at all tonight? Since his performance? *Lord, I couldn't have done it without You. Thank You . . . really.* But the prayer brought him no peace.

He stood and paced again. What were the other contestants doing? And why wasn't he with them? If Reese were here, she'd tell him to have fun. He'd made it this far, so why hide in his room? This roller coaster wouldn't last forever, so for now he needed to be downstairs in the private lobby. With his *Fifteen Minutes* family.

He slipped into a white T-shirt and sweats and made his way back to the lobby. Zoey was gone, but a dozen of the others were still there. He joined the circle. The gospel singer grinned at him. "So what's going on with Zoey? People wanna know."

"Nothing." He chuckled as he shook his head. "Really. It's all made up. You know. TV can make it look a certain way."

"Doesn't look made up." One of the older girls grinned. "You two have crazy chemistry."

"Yeah, well, I love my girlfriend."

"So . . . your girlfriend flying out for any of the live shows?" His roommate clearly felt it was okay to prod. They were all close now, too. Any conversation was fair game. The guy raised one brow. "That could be interesting."

Fly Reese out to watch a live show? Zack hadn't even thought about it. "I guess it depends how long I stay on."

"Okay." One of the teenage guys laughed. "Can you hear yourself when you sing?"

"Yeah, man." Zack's roommate laughed and the others joined in, the happy sound rising from around the circle. "Tell her to book her flight for the final."

"Come on." Zack didn't want to talk about himself. "Let's be honest. Anyone here could win." He was about to go into detail, but something caught his attention at the back of the room. He turned and saw Zoey. She seemed to be in her own world, staring out the dark window, her expression distant.

Hank followed Zack's gaze. Rather than joking, his face grew serious. "Hey, man. Maybe you should talk to her."

"Yeah. Maybe." Zack looked back at her. If she needed someone to talk to, he would go. He stood and crossed the room.

Her eyes met his and then she looked past him to the other contestants, all watching. "Hey." She ran her fingers through her long blond hair.

"Hi." He would've hugged her but he could feel the eyes of the group on them.

Zoey looked uncomfortable. She glanced at the others. "Can

we go upstairs?" A nearby stairway led to a smaller private lounge one floor up.

"Sure." He steeled himself against whatever was coming. He couldn't let the moment become a repeat of what happened before. He followed her up the stairs where the lounge was dark except for the lights from the city. They walked to the far corner and sat on opposite ends of a leather sofa facing a floor-to-ceiling glass wall.

"After you went to your room . . . I felt so alone."

"You weren't." Zack was struggling. Whatever this feeling was, it was stronger than the attraction he'd felt that night in the hallway. "You . . . could've sat with the group."

"It's not the same. I wanted to talk to you." She ran one hand over her arm and looked his way. "But I think I get it."

"Get what?"

"The reason you didn't stay . . ." Tears filled her eyes. She leaned forward as if she was searching for a way to understand. "It's because you . . . aren't attracted to me."

"Zoey . . ." She had to know how ridiculous she sounded. Half the young guys in America would line up to be in his place right now. "I love my girlfriend. You know that."

"To be honest . . ." She looked out the window at the city. "Sometimes I think you're in love with me." Her eyes found his again. "The way you look at me and talk to me. How we laugh at the same things."

A simmering desire stirred within him, frustrating him. She was right. Sometimes he actually did feel that way like he was falling for Zoey. But that was the whole *Fifteen Minutes* thing. The insanity of it and the close quarters. He and Zoey were together constantly. He was bound to feel something for her some of the time. But that wasn't real. Not the way Reese was real.

He stood and moved farther away, to the arm of the sofa. Distance. That's what he needed. He sat there, his feet on the cushion, facing her. "I'm sorry . . . if I made it seem like that."

"Don't be sorry." Adoration filled her eyes. "Whatever this is . . . Maybe we need time to figure it out."

He wanted to explain himself again, but he couldn't find the right words. She looked so pretty, watching him from her side of the couch.

After a long minute she faced him again. "Thank you, by the way." Slowly she walked around behind him. "For coming here."

Whatever she was up to, he had to be smarter. One step ahead of her. But before he had time to move away again he felt her fingers at the base of his neck. With great skill, she pressed her thumbs into his muscles and worked them in circles, easing the tension from his muscles. His body relaxed against the pressure. "Mmmm . . . man. That feels good." The words slipped before he could stop himself.

"We're all so uptight, so tense." She moved her hands down a few inches, pushing her thumbs into his back muscles and working her fingers into the knots near his neck. "Sometimes I wonder . . . how things would be if you and I had met before Reese."

He was still sitting on the arm of the sofa, and as her backrub continued, her body made contact with his shoulders. At first only here and there, and then in a way that felt very intentional. A subtle pressing against him.

The feeling consumed him and swept him away, a wonderful mix of physical release in his tense neck and a desire stronger than his resistance, one that was taking over his senses. "Zoey . . ."

She leaned in closer and whispered against his neck. "Relax."

He had no response. The rhythm of the backrub filled his body and soul.

"You think because we're on this show"—she straightened again, but her voice remained a whisper—"that what we feel isn't real?"

"I . . ." His control was dissolving.

"You feel something now, Zack. I know you do." The sound of her whispers and the feel of her body against his, the way she kept pressing her fingers and thumbs into his back, all of it stirred his desire to an even greater level. He could see himself turning around and taking her in his arms, kissing her the way he wanted to kiss her. He gritted his teeth. No . . . he couldn't. He wouldn't do that to Reese.

Gradually the backrub stopped and she moved her soft hands to his bare arms. With the lightest feather touch, she ran her fingertips down his triceps all the way to his elbows. The feeling pushed Zack closer to the edge. *Run,* he told himself. *You can't do this.* But he stayed. He stayed and he loved every second, every feeling her touch ignited in him. She leaned her face closer to his again, their bodies making full contact. "We both feel it . . . and it *is* real."

That was it. The physical pull was like an assault, a full-blown attack against which he was completely defenseless. Every cell in his body wanted to go with the wave instead of fighting it. He squeezed his eyes shut. "Please . . . Zoey."

"Come on." Her lips touched the skin on his neck, and again her fingers traveled down his arms. "Turn around and tell me you don't want me."

His head slowly fell back against her. He was losing the battle, failing the test. Then he remembered something Reese had said before his audition. Something about time apart. So that they could figure out who they were. Zoey ran her hands down his arms again. Zack clenched his jaw, barely able to breathe. Maybe Reese was right. Maybe he needed this so he could be sure.

"Zack . . ." She came around in front of him and took his hands and gently turned him so he was facing her, his feet on the ground.

He slid to the edge of the sofa arm.

It was happening . . . he couldn't fight his desire another second. He moved his feet slightly apart and she easily took the spot between them. Like that they were face-to-face and her arms came around his neck. "Hold me." She touched her lips to his neck. "Please, Zack."

He did as she asked, pulling her closer and wrapping his arms around her back, her waist. The hug didn't last long before he was kissing her. Making out with her the way he had longed to do since they walked upstairs. His desire doubled and the kiss grew more intense, more passionate.

"Don't stop." She spoke softly against his neck, kissing him several times there before returning to his lips.

He moved his hands along her back and thought about the dark-lit room and the sofa and how easy it would be to lie down with her here and—

Suddenly he slid back. What was he thinking? How had this happened? He created distance between them. With a strength not his own he worked his legs over the sofa arm onto the other side and moved three steps away from her. "Wow." He laced his fingers together at the back of his neck and hung his head. For a long moment he only focused on breathing, desperate for control. *Stay here, Zack. Don't go back.* How had things gotten so out of control? He waited until the fires coursing through him cooled a little. Then he lifted his eyes to hers.

"I can't . . . do this." He shook his head. His breathing was nowhere near normal.

She was out of breath, too, and shame colored her expression—even in the dark-lit room. "You just did." She knit her brow, clearly hurt. "Think about us, Zack. Stop lying to yourself."

Thoughts of the kiss consumed him again. His body screamed for her, but this time he ignored the demands. He stood a little taller. "There is no us."

For a few seconds she stared at him. Then slowly she nodded. "Fine." She crossed her arms. "Friendship? Is that what this is?"

"You don't make it easy." He exhaled, frustrated more at himself. "Look, I'm sorry." He kept his distance, not wanting to be drawn in again. "I care about you."

"Care? Concern? Those were your feelings a minute ago?"

"How do you expect me to feel?" He felt beyond defeated. "Nothing's normal. The show . . . all of it." He still felt drawn to her, but he held his ground. "You're very beautiful, Zoey. You needed someone. The backrub . . ." He held his breath for a few seconds and then exhaled hard. "The lines get blurred."

"Yeah." She pulled her hair to one side and stared at him, pride flashing in her eyes. "For both of us."

"Okay." The reality of what he'd done was hitting him. He felt awful. Not only because of Reese but because his actions had clearly confused things. Before another moment passed he had to be absolutely clear. "Look, I do care for you. But before this show and after it I will love the same girl."

Once more tears shone in her eyes. "Fine." She found a sad smile and some of her usual composure. "I'm going to sleep."

Another realization hit Zack square in the heart. This would've been a perfect time to talk about God. But in light of his weakness, the conversation would clearly have to wait. "Good night."

She hesitated and her expression said it all. If he wanted to stick by his girlfriend, then she would stop trying. And she certainly wasn't going to hug him good night the way she usually would. She took a few steps toward the hallway, the one that led to the elevators. "Good night."

He watched her walk off. The moment she stepped out of sight he remembered the cameras. He searched the room but couldn't see one. That didn't mean someone wasn't watching. Why hadn't he thought of that when he started kissing her? He walked to the window and stood there. Just stood there and wondered what had happened.

He had told her the truth. He loved Reese. But in those minutes all he'd wanted was Zoey Davis. How was that possible? And what did it say about him? He leaned against the windowsill and tried to make sense of it all. But he couldn't.

Exhaustion seized him. How could he have let things get so crazy? He closed his eyes, disgusted at himself. What had happened here wouldn't happen again. He would be more careful. *God, I'm sorry . . . I failed tonight.* A shiver came over him and he stared up between the buildings at a sliver of the dark sky over New York City. He was slipping. He could feel it. *I thought I could do this, Lord . . . what's wrong with me? Please make me stronger.* Despite the highs and lows of the day, he felt a hint of inner strength, one that wasn't his own. The pace was so crazy, the situation so extreme. Of course he had kissed her. Next time he'd be smarter. He would avoid going anywhere alone with her, and late nights would be with the group only.

He remembered the warning from Chandra Olson. How she'd lost her fiancé during her run on *Fifteen Minutes.* Sure, God would forgive him, and Zoey, too. But the question that remained, the one that kept him awake and broke his heart long after he turned out the lights, was this:

What about Reese?

chapter 24

Reese didn't get a call from Zack until early the next day. It was well before lunch and she was teaching when she felt her phone vibrate. She glanced at the screen and saw that the message was from him. Walls in her heart shot up. He could wait. Her session was with Toby, and she wasn't about to cut it short just because Zack finally responded.

Half an hour later she read his text. *Baby, we need to talk. The contestants didn't watch last night's show until early this morning and then we had some appearance in Washington Square. I couldn't use my phone till now. Anyway . . . I saw the Romeo segment and I'm sick. Baby, everything's turned around and I need to explain. I'm so sorry, Reese. Please . . . call me.*

Reese didn't feel anything. Zack had changed—the video had told her that much. He followed his first text with three others. *Reese, are you there?* A few minutes later, *Baby, please call me.* And two minutes after that, *I know you're upset. I'm sorry. We have to talk.*

Had he been gone so long that he forgot she worked on weekdays?

She finished with Toby and had an hour before her next student, a new little girl with physical limitations because of a brain tumor. She went to the edge of the field and leaned on the old fence. Her fingers flew over the virtual keyboard. *I'm at work. I have an hour. I really don't want to text. Some things need to be said face-to-face. Can you Skype?*

She lowered her phone and stared out at the hills. The sooner she cut things with Zack, the better. In some ways it was good he'd gone to the audition, good he'd made it through this far. That's what her dad had told her last night when he got home and saw the segment. "Tough situations have a way of showing a person's true colors." He had sounded sad. Her parents both liked Zack. "I'm sorry, honey. I didn't see this coming."

They had all thought Zack was different, with a deep devotion to God and the rare kindness of a gentleman. But no one thought it more than her. She had laughed with him as they rode horses through endless Kentucky hills and worked beside him while he fed homeless people in Costa Rica on a mission trip. They had talked all night about their love for God, their belief that He had great plans for them. She'd seen Zack take Grandpa Dan's arm to help him walk or sit for hours reading to AJ. Yes, Reese had known the very best of Zack Dylan. But the guy featured on last night's show was someone Reese didn't know at all.

Zack's text response came a few minutes later. *I knew you were at work. I'm sorry . . . and yes, I can Skype. But it might take ten minutes to get set up. Is that okay?*

Part of her wanted to celebrate the way she usually would because this was Zack texting her, Zack sitting somewhere near Carnegie Hall reaching out to her. The Zack she loved and missed. But she couldn't think of him that way. He had become someone different. She read his message again. Since yesterday she had dreaded this conversation, dreaded it more than any in all her life. Sure, she could wait ten minutes. *That's fine.* Her fingers moved across the phone. *Like I said, I only have an hour.*

Again his response was instant. *I'll hurry.*

She stared out at the fields again. She could no longer see her future here. In a few weeks she would move to London and discover what God had for her there. But first she had to end things with Zack. Not because he was caught up in the show or because of the kiss or because he'd allowed the producers to find enough material for their Romeo and Juliet piece. But because he had done the one thing he had promised he would never do.

He had changed.

ZACK WAS DESPERATE and angry and scared.

That morning when they had gathered in pajamas in the new living space to watch the show, Zack saw for the first time the Romeo and Juliet piece. Until then, the twenty contestants had been upbeat and vocal, running a constant commentary about how talented this one or that one truly was and wishing all of them could stay even after tonight's kickoff show. But when the piece on Zack and Zoey came on, an uncomfortable silence settled over the group.

The entire time it played, Zack felt like he was falling. Falling into a deep, dark, bottomless pit. The image in his mind flipped from what was playing on the big screen to flashes of moments from last night, when the kiss had almost gotten out of control. The footage was contrived, no doubt. Everyone on the show knew how he felt about his girlfriend, no matter how he'd failed her. But the photos didn't lie. Clearly he had shared those moments with Zoey or no camera could've caught them.

The judges had been in the room. Halfway through the piece, Zack glanced at them. Kelly and Chandra stared straight ahead, unsmiling. Only Cullen seemed to enjoy himself, grinning as the segment played on. Zack felt his fury begin to build. Which of them had encouraged this? Was it a judge or William Gaines? Or maybe even Samuel Meier? Zack felt betrayed by everyone, somehow even Zoey.

She was seated beside him again, leaning over her knees, seeming as shocked as he was. When it ended, she looked at him, like she wanted to see his reaction before showing her own. He couldn't talk to her. Not after watching their kiss play out for all of America. Without waiting another moment he stood and walked to the back of the room where Gaines was standing. "Whose idea was that?" Zack's voice had been more of a hiss. The show played on for the rest of the contestants, although the mood in the room had definitely changed.

Gaines folded his arm and looked toward the door. "Mr. Meier is out there. Talk to him."

Zack stormed into the hall and found the producer surrounded by a team of assistants. Zack didn't care. He waited till the producer looked at him, puzzled. "You and I, we need to talk."

Samuel Meier stared at him, unrushed. "Zack." He excused the others with a nod and then sauntered closer. "Something on your mind, son?"

"Why'd you do it? The Romeo piece?" Zack's breaths came fast, his forehead beading with sweat.

"What do you mean?" Meier relaxed and allowed a gentle laugh. "That was you in the pictures, right?"

"The way you played it . . . that isn't the truth." Zack's anger stayed barely controlled.

"You didn't walk with her and talk to her and hug her?"

Zack clenched his jaw, trapped. "You know what I mean."

"Was that you kissing her or not?" Meier's tone grew harshly cool. He didn't allow time for a response. "Really, Zack. You are what you spend your time on. You're supposed to be this strong Christian, right?"

"Yes." Zack thought about last night and conviction shot arrows at his soul. "My faith is important to me. That's why this segment makes me so—"

"Hold on." The producer raised his voice. He came a step closer and pointed at Zack. "If your faith was so important, why didn't our camera guys get shots of you reading your Bible?" He leaned back, studying Zack. "By the way, you'll be doing a duet with Zoey next week." He shrugged, his eyes hard. "Don't complain about the segment, Zack. You gave it to us."

With that he turned and walked at a determined clip down the hallway where the assistants had gone. He didn't look back once.

In some ways, Zack wanted nothing more than to run back to the hotel and grab his things and head home to Kentucky where he belonged. But he'd been hit by a strange and stark reality. He didn't really want to go home. Not yet. Regardless of the Romeo and Juliet piece and the producers manipulating his time with Zoey. Even after what happened last night, he'd come too far to quit.

When the ride was over, he would talk to Reese and work things out.

He kept to himself the rest of the morning and into the afternoon as the group did another Jeep commercial and a photo shoot in Washington Square. Zoey tried to talk to him once, but he shook his head. "Not now. Please."

After that she left him alone, finding her place amid the group. With every passing hour he thought about what he'd say to Reese, how he'd explain the piece with Zoey, their time together, and the kiss. Not just that one but the one from last night. Especially that. On the bus ride back to the practice hall they were given permission to use their phones. Zack texted Reese immediately.

Now that she'd finally answered, he was desperate to find a way to Skype her. That way he could look into her eyes and explain at least some of what had happened. They filed into the building for what was supposed to be another rehearsal of the group numbers. Zack found Gaines at the back of the practice room. "I need thirty minutes. It's an emergency."

Gaines narrowed his eyes. "We don't have thirty minutes. We tape in two hours."

"I'm sorry, sir. I have to make a phone call."

Ten full seconds passed and then Gaines slowly picked up his megaphone. "Take twenty, everyone. We'll meet here after that."

It was the first real break of the day and Zack thanked him as he sprinted for the door. He grabbed his laptop on the way out but was stopped by a line of bodyguards at the door. "Hold up." One of them stood in his path. "Where do you think you're going?"

"Across the street." He pointed to the Starbucks. "I need to make a call."

"You have permission from Mr. Gaines?" The guy peered past Zack into the building.

"I do. Please." He checked the time on his phone. "I don't have long."

"All right, then." The bodyguard nodded at one of his peers. "Let's do this."

Zack couldn't believe he'd need two bodyguards to cross the street and Skype from Starbucks. But he didn't have time to argue. The hot sun beat down on his shoulders as they walked to the nearest intersection and crossed at the light. Before they reached the other side, a van full of teenagers screeched to a stop and the door flew open.

"Zack Dylan!" One of the girls ran from the van and was nearly hit by a cab as she raced toward him. She screamed, waving her arms at him. "It's Zack Dylan!"

"Zack! Wait for us!"

Zack and the bodyguards stepped onto the sidewalk and the girls surrounded them. They managed to reach in and touch Zack, tug at his shirt and put their hands on his arms and shoulders. The moment was easily one of the most out of control since the competition began, and Zack waved them off. "Hey, I gotta go! Sorry!"

"Just one picture, please, Zack?" Half the group was screaming, and as he and the bodyguards continued toward Starbucks, the girls stayed close. Zack could see where this was going. The girls would follow him into the coffee shop and he'd never get the chance to jump on Skype.

"You're drawing a crowd." The bigger of the two bodyguards turned to him. "What do you want to do?"

"I say you take a few pictures and get rid of them." The other bodyguard shrugged. "You wanted to do this."

The guy was right. Zack stopped and turned to the girls. As he did, the bodyguards took up their places on either side of him. "Okay, come on." He found a smile that had become practiced in recent weeks. "Let's take a picture?"

Again the girls screamed and squealed, but once he began taking photos, they quieted down. Each of the girls wanted a single shot, and then there were several group pictures. The girls had their hands all over him, and one of them leaned in to kiss his cheek before the nearest bodyguard put his hand up. "That's enough. We have to go."

The girls waved and squealed as he walked away. "Marry me, Zack!" one of them shouted. He could still hear them as he entered the coffee shop. One of the guards stayed outside. He couldn't keep the public away, exactly. But he could try.

Zack checked his phone. He was ten minutes late at least. He took a table in the back corner, opened his laptop, and frantically logged in to Skype. "Hurry," he whispered. He was still catching his breath from the commotion outside. "Be there, Reese. Please."

After the first ring, she picked up, and like that he was looking into her eyes. "Hey . . . sorry I'm late."

"It's okay." She didn't seem angry. But her expression was so sad he could barely look at her.

He could sense the crowd gathering outside. The girls remained, and more were joining them. So far the bodyguard had kept them at bay, though Zack could hear the commotion building inside with the employees. Zack shut all of it out and tried to focus. "Reese, I'm sorry." Their connection wasn't perfect. She was probably using the Skype app on her phone. But it was better than they'd had in weeks. He had to hurry. "The video piece, that's not how it is."

Reese hesitated. She looked down for a long moment and then straight at him. "You kissed her."

"It was a crazy night. She pushed me. I . . . I didn't mean it."
He kept his voice low. People behind the counter were watching.
"Reese, the whole thing lasted only a few seconds." His words
tumbled out, one on top of the other and he caught himself. Excuses would get him nowhere. Especially since at some point
he'd have to tell her about last night, too. He pushed his fingers
through his hair and breathed out. "I'm sorry. It was my fault. I
was wrong. I . . ." Another sigh. "I'm sorry."

Tears shone in her eyes, but she didn't break down. "Thanks.
For saying that." So many details remained, but clearly she
wasn't interested. "Zack, I need to tell you something."

His heart slammed against his chest. Outside he could hear
the girls squealing his name, and inside, the workers had formed
a half circle, whispering and staring at him. Zack was glad he had
his back to the wall. No one else could see the computer screen.
"Try to understand, please. I'll fly home tomorrow if you want."

"No." She shook her head. "I don't want that."

"What, then?" Time was running out. If the girls got past the
bodyguards, his conversation would be over.

"Zack . . . I'm moving to London. I leave in three weeks."

"What?" The room began to spin, and Zack had to grab the
edges of the table to steady himself. "Reese, don't do this. Not
until I get home so we can talk."

"I've made up my mind. I already gave my word." Until this
point she had sounded strong. Now her eyes welled up. "It's
over." Her voice cracked and she shaded her eyes. He'd done this
to her, hurt her this way. Zack would've given anything to climb
through the screen and take her in his arms.

"Reese, don't! It's not over." He lowered his voice. Already
everyone in the place was listening. He had no privacy, but he
didn't care. "I love you."

She wiped her eyes with her knuckles and looked at him again, to the deepest places of his heart. "I'll always love you. But it *is* over. I wanted to tell you to your face."

Lines began to run horizontally across the screen and the sound crackled. He shifted the laptop a few inches each way. "No, Reese . . . you can't do this. Please . . ."

"I already did." Her tears spilled onto her cheeks, but she remained composed even as the connection grew worse. "It's over. Don't text me. It'll be . . . easier that way. I can't—"

The screen went dark. At the same time the bodyguard keeping watch inside stepped up. "We need to go. Just got a call from Gaines. Rehearsal starts in five."

"Not yet." His fingers flew across the keyboard, desperate to bring Skype back to life. He was too late. The signal was gone. Zack held his breath. He could've thrown his laptop through the window. Instead he had to smile. Devastated and in shock, unable to believe what had just happened, he gathered his laptop and followed the bodyguards out onto the sidewalk.

Like an actor playing a part, Zack smiled and waved and paused for photos with a crowd that had doubled while he was in Starbucks. He kept his easy grin in place while he crossed the street and returned to the practice hall. For the next hour, he danced with the group and acted excited about the upcoming show. But his broken heart was in Kentucky.

Only Zoey seemed to know something was wrong. She was still his dance partner, and though the two of them had been awkward since last night, she looked worried. She caught up to him during a five-minute water break. "What's wrong? Tell me." She hesitated. "You're mad."

"I'm not." He took a long swig of water and stared at her. "Reese broke up with me."

Her expression fell as if she were genuinely upset for him. "Can you . . . Will you try to change her mind?"

"Yes." He held her gaze, keeping control on his anger. "As long as I'm breathing." He turned and walked back to the dance floor. He had no right being mad at Zoey. None of this was her fault. He hadn't seen his friendship with Zoey coming, let alone the attraction he'd felt last night. And by the time he realized how the producers were playing the situation, it was too late. He could only blame himself for the video segment and the kiss. Both kisses.

For all of it.

The kickoff show happened in a blur, like something from a dream. They performed their numbers and sat through a painful few hours while ten contestants were eliminated. The whole time Zack wanted to stand up and volunteer. A ticket home would mean he could start piecing his life back together. He was kept, like everyone expected, and when the final cuts were made the remaining ten erupted in hugs and celebrations. Zoey wrapped her arms around his neck, but he quickly turned and hugged someone else. He'd given the producers enough footage.

As the show ended, they signed a new set of papers, promising a portion of their earnings over the next three years to the show. Then they were escorted to a waiting Mercedes Sprinter van and taken to Del Frisco's on Avenue of the Americas for a private dinner. After that they attended a front-row performance of *Annie,* complete with ten bodyguards, a red-carpet arrival, and throngs of screaming crowds.

Zack felt numb through all of it. They sat him next to Zoey, but Zack might as well have been on a deserted island. His body was merely going through the motions. He kept smiling. Kept laughing. But he couldn't keep track of the conversations around him. Couldn't pray.

As if God Himself was back in Kentucky with everyone else he loved.

All he could think about, all he could see, were Reese's beautiful, broken eyes and the certainty there. She was moving to London, yes. More than that she was moving on with her life. He could see that much even with the poor Skype signal. She didn't want an explanation or a way to make things work or for him to get on the next plane.

She wanted to get as far away from Zack Dylan as possible.

Everyone could see the difference in Zack, but Chandra felt like she had a special window to it. Zack was changing before their eyes. Despite her warnings, he was letting the attention get to him, like everyone else. The show had mocked his convictions and manipulated his friendship with Zoey, and now he was left trying to find his way through his new life.

The one that no longer included his girlfriend.

Three weeks had passed, and everyone knew about the breakup. Chandra had watched from a distance, wondering if Zack would lose the will to compete and wind up getting kicked off earlier than any of them had expected. Instead, he seemed to have doubled his efforts to win, while his friendship with Zoey appeared only to have grown stronger. As if the two of them together had become victims of the show's producers.

Star-crossed friends, if not lovers. The two of them against the world.

His breakup alone didn't prove that Zack was a different person today. Relationships ended all the time. It was the other things. The fact that Zack had all but stopped mentioning his faith. Back when Meier gave the edict about avoiding faith talk, Zack had been determined to carry on anyway. Not anymore. His last dozen tweets were shout-outs to his fans, gratitude for their votes, and thanks to the show's sponsors. Nothing about the God he served.

The competition was down to six contestants, and tonight each of them would sing two songs and a duet. They were set to compete in a few hours, and Chandra was worried. She'd seen Zack in wardrobe and watched him during rehearsal. His style had gradually changed, his clothes and hair edgier than before. One of his songs tonight was about getting drunk on a beach, and the duet was a racy love song. She pictured the way Zack and Zoey sang it during practice. If America didn't believe they were a couple before tonight, they would soon. And maybe they really were, the way they acted.

Zack didn't talk to Chandra like before.

Chandra finished her lunch and walked to the rehearsal room. For more than a week she'd looked for a chance to talk to Zack again, and now she couldn't wait. The contestants had ten minutes left on their break. Chandra found him sitting next to Zoey, the two of them looking pensive. She walked up and made small talk at first. Then she looked at Zack. "Do you have a minute?"

Zack looked like he'd expected this. He stood. "Definitely." He left his things with Zoey and followed Chandra to the back of the rehearsal space, down a hall to her private suite. She shut the door behind them and directed Zack to the sofa. She took the chair. For a long moment, she studied him, willing the right words to come. "Your memory isn't very good, Zack?"

"Ma'am?"

She raised her eyebrows and her pointer finger at the same time. "Chandra." Frustration filled her voice. "I told you that."

Zack paused. "Sorry." He sat a little straighter.

She had his attention. "We need to talk."

"Okay." He looked confused, not sure what to make of her anger.

She sat back hard in her seat and stared at him. "You didn't hear me the first time, is that it? That why you're letting fame suck you in?"

"I . . . I'm not sure I understand."

"I warned you." She crossed her arms, her voice louder than before. "Of *course* they were going to make some love story out of you and Zoey Davis." She threw her hands in the air. "Look at you two. Like something off a movie set."

Zack blinked. A fight stirred in his eyes. "Was that my fault?"

"You care about that girl back home?" Chandra leaned over her knees, too worked up to stop herself. "Do you?"

"You know I do." Zack shifted, clearly uncomfortable.

"And you care about that *God* you used to talk about?"

"What do you mean *used* to talk—"

"Zack Dylan!" Chandra angled her head, shooting her best warning look at him. "Don't go all innocent on me. You know what I'm saying. Check your tweets. When's the last time you mentioned God or prayer or faith in Jesus?" She waved her hand in front of her face. "Don't answer that. Just look later. When we're done."

"You called me back here to talk about Twitter?" Zack rested his forearms on his knees, his eyes intent. "Is that what this is about?"

"It's about you." She emphasized each word, her voice

marked by disappointment. "You're not the same Zack. Right before our eyes, you're changing."

He stared at her, and the anger in his expression grew. He stood and walked until he faced the far wall, then he slammed his fist against it. Hard as he could. His forehead fell against the cool brick and he stayed that way. Several seconds passed before he spun around and glared at her. "How is any of this *my* fault?" he yelled. "Could you tell me that, Chandra?" He clenched his fists and made a move to hit the wall again, but at the last second he changed his mind and found a level of control. "How is it my fault?"

"Because." She stood and pointed straight at his chest. "You love it, Zack. The cameras and autographs and stanchioned-off crowds. The staged photo shoots and live shows. You love all of it." She grabbed a quick breath. "And you know what I think?"

He didn't answer. His chest still heaved from hitting the wall with his hand.

Chandra let her hands fall to her sides. "I think . . ." her sudden calm made every word more pronounced, "you love it more than everything and everyone back in Kentucky."

"Don't say that." Zack looked like he wasn't sure whether to storm out of the room or break down and cry. "I didn't stop loving anyone."

"But . . ." she pointed at him again, her voice a whisper. "You love this more. Otherwise, you would've gotten on a plane and gone after the girl." She held his eyes for a few heartbeats. "Look at this." She pulled her laptop from a nearby desk. She took the computer to the sofa and pointed to the seat beside her. "Sit."

Zack did as she asked. She opened the computer, pulled up her iPhoto library, and brought up the first picture. A photo of her with her mom and dad at what looked like a middle school graduation. "Those are my parents. Take a good look, Zack." She peered at him. "You see them? See how happy we look?"

"Yes." He sighed. "Look, Chandra . . . I need to get back."

"No!" She raised her voice again. "You watch. This could just as easily be your life. The life you had before you auditioned."

A stream of pictures followed. Chandra and her parents on a beach vacation, the three of them at the park playing with their family dog. There were other photos, pictures of Chandra and her fiancé when they were teenagers, back when they first fell in love and more as they grew older and the relationship grew serious. Near the end of the file was a picture of her with her parents and fiancé, all of them standing around her car.

"I keep a copy of that photo with me always. In my car, in my purse. On my phone. It's always there." Sadness consumed her. "Know where I was going?"

Zack looked at her, but again he said nothing.

"That's right." She stared at him. "I was leaving to audition for *Fifteen Minutes*." She stared at the picture and her heart broke. The way it always did when she looked at this photograph. "Sometimes . . ." She heard tears in her voice. "When the world spins out on its axis like it does . . . I call up this picture and climb into it. Just *live* in it for a few minutes. However long I can. You know why?"

Anger marked Zack's expression, but his eyes were filled with unshed tears. He clenched his jaw and shook his head.

"Because I would do *anything*," she jabbed her finger at the photo on the screen, "anything at all to be back in that moment."

She was almost finished. The next photo showed a ring in a box. "That's my engagement ring, the way it looked when I gave it back to him. Never loved anyone like I loved him. But this"— she waved her hand at their surroundings and toward the door—

"all of this won out over him. I didn't think that's what was happening at the time, but it was. What we used to have was never the same after the show."

One more click and there they were. Her parents' tombstones.

"Take a look, Zack." She turned the computer so he could see more clearly. "Take a good hard look. See their names on the grave markers. See the dates." She breathed in sharp through her nose, ignoring the tears that made their way down her face. "After a loss like that, there is no going back. There just isn't."

Zack hung his head, and Chandra watched a series of tears splash onto his faded jeans. He rubbed the back of his neck and then looked at her, angrier than before. "Why are you showing me this? I'm not you."

"Look there." She pointed at the name of the file. "Look at what I call this photo album."

He squinted at the word, following her orders even when he clearly did not want to.

"See what it says? It says, 'Cost.' This file . . . these thirty-six pictures . . . represent the *cost* of my success. The price of my *fame*." She shut the computer and returned it to the desk. Then she took the chair across from him. "You have that file, too, Zack. Even if you haven't created it on your laptop yet." Her tone was soft, every other emotion giving way to sadness. A sadness that was always beneath the surface for Chandra. "What's in your file, Zack? What pictures?"

He worked the muscles in his jaw. "Nothing. I haven't lost anything I can't get back."

"That right?" She nodded, her attitude showing again. "Well, let me tell you what's in that file already, just so you know." She stood and waved her hands in front of her. "A photo of a sprawling Kentucky horse farm you'll never go back to. That should be there. And a picture of you and your family, sitting on the front porch like you had forever to watch a sunset. Oh, and your favorite picture of you and your girlfriend. Start there." She lowered her hands to her sides. "Leave room, Zack. Because the file of what it costs will keep growing. Every year it'll grow."

"I need to get back." Zack stood and reached for the door.

"Not yet!" she yelled. "Turn around and look at me." He kept his hand on the knob, but he did as she asked. "When you leave here, you take a minute and think about what I said. Think about how you've changed. How the wide-eyed guy from Danville, Kentucky, disappears a little more with every performance." She came a step closer, pointing at him one last time. "Think about it while you sing your drinking song and that love duet with Zoey." She hesitated, her passion getting the better of her. "You've changed. You're buying in to the fame as fast as anyone on this show. But you mark my words, there will be a cost."

He hesitated, their eyes locked. "Thank you. I'll . . . keep that in mind."

"You do that." She crossed her arms. "And when you hit the pillow tonight, I want you to think about something else. I took this job for two reasons." She hesitated, making sure he heard this last part. "So I could find meaning in all this. Meaning, because by winning . . . I lost everything." She paused. "You wanna know the other reason?"

"What?" His tone was just short of rude.

"So I could warn someone like you." She came to him and found control once more. Gently, she took his hands in hers. "I promise you something, Zack Dylan. Right here I promise you. I haven't prayed to God since my parents died. But tonight . . . to-night when you perform in front of America I will be praying for *you.* Praying that despite all the madness, you might find a way to win." She released his hands. "Go."

Zack held her eyes for another few seconds, then disappeared down the hallway. Chandra shut the door, grabbed her computer, and sat down. She found the photograph again, the one of her and her parents and her fiancé in the moments before she drove off to audition.

For the next ten minutes she didn't want to live anywhere else.

ZACK COULDN'T RETURN to the rehearsal room. He wasn't even sure he could compete after that. He walked blindly to the end of the hall toward the emergency exit. That's what he needed, right? An emergency exit. So he could stop the madness and think about his life, about what Chandra had told him.

He hated her approach, how she had yelled at him and blamed him. But somewhere deep inside he had the horrible suspicion that she was right. That every single word was the truth. The absolute truth.

Facing the wall, his forehead pressed against the cool brick, he let the singer's warning play in his mind again. She was right about Twitter. He didn't have to check. Gaines had warned him enough times that he'd convinced himself his faith could wait. As if he could put God on hold while he finished the show run and then later . . . after he won . . . he would tell the whole world about Jesus.

The plan disgusted him now, made him want to burst through the door and run as far and fast as he could. He thought about her accusation that he loved this new life more than the old. That couldn't be true, right? But how else could he explain some of the changes he'd made? Changes that were intended to please the producers and the audience without thought for how they might affect Reese or his family back home. One at a time he examined Chandra's statements and he could only admit what was painfully obvious.

She was right.

The realization shocked him. How had he allowed it to happen? And if a stranger could see it, what about his family? His parents and his brother and sister? Grandpa Dan?

What about Reese?

No wonder she was moving to London. He'd texted her every few days since she broke up with him, but she never texted back. With each ignored attempt, he felt his heart grow colder toward her. Zoey understood. She was here and she was his friend. No more private moments or make-out sessions. They had reached an understanding after that first live show, and now they were more careful.

Not that it mattered. The cameramen caught what they wanted. Nearly every week the show ran some sort of update about the two of them—either how they were fighting or hiding from the others or falling more deeply in love.

But somehow along the way he had called home less often. The drama with Zoey had begun to feel real, while his life in Kentucky faded a little more each day. Chills ran down his arms. So much drama, so much public scrutiny.

He thought about the lyrics of the song he would sing that night. They were about being too drunk to remember last night's girl and maybe even last night's fight. Drinking until he couldn't see the stars and waking up under the sun. It was a song William Gaines had suggested. "People need to see the edgy cowboy," he'd told Zack when they were picking songs.

"You're a guy's guy. Like David from the Bible. Time to show a little of that muscle."

Zack had found himself nodding along with Gaines, agreeing. Who wouldn't want to be like King David, ready to slay any giant who got in his way on *Fifteen Minutes*? But a drunken-cowboy song couldn't point people to the Bible. How could he have thought that for even a moment?

Then there were his clothes. Tonight he would wear a cutoff T-shirt and tight jeans—an outfit the wardrobe assistants said was inspired by an Abercrombie ad. Both decisions had seemed right at the time. Anyone would want to be a handsome, well-dressed guy's guy. The most masculine voice on the show. The at-home audience would go crazy for both the song and the look. Those were Gaines's words. "You'll be through with more votes than everyone else combined."

Nausea tightened Zack's gut. How could he have agreed to any of it? What had happened to praying about his performance and asking for God's will, whatever it might be? Zack stood straighter and stared at the emergency exit. He couldn't leave now. News crews and police would spend the evening searching for him. He'd embarrass his family and the show and probably wind up being sued.

No. He had to go on. He'd made his decision long ago.

When he couldn't wait another minute, he returned to the rehearsal room. The other contestants were seated in the front row and Gaines was about to use the megaphone. When he spotted Zack, he threw his hands in the air. "You scared us half to death." His shout could be heard throughout the cavernous room. "Get over here."

And like that Zack stepped back on the roller coaster from which there was no getting off. He took his place next to Zoey, and in the minutes before heading over to Carnegie Hall, the two of them ran through their duet again. The competition was turning Zack into an actor. He could sing a love song with Zoey and convince just about everyone in the room.

Zack realized something as they were whisked across the street to Carnegie Hall. He no longer found it natural to pray in the moment. The noise around him was so loud, the screaming fans and demanding production assistants, the rehearsals and sound checks and wardrobe issues. All of it had become so overwhelming he could barely think, let alone pray. One more cost to add to the list.

A list that no doubt would be longer after tonight.

chapter 26

The show that night would go down in history. At least that's what Cullen announced as they moved past the individual performances to the duets. Zack's drinking song had been met by thunderous applause. He'd grinned and laughed, but he had never felt more empty in all his life. Now he had changed into his cutoff T-shirt and jeans and stood backstage with Zoey, trying to figure out what to feel, how to feel.

He was there when Gaines found him.

"I have a note for you from Meier." Gaines was all business, a clipboard in his hand. He seemed to read something from the paper. "Here it is." He looked up, serious. "Push-ups. Drop and give me twenty push-ups."

Zack looked around at the other singers. "What?" Was this some kind of joke? He chuckled and took a step back. "What do you mean?"

"You heard me." Gaines's voice turned gruff. "We don't have

much time. Drop and give me twenty. They want you to look more buff during the duet." He gave Zack's bare biceps a once-over. "They look fine to me. But production wants your muscles to pop for this performance."

Zack wasn't sure whether to laugh or tell the man where to take his clipboard. He caught Samuel Meier watching him from the far corner of the room, surrounded by staff. His look told Zack no one was kidding. So with Zoey standing beside him and the other four contestants watching, Zack did as he was told. He dropped down and did twenty push-ups. Twenty became forty and forty became sixty. The push-ups became one sure way to re-lease the anger he felt toward himself and the show and his com-promises.

Finally Gaines returned. "That's enough. You won't be able to sing."

Zack rattled off five more for good measure and then hopped to his feet. He was out of breath, but he felt more alive than he had since his talk with Chandra. Suddenly the noise of the con-testant coordinator faded along with every other sound in the room. *God . . . what am I . . . what am I doing here? What's hap-pened to me?* The prayer came in fits and starts, but it was the first time he had prayed in longer than he could remember. Gaines's mouth was moving, but Zack couldn't hear him. Couldn't hear anything but his pounding heart and the gentle whisper of the Holy Spirit.

I have been with you all along, son. . . . Turn to Me. I know the plans I have for you.

"Zack!" It was Zoey's voice. "You okay?"

He looked around and saw her standing in front of him, searching his eyes. "Yeah, I'm . . ." Her blond hair looked fuller than usual and she wore a short tight black dress and boots. He let his eyes drift over the length of her before he caught himself. She looked gorgeous. If they were alone now he wasn't sure . . .

What was he thinking? He blinked and stared at the ground. Panic seized him. Chandra had just warned him, and still he couldn't stop the slide. A thought hit him square in the heart. Wherever Reese was tonight—if she watched the show—she would be sure she'd done the right thing.

"Zack, what're you thinking?" Zoey moved closer, her voice a whisper. As if she didn't want the others to think something was wrong. "Are you sick?"

"No." He came back to the surface. "I'm all right."

Across the room, Gaines called for them. "You're up in thirty seconds."

Zack took her hand and led her to the stage door. This was how they were supposed to enter, whether he liked it or not. He'd made his commitment to tonight's show. Now he had to follow through. They could hear the countdown behind them and at the right time they walked onto the stage to a standing ovation. Zack remembered Meier's statement from yesterday. *America has never loved a* Fifteen Minutes *couple more than the two of you.*

The lighting became more romantic and Zack noticed the setting, the one they had practiced with. There were trees and a small bridge and a park bench. He almost forgot the blocking. But as the song began, the movements came easily. Hand in hand they sauntered across the bridge, stopping to sing while looking into each other's eyes. Next they moved to the bench and then to a pair of microphones at the center of the stage.

"We'll make love tonight and make love last," Zack sang to her.

"Like we never had a yesterday before today," Zoey added.

They finished the song together. "Like we never had a past. Never had a past."

Again the crowd was on its feet, screaming and applauding and making the walls of Carnegie Hall feel like they might fall from the sound. They each bowed and then Zoey caught his eyes. Before he could stop her, she stood on her tiptoes and kissed him. On impulse alone, his hand came to the side of her face as the kiss played out.

It didn't last longer than a second or two, but it doubled the noise in the building. With that the two of them walked off, still holding hands. Zack didn't take a breath until they were backstage. A production team seated at a distant table began to clap. "Perfect, you two." Gaines added his applause to the mix. "The kiss was brilliant."

Zack couldn't speak. He led Zoey out of the room and down a long cement hall. There was precious little dressing room space in the back of the building, but Zack found a supply closet and pulled her in behind him. When they were alone—definitely alone—he faced her, hurt and seething. "How could you do that?"

"What?" Her own frustration added to the moment. "That kiss?" She glared at him. "Don't worry. It didn't mean a thing." She was shaking. "The audience wanted something extra, so I gave it to them."

"That wasn't your choice. I had no idea."

"Oh, right, . . . and you hated it. Just like you hated kissing me in that upper lobby." She crossed her arms and laughed, sarcasm working its way around her words. "Whatever. Listen, Zack. I want to win this thing. If that means kissing you on a live show, so be it."

"Yeah, well, maybe check with me first. How am I supposed to explain that?"

She hesitated, her silence consumed with what looked like a dozen conflicting emotions. Finally she dropped her voice and took a step closer. "How are you supposed to explain that *kiss*?" This time her laugh sounded bitter. "Come on, Zack. How are you going to explain the song about getting drunk? Or the way you let them dress you like some pinup boy tonight?" She tossed her hair, and her haughty eyes burned through him. "I'm the least of your troubles."

With that she spun around and left.

Zack stayed in the closet another five minutes, fighting for control. Of all the things he hated about the night, he hated this most of all—the fact that she and Chandra were right. He had only himself to blame for the people he'd lost and for the person he had quickly become.

When he finally made his way to the main room backstage, the show was winding down. The last couple was onstage singing their duet. One of the production assistants saw him and motioned him closer. "Zoey isn't doing so great."

"What do you mean?" Zack scanned the room. He didn't see her.

The guy chuckled. "She said you two were in a fight because of the kiss."

More drama. Just what he needed. Zack could've pulled his hair out. "Which way did she go?"

"That way." He pointed down a different hallway. "But don't worry about her. They're paying her plenty for your little love story."

Time and motion and gravity all ceased. Zack stood anchored in place, just looking at the production assistant. "What . . . what do you mean?"

"Come on . . . they must be paying you, too."

Mountains on all sides of him collapsed, burying him in the garbage of three straight months. They were paying Zoey? To give the show the appearance that the two of them were an item? He shut his eyes for a few seconds and then blinked them open. It wasn't possible.

The guy was still talking, but like earlier with William Gaines, Zack couldn't hear him. Suddenly he pictured a number of times when he had seen Zoey talking to Meier or Gaines. Was it really possible? He jogged down the hallway never feeling the floor, searching every doorway for Zoey until he found her in a dressing room that had Gaines's name on it. She was alone, still in her black dress and boots, curled up in an oversized armchair, sobbing.

"Look at me." Zack didn't yell. His shock was too great. "Zoey, look at me."

"It isn't true." She spun around to face him, her feet hitting the floor. "I was standing around the corner. I heard what he told you." Her face was red, her eyes swollen. "You can't believe that."

"What am I supposed to think?"

She stared at him, clearly trying to find control. Sorrow and fear colored her expression, but they didn't come close to the more obvious emotion consuming her. An emotion that could only be defined as guilt. "I've hated keeping this from you, Zack." She breathed fast, on the verge of hyperventilating. "I'm sorry. I'll tell you everything."

Zack sank into the chair across from her. Whatever she had to say, he needed to be seated. Otherwise, he wasn't sure he'd survive it. "Go ahead." He held his head in his hands for several seconds before looking up at her again. "Talk to me."

"I . . . didn't want . . . to go along."

"Are they paying you? I need to know that first." His voice was louder, meaner than before. He had to force himself to find calm. He stood and closed the door and then returned to his spot across from her. "Tell me if they're paying you."

"No." She shook her head fast and sharp. "No, I would never take money to . . . to be your friend, Zack. Never." She hung her head and panic seemed to grab hold of her. Her breaths came even faster and she stood, panic frozen in her face. "I . . . I can't breathe. Zack . . . help . . . me."

His instincts took over and he came to her. With the compassion that once defined him, he held her and stroked her back. "Zoey, shhh. It's okay. Breathe out. You're okay."

"I can't . . . catch . . . my breath."

He held her for several minutes until he felt the muscles along her spine relax. Finally she took a step back and covered her face, her tears flowing once again. When she sat down and lowered her hands, he could see that she was going to be okay. She was broken, but she was breathing.

"I didn't . . . take money." She shook her head, her eyes imploring him. "Please believe me."

"Did they offer it?"

"Only as a joke."

As a joke? Zack turned and paced to the opposite wall of the small room. He stayed there, trying to keep some sense of sanity. "Are you serious?" He turned and stared at her. "Who did that?"

"Gaines. But he was kidding."

"So what . . . what did they promise you instead?" He knew there was something. He could sense it in her panic.

"They said . . . I had a better chance of staying on the show if—" She looked down at her lap.

"Say it. Come on, Zoey." He walked closer, willing her to speak.

She looked up, her swollen eyes locked on his. "I had a better chance if I stayed near you. If people thought we . . . were an item." Tears fell on her cheeks, but this time she didn't look away. "I'm sorry."

There it was, the whole story out in the open. The producers hadn't only worked to find an angle, they had created one. With promises of fame, Zoey had played her part. Zack dropped to his seat and faced her, just stared at her. "I lost Reese for that? So you could fake your feelings for me?"

"I wasn't faking it." She looked horrified. "I *am* in love with you, Zack. Sure, I'm your friend, but that's not all I feel." She stood and threw her hands in the air. "I'm not that good an actress. Not for any amount of fame."

Zack wanted her out of his sight. A memory flashed in his mind. The winter he was sixteen and working at the back of his family's horse farm when a snowstorm came through. He needed to secure the stables, but by the time he did, the storm was a full-fledged blizzard. When he tried to make it back to the house, snow was flying in every direction. Zack had fallen to the ground, no longer sure which way was up. If his father hadn't found him, he might've died out there.

That was how he felt now. No longer sure which way was up and in desperate need of rescue by his Father.

Zoey must've seen what he was feeling because she didn't wait around for his next words. She stood and ran from the room and down the hall. He waited until he could no longer hear her boots on the floor before he slowly left Gaines's dressing room. He had failed his God and his family, and he had absolutely failed his girl. He had no idea what the full consequences would be, but one thing was certain.

His eyes were open now.

One way or another he was headed back home to start re-building what he'd lost. He walked slowly down the hallway, and as he struggled to grasp which way was up, he remembered something. Chandra was praying for him. Chandra and his parents and his siblings, the kids back home at church. Even Reese. Reese, who would leave for London tomorrow. She was praying because that's the sort of girl she was. No matter how he'd hurt her, she would pray for him. And with all those prayers, he could hope for only one thing.

That his trip back home might come sooner than any of them expected.

THE EPISODE WAS mercifully over. Reese felt like she could breathe for the first time in an hour.

Grandpa Dan turned off the TV. "I don't recognize him." He leaned on his cane and looked at Reese. "I have no words."

None of them did. "It's okay." Reese couldn't think of anything else to say. "It was my choice to be here tonight."

She had to watch the show with them this one last time. Her flight to London was scheduled to leave tomorrow night. Once she landed, she would stay in an apartment at the horse facility and spend a few weeks getting to know the instructors and students. Then she'd begin teaching. In her spare time she would tour the city and get familiar with the underground. Her life ahead gave her hope in the darkest hours. God wasn't finished with her.

But she couldn't leave life here without this night. All day she had prayed for God to show her if she was wrong. If leaving Zack wasn't part of the Lord's plans, then she needed to know now. Before her plane took off. She imagined Zack singing some-

thing with a faith message and admitting to America that he'd
made mistakes leading up to this point. She even wondered if
maybe he would talk about missing her and his home back in
Kentucky.

Instead . . . well, instead Zack's performances had only
shredded what was left of her heart. The guy singing on the
TV screen wasn't remotely like the one she'd kissed good-bye
three months ago. He acted different and looked different and
dressed different. And when he and Zoey sang their love song,
Zack's dad nearly turned off the TV in the middle of the performance.

Reese's shock had held off her tears. But now she could feel
the dam in her heart breaking. She needed to leave, needed to
get home and finish packing. So she could cry in private. She
stood. "I need to go."

"I'm sorry." Dara came to her and the two hugged.
"Please . . . keep praying for him." She looked deep into Reese's
eyes. "This isn't him. You know that."

Reese nodded. Of course it wasn't him. The fame, the overnight success, had done to Zack what it did to nearly everyone in
his position. It had changed him. No matter what promises Zack
had made back at the beginning. She smiled at Zack's mother.
"I'll miss you." Tears stung her eyes. She wanted one thing—to
feel the plane lifting off the ground, taking her to a new life far
from this one.

Reese hugged Zack's dad and Duke and AJ. The girl was sick
again. She struggled to make it down the stairs, let alone to the
stable. "You get better, okay?"

"Okay." AJ took a step back. "We'll go riding again when you
get back."

"We will." This was the hardest part. Reese never imagined

she'd say good-bye to these people. They were like her own family. "I'll see you next year."

AJ nodded and moved across the room to her mom. The two of them held on to each other, the sadness like a wave pulling them under the surface of all that once was.

Reese said good-bye to Grandpa Dan last. Here was the man who had promised Grandma Lucy that he'd take care of her. The man who had prayed for her and been certain when Zack brought her home that God had meant them for each other. Not anymore. He took her in his arms and held her the way her own father might. When they drew back, Reese saw tears on his cheeks. "I'll pray for you. Every day." His voice was scratchy beneath the obvious weight of his sorrow. "I promised your grandmother, and I'll keep my promise." He kissed her forehead. "God has good plans for you, Reese. Go find your life." He stopped, gathering his composure. "Don't forget us."

She could hardly see through her own tears. "I won't." Once more she hugged him, and then she picked up her purse and said a final good-bye. She left without looking back. Zack Dylan and his world were behind her now. Every step put distance between them, the sort of distance she needed if she were going to find a new life apart from him. Her heart ached, because this wasn't what she had wanted. She was leaving, but she still missed him. She climbed into her car and covered her face with her hands. The tears washed over her, tears for her shattered dreams and tears for the guy she loved. The one who no longer existed. Only one thought brought her comfort as she dried her face and started her car.

Tomorrow night at this time she would be boarding a plane to London.

chapter 27

The one o'clock meeting was for brass only. Samuel Meier kept the details hushed and invited only Gaines and the three judges. Chandra arrived at the same time as Kelly, and they swapped a look. Whatever was going on, it was serious. Only Samuel remained standing as they took seats around a small table.

Without any fanfare, the producer got started. "As you know, the ratings this season have been the best yet." He had a number of documents in front of him and he sorted through them now. "Our ad rates have nearly doubled and everyone at the network is thrilled. We all know the reason—Zack Dylan and Zoey Davis have the talent and they give viewers a story they can't resist." He sighed. "We counted on both of them making it to the final. We were sure about it." He stopped and stared at them, the lines on his face deeper than before. "Until last night."

Chandra felt something strange in her heart, adrenaline

maybe, or something almost divine. She held her breath while Samuel struggled with whatever he needed to say.

"Don't tell me he got kicked off." Cullen leaned his forearms on the table. "That's insane. It was his best night."

Samuel nodded, his lips locked in a frown. "I asked the accounting firm to do an audit. The results were the same. He'll go tonight."

Heaviness hung over the table. Chandra stared at her hands, trying to contain her joy. Zack had been kicked off? The idea was outlandish, impossible. But the truth remained. She had prayed for Zack, that he would make it out alive. And America had voted him off.

Kelly had to feel the same way—happy about this latest development. Not for the show but for Zack. Cullen was going on about how there had to be a mistake. "America will turn off their TV sets for good if the bloke gets kicked off."

"Which is why"—Samuel dropped to his chair, picked up a small stack of papers, and handed them out—"this is our newest policy. Other shows do it. But tonight will be the first time it's been done on *Fifteen Minutes*."

"Ahhh, a judges' save." Cullen relaxed into his chair. "Perfect. I love it."

"Yes." Samuel smiled, fully in control. "We need Zack on this show. Ideally it's him and Zoey Davis in the final. We could ride those ratings for another three seasons."

Chandra couldn't believe it. Why have a voting system if it came down to this sort of manipulation? "So we'll vote tonight, is that how it'll work?"

"Yes." Samuel leveled his gaze at her, his eyes intense. The unspoken message was crystal-clear. "All of us are shocked about this. Cullen will lead with the announcement of a save. Zack will sing for his life. Then we'll break for a commercial and the three of you will vote to keep him." He shifted his attention to Kelly. "We'll come back from the break and you'll tell America the good news—Zack is safe for one more week."

"And we'll vote off three the next week, right?" Cullen chuckled. "It's perfect." He narrowed his eyes, his focus on Samuel. "What do you think happened?"

"Honestly?" Meier shook his head. "I've only seen this a few times, but I think until now he's been too good. His loyal audience sees him as a nice boy. The token Christian. He sings a song about getting drunk and they stop voting."

"Come on." Cullen couldn't have been more shocked. "No one's that narrow-minded."

Samuel frowned. "You'd be surprised."

Kelly stood. "If that's all, I need to call my dad. He's expecting me."

Chandra watched her colleague leave without waiting for permission. Was it a coincidence, her timing? Or was she as fed up as Chandra? Of course people hadn't voted just for Zack. They'd voted for his faith and values. When he stopped being defined by them, the people stopped voting. Chandra wondered why Cullen and Samuel were so surprised.

She excused herself and found Kelly in the hallway. "Hey."

"Hey." Kelly's eyes were soft, deep.

"How's your dad?"

"He's still . . . terminal." Sorrow fell like a shadow over her face. "But he's in remission. He might have longer than we thought."

"Good." Chandra had come to enjoy talking to Kelly. The changes in her fellow judge were dramatic. "What about Cal?"

"We're trying. He and the kids moved in with me." She

leaned against the wall. "I mean, we're not rushing to church or anything. But we need each other." Kelly hesitated, thoughtful. "The last few weeks have taught me that."

"Hmmm." Chandra stared at her high heels for a long moment before lifting her eyes to Kelly. "About tonight . . . looks like it'll be up to us."

"Yeah." Kelly stared out a distant window at the end of the room. "I liked Zack better at the beginning. Before everyone knew who he was."

Chandra nodded. "Me, too." She put her hand on Kelly's shoulder. "Do me a favor?" She didn't wait for a response. "Tonight . . . when it's time to vote . . . don't let anyone decide for you. Never mind the ratings. *Fifteen Minutes* will always be strong."

"True."

"They'll ask you back." Chandra lowered her voice, looking as deeply into Kelly's heart as the woman would allow. "Vote with your gut. With your conscience." She straightened. "A lot's riding on our decision."

Kelly nodded slowly. "I'll keep it honest." She took a step toward the dining hall. "I promise."

Chandra stayed, thinking about her words. They were true. Zack's future depended on tonight's vote. Now that Chandra had started praying for him, she couldn't stop. It wasn't too late for Zack. Only the top four contestants toured after the show was over. Everyone else was on their own. Some were offered deals, others had to find their own way. Back to waiting tables or leading worship at their local church.

The judges each had a vote. She had no idea what Cullen and Kelly were going to do with theirs.

But she was absolutely sure how she would cast hers.

* * *

ZACK HAD BLOWN it. He knew as soon as he woke up that morning. Like always lately, he jumped on Twitter before he was fully awake. At first he thought someone was playing a joke, or maybe someone had hacked his account.

It took two minutes to figure out that wasn't the problem.

He hadn't checked last night, too exhausted from the drama with Chandra and then Zoey. Now he scanned back through his @s and realized the truth. The comments had turned sour right after his performance aired on the East Coast and they continued that way through the night and into the morning.

One after another they shouted at him, reminding him of the person he'd become. He read as many as he could stand.

What happened to @ZackDylan? I thought he was a Christian? #hypocrite

Figures. Everyone changes when they get famous. Even @ZackDylan. #toogoodtobetrue

Really? @ZackDylan singing a song about getting drunk on a beach? What a joke!

Not every tweet was negative. But the positive ones seemed focused on the wrong thing.

If you're gonna show us your arms @Zack Dylan, take off the shirt. Give us what we want! #hotbody

Don't you just know @ZackDylan is spending hours rehearsing with
@songleader? Zoey Davis you're a lucky girl. #jealous

He felt sick to his stomach. Some of the tweets were crass—
more so than ever since he'd made it on the show. Zack winced
as he read the next tweet on his feed.

Come find me @ZackDylan. The spot next to me in bed is all yours.

A few were so vulgar, with cussing and descriptive sugges-
tions, that Zack skimmed over them. Others expressed outrage.

Anyone who votes for @ZackDylan after that performance doesn't
remember who he was at the beginning. #changed

Disappointed in you @ZackDylan. Who are you, anyway?

After ten minutes, Zack exited out of his account. He had
known he was making a mistake last night even before he took
the stage. Chandra's warning, and then the whole twenty push-
ups thing. Finding out about Zoey and the promise of fame from
the producers had been the last straw.

Now he wondered if he'd get sent home. A thrill of anticipation ran through him. It would be the happiest exit moment
the show had ever seen. Not that he could celebrate yet. He
had damaged his reputation and his witness and no doubt em-
barrassed his family. And what about Reese? Wherever she
was, packing for Europe, she must think him the most insen-
sitive jerk alive. He had so much damage to undo. If that were
even possible.

Zack stood and filled his lungs. *God, I give You this day . . .*
I'm sorry. I've made a fool of myself. He thought about the first kiss
with Zoey in the hallway. That never would've happened if he'd
stood by his convictions, to bring glory to God. *I fell in love with*
the attention, Lord, with being popular to the world. Everyone's
right. Being on the show changed me.

The change hadn't happened all at once, of course. But it had
absolutely happened. He had started the show defined by his
faith. The Christian guy in love with his girlfriend back home. Not
anymore. Now the world saw him as some hunky heartthrob dating his fellow contestant. *How did everything get so bad, God? I let*
the show define me.

Defeat threatened to consume him. *Help me find my way*
back. I'm sick of this life. I want to be Yours again. Completely. He
gritted his teeth and felt a resolve he'd never known, not in all
his life. Before the show his faith was easy. Untested. Now he'd
been through the fire. And even though he'd failed, he knew this
much—Jesus loved him. Even now. *Please . . . please take me*
back. Forgive me.

A picture of Christ's outstretched arms filled his soul. The
Lord was here. He hadn't abandoned Zack and He never would.
His grace was sufficient, even now. God had been with him all
along. Using Chandra and Zoey and even Twitter to show Zack
what would happen if the madness didn't stop. Because that's
how the Lord was. He never forced Himself on anyone. Rather,
He simply remained, leaving signs and clues so His people might
find their way back.

Where He would always wait with open arms.

Zack picked up his phone and gathered his nerve. Before he
could report for breakfast and a packed day of rehearsals and in-

terviews, he had to take care of something more important. He clicked his phone a few times and did what he hadn't done in far too long.

He called home.

MINUTES BEFORE THEY were set to take the stage for the kickoff show, Zack was praying in the empty hallway behind the stage when Zoey found him. She looked beautiful, ready to move ahead. The way she'd been promised.

"Hey . . ." She approached him slowly. The two of them hadn't talked since she ran out of Gaines's dressing room. "Can I say something?"

"Sure." He was no longer angry with her. None of this was her fault. Why wouldn't she take the producers' deal? Besides, he was well aware of her feelings for him. She couldn't fake that, even for a spot in the final.

She came up beside him and pressed her shoulder to the wall, facing him. "I'm sorry. About last night. The kiss."

Her apology surprised him. He figured she'd be sorry for her deal with the producers. "Thank you." He nodded and slid his hands in his pockets.

"I mean it. The whole time I never respected the fact that . . . that you had a girlfriend."

He could feel the walls rise around his heart. He shrugged. "You had your reasons."

"No." She shook her head, her eyes damp. "Never mind the producers. What we have between us—what we had—it was real."

He smiled, though his eyes felt flat. "Sure." He took a deep breath. "We better go. Call's in a minute."

She looked awkward, like she wanted to hug him. But it was too late for that. "I'm just sorry. That's all."

"Thanks." He gave her a long look. As he did he remembered his own prayer from earlier. "Forgiven."

She hesitated. "You never taught me how to pray. Remember? You said you were going to."

"Yeah, well . . . I might be the wrong guy for that."

"You're not." She held her ground. "You're everything good and right and true, Zack Dylan. I messed it all up for you, but it was never your fault."

"It was." He allowed a sad, quiet laugh. "I didn't fight for what I believed in. That was all my fault. My faith should've been stronger."

"You'll find your way out of this. I believe that." Her expression said she knew she'd lost, that nothing between them would ever be what it had been. Still, she seemed compelled to finish her thought. "When you do, when you land on your feet on the other side, somewhere in Kentucky, there's going to be one very lucky girl waiting."

"Maybe." He shrugged. All he could do was try. Reese hadn't responded to a single text. "Come on." He motioned to her and they walked together to the stage door. "It's showtime." Even as they walked toward the crowds and lights and cameras, Zack could only hope one thing.

That he was taking this walk for the last time.

The hour-long show was nearly over. They'd performed several group numbers and hung around onstage while new features were aired on each of the remaining six contestants. Kip Barker was in fine form, using dramatic sweeping statements to keep viewers glued to their seats. "What will happen when we take a look at the votes? Will your favorite sweethearts be separated? Or will they go through? And what about the greatest gospel singer to grace the *Fifteen Minutes* stage? Will you give him another week?" He paused and pointed at the camera. "All this and more . . . when we return to *Fifteen Minutes*."

Zack felt strangely calm. Whatever was about to happen, he was ready. Contestants kicked off this evening would fly home tonight. It was part of the process. Like everyone remaining on the show, Zack had his bags ready.

As for the mess he'd made of his reputation and his life, God held his future. It might lie in a ball of tangled knots and consequences for his compromises. But one day soon he would have his second chance. When he did, he would never look at love or life, faith or family the same way again. Tonight only one thing terrified Zack.

The idea of winning.

Chandra had said it best. She would be Chandra Olson until the day she died. Even after. History would talk about her and compare other singers to her and if she ever married and had a family, her kids would forever be defined first as the sons and daughters of the famous singer. They would be objects of scrutiny with bodyguards of their own. There was no escaping it. If Zack won season ten, there would be no way back to Reese Weatherly. She would find her life in the freedom of anonymity—maybe in London for good—and every sunrise would create more distance between them. If he won, he would be a slave forever to the fame of *Fifteen Minutes*. Even making the final four would mean being recognized and placed on a pedestal for all time.

Not so for those who went home today. History would leave them alone.

You're in charge, Lord . . . I'll go where You lead.

Before the break was over, Zack made eye contact with Chandra. She looked intently at him, as if she had something she wanted to tell him. Instead she only gave him the slightest smile and then turned her attention back to the other judges. The production assistant counted them in to the live show and on cue the audience erupted in applause.

"We're back with the news you've been waiting for." Kip looked at the contestants. "If I can have all six of you here next to me on the stage."

Zack could feel Zoey shaking beside him, breathing fast the

way she had in Gaines's dressing room. When she caught his eye, her fear was almost tangible. He smiled, as if to tell her not to worry, she was going to be okay. She seemed to relax a little and Zack was glad. He held nothing against her. What had happened between them was his fault.

Kip talked about their performances, heightening the drama as much as possible and referring to Zack's cutoff T-shirt. "But was it too much for the guy who got his start singing at church?"

Zack felt the blow to the center of his soul. But all he could do was take the heat. His decisions had led to this. He had no one to blame but himself.

Like always, Kip started with the two contestants who had the most votes. Zack had been in this group every week. Not this time. Zoey and Kent, his married roommate, were ushered onto the Winning Sofa, as it was called. Next, one of the singers was let go, and his exit video was played.

That left just two of them. A woman whose marriage was falling apart back home, and Zack. The buildup seemed to last forever before Kip delivered the verdict. "I can't believe this, America. But . . . the singer going home tonight . . . is Zack Dylan."

A chorus of boos came from the audience as Zack and Kip congratulated the woman. She joined the others on the sofa, clearly overjoyed at going through. At this point Kip was supposed to talk about Zack, his run at the title or his family's horse farm or his "romance" with Zoey. Instead, Kip looked straight into the camera and said something that caused Zack's heart to skip a beat.

"Coming up next . . . a dramatic surprise . . ." He paused. "Something never done on a *Fifteen Minutes* stage . . . until tonight. After the break."

When the cameras cut, Kip came up beside Zack. "You ready?"

"For what?"

"To sing. The surprise involves singing."

Zack felt dizzy. They'd been told often to always have a song ready. But so far the kickoff shows hadn't involved anyone performing. Just the exit videos.

The break was over before Zack understood what was going on. Kip launched into the big surprise. They had created a "judges' save" that would last for the rest of the tenth-season run. "And tonight"—Kip stared into the camera—"the judges have decided to possibly use that save on one of your favorites—Zack Dylan."

Across Carnegie Hall, the crowd went wild. They might've been disappointed by Zack's choices, but they didn't want him to leave. Certainly the fans here tonight didn't want that. Kip was still explaining the situation. "Before the judges vote, Zack's going to sing for his life. Right after the break."

When the cameras were off, Kip turned to Zack. "What are you singing for us?"

"Uhh." The question caught Zack completely off guard. He had given the production team a few choices of what he might sing if called on. That conversation had been weeks ago. Now . . . in light of his pending departure, there was only one song he wanted to sing. "Can someone get my guitar?"

"Of course." Kip shot the order to one of the grips. He didn't look flustered, but this was off script. The task proved harder than it sounded. The guitar was across the street in the rehearsal room. One of the production assistants ran for it and had it in Zack's hands ten seconds before cameras rolled.

"We're back with one of the most exciting moments in *Fif-*

teen Minutes history." Kip's expression remained dramatic as he stared into the camera. Then he turned to Zack. "Okay, it's up to you." Kip paused. "What are you going to sing for us?"

"A song I wrote. It's called 'Her Blue Eyes.'"

"Okay, then." Kip turned to the camera. "You sure that's not called 'Zoey's Eyes'?"

Zack smiled, the way he was supposed to. "No." He could feel the eyes on him, those of Samuel Meier and William Gaines and Zoey Davis. All of them were waiting. "I wrote it for my girlfriend, Reese."

Zack was breaking the rules one after another. He'd been told never to mention God or his girlfriend again. Tonight he was finished taking orders. "Ladies and gentlemen, Zack Dylan singing 'Her Blue Eyes.' While he's singing, our judges will make their final decision. Will they save your favorite heartthrob? Or will Zack leave *Fifteen Minutes* tonight?" He pointed to Zack. "Here we go."

Someone had brought a barstool to the stage and Zack sat down with his guitar. He missed the way it felt in his arms. Zack closed his eyes as he began. Despite the tens of millions of viewers and the packed house at Carnegie Hall, he was back on Reese's front porch steps, singing this song the morning he left for Atlanta.

As the words came, he felt himself becoming the old Zack again. The guy he had forgotten somewhere along his *Fifteen Minutes* ride. A few seconds into the first verse he opened his eyes and looked into the camera. She might not be watching, but he had to sing as if she were. As if he still had a chance. In what felt like the performance of his life, Zack sang with everything he had. The audience was on its feet as he sang out the final lines of the last chorus.

I always want to see me there
Under a Kentucky sky
There in her blue eyes.
Lost in her blue eyes.

The response wasn't the thunderous applause that had come to define Zack's previous songs. As he looked out at the crowd he understood why. They were on their feet and many people had tears on their faces. They understood that this song was different, and the sense throughout the building was that everyone had witnessed something they would never forget. Zack had found his way back.

Zack set his guitar down against the barstool and pointed up. Something he hadn't done since his audition in Atlanta. Then he turned to Kip. "Thank you."

"Well." Kip blinked back tears as he looked to the camera. "If that didn't get you, check your pulse." He turned to Zack. "Obviously your motivation for that one is very personal. What was going through your head as you sang?"

Zack couldn't have rehearsed his response. The words simply spilled from his heart. "Over the last few weeks I sort of forgot who I was. My faith . . . the people who are important to me." Regret weighed heavy in his tone. "I'm sorry for that." He hoped Reese was watching. "I get lost in that song." He hesitated, almost unaware of the cameras. "I sang it because it helps me remember what really matters."

"You heard him. Zack Dylan . . . finding his way back." He pointed at the camera. "The judges' vote coming up . . . after the break."

During the commercial someone took Zack's guitar, and he was directed to the spot beside Kip. Once he was set, he looked at each of the contestants on the sofa. When he reached Zoey, their eyes held a few seconds longer. He could see in her now what he'd felt earlier in the hallway before the show. What he still felt. They would always share the journey they took together on *Fifteen Minutes*.

But the charade was over.

In the final seconds before cameras rolled again, Zack studied the judges. They were deep in what seemed to be a quietly heated conversation. As the production assistant counted them back to live action, the conversation stopped abruptly. The tension could be felt to the top level of Carnegie Hall.

"The judges have voted," Kip told the camera. "It's time for the moment of truth. Will Zack Dylan stay? Will Romeo and Juliet go on together? Or is this the end for our boy from Kentucky?" He turned to the judges' table. "Cullen, have you reached a decision?"

"We have." Cullen scowled. "I have to say, our choice was not unanimous." He looked from Kelly to Chandra and back at Kip. "My fellow judges did not see what the rest of us saw in that unforgettable performance."

Zack's heart began to soar. He stood a little straighter and tried to look concerned. He could feel the jet engines beneath his feet.

Cullen shook his head. "Unfortunately, we've decided to send Zack home tonight."

The audience sent up a collective and drawn-out "Boo!" Several of them shouted, "Nooo! Don't do it!"

"Wow." Clearly Kip was shocked. "Let's hear some feedback. Kelly? You didn't like Zack's song choice with 'Her Blue Eyes'?"

Kelly looked at Zack. "The song was beautiful." She cleared her throat, as if she were struggling to find the critical voice she had become known for. "A lot goes into a vote like this." She shifted her look to Kip. "I had to think about Zack's past performances along with this one. I also had to consider whether Zack had a chance at being the next *Fifteen Minutes* winner."

"You didn't think so?" Kip still sounded stunned.

"No." She looked at Zack. "He . . . doesn't have that star quality we're looking for." She smiled, and something in her eyes told him she was talking in code. Like there was much more involved in her decision. "You might have a songwriting career ahead, though. That last number was truly beautiful."

"I don't think anyone at home could've seen this coming." Kip shook his head and frowned into the camera. Then he turned to the judges again. "Chandra? Your vote?"

She stared at Zack, straight through him. The look was for him alone, a look that recalled their intense conversation just yesterday. Chandra cared enough to share her own heart, her own misery at being forever famous. Now her look told him she was silently celebrating. Instead of smiling, she shook her head and gave a sad shrug in Kip's direction. "I have to agree with Kelly. Zack's a good guy, a decent singer. But he's not cut out to win the whole thing." She looked back at Zack. "My vote came down to that."

"Well." Kip turned dazed eyes to the camera. "You heard it. The decision is made. Zack Dylan will leave us tonight." He paused, milking the drama. "Let's take a look at Zack's journey on *Fifteen Minutes*."

The segment cut Zack to the heart. His eyes and attitude at the beginning—humble and looking to bring glory to God, hope to his family's horse farm. The change from that to his performance yesterday. The shots of him and Zoey played again, including the kiss. The piece ended with Zack's interview and his words, "All good things end eventually. I don't want to go home, but if I do, this will always be the highlight of my life."

He felt sick. Had he actually said that? Kip gave him one more chance to say something before the show ended. This time the words came from his heart. The heart that remembered who he was before the show, who he wanted to be long after it was over. "I want to thank everyone at *Fifteen Minutes* and the audience back home." He looked at Kelly and then at Chandra. "And I want to thank the judges. A few months ago my grandpa told me it's easy to lose yourself on a stage this big." He smiled. "Tonight I feel like the winner." He held Chandra's eyes for a few seconds and then looked at Kip again. He shrugged, a grin playing on his face. "I get to go home to the people I love."

The audience cheered as the music played and the show wrapped. Zack went straight to the judges' table. He shook Cullen's hand. "Thanks for believing in me."

Cullen's disappointment darkened his expression. He shook his head and glanced at his fellow judges. "This is rubbish. You're the most talented bloke we've had. I'll never understand what happened tonight." He grabbed his things and headed up the stairs and off the stage.

Zack turned to Kelly next. "Good-bye."

"You understand, right?" She looked nervous. "I voted for you as a person. Not you as a singer." Her smile softened her face. "As a singer, you should've won the whole thing. Just know that."

"Thanks. That means a lot."

She nodded and followed Cullen. Next, Chandra stood and came to him. Zack faced her. "You . . ." He took her in his arms and hugged her. She had become a friend in the last two days. As he stepped back he looked deep into her eyes. This was their moment. Never mind the mass of fans being kept at bay by the bodyguards. "You were praying."

"I was." Tears sparkled in her eyelashes. "You were my reason." She put her hands on his shoulders and grinned at him. "You gave me meaning, Zack."

They hugged again, and one last time Zack looked at her, into her very private heart. He didn't have time to say everything he felt, but he sensed she understood. With that he waved to the crowd, and two bodyguards walked him offstage. Before he reached the door, he stopped and looked back.

The crowd was no longer trying to get to him.

Zoey and the other three contestants had come to the edge of the stage, smiling for pictures and hamming it up for the audience, their arms around one another's necks. The packed house screamed and waved at them.

Zack smiled at the bodyguards. "Looks like *they* need you more than I do."

The guys nodded and patted him on the arm. "Take care, Zack."

"You, too." He shook their hands. Then he watched them hurry to the front of the stage to help the winners.

In a rush, Zack felt a mountain move off his shoulders. He was free. Ready to go home. He walked backstage, found William Gaines and asked the only question that remained. The one burning in his mind.

"How soon can you get me to the airport?"

chapter 29

The kickoff show played on every television in the airport. Reese couldn't get away from it, so she settled in at Gate C21 and watched. Zack and the other remaining contestants performed three group numbers, and Kip Barker showed clips from each of yesterday's performances. She didn't look away when they showed Zack's highlights. She needed to see again who he'd become. She needed that as often as possible.

London beckoned to her, and she had made her commitment. But her life, her future . . . everything she had hoped for was here in Kentucky. Seeing Zack now reminded her she had made the right decision. She could hardly wait to board the plane. Only ten minutes of the show remained. The part where two contestants would be sent home.

Reese had figured Zack would be golden with the audience. At Carnegie Hall that night, girls had practically fainted at the sight of him in a cutoff shirt, and they went crazy for his duet with Zoey. But Reese had spent a few minutes on Twitter earlier and now she wasn't sure. Overall, his fans seemed disappointed. Apparently she wasn't the only one who could see how he'd changed.

A voice came over the speaker system, interrupting the show. "This is our first call for Flight 449 to Atlanta. First-class passengers are welcome to board now."

Reese slid to the edge of her seat. She was in the final boarding group, and now that she had watched this much of the show, she wanted to know if Zack had survived. Zoey and one of the married singers were saved right off, and then one of the contestants was sent home. That left three of them. Kip Barker drew out the drama as he sent another singer to the sofa. Only Zack and one of the remaining women stood on the stage next to Kip.

One would go home and one would stay.

"Attention, passengers. Groups one through three are now boarding at Gate C21 for Flight 449 to Atlanta. Groups one through three, please board now."

Reese was in the fourth group. She stood and pulled her carry-on bag close to her side, her eyes locked on the television screen. She could hardly believe what she was seeing. Zack was in the bottom two? This hadn't happened since the live shows started.

Next to her, she heard a man talking to his wife. "That Zack kid's the most talented of all."

"Yeah, but he's changed. You should've seen him last night." The woman shook her head. "Wouldn't surprise me if he goes home tonight."

For the first time Reese considered the pressure Zack had been under. Half the country was talking about him, analyzing him, judging him. Declaring that he was or wasn't worthy of continuing on the show. A commercial break ended and Kip made the announcement.

Zack Dylan was going home.

"Attention, passengers, group four is now free to board. All passengers for Flight 449 to Atlanta, you may now board through Gate C21."

Reese walked a few steps closer to the TV, her eyes locked on Zack's face. *What happened to you? Where's the guy you used to be?* She searched his eyes, his expression. What was he feeling? Was he devastated after coming this far? Or was this God's way of rescuing him? If this were the old Zack, she would've said he looked almost relieved. Happy, even. But Reese could no longer be sure. She was still studying him, missing him, when Kip delivered a shocking update. The judges were being given permission to save Zack.

"Final boarding call for Flight 449 to Atlanta."

Reese hesitated. So this was how he was going to stay on the show. She wasn't surprised. The press had talked often about Zack and Zoey helping ratings. Reese took a last look at Zack as the show broke for another commercial. Then she pulled her bag to the gate and boarded the plane. She was glad she wouldn't be here to see next week's show, what songs he would perform and how he would leave a little more of the old Zack behind him.

She took her seat and checked the time on her phone. She had a five-hour layover in Atlanta. Not ideal, but then she'd be on the flight to London. She could hardly wait. But over the next few minutes maintenance workers discovered faulty wiring in the cabin door. A repair team was brought on board, and an hour later they finally pushed back from the gate. But they didn't move two feet before they stopped and once more the mechanics were called in.

Another thirty minutes passed with occasional updates from the cockpit. Finally the plane seemed to be fixed and they were about to find their place in line for takeoff when the captain's voice came on. "Sorry for the inconvenience, folks. We're looking at big storms in Atlanta. I'm afraid we'll have to sit and wait a while. Thanks for your patience."

Reese sighed. She hated the delay. Here on the ground in Kentucky, she could feel Zack Dylan. Her memories were alive and everything about yesterday still seemed possible. Not until the plane took off could she truly give herself permission to move on.

After nearly another half hour the captain came on again. "Folks, we have some bad news. Our crew has timed out. We'll have to return to the gate to switch crews. Again, thanks in advance for your patience."

A chorus of grumbles rose from the crowd. Reese peered at the Kentucky night sky and her heart ached. *Please, God . . . get me out of here. I can't stay much longer.*

Her flight was supposed to leave at eight, but as she got off the plane and turned on her phone, it was nearly ten o'clock and some sitcom was on the TV. Reese bought almonds and water at Hudson News. As she returned to the gate, the airline agent was giving another update. Her flight was now leaving out of C11.

She gathered her things and walked with the other passengers to the new gate. She took her seat and felt the weariness in her body. She had never felt so exhausted. Missing Zack, wondering why he had done the things he'd done, walking through the days alone. Getting ready for her move. All of it had drained her energy. She closed her eyes. At least her layover in Atlanta would be shorter. And then finally she would be on the plane to London, where she could get some rest.

And put the last few months behind her.

ZACK COULDN'T SLEEP. He had begged God from the time he left LaGuardia until now as his plane was landing that maybe . . . just maybe he might see her. They would be on the ground in five minutes, sometime around eleven o'clock. He wasn't sure when her flight took off, but his mom said Reese was on a red-eye through Atlanta.

Every minute would count.

When the plane parked at the gate, Zack barely reached the concourse before a group of *Fifteen Minutes* fans ran up to him. He had no seconds to spare, not if she was still in the Kentucky airport. But the fans didn't know that. *God, let me shine for You. This is a privilege. I realize that now.*

The moment was profound because it stood as a beginning for Zack. Here in this moment he could do nothing but treat it that way. If he wanted to return to the person he'd been before the show, if he wanted to glorify God in moments like this, then he needed to be intentional. He signed autographs and took pictures for ten minutes.

The group was clearly upset with his elimination. "You should have won the whole thing." One young guy shook his head.

"That's what I thought," another chimed in.

A girl with them crossed her arms. "Yeah, I was so mad tonight."

"Thanks." Zack smiled. "I appreciate your support." He took a final picture with a couple of the girls. Then he turned and smiled at them. "God must have better things for me back here." They nodded, happy with that, and Zack waved. His answer felt wonderful because it was the truth. Here at the airport he was free. No one from the show was watching him or pushing him to say what was best for ratings.

Like before this journey, he didn't answer to anyone but God. That new reality filled him with hope. A flight board hung on the wall down the concourse. Zack ran to it, frantically searching the departures. *Please let her still be here.* He spotted the one that had to be hers. A red-eye to Atlanta. His heart sank. The flight was scheduled to leave hours ago. One word next to the gate number gave him hope. *Delayed.*

In a full sprint he took off toward the C concourse, but by the time he reached her gate, the seating area was empty. He was out of breath as he walked up to the gate agent. "Flight . . . 449?" He looked around, desperate. "Did it leave?"

"It moved to C11." She checked her monitor. "They're boarding now."

Zack could have hugged the woman but he had no time to waste. He ran as fast as he could back down the concourse. The gate was crowded, and people were boarding. He wanted to scream for everyone to stop. She couldn't slip away from him now that he'd come this close.

Like a crazy person, he darted about trying to find her. Some of the passengers definitely recognized him, but they left him alone. As if they could see he was caught up in some deeply personal moment. Zack looked over everyone in the crowd before he realized the awful truth. She must've already boarded. He dropped to the nearest chair and hung his head. How could he have come this far and missed her?

He stayed there, his head in his hands, eyes closed, while

the rest of the passengers boarded. Just when the reality had taken root in his heart, when he had come to terms with the fact that he wouldn't have this last chance, he felt someone walk up to him. He couldn't take another picture, couldn't sign another autograph. Not when the girl he loved was leaving.

"Zack?"

His eyes flew open and he was on his feet. It was Reese. Standing in front of him for the first time in months. "I . . . I thought I missed you."

"I was in the restroom." She smiled, but it didn't touch the sadness in her eyes. "I thought they gave you another chance."

"No." He came a step closer. "They sent me home." He held up his hands and then dropped them at his sides. "I'm finished with the show."

"Hmmm."

A voice came over the speakers. "All remaining passengers for Flight 449, please board at this time."

Reese looked over her shoulder and then back at Zack. "I have to go."

"No. Please . . ." He set his backpack on the seat beside him and came closer, so their faces were inches apart. "You can wait a week, Reese. We need to talk."

In his mind, he had pictured this moment a hundred times. He would find her in the airport and tell her how sorry he was. She would understand and she'd cancel her flight. But now . . . the walls around her heart were locked in place. She shook her head. "I made a commitment."

The message was clear. She kept her commitments. Zack's heart raced and he searched desperately for the right words, anything to make her stay. "Reese, listen." He put his hand alongside her face. "I love you. I'll never love anyone the way I love you."

Fear made his voice shaky. "Please, don't go. I need to talk to you. I need to explain what—"

"Last call for Flight 449. All remaining passengers please board at this time."

"Zack . . ." She covered his hand with her own. "You don't need to explain. We have different lives."

"I don't want that." His words came like rapid fire. He was running out of time, and she wasn't hearing him. Wasn't budging. "Please, Reese, come home with me. You can go next week."

"I can't." Her eyes softened. She came to him and put her arms around her neck. "Good-bye, Zack."

"Please . . ."

She pulled away and walked with her things toward the gate.

The airline agents were watching them, anxious for Reese to board. Zack felt himself giving up. He couldn't chase her onto the plane. She had made up her mind. He stopped and watched her leave, his sides heaving from the way his heart was breaking. "Reese . . ."

She turned around one last time.

"I love you. I'm sorry."

Her eyes told him that somewhere inside she felt the same way, that she loved him and was sorry it had come to this. But she only held his eyes for a few seconds and then mouthed one last word. "Good-bye."

With that she boarded the plane and the gate agent locked the door behind her. Zack shuffled to the window and put his hand on the cool glass. He stayed there while the jetway pulled back and the plane taxied out onto the runway. *How can this be happening, God? It wasn't supposed to go like this.*

When the plane moved out of sight, Zack grabbed his backpack and walked slowly down the empty concourse toward baggage. He had lost her. Because of his careless actions and self-centered motives, he'd lost the only girl he ever loved. Reese wasn't only moving to London. She was moving on. Her eyes had told him that much.

As he collected his bags and waited out on the curb for a cab, Chandra's words came back to him. *There's a cost to fame. You may not see it now, but it's there. Everyone pays something.* Yesterday Zack hadn't wanted to hear that. He had insisted his life and Chandra's were different. Certainly he hadn't lost anything he couldn't get back. Even Reese was bound to forgive him. That's what he thought. But now, with the humid summer night air surrounding him and home a half hour away, he understood her words better.

The cost was not only real. It was almost more than he could bear.

chapter 30

They had reached the finale, and Chandra wasn't surprised when Samuel Meier gathered them an hour before the show and told them the results. The winner they would announce that night was Zoey Davis. The girl who had captured America's hearts with her face and voice, the other half of the Romeo and Juliet team.

The second finalist was Kent Jordan, the married guy whose goal had remained the same throughout the show. He had told America that if he won, he'd sing for a Christian label. He knew who he was, his style, his genre. The show hadn't changed him.

Chandra took her place on the panel with the other two judges. Cameras would roll soon and excitement buzzed through Carnegie Hall. From her place, Chandra waved at the audience and then spotted Kent near Zoey, the two of them talking to Kip. Since Zack's departure, Chandra had taken to praying for Kent. His second-place finish was an answer, she had no doubt.

Suddenly she remembered Zack. He had to be in the audience. The top ten contestants had been brought back for tonight. They would perform as a group early in the show, and then after Kip Barker crowned Zoey as the season's winner, the group would join her onstage for the final song while confetti rained down. Chandra scanned the audience, but she couldn't see Zack or the others in the front section. They were probably backstage preparing.

Chandra looked at the stage and studied Zoey Davis, the girl who was about to win it all. Zoey would have a much harder time with the fame than Kent would have. Chandra didn't like to think about the pressure and changes and celebrity that awaited Zoey in the pop world where she planned to make her mark. Her win hadn't even been announced, and already every talk show and variety magazine wanted a piece of her. The teenager had no idea how her life was about to change.

The frenzy onstage and in the wings continued to build, but Chandra remained quiet, reflecting. Remembering. In Zoey's interview last week, she had said the same thing Chandra had said the week before her own win. "This means everything to me. It's all I've ever wanted." Chandra narrowed her eyes. Would the girl look back and regret those words? How badly would she wish to climb into some special moment from her past, before her first audition?

Chandra clicked open the photo album on her phone. She pulled up the picture. Her parents and her fiancé standing beside her. The moment she still tried to live in. Tears stung her eyes and she shut her phone. Often she had wondered how it had happened, how she'd become so famous overnight. Here at the end of her ride as a judge, she had the answers. The show needed to create a celebrity each season. Someone to stir interest and drive ratings and draw another hundred thousand kids out to auditions when summer came around again.

She was part of a machine. All of it made sense now.

She took a deep breath. They had a little time before the show went live. The energy onstage grew more intense and every seat in Carnegie Hall was filled. As Cullen told them about a few added commercial breaks, Chandra felt someone come up beside her. She turned and there he was. "Zack! You're here!"

"I got in a few hours ago."

"You'll sing in the group number?"

"I will." He looked deeply at her. "You were right. About the cost."

"Yes." She searched his eyes. "Did you make it home before she left?"

"I did." He leaned closer, keeping it private. "I told her I was sorry."

"And . . ." She wanted to believe the girl had changed her mind, that she'd forgiven Zack and stayed in Kentucky. But she could see that wasn't the case.

"We had a few minutes in the airport, but she left. She . . . doesn't want me."

Chandra's heart felt heavy. "I'm sorry."

He smiled. "My family and I, we're doing well. I'm so grateful . . ." He looked up to the stage where Zoey and Kent were getting final makeup touches. He didn't have to finish his sentence. He looked at Chandra again. "Thank you."

She nodded. "I heard you got a publishing deal."

"I did." His smile reached his eyes, and for the first time since his Atlanta audition she could see all the way to his soul. "I'll be songwriting from Kentucky, driving into Nashville once a month to meet with the label."

"Perfect." She wanted to raise her hands in a victory dance. Zack had lost his girl, but he had escaped with his life. There would be no prison cell for Zack Dylan. She'd seen him in a number of interviews since his exit. He would be fine. She smiled at him. "Your family?"

"The publishing deal came with an advance. We saved the farm."

Chandra couldn't speak. Happy tears welled up and she nodded.

"Oh, and AJ's doing better. She has a new doctor."

Chandra took Zack's hands in her own. "All of that . . . it's exactly what I prayed for."

"God is good."

She felt the words to her core. The phrase was something she remembered from her parents, back when she was growing up. She finished the saying. "All the time." No words could've touched her heart more.

Zack had to take his seat in the front row with the other finalists. As he did, Chandra was overcome with a feeling as fulfilling as it was unfamiliar. Despite everything she'd lost, and regardless of the fame she would never escape, something was true that hadn't been true before.

Her life had meaning.

ZACK FELT THE cameras on him and the others as the final show began. Something was different now. The cameras didn't linger. He was no longer the one everyone talked about. That honor belonged to Zoey and Kent.

A few minutes into the program a production assistant led the group backstage. For the first time, Zack saw Zoey. She had makeup and hair people on either side of her, and a body-guard giving her instructions for the moment the show was finished. Somehow amid the chaos she must've sensed him watching her, because she turned and their eyes met. She mouthed, "Hi."

He raised his hand and did the same. The two of them hadn't talked since his departure, and Zack doubted they would. Their run on the show was the only thing they'd ever had in common. He wondered if anyone had told her about Jesus. It was still something he wanted to do—though now he didn't know when he'd get the chance. He did pray for her now and then.

But they had both moved on.

"Okay, people, you're on in five." The production assistant was the same. All of it was familiar—the setting and people and frenzied minutes backstage. But something else was different. Zack smiled when he realized what it was.

He no longer belonged.

The group number was one of their strongest yet, and Zack returned to his seat with the others to watch the show. Seated beside him were the newly married Nolan Cook and his wife, Ellie. Nolan was a star NBA player with the Atlanta Hawks, a guy known as much for his faith and good works as his jump shot. Not long ago Nolan and Ellie's story had run in *People* magazine, and Zack had read it. Nolan was the real deal, a guy who had never compromised his faith or his love . . . despite the crazy temptations of the world he lived in. When he and Ellie were seated, Nolan introduced himself. Then he talked to Zack about joining his online Bible study. "Us guys need it." Nolan had his arm around his pretty wife. "The world will eat you alive otherwise."

"I'm in, definitely." Zack had been surprised that Nolan Cook even knew who he was. But he jumped at the chance to join the athlete's Bible study.

Now during the commercial break, Nolan leaned closer. "You were awesome in the group number."

"Thanks." Zack raised his brow. "I was afraid everyone could see. You know, that my heart isn't in it anymore."

"Not at all." Nolan slung his arm around Zack's shoulder and spoke lower than before. "Can I confess something?"

"Sure, man."

"I was praying you'd get kicked off."

Zack chuckled. "You and everyone I know."

"And me." Ellie leaned over her husband's knees. "Add me to the list."

They all laughed and Nolan leaned back toward Ellie. The couple was beautiful, the picture of young married love. They were exactly how Zack had hoped to look when he married Reese. He held the image of the two for a few seconds and then looked away. He had lost too much to think about.

The show continued and a number of celebrity guests performed including Chandra, whose new single would release tomorrow. Zack watched her perform, the grace and confidence, the way she owned the stage. She had told him once that she felt most alive when she was performing. When no one stood guard over her, no one could get to her.

Moments like this.

Zack watched one famous singer after another take the stage. What were they thinking? Deep inside when the noise grew dim? He shivered, thinking how close he'd come to being one of them. While Selena Gomez sang her new hit, Zack's mind drifted back to the first days after he came home. He had held a meeting with his family and apologized. He told them how he hadn't represented them well, and how sorry he was. Everyone forgave him. Grandpa Dan remained the most upset, but more because of Zack's losing Reese. "I'll believe she's the girl for you as long as I live," his grandpa had told him when the others left the room. "Don't give up."

Zack had promised he wouldn't. He didn't deserve it, but he prayed every day that God would give him another chance with Reese Weatherly. He wondered if she'd seen his interviews after his kickoff. His comments that next week made headlines, even though that wasn't his intent.

Someone had asked him about his thoughts on shows like *Fifteen Minutes*, the wonderful opportunity provided for people who might not be discovered otherwise. It was a chance to simply nod and smile and confirm that singing competition shows were a tremendous gift to singers everywhere.

That wasn't what he said.

"The whole thing kind of troubles me, actually," he had said several times that week. "People were never meant to be idols. We aren't supposed to be worshipped. Only God deserves that kind of praise."

For a full day that was all the news could talk about. "Zack Dylan Criticizes Fifteen Minutes." Pundits called him a hypocrite and a sore loser. Then the commotion died down and the media tired of him. Zoey quickly became more interesting.

Nicki Minaj joined Selena onstage, but Zack was too lost in thought to hear their song. He turned his eyes to Zoey, sitting to the side of the stage with Kent. The battle for her sanity had only begun. There was no telling the traps and pitfalls that lay ahead for her whether she won or not.

Zack thought about his own future in music. His first song had already been picked up by Keith Urban—"Her Blue Eyes."

Radio hosts were saying the single could be the singer's biggest hit in a while. Zack couldn't get over God's grace, the way he was being allowed to do what he loved and stay in Kentucky with his family and his church.

But he would never get over what he'd lost for the sake of *Fifteen Minutes*.

His Reese.

She had texted him just once since she left. He had read the message so many times he knew her words by heart. *We both lost over all this, Zack. But I have to ask you to respect my decision. Please . . . don't contact me. I have to move on to whatever God has next for me.*

Her words had all but destroyed him. Though he would respect her wishes, he wouldn't give up. Not until he heard she was engaged or taking up permanent residence in Europe. Until then he would keep praying, keep believing that somehow, somewhere down the road they might have a second chance.

The show was winding down, the buildup leaving everyone in the audience on the edge of their seat. Again he and the other finalists were escorted to the backstage door as the announcement was made.

Sure enough, the winner of season ten was Zoey Davis. On cue the group ran onto the stage as fireworks exploded and confetti fell over Carnegie Hall. They surrounded her, congratulating her the way they were supposed to. Then they took their places and joined her in the song that always ended a season of *Fifteen Minutes*. "Tell Me to Breathe" filled the concert hall. The song talked about being caught up in a dream, unable to believe that this moment was actually happening.

As the song ended, Zack spotted Kelly Morgan's husband and kids in the front section of the audience. Beside them were two older people, a woman and a frail-looking man. Kelly's parents, no doubt. Last Zack heard, Kelly's father was still in remission. So much had happened in the last three months, not all of it bad.

When the show ended, the audience was ushered out and the finalists and judges and production team gathered onstage. The celebration continued, everyone congratulating Zoey and wishing one another well. Zack thought about approaching her, congratulating her or telling her that he'd been praying for her. But she was surrounded by far too many people, already being pulled into the life she would live from this day on.

Zoey Davis, superstar.

Zack slipped through the door to the backstage. He was ready to leave, but there was one thing he had to do first. He found a quiet corner and pulled out his phone. In no time he was on Zoey's personal Facebook page. Through private message he wrote her a note that said what he hadn't said earlier, what he hadn't found time to say.

> Hey, it's me. Zack. You were busy tonight, so I thought I'd tell you congratulations this way. Mostly because I have something else to tell you. First, I owe you an apology, Zoey. I didn't want to wait another day before I said so. I'm sorry. How I acted over the last few months was wrong, and it wasn't me. I should've been a better friend to you. A better boyfriend to Reese.
>
> Also, you asked me a couple times about Jesus—how to pray and all. I told you it's easy. You just talk to Him like you'd talk to a friend. But I guess I wanted to be more specific. Talking to God isn't the biggest part of it. The biggest part is getting right with Him, asking Him to be your Savior. Basically none of us can get to heaven on our own. We're

too messed up—I'm proof of that. So we need to admit the things
we've done wrong and ask Jesus to forgive us. Then we need to ask
Him to be our Savior.

That's what I should've told you when we were together.

Living for God is a little more complicated—that's why it's good to find
a church and a Bible. It's a journey, for sure. Along the way you can talk
to God whenever you want. I hope that makes sense. I'll pray that you'll
look into it. Jesus is the only way out of here alive.

That's all, really. Again, I'm sorry. Be careful with all that's ahead. And
remember this—no one loves you as much as Jesus does.

Your friend, Zack

He read the note again before he sent it. As he did, a weight
lifted from his shoulders. He pulled a beanie from his backpack
and slipped it on. Then quietly he stepped out the side door onto
West Fifty-seventh Street. He blended into the crowds as he
walked in the other direction. A few blocks away he hailed a cab.
"LaGuardia, please," he told the driver. He would be home before midnight, which was good. Tomorrow would be a busy day.

He had breakfast scheduled on the front porch with
Grandpa Dan.

chapter 31

ONE YEAR LATER

Zack pulled into the Kroger parking lot and killed the engine. It was his turn to make dinner—chicken and rice with steamed broccoli. One of the few meals he knew how to cook.

He had moved into the house at the back of the farm, but he still shared meals with his family. Their time together was more special now—the way it had remained since his time on *Fifteen Minutes*. Life had found a normal rhythm, something Zack loved. He and Grandpa Dan shared coffee nearly every morning, and after that Zack did most of his songwriting on the front porch. His father had hired a foreman to help run the horse farm, which was back in business and doing better than it had in years.

Every now and then Grandpa Dan asked Zack the question he dreaded most. "What do you hear from Reese?"

The answer was always the same. "Nothing, Grandpa."

"Keep believing. She'll come home someday."

The conversation was part of their routine, but it made Zack sad. Believing Reese might be part of his life again was more difficult all the time. Clearly she had moved on. Whether he ever heard what happened to her, whether she'd fallen in love with someone in Europe, her silence spoke louder than anything she might've said. She wasn't interested. Period.

Zack missed her still. Especially when he took AJ to the Lowell Center for her riding lessons. They'd hired someone to replace Reese, a guy with a decade of experience. AJ loved him, but even she brought up Reese once in a while. "She said she'd come back." AJ remembered details like that.

Always he tried to explain. "Sometimes people change their minds."

"Sometimes." AJ didn't stay sad long. She loved being around Zack, and she loved that he was leading worship for the youth group at church again. Now that she was healthier, his sister was in the front row every week.

Zack didn't take a single day for granted.

He headed into the store and found a bag of broccoli and a few pounds of apples and bananas. He was trying to remember what else his mother needed when it happened.

He spotted her halfway down the canned-food aisle.

She had her back to him, but he would know her pretty dark hair, her graceful walk anywhere. For a moment he stopped, not sure if maybe he was dreaming. Could it really be? Was this happening? She was reaching the end of the aisle when he jolted into action. He couldn't miss this moment. Not after a year had gone by.

"Reese!" He left his cart and jogged toward her. "Reese, wait!"

She hesitated before turning around. As she did, their eyes met and Zack froze. It was her . . . it really was. She had returned home and she was here at Kroger. As if no time had passed. As if she hadn't spent the last twelve months in London. "You . . . you're back." He walked slowly toward her.

As he did, he saw something that gave him the slightest bit of hope. Her eyes looked damp. "Zack."

"I . . . I can't believe you're here." He went to her and slowly took her in his arms. The hug didn't last long enough, but the feeling brought back yesterday. Maybe for both of them. He allowed distance between them again and searched her eyes. She looked different, more beautiful, if that were possible. The walls that had been there a year ago were gone now. And an alluring confidence shone from her soul. Zack wondered if he could even breathe, standing this close.

She spoke first. "You look good. I hear your song everywhere."

He hesitated, not breaking eye contact. "It's your song."

She smiled. "Keith Urban's song, right?"

"No." He shook his head. He could feel a smile starting in his eyes. "It'll always be yours, Reese. I wrote it for you."

"Well . . . I think of you when I hear it." She looked at the time on her phone. "I'm sorry. I have to be somewhere."

Panic coursed through his veins. She couldn't leave him again, not this soon. "When . . . when did you get back?"

"A few weeks ago." She angled her head. "London was wonderful. I might move there for good." She shrugged one shoulder. Everything about her looked irresistible. "I'm still praying about it."

He wanted to shout that she could never move there. Not forever. Not when he still loved her. He had so much to tell her, so much to know about her time away. But she needed to leave. So he did the only thing he could. "I have the same number."

"Me, too." Her eyes looked to the places in his heart that would never forget her. "We should get coffee."

"Yes." Zack felt dizzy with the first real possibility he'd felt since he left for Atlanta more than a year ago. "I'll call you." He took a step back toward his cart. "Tomorrow?"

She laughed. "Okay. Tomorrow." Her smile faded. "Good seeing you, Zack."

"You, too." He watched her go and tried to remember to breathe. She was home and she was here and maybe tomorrow she would get coffee with him.

His heart soared ahead of him down the aisles of the store. The chance meeting here at Kroger was a start. The miracle he'd been praying for.

He could hardly wait to tell Grandpa Dan.

HIS TRUCK WAS filled with groceries, but Zack wasn't ready to go home. He couldn't stop thinking about Reese. The look in her eyes, the way he could see all the way to her heart. Just like before.

He needed to sort through his feelings before driving back to the farm. Instead of getting on the freeway, he stopped at The Coffee House, the place where he and Reese once shared a hundred private moments. He parked his truck and went inside.

The host was a teenage kid Zack hadn't seen before. He smacked his gum a few times as he walked up to Zack. "Can I help you?" The kid clearly didn't recognize him, something Zack appreciated more all the time.

"Table for one." Zack followed the guy to a booth and sat

down. He ordered coffee but when it came, Zack barely sipped it. He couldn't believe what had just happened. There was no way running into her was pure coincidence. Not when he prayed for her and for the two of them every day.

Could it really be, God? Could we still have a chance?

No answer came, but a verse spoke quietly in his heart. The one from Jeremiah 29:11. God knew the plans He had for Zack and for Reese. Plans to give them a hope and a future. Whether together or apart.

But now . . . now Zack had to believe this was a beginning. Reese hadn't made up her mind about moving permanently to London. There was still time to change her mind. Zack breathed in, happier than he'd been since before *Fifteen Minutes*. He could hardly wait for tomorrow.

The host was back at his table, bringing the check, but something had caught the kid's attention. Zack followed his gaze and there on the nearby TV screen was a segment of entertainment news. An announcer was talking about *Fifteen Minutes*. "It's that time of year." He smiled into the camera. "Around the country hopeful singers are packing up and heading out to six major cities for the chance at being the next *Fifteen Minutes* winner."

"That's so cool." The guy set the check on the table, his eyes glued to the screen. "Winning that show . . . that'd be a dream."

"You sing?" Zack looked at him.

"Yeah." He glanced at Zack and back at the screen. "I'm decent. I'll probably audition next year. Gotta save up some money first."

"Hmmm. Well, good luck." Zack watched the guy go. He could only hope he wouldn't see the kid on the show next year or any time after.

The segment was still playing. The announcer was talking about Zoey Davis. "Last year's winner continues to grab headlines." Images flashed across the screen, Zoey on *Ellen* and *The Tonight Show*, articles declaring that she was breaking record sales. "Of course," the announcer said, his voice concerned, "not all news about Zoey Davis has been good." They cut to a short video feature showing a different series of headlines about Zoey Davis. She was too thin or addicted to drugs or cutting herself. A few months ago she'd spent a week in rehab.

Zack felt his heart sink. He had only heard a quick thank-you back from her after his private Facebook message a year ago. Since then they hadn't talked, though Zack followed her on Twitter. Last week Zoey had tweeted that she'd completed rehab for her "struggles with exhaustion." Another of Zoey's tweets appeared on the TV screen now. *Thanks for your prayers, everyone. I've learned how to pray. It helps. I may have finally figured out how to live.*

The tweet made Zack smile. Maybe she'd had the talk with Jesus he had told her about. It was what he had prayed for. But the struggles and pressures of fame would remain, whether Zoey prayed or not. Like Chandra had told him, the prison of celebrity was unbending no matter who was trapped within its walls.

On TV they were showing contestants lined up in New Orleans, home of the first round of auditions. An on-site reporter spoke loudly against the backdrop of excited contestants. "I'm here in New Orleans where tens of thousands of hopefuls have gathered for the first round of *Fifteen Minutes* auditions." He motioned for two teenage girls to join him. "What brought you here today?"

In unison the girls squealed. "We want to be the next winner of *Fifteen Minutes*!"

"There you have it." He looked into the camera. "And so season eleven begins. Back to you in the studio."

Zack had seen enough. He paid for his coffee, and as he headed out the door, the announcer on the TV kept talking. "In other news, one of America's favorite teen actresses is back in jail after being arrested again for drunk driving. Prosecutors say this is her final strike in her ongoing battle with . . ."

Zack walked out and the door closed behind him.

He didn't want to think about *Fifteen Minutes* or the upcoming season or the trouble with another teen actress. He'd lost enough time on such emptiness. Lost more than he ever could've dreamed the day he drove off to Atlanta. Chandra had been right about the cost.

But he couldn't think about that now.

Instead, he walked across the parking lot, breathing in the sweet Kentucky summer air. He had groceries to put away and news to share with his family and a song to finish. Then tomorrow . . . maybe a coffee date with Reese Weatherly. And if God allowed a miracle to play out, sometime in the weeks ahead he might have something else.

A horseback ride at dawn with the girl he still loved.

About the Author

Karen Kingsbury, #1 *New York Times* bestselling author, is America's favorite inspirational novelist with more than twenty million copies of her award-winning books in print. Karen has more than a dozen novels that have hit #1 on national lists. She lives in Tennessee with her husband, Don, and their five sons, three of whom are adopted from Haiti. Their actress daughter, Kelsey, is married to Christian artist Kyle Kupecky.

Fifteen Minutes

KAREN KINGSBURY

Z ack Dylan had a dream—to make it to the big stage as a singer. Even though life on the horse farm in Kentucky was somewhat idyllic with his college sweetheart and family closely connected, the farm's financial future was hanging in the balance. Zack saw a chance to save the farm, fulfill his dream as a singer, and proclaim his faith in Jesus Christ all at once. *Fifteen Minutes* would change his life in ways he never imagined, but would the chance of a lifetime end up costing him more than he bargained for? *Fifteen Minutes* is a cautionary tale about fame, fidelity, and faith, and the journey of discovering where loyalty will land when the chips are down.

Topics & Questions for Discussion

1. What did you enjoy most about *Fifteen Minutes*? Which character was your favorite? What was it that you most appreciated about him or her?

2. Do you watch reality TV talent competition shows? What are your thoughts about the opportunity for people to advance from "unknown" to "celebrity" throughout the course of a season? Do you think it is a positive or a negative?

3. When we first meet Chandra Olson, she is walking through a cemetery contemplating how much fame has cost her. Like Solomon, what was she chasing in the wake of her great loss? Have you ever achieved a goal or realized a dream but didn't get the fulfillment and meaning you thought would come with it? How did you respond?

4. Zack Dylan's grandfather tried to persuade him to stay on the farm instead of pursuing his dream of singing on *Fifteen Minutes*. Do you think Zack should have heeded his grandfather's advice? Why or why not?

5. On page 14, Zack says: "What if I could shine brighter for God on a bigger stage? In front of the whole world?" Com-

pare this "big stage" strategy of witness with the ministry of Jesus. Why do you think Jesus chose *not* to use a "big stage" strategy?

6. Grandpa Dan warned Zack that "fame is a demanding mistress." What were some of the things that fame demanded of Zack as he made his way into the spotlight on *Fifteen Minutes*?

7. Describe your impression of Zack and Reese's relationship before he left to audition for *Fifteen Minutes*. What qualities about their relationship did you admire? What advice would you have given them on the eve of Zack's departure?

8. What were some of the patterns in Zack's growing friendship with Zoey that set the stage for unfaithfulness in Zack's heart? Make a list of each person who suffered as a result of his unfaithfulness. Discuss your observations about the options Zack had to change some of his choices. Do your observations provide insight into your own patterns of interacting with people, especially members of the opposite sex?

9. What words would you use to describe Kelly Morgan when you first encounter her in chapter five? What are some of the things she is most concerned about? Do you think you would have enjoyed working with her? Why or why not?

10. Describe the role Chandra Olson played in Zack's life during his time on *Fifteen Minutes*. How did Zack respond to her

counsel? Is there someone who has played a similar role in your life—praying for you, speaking with you, challenging your beliefs and assumptions? How did you respond to their input?

11. Compare how Kelly Morgan and Zack Dylan change throughout the novel. How are their journeys of transformation similar? Different?

12. What did you feel when Reese made the choice to move to London? Do you think she was reacting to her hurt or responding to God's call for her life? How can you discern the difference between running from a hurtful situation and following God's lead?

13. How did Zack and Zoey's "love story," scripted by the *Fifteen Minutes* producers, impact you? How did you feel about the way Zack and Zoey responded to the demands being made of them? Have you ever been in a situation where you acted in ways contrary to your true values in order to advance or gain the approval of others?

14. One of the themes in *Fifteen Minutes* is the impact that small, seemingly insignificant choices can have over the course of time, especially in the midst of competing values and priorities. How does Scripture speak to this struggle? Can you think of an example from Scripture where a person (or people) took small steps that ultimately resulted in a significant distance in their relationship with God? What are some seemingly "small" things (inconsistent with God's

ways) that may slowly be creating distance in your relationship with God?

15. How did you feel about the way the story ended? How did it
compare to the ending you anticipated?

16. In what ways does the title *Fifteen Minutes* reflect one of the
primary messages of the book?

Enhance Your Book Club

1. Read the story of Saul in 1 Samuel 12-13. Compare Saul's choices with those leading to significant consequences in *Fifteen Minutes*. What did Saul want more than loyalty and obedience to God's commands? Discuss the things that you are tempted to desire more than your relationship with God, and some possible ways to feed your desire for God.

2. Read Timothy Keller's book *Counterfeit Gods*. Discuss the contrast between the passionate pursuit of dreams and goals and making the dream or goal an "ultimate" thing.

3. If you know someone who has achieved a level of fame or prominence, invite them to come to your next book club for a Q&A about how they navigated the temptations and costs of being well-known and admired.

4. Watch a season of one of the current reality TV talent competition shows. Pick one person on the show to follow, and each week take note of what changes you observe in them.

A Conversation with Karen Kingsbury

What prompted you to write about the temptations and costs of fame in *Fifteen Minutes*?

Our family doesn't watch much TV, but we do watch *American Idol*. We've watched it from the beginning. Over time I found myself remembering not so much the singers as their stories. Some flashed bright and burned out, some shone for Christ in their newfound fame, and some seemed better off before they ever auditioned. The latter intrigued me and caused me to begin dreaming up a fictitious show with fictitious judges and characters. A few years ago I outlined *Fifteen Minutes*, and as soon as my schedule was clear I wrote it.

Are you a fan of talent competition shows like *American Idol, The Voice*, etc.?

Yes, I love these shows—but again more because of the stories than the singing. There's something compelling about a person who had a very normal life by the world's standards, and then virtually overnight they have throngs of paparazzi capturing their every move and hundreds of thousands of fans. How does a person deal with that sort of fame? What happens to their relationships back home? And what about those young people who were better off before they auditioned? These ideas compelled me to write *Fifteen Minutes*.

What kind of television shows do you most enjoy watching?
We watch football and basketball, and beyond that we watch *American Idol* and *Duck Dynasty*. The endearing qualities of those shows resonate with our family and bring us together. But part of what makes our family special is that most of the time the TV is off.

Did you visit the set of an actual talent competition show prior to writing *Fifteen Minutes*?
No, I never did. I have several friends who were successful on *American Idol* or *The Voice*, and several who auditioned and made it several rounds before being cut. All of them have a similar story to tell about the pace and demands of the experience. It's crazy busy, intense, and surreal—and always a little difficult to transition back into real life. Those who were the most grounded going in tend to do the best in their post-show life. I don't know this for a fact, but there seems to be a wistfulness among the winners that the fame and success comes at a cost. For some it is a very great cost, indeed. That much we know. My characters are not based on any real-life singers or competitors on these shows. But there is no doubt that my years of watching *Idol* influenced my decision to take a fictitious look at the phenomena of singing competitions.

Which character was the most enjoyable to develop?
That's a toss-up between Zack Ryan and Chandra Olson. Zack is wide-eyed and innocent, believing that he can remain unchanged no matter what happens. Chandra has seen the cost of fame, experienced it on a painful level that sets her apart even in a world of celebrity. Both are searching for purpose and meaning, for God's lead, and for His voice in what's next. These two—

more than anyone else in *Fifteen Minutes*—are living, breathing people to me.

As a popular author, how have you handled some of the temptations illustrated in the book related to fame and the pursuit of the "big stage"?

Authors have it a little easier than other public figures at the top of their field. For the most part we go unrecognized, and—at least for me—I build my life around those things that have nothing to do with me being an author. You can find me in the stands at our son's high school football game or serving up spaghetti for our other boys' soccer team. Someone might come up and say, "I loved your last book!" and it'll take me a few beats to remember, "That's right . . . I'm an author!" Seriously. I credit that to a couple of important things. First, I write for God, for His purpose and His glory. So any good that comes from my work gets credited to Him. That pretty much settles the question of ego. Also, my dad told me a long time ago, when he was still with us, something I will remember always. He said, "Karen, there will be no autograph lines in heaven. Remember . . . you are only meeting people and making friends along the way."

Are there safeguards and/or practices you have in place that help ground you in your relationship to God rather than in the approval of your fans and readers?

Again, those words of wisdom from my dad have provided the best safeguards. He also told me there will always be someone who does not like your work, and there will always be someone who does. Neither voice matters as much as God's, who called you to write in the first place. When I write, I have an audience of One. His lead and approval are all that really matter. When I release a book, I pray it will touch hearts and change lives, some-thing only God can do. I feel grateful to be even a small part of that process.

What was the hardest part of writing this story for you?
Treading carefully with the concept. *Fifteen Minutes* is entirely fiction, as are all the characters. But I was super aware of the real-life stories that have come from shows like *Idol* and *The Voice*. Many people do well on these shows and go on to make a great impact on the world for God. This story wasn't about the good that can come from a singing competition, but the cost it takes to find a place so quickly on such a big stage.

What advice would you give an "unknown" Christian au-thor who wants to "make it big"?
Hmm. I smile at this question, because the question—in and of itself—is flawed. As a believer in Christ, our goal needs to be to make His love and salvation "big," not ourselves. Any marketing I do, any publicity, any ideas meant to expand the number of read-ers who know my work must first be rooted in ministry. I love my readers. I care about their hearts and lives and families. God puts a story in my heart, but He has their hearts in mind. When I pray for an idea to expand, it's so others might see Him at work in the story. If they see that, then they are more apt to see Him at work in their own story. My advice would simply be, "Write for Him." Write the story He is calling you to write. The more keyed in you are to that calling, the more likely you'll reach a lot of readers. If your goal is to "make it big," you probably won't. Early on, when I first started writing novels, I would scan the best-seller list every week hoping to see my name. I literally felt God convict me of that. He made it clear that my motives were

wrong. I gave up looking at bestseller lists, and I've stayed away from them ever since. Sure, I hear that a book has made the list, and I hear about sales. But I don't seek out the information, and it's not what drives me. The reason needs to be rooted in His purpose. Only then will the books become all they can be. That's been my experience.

Would you like to be a judge on a show like *Fifteen Minutes*? Why or why not?

I would LOVE to be a judge on such a show. I would be the compassionate one, the one encouraging someone to keep searching for their passion, the thing God is calling them to do and be. It'd be super fun to see firsthand some of the talent that will one day reach the world. I'd love to be a voice of reason and direction for those singers—helping them to stay grounded and never believe in the fame. Once you believe in it, you've lost what matters most.

The ending of the book is left to the reader's imagination. How would you like to see Zack and Reese's story end?

I don't think the answers will come easily for them. There's lots to work out, lots to talk through. Reese has reason to doubt Zack now. Not just the mistakes he made along his run of *Fifteen Minutes*, but also the motives that led him there in the first place. Still, that said . . . I see them together. Right? Don't we all see them together eventually? Hmm. Might have to write a postscript at some point. ☺

What can we expect from you next?

I pray God allows me to continue writing a big novel each year, maybe two, depending on the season of life. Also, I will be writing a Bible study series soon. It's called "Heart of the Story," and it will be four books over four years. Each will feature short novels on characters in the story of Jesus. The first focuses on the *Family of Jesus*, then the *Friends of Jesus*, the *Followers of Jesus*, and the *Firsthand Encounters of Jesus*. I'm partnering with our pastor at church—Jamie George—who is one of the great storytellers for Jesus of our day. He will write the teaching part, while I provide the short novel on each character. The goal is to make people fall in love with Scripture, with the great story of the Bible, so that we each see that we are a part of His story more than a part of history. I also have another series stirring in my heart. Beyond that there will be movies based on many of my books, and for the first time I'll be screenwriting—playing a major part in bringing the stories to life on the big screen.

Keep reading for an
excerpt from
Karen Kingsbury's
upcoming Bible study,
The Family of Jesus!

A Brother's Love

A fictional tale of Jesus and his unbelieving brother, James

All of Nazareth was in an uproar, and James was sick of it. He stepped outside his house and leaned on the doorframe. Craziness. Jesus was having dinner down the street, and even from this end of the block James could see the multitudes gathering around the dwelling, pushing their way inside.

"Jesus! Help us . . . Jesus, over here!"

"Let me through!" A man came screaming down the street, a child in his arms. "We have to get to Jesus! Please . . . let us through!"

James scowled. Ridiculous. This whole Jesus thing made absolutely no sense. James wiped the sweat off his brow and peered at the distant chaos. Five men were shouting at the followers of Jesus, telling them they were crazy. A long sigh rattled from James's chest. Every time Jesus came through town, people picked sides. There were the sick, the lame, the down and out, clamoring for his attention, looking for healing or some sort of inspiration, jumping on the bandwagon. The other camp was just as loud. Family mostly, to be honest. Cousins, aunts, uncles. People who knew the truth about Jesus.

He was a carpenter's son.

Not God in the flesh the way his crazy disciples seemed to believe. James should know. Jesus was his brother, after all.

He stepped back inside the doorway and rolled his eyes.

Maybe it was time to put an end to the madness. He had authority with the people of Nazareth, and he could get his mother and brothers to come along. His mother believed Jesus's claims, or at least James thought she did. But she didn't like hearing him mocked by the rest of the family. She would come along. And his brothers felt the same way he did. Jesus was embarrassing himself and, worse, he was embarrassing the entire family.

A quiet chuckle came from James. The savior of mankind—the Emmanuel spoken of in Isaiah—a carpenter's son? In a town like Nazareth? He grabbed a cup of water, downed it, and slipped his cloak on. Yes, it was time. Enough was enough.

He walked outside onto the hot, dusty street and shut the door behind him. Fifteen minutes later he had gathered his mom and three brothers and hatched a plan. They would stay in a tight group, push their way through the crowd to the front door of the house and tell the owner that Jesus's family needed a word with him. Then with loud, dramatic discussion, they would fully and finally put Jesus in his place.

"It's the only way," one of his brothers agreed. "The kindest thing we can do for the people of Nazareth . . . and for Jesus."

On the walk down the street, James was seized with a mix of anger and sorrow, distressed that his relationship with Jesus had come to this. When they were younger, James and Jesus had been the best friends two brothers could be. James looked up to Jesus in every area of life. When Jesus studied the Scriptures, James studied them, too. When Jesus told a funny story, James was the first to laugh. They went everywhere together. No better big brother anywhere, that's what James grew up thinking.

As far as he was concerned, Jesus could walk on water.

But as soon as Jesus left the carpenter's shop, he began to think he really could. He even told people he'd done just that—

walked across the Sea of Galilee in the middle of the storm. On top of the water.

James coughed again. At first he figured it was just a stage, a strange season in his brother's life. Jesus would come to his senses, come home, and they could go on being a family. Making memories and sharing meals. James and his best friend, Jesus. His big brother.

But Jesus continued the madness, spinning the insanity until now it was out of control. Jesus made his way throughout the entire region, doing some sort of magic nonsense and causing people to believe he was the Messiah. The Messiah, of all things!

It had been a year since he and Jesus had laughed together, shared a conversation, just the two of them. James had tried to make light of the situation. "Come on, Jesus, we miss you back home. Don't you think it's time to stop the traveling?" He gave Jesus a light slap on the shoulder. "I need you, brother. You and me, like it used to be."

But Jesus only looked at him—that same unconditional love he'd always had for James—and a smile tugged at his lips. "I have to go. It's what my Father has called me to do." His smile fell off a little. "It's my calling. Please, James . . . try to understand."

Now, though, Jesus had forgotten him. What sort of calling would take him away from the people he loved most? James wiped the dust from his mouth as they reached the house. "Let us through . . . we're his family!" James used his loudest voice. "We need a word with Jesus. Please get out of the way."

They reached the front door and the master of the house was called in. "Yes." He looked bewildered. "You want to talk to Jesus?"

"We do." James took the lead. He stuck his chest out. "We

are his family. Tell him that his mother and brothers have come."

The man was gone for less than two minutes. When he returned, he shook his head. "Jesus says he cannot talk. He said his mother and brothers are those who . . . hear his word and obey it."

James felt his face grow hot and the ground shift beneath his feet. All around them, people stared. A few even snickered. Jesus had completely and utterly rejected them, his very own family. James hesitated, but only for a minute. The man wasn't going to let them through. Even if he did, Jesus had basically just disowned them.

They left in shame, the whispers and stares of half of Nazareth following them all the way back to James's house. Not until Jesus left town again did James feel good about leaving his house. Even then there was talk. Rumor had it Jesus had gone so far as to say that only in his hometown was a prophet without honor.

Of all the nerve.

For the most part James was angry, an anger that stayed and brewed within him through summer and into fall, that year and the next. But his anger was surpassed only by his sorrow. He never could've imagined Jesus—the one who loved him the most—doing this to him, to their family.

Not until Passover that year did James catch wind that things weren't going so well for Jesus. It was their mother who convinced them that maybe it was time for a reconciliation. "We're going to Jerusalem," she told them. "If we can see him, we should. I love him and I miss him. I know you all do, too." She paused, her heart clearly heavy. "Besides, Jesus is in trouble. He needs us."

It was a quiet trip to the city, and along the way James found himself torn by his conflicting emotions. The anger and rejection, the sense of betrayal Jesus had brought by his actions. But also a simmering fear. Because the closer they got to Jerusalem, the more they heard the murmurings. The people of Israel wanted to kill Jesus.

Heated tension, mobs of angry Israelites, days of protests, then everything spun wildly out of control. Jesus was arrested and word on the street was that he'd been beaten—almost to death. James could hardly console their mother. "Please, James," she told him. "I need to see Jesus . . . tell him I love him . . . just one more time."

James took the matter personally, and he desperately wanted to help her. But it was Friday and the decision had been made. Jesus would be crucified—his crime, the one James had feared would eventually be Jesus's undoing. His claim to be the king of the Jews. Jesus the Messiah. He had taken the whole act too far, and now he was going to die because of it.

"I'll get you there," James told his mother and brothers. "We'll go to him, see if we can stop the soldiers." Jesus might've been crazy, but he wasn't dangerous. He'd done nothing worthy of the death penalty. They ran, pushing their way through the throngs of people. As in Jesus's life, the crowd was split—some people wailed, begging for the soldiers to have mercy. Others mocked Jesus, demanding his crucifixion.

Here in Jerusalem, no one recognized James and his brothers, no one pointed and stared at their mother. James wasn't sure he would've cared if they had. The shock was wearing off, reality setting in.

His brother, his best friend, was about to be killed on a cross.

Finally, they jostled their way to a position where they could see him . . . they could see Jesus. They reached the spot just as the first nail was being driven into his wrist. Next to James, his mother cried out. "No . . . no, not Jesus!"

The wailing grew louder, but the soldiers carried on. His other wrist—his feet—nailed to the cross. James couldn't talk, couldn't draw a full breath. What was happening? Jesus might not be God, but he was still his brother. "Let me go to him," he shouted at the soldier in his way. "He's my brother!"

"Get back!" The soldier hit James, knocking him to the ground. "One step closer and I'll lock you up!"

James scrambled to his feet, but before he could try once more to force his way past the soldier, his mother took his arm. Tears streamed down her face. "No, James. This is his choice . . . the reason he came to us." She trembled, barely standing beneath her breaking heart. "He must finish his work."

For a long moment James looked at her, understanding fully what he had always guessed to be true. His mother believed Jesus. She, too, was one of his followers. James slowly put his arm around her shoulders, and for the next two hours he did the only thing he could do. He held his grieving mother and prayed to God for the soul of his brother Jesus.

Tears streamed down his face as Jesus gasped for breath, dying on the cross. Every wonderful time, every childhood memory played again in his mind and he wondered if he could take the pain. Jesus had always been there for him when they were growing up. Now James wanted to be there for Jesus, but he could do nothing. Nothing at all.

When at last Jesus drew his final breath, broken and battered, he cried out from the cross, "It is finished . . . Father, into your hands I commit my spirit."

James turned to his mother and brothers and pulled them close, crying with them, holding them. Before he could say a single word, the ground began to shake . . . a menacing, terrifying earthquake. All around people began to scream, and as the ground split and opened up, there was a terrible sound.

Like everyone else, James turned to see what horrific thing might make such a noise. What he saw brought him to his knees. The curtain of the temple was being torn in two from the top down. But not a thing was touching it.

In a rush, like wind through a canyon in a sudden storm, the truth came upon James. Jesus had been right all along. The miracles, all of them had been true stories. Not fables. Jesus really *had* walked on water. In the distance James heard one of the soldiers call out, "Surely, this was the son of God."

But it was too late to tell Jesus, too late to make things right. James buried his face in the dirt and cried out, "Forgive me . . . please, Jesus . . . forgive me!"

The days blurred together in a dark and painful montage of memories and regret, and finally it was Sunday, the first day of the week. James was at his home, wishing for one more hour, one more chance, when he heard a sound behind him. With a start he turned, and though the door remained locked, there stood—

"Jesus! You're alive!" Of course he was alive! He had risen from the dead, just like he had talked about doing while he was alive. James came to him. He fell to his knees and hung his head. "Forgive me, Jesus . . . please . . . I was wrong."

"James . . ." Jesus touched his brother's shoulder. "Look at me."

James did as he was told. He lifted his head and for a long time he looked into the eyes of Jesus. Never in all his life had James felt such love, sensed such grace and mercy in a single heartbeat. "Stay, Jesus . . . live with me." James brought his hands together, pleading. But even as he said the words, he knew the answer.

"I cannot stay." Jesus helped James to his feet, and for the most wonderful moment the two of them embraced. Brother to brother, like old times. "You will always be my brother, James." Jesus stepped back. "But now you will be my disciple. And you will lead my church in Jerusalem."

"Yes, my Lord." James bowed again and their eyes met once more. "I will serve you all the days of my life."

And with that . . . Jesus was gone. But as James stood there, he vowed to make good on his promise. He would serve Jesus all the days of his life. He would tell the stories of Jesus and lead people to follow his teachings. He would do so every day, all the while remembering their times as children, and this, their final meeting. Because until the end of his earthly life, Jesus would be his brother . . . his best friend.

His God.

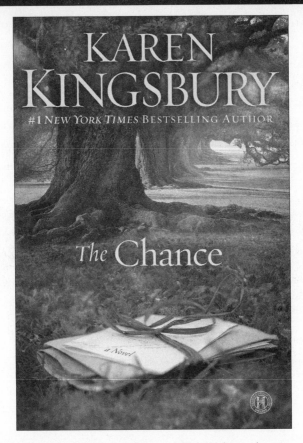

KAREN KINGSBURY

POSSIBILITIES™

with daughter Kelsey

In the spring of 2013,
Karen Kingsbury and her daughter, Kelsey Kupecky,
dreamed of the possibility of a card & gift line
that would breathe life and love into your stories.
They took their dream to DaySpring and a plan was formed.
The dream came true.
Now it's your turn. Follow your dreams.
Write your story.

COMING IN 2014